THE SOUL OF SCOTLAND

Kyra mounted her horse and took her place in the line of men, baggage, horses, and foot soldiers. She saw Arryn mount Pict. He shouted a command, and they began to move.

She passed beneath the portcullis, and kept her eyes ahead. She didn't look back until they came to the crest of a hill.

The sun was setting. The fortress was bathed in a red glow. Seacairn was beautiful, caught in the dazzle of the sunset and the glitter of the river sweeping around the stone. Kyra lowered her head, afraid that she would burst into tears.

"It is stone, my lady," she heard, and she lifted her head. Arryn had ridden back to her. "You have left walls of stone behind, but you've left them to join with the soul of a people."

When he rode on, Father Corrigan reined in at Kyra's side.

"Will I find the soul of a people?" she asked him, aware that he had listened to Arryn's words.

"If not, my lady, I believe that you will find your own. He smiled. "A worthy trade." He reached for her hand, and squeezed. "God bless you, Kyra."

"Aye, and may He protect us all!" she said.

She looked at Seacairn against the setting sun one last time.

Then she turned and rode forward, and she did not look back again.

More titles by Heather Graham

CONQUER THE NIGHT

HEATHER GRAHAM

ZEBRA BOOKS
KENSINGTON PUBLISHING CORP.
http://www.kensingtonbooks.com

ZEBRA BOOKS are published by

Kensington Publishing Corp.
119 West 40th Street
New York, NY 10018

All Kensington titles, imprints, and distributed lines are available at special quantity discounts for bulk purchases for sales promotion, premiums, fund-raising, educational, or institutional use.

Special book excerpts or customized printings can also be created to fit specific needs. For details, write or phone the office of the Kensington Sales Manager: Attn.: Sales Department. Kensington Publishing Corp., 119 West 40th Street, New York, NY 10018. Phone: 1-800-221-2647.

Zebra and the Z logo Reg. U.S. Pat. & TM Off.

First Printing: July 2000
ISBN-13: 978-1-4201-3639-5
ISBN-10: 1-4201-3639-9

10 9 8 7

Printed in the United States of America

PROLOGUE:
THE ABYSS

March 18, 1287

Storm clouds filled the day, puffing, bellowing, haunting the sky. As the hour changed, so did the clouds, altering with time from a deep and angry blue to gray, and then the gray began to turn to a strange, misty crimson, the color of blood. Indeed, some of the king's courtiers, departing Edinburgh in the evening, commented that Alexander must not travel that night— all day, the sky had been like an artist's palette splashed with blood, and that deadly color had dripped along over the light of day until all was swept into the darkness of a still, strangely crimson night.

And still, the night was not wholly dark.

The storm that had threatened had come, and what might have been the ebony of evening was highlighted by the white of a raging snow, swirling, sweeping, blanketing land and air, blinding men and beasts alike. Breaking from the king's council that night at Edinburgh, the king's men duly noted the weather. His council was composed of intelligent men, bright fellows aware of the world around them, sophisticated. Alexander ruled over a kingdom that had been basically formed for centuries, and the people, drawn from so many backgrounds, considered themselves Scotsmen now, even those with English leanings— men with property in England, rich barons, owing fealty to two kings. It was often because of their Norman influence that they felt themselves so informed, learned and well-read.

And yet, there were enough vestiges of the past among them—remnants of the old Picts, Scotias, Britons, Gaels, Celts, and more—that they felt very superstitious that night.

Bishop Wishart, well regarded by the king and a man who loved and honored him in return, urged him to remain in Edinburgh. "You should stay here. A storm comes, a red storm, dark and fierce, sire, and dangerous."

The king clapped the bishop upon his shoulder. "Ah, but, my friend! I have a new bride, and what man would not defy the wind to reach such a young beauty as my Yolande?"

Wishart gazed at him shrewdly. Standing tall and solidly built at forty-four, Alexander III of Scotland was a handsome and robust man in the prime of his life. His first wife, the sister of Edward I, king of England, had died, as had their young sons and their daughter, the late queen of Norway. His heiress was his grandchild, Margaret, born to his daughter and Erik of Norway. He'd had his barons sign a compact that they would honor her as queen of Scotland, should he die. A regency of six would guide the lady, should she become queen while still a child. Six—with none of them a contender for the throne himself, though he might well have a favored man among the king's many second cousins.

But now the king had remarried. His new bride, Yolande, was young and beautiful, and as the king was indeed feeling himself a young enough man still—a man of healthy appetites—it was rumored that he might produce a son. He was enamored of the young woman now awaiting him in their marital bed, and though his barons had sworn to honor his granddaughter's right as heiress to the throne, it was still a king's duty to sire sons—sons strong enough to fight for the kingdom and wily enough to hold it against greater strength. And God knew, that would surely be a pleasant enough task; indeed, too pleasant, for the king seemed now to have no interest in listening to common sense.

"Your bride will wait another day, sire," Wishart said.

"Ah, my good friend!" Alexander replied. "A storm comes, aye, as fierce as a Scotsman himself, like as not! This is my country, Wishart. I love it for the bogs and marshes, hills and craigs, the beauty of colors in spring and summer—and the very fierceness of a winter storm, as wild and blustery, craggy and windswept as we be ourselves!" He looked at the learned bishop and spoke again, more forcefully. "There must always be a Scotland, Wishart. There must always be a Scotland."

"Sire—" Wishart began again, but the king ignored him.

"My friends!" the king called loudly to his companions, knights of the realm, brave and hearty fellows all, "we ride hard for the crossing at Queensferry! We will ride to Kinghorn at Fife, and I will sleep beside my new lady wife!"

"Aye, sire!" his escort called in return.

One of the men, the very young and newly knighted Sir Arryn Graham, did not reply. Mounted upon his destrier—a gift from the king—Arryn studied the sky.

The king's page hurried up with his own horse. The king mounted and looked over at young Graham, a lad still not near his majority, yet already tall, honed in the pursuit of a knight's battle expertise, and at the moment, as grave as Wishart as he gazed upward.

"You don't think I should ride, my lad?" the king inquired,

smiling. It was rare to see such careful deliberation in one so young.

"Nay, sire," Arryn said gravely.

"And why is that? Speak up, boy!"

"The sky, sire, throughout the day, gave warning. And now . . ."

"Aye, the sky. So go on."

"My mother hails from the Highlands, sire, and there the chieftains and the shepherds alike know the sky, as they know the country, and they know when the sky makes the land treacherous, my lord, and so it is now."

"Good counsel. Aye, Highland wisdom is always good counsel, but as I just told my very good friend, Bishop Wishart, there must always be a Scotland."

"Sire?"

"We are this strange blend of cold and wind, flowers, thistles, moors, colors, barren rock, soaring cliffs. We are Picts and Scots and Britons and even Normans and Vikings feeling new roots. We've blended, boy, to something different, and so there must always be a Scotland. We are a lion, a lion triumphant. I make no sense, eh, lad? Still, I must travel on tonight." The king smiled, a jovial smile, waving a salute to Wishart. He lifted his arm high and started off at a lope, his escort riding hard behind him.

The bishop, already feeling a deep chill in his bones, watched them go. He was still deeply disturbed. He was a man of the cloth, no Highlander to feel the old superstitions claw at his heart. He was cold, as if the late winter wind had swept beneath his skin. Aye, and why not? The wind was shrieking like an old woman; the snow was flying with a vengeance. And still, though the white flakes fell and the night had come, the sky seemed to be the color of blood.

The bishop turned and reentered the castle.

* * *

The king, at the head of his men, had no misgivings. Duty and pleasure had never so sweetly combined as in Yolande, daughter of the Conte of Dreux. After the grief of losing his first wife and their children, he had reason to rejoice in Yolande. Aye, the barons were good men, but Scotland was a place for the hard and hearty; they were sworn to honor Margaret, but he needed to leave them a male heir, a leader to ride hard when needed, to swing a sword, to fight with the best of them. He needed a son. Though Scotland had not been at war now in some time, and he was proud to say that men considered his a golden reign, he knew how fickle life—and men—could be. As an eleven-year-old boy, newly married to ten-year-old Margaret of England, he'd been kidnapped by old Henry of England, then kidnapped again by Scottish guardians. He was on good terms with Edward; he'd been honored in London, as he had given honor to the English king. Nothing was certain in this world.

Aye, he needed a son. For Scotland's future. That was why he rode so hard tonight, he thought. For Scotland's future.

"The snow flies harder, sire."

He turned. The others had fallen back, but Sir Arryn was still at his side. "Are you afraid to go on, young sir?" the king demanded.

"Nay, sire. I'm not afraid for myself. I fear for Scotland."

The king smiled. "How old are you, lad?"

"Sixteen, sire."

"Indeed, you are wise for your youth. Remember this, then: Scotland is never one man. She is the heart and pulse and soul of those who claim her through their blood, and by their blood. Kings are created by the whim of noble breeding. Scotland is this earth we tread, both wicked and beautiful, just as she is the people you know, young sir—wicked and beautiful as well.''

He spurred his horse, spewing up dirt and snow, aware that he had blinded the young man behind him, and that his escort fell even farther behind. But most of the five who had ridden with him tonight were the sons of his nobles, lads still wet behind the ears, boys who probably thought him old. Nay, he was in excellent shape, and God knew, he was an expert horseman, and beyond the prowess of his physical abilities there was something poetic and stirring in his determination to reach his bride. By God, he would defy heaven and earth to get to her.

He gained the crossing. The others rode up behind him, winded, anxious. The ferry keeper had retired to his hut, not expecting to bring men across the Firth of Forth at such a time, but the king banged on the door. ''Eh, man! Come to duty, my fellow!''

The ferry keeper was a coarse and hale soul himself, thick in the shoulders, strong in the arms. He cracked the door, saw the king, then threw it wide. Alexander's men gathered in close around him, huddling for what shelter they could find from the keening wind and the fiercely blowing snow.

''Sire!'' the man said, bowing to a knee. ''Sire, a crossing cannot be made—''

''My man, a crossing shall be made!''

''*Cha bu choir dhut!*'' the ferry man said, eyes wide, insisting that the king should not cross.

''A crossing shall be made!'' Alexander repeated.

When the king spoke so, there was no denying him. The ferry master reached for his heavy mantle and, bowing to the king, started ahead to the ferry. The storm was so ferocious by then that the king's courtiers had to help the man untie the ropes.

The ferry master, a massive bulk of a man both grizzled and fierce, struggled against the wind, grateful for the help he received. He looked up at one of the young men assisting him and muttered beneath his breath, 'God help us all that we must honor kings who would be fools!''

"Will we make the crossing?"

"By the grace of God alone! Ah, sorry, lad ! Forgive an old man his fondness for living. You can swim, boy?"

"That I can."

"You'll be fine."

"I wasn't afraid for myself."

The ferry master cast him a quick glance. "Aye, young sir! Stay with that madman who has forgotten sanity to be a lover before being a king!"

What they spoke could be construed as treason, so they fell silent as others came closer and they struggled with the ropes. The waves tossed; the wind rose to a new frenzy. Men shouted instructions and warnings above the roar of wind and snow and waves lashing against earth and wood.

Horses and men at last boarded the ferry. Again, with their weight upon the ropes that guided the vessel, the courtiers were put upon to assist, and even then they battled the wind to reach the shore. Men looked to one another with cold, bleak faces. With the way the snow blew, they were soaked to the bone. With the sharpness of the cold, their noses were frozen, their cheeks were brittle, their faces hurt.

At length, though, they made the crossing, and the king's men, greatly relieved, cheered him.

He was pleased to have proven his point: that he would ride when he chose. He was Alexander, powerful, virile, a king to lead men. A man of strength and stamina, he would reach his bride, and give that strength and stamina to the future.

"Aye, sire, here we be," the ferry master told him, and Alexander rewarded the man with a coin cast in his own likeness. The ferry master caught the coin, nodding his thanks, bowing deeply. He heaved from his exertion; there was sweat upon his lip despite the cold.

"Aye, my man, and here we be, as I said!" the king reminded him, but his humor was good; he defied the cold, throwing his mantle over his shoulder. *"Creasaibh oirbh!"* he ordered, commanding his men to hurry.

They mounted their horses, waved to the ferry master.

The ferry master lifted his hand in return. There was something strange in his face that caused Sir Arryn, the youngest knight among them, to turn his horse quickly in pursuit of Alexander.

Aye, kings could be fools! he thought. And his heart hammered.

The king rode ahead, hard and fast, with such eagerness and urgency that his men could not keep up.

"Finn, sweet Jesu! Can you see him?" Arryn cried back to the rider closest behind him.

"Ride harder; follow the king!" called Finn of Perth impatiently. "We are behind!"

"I canna see him; nae, I canna see him!" shouted John of Selkirk in distress.

Fear and foreboding had come over them all.

And indeed, the snow came more blinding than ever. Now it was like a wall of white, and the world was white and black; there were no markings. The men reined in, frightened and confused, and called to the king as their horses pawed the ground and moved in restless, uneasy circles.

"My God, we've lost him!" Finn shouted over the wind.

"We canna lose him!" John protested. "We take different trails! We canna lose the king! If we lose Alexander . . ."

"We lose Scotland!" Arryn murmured, and spurred his horse and soared on through the wind.

* * *

Alexander was unaware. Already his heart was pounding. He thought of a warm fire, mulled wine, the silken flesh of his young bride. He thought he could see, as many a blinded man has done.

He thought he knew the path, and that his horse was as surefooted as he was swift.

He thought curiously that the red had left the day, that the night was silent, beautiful and white against the abyss of darkness. . . .

Then his horse lost his footing, stumbled, and fell. The king, swearing, was thrown. He did not hit the ground.

Every man denies his own death. Even as his horse sent him hurtling over the cliff, Alexander denied the fact that he was plunging to his death. The crimson storm that had burned the sky and raised such a tempest had not sent him into an abyss. . . .

The crimson had left the sky, he thought. . . .

Because the red would bathe the land. Crimson, aye . . .

For the future of Scotland! He had ridden for the future of Scotland! He was a mighty king, a virile king, a powerful man in the prime of his life!

He raged! And still . . .

The king was cast upon the rocks.

Pain, ungodly pain, pain. Darkness.

His body, broken, torn, bounced, flew, plummeted farther, farther.

And it was true. The crimson that had splashed across the sky was indeed a foreboding of the blood that would come to bathe the land.

Aye, indeed. The color of blood.

It was a herald of all that was to come. . . .

The future of Scotland, like the body of the king, lay in a dark abyss—a future now doomed to be painted in blood.

CHAPTER ONE

Seacairn Castle, near the forest of Selkirk
The Year of Our Lord 1297

Kyra stood before the fire in the main hall of the old stone tower at Seacairn, watching as the flames rose and leapt, crimson and gold, dancing exotically to the whim of the drafts that ceaselessly filled the fortress.

No. No. Never.

The simple words filled her soul. She longed to shout, scream, cry out so loudly that the rafters would tremble with her denial, that the stone itself would shake and shudder with the force of her words.

She turned from the fire and raced up the curving stairs to the chapel above the main hall. She stared at the main altar, but turned from it. Far to the right of it was a shrine to the Virgin, and it was there that she fled, falling to her knees, her skirts billowing out around her. "No, no, no! Don't let it happen.

Blessed Mary, give me strength! I will enter any bargain with God, or so help me, Lady, forgive me, but I would deal with Satan himself, to escape what fate destines for me. Dear Lord, but I'd rather die than—''

She broke off, startled by the thunderous sound of a ram slamming against the main gate of the castle. It was an ancient fortification, strengthened and enlarged by each power to lay claim to the land, for it lay in border country, where it seemed that every race known to Scotland had once ruled. Now, under the ruthless determination of Edward I, the castle was in English hands. And with Scotland in turmoil since the death of the Maiden of Norway, vicious battle could come at any time, and the man who held a castle was he who ruled it, no matter what his nationality.

''My lady!''

Kyra rose and spun around as her maid, Ingrid, tore into the chapel.

''What is happening?''

''They've come, milady! Marauders, murderers, wild men, savages! Horrible, heathen Scots out of the Highlands!''

Ingrid was young, a buxom girl who had been raised in a convent. She was convinced that most men were savages and that Scotsmen were little more than the lowest, most barbarous beasts.

Kyra rushed to the arrow slit and looked down. It was true. Mounted men, some in chain and plate armor, some in leather, some with little more than sharpened shovel poles or sickles as weapons, were shrieking out fierce battle cries and bearing down upon the castle. They had already breached the outer gate and were in the bailey, fighting the meager forces left behind by Lord Kinsey Darrow, the Englishman granted rule here by Edward of England after her father's death.

She could see the hand-to-hand combat being waged. She could hear the screams and cries of the dying, see the spatter of blood as battle-axes and swords met flesh and bone. Someone cried out that those who surrendered would be granted mercy, more than the Scots had received at the hands of the Englishmen.

"God help me!" she said softly, backing away from the window.

"They've come for you, my lady!" Ingrid said. "They've come for you, because of what Lord Darrow—"

"Ingrid, enough!" came a firm masculine voice. "Say nothing more to your lady!"

Again Kyra spun around. His head hooded, face shrouded by the wool of his garment, Father Michael Corrigan had come quietly into the chapel. She had long thought that as an Irishman, the spiritual leader of this fortress would give his sympathy—and his prayers—to the Scots.

"What does it matter what she says?" Kyra asked him, fighting to remain calm. "They have breached the walls. They are here, quite simply. Lord Darrow's men have fallen or surrendered. The enemy will be here any minute. The truth is that we're all about to be murdered by heathens—"

"I rather doubt they've come to do murder."

"Oh, come, now, Father, do you see what happens below?"

"Indeed, my lady, they've come for vengeance. They've come for the castle, for its origins are ancient and Gaelic, and—I dare say—they've come for you."

His face lay in shadow, yet she knew that he watched her. Was there vengeance in his heart as well as in the souls of the enemy below? Or was he simply detached, wondering if she would dissolve hopelessly into tears or attempt to throw herself from the battlements in despair.

"The soldiers out there will die for you," he said, and she wondered if he applauded their valor, or mocked her worth in return for their lives.

She lifted her chin. "They must not do so. If the barbarians can be induced to offer mercy in any way—"

"Darrow herded fighters and farmers alike into a barn and set fire to it, Lady Kyra. Difficult to ask mercy in return."

"It is never difficult to ask mercy, Father. The difficulty may lie in the enemy's ability to give it."

"Lady Kyra!"

She turned. Capt. Tyler Miller of the castle guard had come. He fell on a knee before her. "Sweet Jesu, lady, we will gladly die in your defense, but I'm afraid there's no help in it. Perhaps there's a way for you to flee. . . ."

"Captain Tyler, I beg you, get up. And I command that you surrender your men if you believe there's any hope of mercy."

"But, my lady, perhaps we can buy time with our lives. . . ."

"I'll not have you imperil my soul with your lives, Captain Tyler, please. Leave me to my defenses. Hold the wild men off if you can, but in Lord Darrow's name, I command you to surrender when all is lost."

Tyler bowed, then turned to go.

"They will be quickly bested," Father Corrigan commented.

"God help me then!" Kyra said fiercely. God help her, yes. How strange that she had just come here, so desperately seeking intervention from the Virgin for the life she had been destined to lead.

How strangely prayers were answered! What in God's name was she going to do?

"God help me!" she repeated to herself in a whisper. But Father Corrigan heard her whisper; he was listening, if God was not. He smiled. "Remember, my child—God helps those who help themselves."

"Indeed, Father? Then by His grace, and certainly with your blessing, I will seek to help myself!"

* * *

"Lay down your arms!" Arryn cried. His first opponent inside the bailey, once they had breached the outer walls, had been a large, well-muscled, and experienced warrior, but the man he now faced was no more than a lad, and the way he swung his sword showed training, but no experience.

"Nay, I cannot!"

The lad swung—a noble gesture. His sword fell short of its target, that target being Arryn's midsection. Arryn sat atop his great bay destrier—obtained several years ago from a fallen English cavalryman—and could easily have brought his own weapon down upon the fellow's neck and shoulders.

"Lad, give it up! You're beaten."

"Aye, I'm beaten. But give it up, sir? To perish in flames, or meet the hangman, or find death at a stake, or—"

"Lay down your weapon, you fool! I don't punish children for the misfortune of their birth!" Arryn cried.

The lad hesitated, then laid down his sword. As he did so, Arryn heard his name called. He swung the handsome bay around. Jay MacDonald, head of the fighting members of his clan, was rushing through the bailey to reach him.

"He's gone—Lord Darrow is gone. They say he heard that an army of wild men was nearly upon him—and he ran!"

"Aye, so 'tis true; the rat has sprung the trap!" Arryn said with disgust, spitting down into the dirt. God, it hurt! His anger and frustration were so great that they actually created a physical pain within him. His heart hurt; his soul hurt. What Kinsey Darrow had done was unforgivable, not to be forgotten. And all under the full blessing of the English king! There was nothing to do when such atrocities were law, except to defy the law. In a land where there was no justice, there was little left to a man except the pursuit of revenge. And by God, if not today, he would have his revenge one day. Kinsey Darrow would die, and die by his sword, or else his own life would be readily, gladly given in forfeit. As it was, by God, he could not live with his dreams. He heard her screams into the night, and even into the dawn, and they would rip him apart as long as he lived, perhaps even through all eternity.

"Arryn, did you hear me? King Edward of England's wretched coward of a lackey is not here!" Jay said.

"You're certain?"

Jay indicated the corner where the castle guards stood, their weapons cast into a heap before them as they waited, eyes darting nervously as they surveyed their Scottish foes. "Ask the lad, Arryn. Lord Darrow rode out this morning."

"It's true?" He had yet to see the boy's face, for Kinsey Darrow was a rich, landed knight with the resources to arm his men well. The lad wore a helmet with a fitted faceplate and tightly knit mail with heavy plates as well. A tunic with Darrow's colors and crest lay over his armor, but didn't conceal its fine workmanship.

The lad lifted his helmet from his head. As Arryn had suspected, he was very young. He stood tall and, though obviously afraid, he meant to stand his ground. He looked at Arryn and nodded. "Aye, sir, 'tis true. Lord Darrow came here to meet his lady, but received a message soon after from the Earl of Harringford, and departed with more than half his forces."

Arryn arched a brow, leaning down against the bay's neck to better study the boy's freckled face. "Came here to meet his lady?"

"Aye, sir."

"And he met with her?"

"Aye, sir."

"And he rode out with her?"

"Nay, sir, he did not."

"Then she remains?" Arryn queried, glancing over at Jay.

"Aye, sir, she remains."

"This is the Lady Kyra we're speaking about?" he stressed.

"Aye, sir, the Lady Kyra." He appeared flushed and unhappy at that. "Aye, sir, Seacairn was always her father's holding, through Edward, and in his time, through Alexander. With our king long dead and Balliol humiliated and a prisoner . . . well, the castle has remained in English hands."

"I know the history of the castle, lad. It is Lady Kyra who interests me now."

"But, sir—" the lad protested, red and afraid, his voice trailing. Yet, why not? He should fear for his lady. Darrow's sins were such that they could not be forgiven, and there were those who suggested that he destroyed and pillaged with her full support and agreement.

"Lad, get to the wall with you, and no harm will befall you," Arryn said.

"But, sir, I don't think you understand—"

"Go to the wall now, boy," Arryn said, his voice low, a warning note within it.

The lad turned, still tall, proud, and headed toward the other prisoners grouped against the inner wall of the tower.

"Arryn," Jay said, "I can only assume you'll be going for Darrow's lady."

"Aye, Jay."

"I know you've been thinking of little other than revenge, and with just cause—"

"Aye, that I am."

"—to take what is his. But still, I implore you to remember, you are not such a creature as Kinsey Darrow."

Arryn lifted a hand with a gesture of impatience. "I intend to take the castle and the woman. What else would you have me do?"

Jay grinned suddenly. "Ah, Arryn! So we have the castle; you'll shortly have Darrow's woman."

"Aye . . . ?"

"Well, she could be ugly as sin, of course."

"Indeed."

"Wrinkled beyond all measure. She is rich, but wealth is certainly not always accompanied by youth or beauty."

Jay studied his friend for a moment, wanting to feel the same sense of humor. He could not.

"If she is as ugly as sin, as wrinkled as a prune, it will not matter. She is Darrow's, and that is all that counts. Was Darrow's. No more. The boys who were left to defend this place will have mercy, but . . ."

"Aye?" Jay demanded.

Arryn shook his head. "What more is there? She, too, is at my mercy." He inhaled and exhaled, feeling as if he breathed in bitterness. "Nothing here is for pleasure. It is vengeance, Jay. She is simply to be used, ruined."

"Aye, but . . . is such vengeance humanly possible if such proves to be the case? I mean, if a maid is preposterously ugly—"

"You have mercy, Jay."

Jay, his helmet in his hand, smoothed back his rich brown hair. "Ah, there's the word! Mercy! Such a virtue, and lost to Scotland and Scots for so very long, so it seems. You've granted mercy to these men."

"But you would have me grant mercy as well to the woman who encouraged Darrow in his vicious and bloodthirsty behavior?"

"Arryn, perhaps—"

Arryn leaned downward, his gloved hand curling into a fist that he slammed against his chest. "Sweet Jesus, I cannot forget or forgive what happened!"

"But she could be quite simply repulsive!" Jay stated.

"Then I will meet her in the dark, with a sack upon her

head! Come, we've taken the bailey· now the towers must fall
to us!''

He spurred his horse, leaving Jay to rush behind him to his
own mount. Angered, restless, still feeling the pursuit of inner
demons, Arryn rode hard to the great gate at the main tower.
He called out orders, commanding his men to bombard the
structure with a ram. Defenders overhead shouted, threatened;
they would hurl down oil and flaming arrows to set them all
ablaze. One fellow, in particular, shouted down that he would
burn with them in hell.

''Seize the great oak shield and continue ramming the gate!''
Arryn commanded, and his men quickly backed away toward
the shield they had fashioned of heavy oak, a piece of siege
machinery that protected them like a wooden roof from the
missiles cast down from the arrow slits in the main tower that
stretched above them.

The door shuddered.

The flames cast down burned, smoked, and went out. The
oil dripped off the curve of the shield.

The ram thundered against the door.

''Hold! For God's sake, we will surrender!''

Arryn lifted his visor and looked up. The same fellow who
had sworn to burn with them all in hell was the one offering
the surrender.

''You protect Lord Darrow's lady, sir. You would give up
so easily?'' he queried mockingly.

''You've granted mercy to the soldiers in the bailey. I am
Tyler Miller, captain of the guard, and I've heard, Sir Arryn,
that you keep your word. Swear mercy to us and I will open
the gates; thus you will have taken a castle you can still defend.''

''Aye, I swear mercy. But I ask again, what of your lady?''

''It is her command that I surrender,'' he said, his voice
suddenly tremulous. ''She, too, must cast herself upon your

mercy. We are too few, we have no more oil, no arrows, and we are poorly armed. And . . .''

He hesitated, looking down. ''Sir Arryn, we've heard of the fate befallen so many of your people. We humbly beg pardon, and swear we were not among those who attacked your holdings. God help us, we were not. These are Lowlands here, and aye, we've English in our blood, but many of us are Scotsmen as well, sworn allegiance to the old lord here, the lady's good father. Aye, he was an Englishman, but . . . we're not all vicious dogs, sir.''

''Open the gates then,'' Arryn commanded.

''Your word?''

''I've given my word.''

The great gates to the main tower of the fortress creaked open. Arryn nudged his horse forward, only to realize that Jay had ridden behind him. ''Take care—it could be a trap.''

''I must lead the way in,'' Arryn murmured.

He spurred the bay lightly; the horse pranced prettily and swiftly, making its way across the threshold and into the stone entry. Arryn held his sword at the ready—it still dripped the blood of Englishmen—but the threat was not necessary. The soldiers from the inner courtyard had laid down their weapons. There were only five of them. One stepped forward, helmet in his hand, offering his sword to Arryn. Arryn dismounted from the bay and accepted the sword. Jay came behind him, along with Nathan Fitzhugh and Patrick MacCullough. The other guards turned over their weapons in total surrender.

''Where is the Lady Kyra?'' Arryn asked, careful to continue speaking his native Gaelic.

Tyler hesitated, wincing. ''In the chapel.''

Arryn dismounted and started to walk past him.

''Sir!'' Tyler called.

Arryn paused, looking back.

''You swore mercy.''

"To you, I swore mercy."

"But—"

"Get these five outside, to the wall with the others," Arryn commanded Jay.

"Aye, Arryn," Jay agreed, watching as Arryn strode toward the wielding stairs. "Arryn, there might still be danger."

"This danger, Jay, I'll face alone. Secure the fortress." Arryn continued on up the stairs to the chapel, anxious, his blood racing and burning in a turmoil.

He reached the top of the stairs, and through a short hallway, came to the chapel.

And there, before the main altar, a woman kneeled.

Her head was bowed; she was deep in prayer. But she heard him. He saw her back stiffen. It was a broad back.

"Lady Kyra!"

Slowly she rose. Even more slowly, she turned to him.

She wasn't repulsive. That would be far too strong.

She was simply . . . serviceable.

She reminded him of a good draft horse. She was as broad at the shoulders as she was at the back. Her cheekbones were broad. Her jaw was broad. She was . . .

Broad. Aye, yes, broad.

The fever of fury that had brought him here seemed to momentarily still. His blood seemed to run like ice. No, she was not repulsive. She was as appealing as a solid cow.

Cruel, he told himself. She had her good points. Her eyes were powder blue; her hair was white-blond. Her little lips were quivering away. She didn't look like the cunning woman who might have made demands upon a man like Lord Darrow, forcing him to heinous and cruel excesses in his bid to gain greater riches beneath King Edward.

No, she did not look the type. . . .

He had come for revenge. She had been party to brutality and tragedy; nothing in life came without a price. She belonged to Darrow—she and her estates. He meant to see that she and her property did not become important additions to Lord Kinsey Darrow's quest for ever greater power, a power that allowed him to torture and murder the Scots at will.

He removed his helmet and neck defenses, setting them down on a pew.

"So . . ." he stated, sword sheathed, hands behind his back as he walked toward her. "You are Lady Kyra."

She was silent, not understanding his Gaelic, he thought.

Approaching her, he felt all the more ill. Seize Darrow's woman, use her, hurt her, cut into Darrow's flesh and soul the way that she and Darrow had cut into his. . . .

Could he ever have carried it all through? He had killed often enough in battle. Yet, murder—and the murder of a woman, even if she were guilty of complicity in the most heinous of crimes against humanity—seemed beyond his capabilities.

This would be like slaughtering a shaggy-haired steer.

"No one left to guard you," he mused, shaking his head. He stared at her flat, expressionless, bovine face again. "Oh, I am sorry, but . . . 'tis no great wonder! Nevertheless, you'll have to come with me."

He started to reach for her. Just as he did so he saw a flying shape—like a shadow of darkness—coming toward him. He spun around just in time to ward off a blow as a figure in a dark cloak came toward him, a knife raised high.

"Ah, a defender at last!" he cried out.

Swift movement had allowed him to ward off the first strike, but the cloaked defender was swiftly at him again, spinning around with supple grace and speed to try to stab a knife into his throat, but again he deflected the blow, seizing the man by the back of the cloak, throwing him forward with impetus to allow himself time to draw his sword once again.

He tried to make out the fellow's face, but beneath the hood the man wore a faceplate with a helm of mail.

"Surrender yourself!" Arryn commanded, lifting his blade. The cloaked figure turned.

And from beneath the encompassing garment, he drew his own sword. This defender was well armed, and had no intention of surrendering.

Fine, Arryn thought. *To the death let it be.*

He advanced, ready for the battle, fury and fire filling his veins once again. He dared not think often of what had happened, horrible things beyond the subjugation of a country, a people. Crimes of man against man, crimes he could not believe that God could sit in heaven and allow.

Crimes that haunted him, day and night, that filled his dreams with the screams of the dying . . .

Alesandra!

Nay, he would win here. His enemy would surrender, or perish.

With vicious, furious movements, he strode forward, his sword battering every thrust and swing of his opponent's weapon.

But the fellow was brave. He flew atop a pew, fought from the rim of the altar itself. All the while, the Lady Kyra babbled and blubbered, crying out strange warnings, gasps, screams of panic.

He ignored her.

This was a fight he could fight.

His enemy leapt from the altar to a pew, swinging his sword deftly. Arryn ducked the blow with a split second to spare, as the fellow was giving rise to leap around again with a solid, bone-shattering swing of his sword; once again, Arryn spun to give his weapon impetus.

A smaller man, lean, trim, agile.

But this was a fighter.

Still, strength would win out in the end, Arryn had determined. Strength, and his will to see everything that was Kinsey Darrow's destroyed.

Step after step, Arryn battered his enemy with a rain of blows that sent the fellow falling backward again, again—step by step his enemy parried his blows. But he knew his own strength and his fury. His opponent was skilled, but he knew that he was beating the power from the fellow's arms with every blow. Eventually, as he moved without faltering, he had his enemy against the wall.

His enemy's sword fell to his side.

"So you do surrender!" Arryn whispered huskily, advancing.

The fellow swiftly lifted his blade, nearly slicing Arryn's chin. Arryn ducked backward in the nick of time.

Surrender, no . . .

The fellow sped past him, tearing toward the entry.

Toward escape.

"Nay, my good fellow, nay, I think not!" Arryn cried, and leaping forward, he caught hold of the cloak, giving such a tug upon it that the fellow, a light man, was spun furiously in a circle. As he turned, Arryn stepped forward, tripping him so that the man's spin finished in a heavy sprawl upon the cold stone floor of the chapel. Oddly enough, they were directly beneath a beautifully carved statue of the Virgin Mary.

"Now do you surrender?"

The cloaked figure shook its head.

The fellow had protected his face and head, but wore no body armor. Arryn raised his sword in a certain threat, lightly placing the tip just above his opponent's heart.

"Now, my good fellow, speak quickly, for though you've been an able combatant, my patience is at a low ebb. Dark deeds have brought me here, and vengeance will be found with the blood of some poor beings!"

"Bastard Scotsman, do it!" the fellow said in a hiss.

Startled, Arryn moved his weapon. "Ah . . . a sword through the heart would be preferable to a hangman's noose? Or disembowelment. Castration . . . a few of the tortures Darrow so enjoys inflicting upon his captured enemies."

"Do it!"

"No!"

The shriek came from Lady Kyra. Arryn kept his sword against the man's chest as he turned with surprise toward Darrow's lady.

His *broad* lady.

"I should spare this fellow? Is he your lover, by chance, milady? A man far more concerned with your welfare than the lord who left you here?"

The lady went suddenly still, in grave discomfort, so it seemed.

Curious, Arryn raised his sword again, as if he would thrust it through the fallen man's heart.

"No!" the blue-eyed, broad, and timid Lady Kyra managed to cry again.

"Who is he? Let me see."

He knelt, wrenching the chain and plate helmet from his fallen enemy.

And there he froze.

For no man gazed up at him, but a woman. Eyes of emerald green fire challenged his in a blaze of hate and fury. A wealth of reddish gold hair tangled around her beautifully formed features. She made a man give pause, forced him to catch his breath.

"Ah!" he muttered, angrily reminding himself to remember his place. "The only man among these English proves to be a woman." He leaned toward her. "So who are you?"

She didn't reply. She had lost her sword, but he realized that she carried a knife still, and was ready to spring for him, attack him. Cut his throat.

He caught her wrist and wrenched the weapon from her. "I am Sir Arryn Graham. Do you know me, madam?"

She didn't reply, but stared stonily at him. He smiled, having no intention of speaking in anything other than Gaelic at the moment. "You will tell me who you are, or I will slice your ears from your head, then your nose from your face. A little trick learned from Lord Darrow."

The woman didn't reply. He started to twist the knife in his hands.

"*She* is the Lady Kyra!" the very broad blond woman suddenly cried out.

Ahh . . .

Was it true? Yes. He could see it in the flashing emerald eyes of the beauty sprawled before him.

Despite himself, despite hatred, anguish, and revenge, he felt his limbs burn, his blood find fire, his body quicken.

"Lady Kyra!" he said softly. Well, she was not broad, and she certainly appeared intelligent, and with a temper—and courage surpassing that of those who would defend her.

This . . . this was Darrow's woman.

No man of flesh and blood could find the need to place a sack over this damsel's head.

"Aye, indeed!" she spat out, thrusting the knife aside, sitting up, and trying to slide back from him. She smoothed a strand of tangled gold hair from her face. "I am the Lady Kyra. But trust me, sir, I do *not* know you."

For a moment, her complete pride and reckless defiance amused him.

He rose, reaching for her hand, wrenching her to her feet. "But you will know me, my lady. You will come to know me very well. Indeed, from this moment onward, you will know no one *but* me." All humor and amusement left his eyes. "Indeed, lady, in payment for those so woefully misused and abused in your name, you will know me very, very well."

CHAPTER TWO

Did she know him? Yes, of course, she did. She had lied.

Yes, of course she had lied. She knew far too much about him, far more than she wanted to know.

She stood now, facing him. He was a tall man, broad and powerful in the rough-hewn and battle-weathered chain and leather armor that adorned his frame. If he had worn a helmet into battle, he had cast it aside now, and she could clearly see his features; like his well-worn armor, they were both oddly striking and weathered. He was a young man with a clean, chiseled face; a hard, squared, and unrelenting jaw; wide-set eyes—large, piercing, and a very deep blue. His hair was as dark as ebony, almost blue-black in its darkness, long to his shoulders, wavy, despite the fact that it was unruly and wild as well. He was clean-shaven, which seemed to make the utter ruthlessness in his eyes and the set of his jaw all the more apparent. Rough, crude, coarse, she told herself. Barbaric, as much a berserker as any of the Vikings who were part of his ancestry, or as brutal as the Picts, the painted men of the north who were equally a part of what made up the Scotsmen of his kind and clan. They were all tribal men, no more civilized than the horses who swept the continent in the dark ages gone by. Not even the Romans had troubled much with them, for they were far too much like animals to be worth the effort.

Yes, this man was definitely . . .

An animal?

Thus Kinsey had described him—as he described all Scotsman. To Kinsey they were one and the same. Especially the Highlanders. This man, though, was from Stirling, so she had been told, and kin to the Sir John Graham who rode so closely to the rough renegade William Wallace, a man who was little better than the berserkers who had ravaged these coasts not so very long ago.

Yes, she knew of this man, one of the Grahams, a clan of born Lowlanders themselves, who led and fought and died with the heathen Highlanders. They hailed from a southern section of the country, where they should have become far more civilized—more Anglicized—but they chose to be a group of Gaelic-speaking madmen who defied God and law and practiced every manner of barbarism known to the imagination.

So this was to be her salvation! she thought, feeling a new rise of panic grow within her. She had prayed for something to happen to change her life. This! This was God's jest, God's irony upon her.

But then, indeed, she had said that she'd gladly meet with Satan himself. . . .

And still, it wasn't so much what she had been told about him that so frightened her.

It was what had been done to him!

All in the name of justice, all in the name of the king, so Kinsey Darrow had said. But Kinsey gave his loyalty to the English king, while the Scots, both desperately and furiously, were fighting against subjugation to that very king, at least Scots such as this one. Fools, Kinsey often said, for Edward I of England meant to have homage paid to him by Scotland, one way or another.

Killing Scots was not like killing people, Kinsey had boasted in the great hall of this very castle. She must always remember: they were animals, and thus killing them was like killing animals; they should be bled, their throats should be slit. Then they should be gutted. Castrated. Quartered. Burned.

Burned, yes, that was what he had done. . . .

A chill swept through her. Like rays of an ice-sun, the cold streaked out into her limbs as she stood, staring at him, feeling the hard, calculating assessment of his cobalt eyes in return. She gritted her teeth very hard, fighting another wave of panic.

She suddenly realized that she very much wanted to live, though she didn't want to admit she was afraid to die. And if she was going to be executed, she should meet her new destiny with all the dignity and courage of her rank and station in life—chin high as she walked toward death!

She *should* know such dignity and pride.

What a pity she was so terrified. It was amazing how much easier it was to be brave and courageous when not facing imminent torture and death.

What else could she be but afraid—very afraid?

The methods used for execution between these enemies were beyond cruel and horrible. If she was tortured, would she suffer in silence?

Most probably not.

God, the way he looked at her was nearly as frightening as knowing what he had decided—and anticipating what was to come.

After what had been done to him. . . .

In the name of Edward I—who wanted to be known as the Hammer of the Scots.

And in her own name, of course, for she was the heiress of an English man, an English lord given dominion in this land. Though her mother had been a Scot, she was an English subject, and subject to the man who would be Hammer of the Scots.

So what awaited her now? Would she be drawn and quartered? Disemboweled? Suffer a fate more fitting the members of her fairer sex, condemned for witchery, heresy, betrayal?

Burning . . .

God help her, she wouldn't face the flames. Some kind executioner would strangle her before the fire scorched her flesh, before she felt the pain, and yet this man must want her to know every dreadful second, after what had been . . .

Her heart thundered. She stared at him. "Sir? Shall you have done with it now? Will you hang me from the rafters in the great hall?"

"Hang you?" he queried. "Hang you? A simple hanging? Good God, my lady! We are barbarians, but surely you must expect that we have some imagination!"

"I'm quite sure you have more than ample imagination. But you have taken the castle. Be advised that the men here had nothing to do with . . ." Despite herself, her voice trailed. She had meant to keep her eyes steady with his. She could not. "The men here were not involved with the events that occurred so recently on your holdings . . . sir."

She wanted to look at him, wanted so badly to raise her eyes to his. Feeling his stare, she wanted so very badly not to appear a coward.

And at last she looked up at him. "If they beg for mercy, I pray that you will remember that in simple justice: they were not involved."

"And we know, of course, that you were," he said, and she wondered if it was a statement, or a question. The words from him, quietly spoken in the Norman French of the court, were more disturbing than a harsh demand in the Gaelic he had thundered thus far. She wondered if it was because there was a more subtle but far more deadly threat in a tone so soft.

She hesitated, feeling the fury that lay within him, feeling it tangible in the air, washing over her in great waves. And she knew that it was more, of course, that it was pain and loss and horror, and she was tempted to scream out her own terror and throw herself at his feet.

"My name was used," she said. "What matters, sir, is that you do not punish the innocent here, that you—"

"No quarter," he said softly.

"What?"

"No quarter, my lady," he answered her, his eyes studying her face, his tone low and even. "No quarter. They are the two words given by your good King Edward at Berwick on Good Friday, March thirtieth, 1296. You have heard of the occasion, surely? He attacked the town and mercilessly slaughtered the citizenry—the estimate of deaths that night ranges from about seventeen to forty thousand. Edward was in a rage—his cousin had been killed by an arrow. His own churchmen begged him to stop the carnage—he would not do so until he had to witness a child being born as the mother was hacked to death."

Kyra knotted her fingers into fists at her sides, well aware that the event had occurred. "Terrible butchery has taken place," she said quietly. "But these people were not part of it. Does revenge justify the murder of innocent men?"

"Innocent men? *Innocent men?* Any man who serves such a master as Kinsey Darrow can hardly be considered an innocent."

"Those who have remained here were my father's retainers. They never rode with Kinsey. They were left to guard the castle when he rode out. I swear to you that they were innocent of . . ."

She faltered. The sudden rise of rage and pain to his eyes were such that her voice trailed to silence.

"The death of my wife and child?" he finished harshly for her.

She was shaking and she knew it. She couldn't meet his gaze.

She had been promised to Kinsey by the king, but as yet, no wedding ceremony had taken place. She had come of age at a time when Edward was ruthlessly destroying Wales and turning toward Scotland, despite his disputes with France. England and Scotland had always struggled for border lands, but never like this. She could not believe the atrocities that took place, the destruction of Hawk's Cairn, Arryn Graham's manor and holdings. Fighting men had been locked into a barn—which had been set ablaze. Then the house itself had been torched.

Kinsey had sworn to her that he hadn't known that Arryn Graham's pregnant young bride was in the residence when his manor was set afire. And still . . .

Had his lady succumbed to the smoke? Or had she died in the fury of the flames?

"None of these men took part," she said.

"Perhaps not. And perhaps you're a liar, praying that they'll find courage and strength and rise again in rebellion when I believe they've been subdued."

Her eyes flew open and she stared at him, surprised by the sudden rise of renewed courage his scornful words had brought to her. "I am the one against whom you should seek your vengeance. Take what revenge you will against me. Turn these men to your own use, for they are far more Scottish than English, and will be grateful for your mercy and perhaps far more useful to you in the future alive than they could ever be now as dead men! Take your revenge against me."

"Oh, I will, lady, I will!" he assured her, spinning around, his strides long as he began to exit the chapel. As he started out, another man, a strapping young dark-haired warrior with his helmet held now in his hand, came bursting in.

"Arryn, did you find—" He broke off seeing Kyra.

"Yes, I found her," Arryn said, turning back to indicate Kyra.

The newcomer stared at her hard, then at Arryn.

"Well," he murmured.

"Escort her to the eastern tower room," Arryn said, his gaze—hard, blue, and passionless—assessing her once again.

"Now?"

"Aye, now." He still gazed at her. He looked at the newcomer once again. "She has suggested that we hang her. I have informed her that, barbarians though we may be, we've imaginations far superior to so simple a solution."

"But Arryn—"

"Jay, you will escort the lady to the eastern tower, where she will await my leisure."

Ingrid came running up to her from the few steps behind her where she had stood. "I will be with you, my lady—"

"You!" Arryn snapped, pointing at Ingrid. "You will descend to the great hall now!"

"No!" Kyra cried, grasping on to Ingrid. "You will not hurt her or abuse her in any way! She is truly no part of this—"

"Madam, she will not remain with you!" Arryn grated. "Who are you? What is your name?" he demanded of the terrified girl.

"In . . . In . . . In—"

"God help us!" he roared impatiently. "Your name! All I've asked is your name."

"Ingrid, she is Ingrid!" Kyra told him.

"Have her go below before I have her dragged out."

"Ingrid, go below to the great hall; see what work needs to be done. He will not hurt you. She stared at him, praying that she told the truth as she looked into the icy pits of his cold blue eyes. Would he hurt her—kill her? Neither women nor children could expect simple decency in this conquest Edward would make. How could she promise Ingrid her safety when she knew what had befallen this man's wife?

It didn't matter. Maybe Ingrid wasn't as aware as she of what horrible cruelties had taken place against their enemy. She stepped forward as Kyra urged her, slowly approaching Arryn, then nervously passing him by.

Arryn watched her go.

"Aren't you afraid she will find a weapon and come back and crush you?" she heard herself say defiantly. Then she was terrified anew, afraid that her reckless words might endanger the girl's life.

"Afraid, madam, of timid Ingrid? Not a whit. While you, my lady . . ." Once again he assessed her. "I'd not trust you for a split second. Only a fool would turn his back on you. But we'll deal with that difficulty later."

Without another word, he threw his mantle over his shoulder and started on his way out of the chapel again. A moment later he was gone, and she was left alone with his man to be taken to the tower room.

"My lady?" the man said.

"How does he know the tower room?" she whispered. "No one has been there since my father—"

"My lady, in better days, he knew your father."

"He never knew my father!"

"Lady, he did."

"I would have remembered—"

"You were very young, and in London, serving at the queen's court. You see, my lady, we would have remembered you as well, had we ever met, I am certain. Will you accompany me?"

"My father was no friend to outlaws."

The tall warrior smiled at her. "We were not outlaws then,

my lady. For Edward of England had not seized this country that is not his.''

"But your leader is—"

"Not a savage, uncivilized barbarian out of the Highlands, my lady. Though he's kin enough among a rugged breed! I swear to you, my lady, he did meet your father, and does know the castle, and was welcomed here once.''

"Sir, whatever the past, you are rebels and outlaws now!''

"Now will you please accompany me?''

He seemed a decent man for an outlaw. She gazed at him, studying him. He was young, with handsome features of a gentler nature than those of his leader, who seemed a rough-hewn, ruthless savage, no matter what this man had to say in explanation.

Aye, if he was savage, he had just cause!

She was not to blame, yet it seemed she would pay the price. There was nothing to do but fight them. . . .

As long as she was able.

"And if I do not do as you say? Follow your orders?'' she inquired. "Will you skewer me here and now? Perhaps I should allow you to do so. I will die an easier death—and you'll not have your barbarian minds taxed in determining a more imaginative end for me.''

The dark-haired man smiled, giving her the first breath of hope she had felt since knowing they had come. "My name is Jay, lady. Will you accompany me, please?''

"Why should I cooperate with you, sir, with men who will decimate my people and destroy me when they see fit? Why should I make things easy and accompany you?''

"Because you have far too much mercy in your own soul to make me go to him with the words that I cannot do so much as accompany an unarmed young woman to a different room within a castle. Then he would come back for you himself. . . .''

Jay allowed the implied threat of his words to linger on the air; then he shrugged. "As it is, unless I must admit to my incompetency, he may be occupied for hours."

"Lead the way, sir. I will follow you."

"Nay, lady, you will go before me."

She arched a brow. "Do you think me dangerous, too?"

"It's best never to trust the enemy."

"The unarmed enemy?"

"My lady, if you will . . ."

He bowed, indicating the door. She exited the chapel and walked down the second-floor hallway, tempted to stop and stare down to the great hall below to see for herself what damage might have been done to the hall and to the folk who worked there. Yet she kept her spine stiff, her chin raised— and walked. From the corner of her eye she tried to see what was happening below; she could not.

She turned around, facing Jay. "Will you tell me, sir, if my priest has survived? His name is Father Michael Corrigan."

"It's not my place, my lady, to tell you anything."

"What of the captain of the inner guard? A brave man named Tyler Miller."

"Lady, what has become of your people is not for me to say."

"You cannot answer simple questions?"

"Again, I say it is not my place."

"Are you a puppet then, sir, nothing more than a plaything for a greater man?"

She was startled when he smiled. "My lady, you will not goad me into betraying Sir Arryn in any way."

He stood steadfast, not at all perturbed, and she was dismayed by the loyalty she saw in his features. She turned and walked again, suddenly half-blinded by tears. This would have been far easier if the man who had set out in vengeance against Darrow were more clearly a monster. Thus far, though they might mean to destroy her, they prepared to do so with courtesy.

They were well-spoken and apparently well educated, for barbarians. Their Norman French was as good as their Gaelic.

She stared at Jay for a moment, weighing her chances to at least know the fate of the two men who had stood by her most loyally—Tyler, who would have fought to the death without her command to seek mercy, and Father Corrigan, who had believed that he had left her hidden in the burial vault of her father, with Ingrid to take her place until he could placate the man who had come for vengeance. Father Corrigan had seemed to think that this man would not bother with Ingrid, that he would set her free, or perhaps force her to do manual labor for his men. She didn't think that Father Corrigan began to understand the depths of Sir Arryn Graham's anger.

Somehow she must defend the people who had defended her. Or die trying.

She would not go meekly to the tower room.

She spun again, tearing for the stairs with mercurial speed. She heard Jay's startled, sworn exclamation behind her, but ignored it, racing down the stone steps to the great landing below, turning to the left, then, to the vast expanse of the drafty great hall.

Several men were there, warriors who had now cast off their helms but remained in their heathen armor—armor not near so grand as that afforded her own men here at Seacairn, but deadlier in its rugged, simplistic style. They were not clad in tunics that proclaimed one great lord or household, but rather in chain and leather protection with metal plates covered by the mantles and colors of their own families, simple plaids that conveyed their allegiance to family and name, rather than to a commander. Four were seated at the large, long planked table that stretched from the area of the hearth; a few were seated upon it. The hounds that supposedly guarded the castle had already given over to the new regime; they lay about in the rushes near the hearth and slept easily—or nuzzled the hand of a conqueror as he drank ale from her storerooms and ate heartily of the smoked meats and fresh bread that had been brought on large trenchers to the table. Already the servants served new masters.

And dinner had come for famished warriors, so it appeared.

She stood still, staring into the room, digesting the sight of the invaders sprawled so comfortably about. Arryn Graham was here. He did not sit with his men as yet, but stood by the hearth, arms leaning upon the mantel as he stared into the flames.

He turned and stared at her. She felt the cold assessment of his deep blue gaze once again, and once again found it chilling.

There had been talk in the great hall—men boasting and laughing, she thought. Now it was suddenly all silence, and like Arryn, they all stared at her.

"Arryn—" Jay began awkwardly, coming to a halt behind her. She could almost feel the rush of warm embarrassment that encompassed him. He had, after all, failed at the simple task of escorting a lone woman from the chapel to the eastern tower room, the isolated master chamber that rose another flight of steps from the second-floor chapel and guest rooms, storerooms, library, and office.

"Aye, Jay, I see—Lady Kyra has come to meet her new . . . guardians," Sir Arryn said. He left the hearth, walking toward her. She felt the frantic beating of her heart as he approached. There was something in him, an energy and a hatred tightly leashed, that frightened her more than all the threats against her life, person, and sanity. It was as if he might, at any second, snap, and then the violence done her would be swift and terrible. Yet suddenly he reached out to her, taking her arm. She felt the strength and tension in his grip, like the lightning of his eyes. She longed to wrench free, to violently shake off his touch, yet she thought better of it—for the moment, at least.

"How rude of me. I failed to ask you to join us for dinner."

So saying, he slipped her arm through his own, a hand upon hers as he led her down the hall to the head of the table. "Men, this is the Lady Kyra of Seacairn, daughter of the late Lord Hugh Boniface and Lady Mary MacGregor of Dumferline—now pledged to one English lackey known as Lord Kinsey Darrow. Lady Kyra, you have met young Jay MacDonald; the fine fellows to my left are Nathan Fitzhugh and Patrick MacCullough. There, to my right, Thane MacFadden and Ragnor Grant. Those strapping lads at the rear of the table are Roger Comyn and Hayden MacTiegue." The men nodded to her as they were introduced. She and Arryn had reached the head of the table. He pulled out one of the heavy, finely carved chairs for her. A hand upon her shoulder, he pushed her down. "Do sit and join us—Lady Kyra."

She sat, having no other choice with his hands on her shoulders, aware of the faces staring her way. Arryn did not sit. His booted foot landed upon his chair. His hands left her shoulders, but he remained close, nearly touching her, as he reached for the tankard of ale in front of her. He drank from it, and pressed it toward her. "Drink, Lady Kyra. Drink with us. We were just about to toast our victory here."

She ignored the tankard.

"Where is my priest?" she demanded curtly.

"Your priest, my lady?"

"My priest. What harm have you done him?"

One of the men at the end of the table made a snickering sound. She bit her lower lip, trying to keep from bolting in a wild panic and amusing them further, for surely they would attempt to stop her, and the attempt would not be gentle.

Arryn's head lowered toward her own. "Surely you are not feeling the need for last rites so soon, my lady?"

She managed to push back the chair and rise, yet found herself hemmed in by him. Still, she found the courage to speak again. "I demand to know what you have done with him!"

"You demand?" he inquired, unruffled, only the dark blue eyes so fixedly upon her betraying any inner turmoil.

"Aye, sir, I demand to know—"

His hand landed on her shoulder. "Perhaps, with all in attendance here, I should fully explain your situation. You will make no demands. You—like the hounds by the fire—will receive whatever courtesies and kindnesses we choose to bestow." He spun her around to see the faces of the warriors in the hall. "Look around you, lady. Every man here had kin at Hawk's Cairn. You have heard of Hawk's Cairn? Ancestral manor and estates of my line of the Graham family. Aye, you know what happened; you know it well. We have established that fact already, haven't we? You say that none of your father's people here had a part in that barbaric act of inhumanity. But you knew of it, by your own admission. You knew that your betrothed was out riding against the Scots. You didn't carry a sword into that battle yourself—or did you? God knows, you handle the weight of a weapon with much greater talent than many a poor man sent to his death on a king's business. It's no real matter here and now. This stronghold will again be held by Scotsmen."

"Aye!" Roger Comyn shouted.

"Roger is one of the Comyn family, a distant relation to John Balliol—the Scottish king forced by Edward to abdicate, my lady," Arryn explained.

"Sir!" she interrupted. "Horrible events have occurred; aye, there is no denying that. But, you should recall, Edward was brother to Alexander's first wife, and the great uncle of the Maiden of Norway. Negotiations were under way for her to marry King Edward's son and heir. He did feel obligated to Scotland—"

"Obligated!" Arryn roared the word in such a fury that she had to fight to keep from falling back when he pressed toward her. "Obligated to wrest Scotsmen from their legal positions and thrust the English in upon us?"

She was shaking, but there were a few matters she had to set straight. "My father was here when Alexander was still alive; he was an Englishman, but he was chosen lord here under King Alexander—"

"Because of your mother. Because of the Scottish blood that flows in your veins—which you seem to have forgotten in your quest to help your intended rise to power in a land he would destroy to conquer, for a king who desires nothing but to destroy and subjugate a people as well."

"Aye, that's the truth of it; you've said it as well. I have forgotten nothing! This land is mine through my mother. Mine! And you—"

"So the land is yours, and not Darrow's! It matters little. By Scottish law then—this land is seized from you, my lady, and from your master, the wretched king of England who would style himself king and overlord here. You have but one function left, lady, and that is to suffer what insult comes your way."

She picked up the tankard he had earlier attempted to thrust her way and slammed it on the table, staring at him, so infuriated by his speech that she was ready to fight again. "At my father's death, I was claimed lady here through the king of Scotland— John Balliol—rightfully chosen king, whom you say you honor, a direct descendent of the ancient kings through his mother's line—"

"Aye, John Balliol had the right and legal claim!" Arryn agreed. "But though he was legal heir, he rots in prison in England, and even his most ardent supporters here"—he paused, glancing at the man Roger—"realize that he tried to be a good king, but hadn't the strength to stand up to Edward."

"You are outlaws, nothing more!" Kyra shouted. "What you don't seem to understand, sir, is that the king of Scotland had agreed that he owed feudal duty and homage to the king of England—"

"The king of Scotland was forced to pay homage—as were

all the Scottish lords and magnates who so foolishly tried to hold on to their titles and their wealth!''

She stepped away from the table. Arryn seemed both angered and amused, and not in the least afraid that she might take flight.

How could she? She realized that his friends had risen, that they formed a circle around her. Jay MacDonald guarded the rear, toward the steps that led up the tower. Ragnor Grant, another heavily built, very tall man, veered to her right. Thane MacFadden, darker, leaner, stood to her left.

She had no intention of running—and letting them toss her about like a sack of dirty laundry. She held her ground, her eyes steady on Arryn Graham. ''If only John had chosen to continue to pay homage—''

Arryn moved in on her, just a shade closer. His companions were at the ready, like hounds eager to make a kill. ''But what you don't seem to realize, my blinded lass, is that John paid homage and paid homage and paid homage—and finally refused when Edward demanded that we give him men and finances for his war against France! That was when the blood began to spill, when Balliol at last stood up against the king of England! And why? Because we are not England; we are Scotland—and he has no real right other than his own determination to be lord over us. We will not submit!''

''You will remember that when the bloodshed began, the Scots raided England first,'' she reminded him.

His sharp blue eyes were narrowed hard on her ''Oh, aye, King John, for once a king of his people, rode south against the English in defiance of the king's order that Scotland should raise men and arms to fight his wars! And the Scots raided and pillaged and did some damage, but there was nothing of a massacre in there.''

''Nae,'' Ragnor chimed in fiercely, brushing back a long strand of his hair, ''it was not a matter of merchants, men, women, and children perishing at the whim of a single man who seemed to think himself as powerful as the Almighty!"

"Nae, it was not murder, wicked, vicious, cold-blooded!" Jay provided.

"Don't you realize," Kyra demanded, "that *Scottish* barons are on the side of the king? The Bruces, with the second most valid claim to the throne, give fealty to the king of England."

Ragnor made a snorting sound of disgust.

"Aye, for they would be kings! But they will learn in time that Edward means to have no true king here but himself," Arryn told her quietly. "Scotland is made up of more than just the powerful who fear what they will lose if they incur the wrath of the English king. She consists of a people who hold freedom very dear, and no matter what devastation he attempts to wreak here, we will win in the end. It is *our* country."

"Aye! It is your country, but there does not need to be this bloodshed!"

"Oh?" Arryn inquired. She didn't hear the change in his voice.

"You and your misguided friends do not begin to understand. Edward is a great king—a great warrior. He possesses courage and strength. He intends to give that courage and strength to this country—"

"Oh, my lady! You are speaking such rubbish! If you'll forgive me!" Jay interrupted, coming forward to face her where she stood at the table. He shook his head with passion and sorrow. "Edward may be a strong king, and a powerful man— but he is an English king, an English man."

"He has practiced treachery against the Scots in the most heinous ways!" Patrick said, joining the group. "You must listen to me and think about what you have said yourself! Scotland has followed a hereditary line of kings for centuries— a bloodline longer and truer than that of the English. But when Alexander died, and the Maiden of Norway so soon after him, we needed to go back a few generations to determine the right man for king. The regency, the guardians of the realm, were afraid that we might have faced civil war.''

Forgetting her rather precarious situation, Kyra felt her temper flare to meet the argument. ''Oh, which you would have! Look at your own barons! They change sides with the fickle nature of the wind!''

''Lady Kyra.'' Jay who seemed the most reasonable of the wild men, addressed her again. ''Our king—crowned king, would-be king—sits in a London prison while Edward tries to fill Scotland with Englishmen governing the castles, with Englishmen given the ancient lands of different men who refuse to bow down to a would-be conqueror.''

''Well-spoken!'' Ragnor applauded.

''Aye, and we shall drink to that!'' Patrick cried.

They were a frightening enough assortment: young men, hardy, well muscled, with both strength and determination. Yet none seemed stronger or more determined than the one facing her.

Arryn smiled, watching her, a smile with no humor. He stepped forward and picked up the tankard once again. Right before her, he pressed the tankard of ale into her hands. She felt the strange power of his eyes upon her, and knew the way that he studied her, with thought and purpose.

''Ah, but then, what does this conversation mean? None of this matters to you anymore, my lady, though we are always grateful for any comprehension of our cause. The castle is no longer yours; freedom is no longer yours. You still try to defend them, but you have cast your fate with devils, madam, and with them, I'm afraid, you must reside in hell. Your anger and pride are sadly misdirected, for, because of the king and the men you would so ardently defend, your own fate is to be used, abused, and perhaps left to the buzzards, though, despite the wrongs done the fine fellows here, we've yet to commit murder in the same fashion as the men you are so determined to follow. So drink with us, my lady. Come, come, drink with us! We drink to Scotland. Scotland, my lady. We are in Scotland!'' He smiled, and still no warmth touched the blue of his eyes. He pressed the tankard of ale toward her once more.

A knife protruded from the meat upon the table. She made a sudden, wild, reckless dive across the table after it, securing the utensil in her fingers before he wrenched her back and all but broke her wrist to force her to release the weapon.

''You'll not get out of your fate by plunging such a weapon into your heart, madam. And you would definitely go to hell for suicide, wouldn't you, lady?'' he demanded, his fingers firm around her wrist, the hard length of his mail-clad body close and cold.

And still she could feel the fever of his heat from within.

She tossed back her hair, narrowed her eyes. ''I had no intention of plunging it into my own heart; it was yours I intended to pierce!''

A cry of amusement, bravado, and warning arose from the heathen warriors who surrounded them.

Arryn wrenched the knife from her, his eyes never leaving hers. ''Drink with us!'' he insisted harshly. ''Drink to Scotland, and a Scottish king! Ah, come, my lady. With us—would you drink with us, drink this? *An oladh sibh seo?*''

Her fingers wound around the cup. Seized by fear, fury, and frustration, she tossed the contents of the tankard into his face.

Unfortunately, there was not much left in the tankard, and he managed to avoid the toss as if he had expected it. Ale flew into his face, but only droplets, and he wiped them aside, staring at her with his eyes glittering with pure fury before he pushed her back—then abruptly threw his shoulder against her midsection and tossed her over his back. His men let out calls and guffaws once again as he strode with her across the hall, but he paused, turning back. ''Jay! Can you watch her now within a tower and not fall prey to her wiles? There's business more important than tending to Darrow's woman for the moment!''

"Aye, Arryn! She'll not escape me again!" Jay said, following behind.

Dazed, afraid, humiliated, Kyra attempted to fight her position. But he moved swiftly, his steps fleet upon the stairway. He reached the second floor and started for the stairs to the eastern tower, and she thought again that he knew the castle— knew it well. Seconds later he was pressing open the door to the master's quarters.

She was suddenly set down.

Staggering, she found her balance and whirled around.

A fire already burned in the hearth; fresh linen stretched across the large bed, and the smell of clean rushes on the floor mingled with the fresh breeze that drifted through the high tower windows, as the tapestries that covered them had been pulled back. He had ordered this place prepared, she thought, and in little time. There were no servants present, this had all been done with remarkable speed and competency.

Naturally, she thought suddenly. He had come here as the conqueror—he meant to take the master's quarters. And he had already told her what her fate was to be: used, abused— and left for the buzzards.

She turned again quickly to find him staring at her. The strangest quickening and tension seemed to seize her limbs. But she was the lady here. And she had endured the taunting in the great hall below because she had gone there with a purpose—to find out about Father Michael and Capt. Tyler Miller.

"Look, sir—you are misinformed, misguided, and, I'm afraid, totally ignorant on many issues. And still, I understand, sir, what you have suffered in this war, and I am ready to pay for the sins done against you with my life.''

"I am glad that you are so resigned, for you will pay," he informed her politely.

"So take vengeance against me."

"I intend to."

She hesitated, watching him, for he made no step toward her. She suddenly felt compelled to defend herself. "What happened at your Hawk's Cairn was horrible, Sir Arryn, but—"

"Beyond all words, my lady."

"But Lord Darrow came after you, sir, you're aware, because of the death of his kin."

It had been a mistake to remind him. She watched the icy steel mask that came over his features. "I didn't murder Darrow's kin or anyone in the path in cold blood, my lady. I met with a warrior, a knight, face-to-face. We fought. He died."

"Sir, still . . ."

"You know exactly what was done at Hawk's Cairn!" he said heatedly.

She had heard the facts of the slaughter often enough. She looked down, not wanting to meet his eyes, wishing she had never spoken.

"Do with me what you will!" she whispered, and found the courage to lift her eyes. "But I beg of you, you must realize that the people here are truly innocent of the crimes that were done against you—"

"While you, my lady, are guilty of an outrageous amount of talk!" he broke in, harsh and impatient. "Guilty of a tiresome, shrew's tongue—among other things. Enough for now. I will tend to you later."

He turned to stride from the room. She was surprised to find herself running after him, throwing herself against his back. "Wait, please! I've tried to explain again and again—"

"You've tried to explain? Ah, lady, at least your Capt. Tyler Miller is a trained fighting man. He mowed down lads and lasses, working in the fields, and he beheaded the smithy, who was surely innocent of any crimes against Lord Darrow.''

"Please!'' she whispered. "I must know what you've done with Capt. Tyler Miller, with the priest, with . . .''

She backed away, dropping her hold on his arm as he spun to her. She stood straight, her eyes raised to his. "I know what happened at Hawk's Cairn. But I don't believe that you will practice butchery upon these people. You wish to taunt, but you will not be so cruel—''

A roaring sound suddenly seemed to erupt from him; she jumped quickly backward again, but not quickly enough. His hands were on her, wresting her to him. He held her, shaking her. She wore no cap or wimple; her hair hung free to her back, and she felt it shake along with her teeth.

"Don't underestimate my determination, lady! And by God, take care! Don't you—you, of all people—dare believe that I will know any mercy!'' She saw the slamming of his pulse at the vein against his throat and cried out from the punishing force of his fingers on her arm. He moved his hand as if he would strike her. She closed her eyes, willing herself not to flinch.

She opened her eyes. He had not struck her, yet seemed the more furious for it. His fingers then fell upon the fabric of her outer gown, soft blue linen beautifully embroidered at the sleeves and neckline, and ripped with such force that the fabric gave way from bodice to hemline. Stunned and frightened, she met his eyes, then turned to flee again—to where, she did not know.

Nor did it matter, for he reached out and caught the cotton fabric of her darker blue undertunic, and her very impetus to flee aided the grasp of his fingers. The garment was wrenched nearly from her; she tripped upon the hemline. Half-clad, she stumbled and fell to the floor, trying to grab the fabric to cover her breasts even as she gasped for breath, and twisted in a desperate movement for defense.

He stared down at her, eyes still glittering cobalt, touched with anger and no other emotion. He was not about to fall on her with lust or unbridled passion. "Don't mistake the need for my time elsewhere as a weakness for having mercy toward you, Lady Kyra. I do not intend to offer any. No quarter. Let there be none asked, for none will be given."

He turned away from her then and exited the tower room.

The door slammed in his wake.

She heard the sliding and grating of the heavy bolt beyond.

CHAPTER THREE

Jay stood just outside, watching as Arryn slid the bolt on the door. "Arryn, it did not occur to me that she would run. She must have known the castle was filled with our men."

"Let any treachery occur to you; she is more devious than Darrow himself, and possessed of a greater spirit," he told his friend and fellow warrior.

"Arryn, in all fairness, would 'devious' best describe the lady?" Jay asked quietly. "My God, I had not expected such a . . ."

"May I suggest the word 'devious' once again," Arryn persisted, aggravated. The lady of Seacairn was not proving to be what he had expected, either. She denied wrongdoing, yet fought like a tigress. She was intelligent, certainly not without courage—and knew how to use arms and armor. It was not unthinkable that she should have known about Kinsey Darrow's exploits, suggested them, or even helped plan them.

Jay shook his head. "No, Arryn. I wasn't about to describe her as devious. 'Beautiful' is the word I was seeking."

"How can you think such a thing about this woman? Have you forgotten—"

"No, I've forgotten nothing, but then, I've never seen the Lady Kyra before. I'd heard the rumor that she was one of the loveliest women on God's earth, but such rumors regarding beauty and talent do seem to go with riches—with which she is also heavily endowed. But it is more than that! She is passionate, ardent; she is loyal to England's Edward because she thinks him a great king, because she was taught that he was her king, and it is natural that she honor him"

"This is Scotland, not England."

"Border country."

"Scotland!"

"Aye, Scotland, then. But her father was English If you listen to her speak—"

"If you listen to her speak, you will find yourself a traitor to your own cause!" Arryn warned him. Then he added hoarsely, "My God, Jay, you must remember what was done! And she knows of it; she hasn't tried telling me she was no part of it, just that the men here are innocent."

"Sweet Jesu, Arryn, I am well aware of the atrocity. How do I forget when my brother perished, when . . . my sister escaped the manor to tell us what had leveled the house to the ground?"

"Aye, it was your sister, Katherine, who related the events that took place. And she would have died with the others were she not so clever and ingenious. And still—you suggest that I forgive this Lady Kyra because rumors of her beauty are true, because she is loyal to the man she considers her king—and because she has the strength of character to *fight?*"

"I suggest that you not practice the same cruelties that make a monster of another man, lest you become a monster yourself."

"I never intended to execute the woman, and you are well aware of that, no matter what my threats."

"Of course."

"But she will not wed Darrow with her honor and riches intact. I swear that as well!"

Jay was sorrowful, looking first to the floor, and then to Arryn. "I ride with you, Arryn, because I know you. I know that you will not hesitate to kill in battle, and I know, as well, that you don't butcher men or women just to prove that you can, or that you are powerful enough to slaughter the innocent. Your strength is in your justice. Whatever you do to her," he said very softly, "it will not bring Alesandra back to you. Or the child that was lost with her."

Arryn didn't reply at first, but after a moment he said, "In all of Kinsey Darrow's offenses, he has cried out that he does justice in the name of the king of England, and the lordships of Seacairn. The lord, Kyra's father, is dead—and until a wedding is carried out and legal, the lordship of Seacairn is a ladyship—the inheritance is hers. She has accepted her king with all loyalty, and such a man as Kinsey, apparently, in the same manner. She is as much the enemy as anyone." He was quiet for a moment, inhaling deeply, fists clenching and unclenching, fighting to conquer the haunting emotions that could seem to paralyze his soul at any given time.

Then he added, "You're right, you do know me. You know that I will not set the lady ablaze." The last was said very bitterly. "But there will be retaliation. For the moment, my friend, you will guard her, and guard her well. I intend to see that we are well secured at this castle. I don't believe, however, that any force would test our own, other than a king's army, and we know that Edward is in the field already. Still, I don't care to be surprised at night by any other faction. I will return when I have seen to the security of the castle."

"Aye, Arryn. Yet can we hold this fortress long?"

"Perhaps not—if Edward himself decides to take it. We can withstand a fairly powerful assault, but still . . . it is important as well that the men immediately begin stripping the fortress of her assets."

"I will guard Kyra well, Arryn," Jay swore. "She'll not escape me again. I promise."

Arryn nodded. He worried somewhat that Jay, usually steadfast in all endeavors, seemed to have weakened toward this woman of Kinsey Darrow's. But she resided in a locked tower with a good long drop to the parapets below. Unless she somehow managed to talk Jay into opening the door, there was no escape—and if she got past Jay, more of Arryn's men were already busy occupying the guest rooms in the castle and staking out their claims to the choice spots in the stables and outer buildings. She could not go far.

At the foot of the stone steps that led to the tower room, Arryn turned to the left, finding the broad passageway that led out to the parapets. From here he could look out at the courtyard of the castle, and to the stone wall some fifty yards away that guarded the outer circle of the defense works. Having seen, earlier that day, that he and his men were coming to attack, the farmers had herded their grazing animals inside the wall. Produce had been gathered inside to protect the inhabitants against siege conditions. Now the gates had been opened once more; animals were being herded back out of the inner tower courtyard, and the courtyard was being set to rights. Darkness had fallen, but after such a day, there was still a great deal of activity taking place. Some men hobbled about, injured in the fracas, but already fishwives were back in the courtyard, trying to make what sales they could of the catch taken even as the defenders had fought to save their castle. To the southeast of the castle, just below the circular walkway of the parapets, there was nothing but water, for that corner was protected by the river. Arryn knew that Seacairn had never been taken in such a manner, for to attempt to enter the fortress from the water would mean coming up the sheer stone of the wall. Stealth would be to no avail. Any assault or danger had to come openly, just as he and his men had come today, riding down hard from the north. It was folly to attack this place without a sound fighting force. It was only in the last months that he had gained a sound enough leadership to acquire the warriors he had needed for such a definitive assault.

Seacairn . . .

He had known the castle, as he had known the old lord, because before Edward had decided that he would destroy Scotland as he had destroyed Wales, there had been a time of relative peace between the two countries. Edward was a strong and crafty king; none had actually realized his true intentions until he had put them into practice.

Arryn walked the parapets and looked out over the large stretch of landscape visible from this height. They had begun their attack at midday; it seemed amazing that a full moon already rode high in the night sky, illuminating the countryside stretched before him.

He studied the slow run of the river, crystallized beneath the falling sun, the rolling green, yellow, and lilac hills, the rich forests beyond. It all appeared so beautiful. . . .

And so peaceful.

No . . . if Edward came with his army, they could not hold this place.

He gritted his teeth and closed his eyes. Arryn had come here to kill Kinsey Darrow, but Darrow had ridden away—at the summons of the Earl of Harringford. It was unsettling to know that Harringford and Lord Darrow were out there somewhere, attacking what village or manor he knew not. Perhaps, he reflected, they were trying to find William Wallace in the forest of Selkirk to destroy him and his men.

He bowed his head, shuddering suddenly, wondering if their

rebellion could ever win them freedom from English domination.

He thought back to the night of Alexander's death. *God rot!* If the king had known just what a hell he would create for his country, would he have risked his life so?

There must always be a Scotland ... Scotland wasn't one man. So Alexander had told him that terrible snowy night, and God help him, he had remembered those words always, even as he had discovered along the way just what defying the English would mean to him.

Ten years since the king's death. Ten years of violence, anguish, defiance, and a fight that they could not relinquish, no matter what tragedy came their way. Ten years ...

Edward had to be defied. And men like Darrow had to be destroyed—along with all who supported them, even such loyal English women as the Lady of Seacairn.

Whether they fought for the imprisoned king who had abdicated, or the lion triumphant of Scotland, did it matter, as long as they fought for their country? Though Edward had taken the king, he had not defeated the Scottish spirit. And rebellions arose: Andrew de Moray in the North, and William Wallace in the south.

Arryn's cousin, Sir John Graham, had, from the start, befriended William Wallace, a man who seemed to some— even among the Scots—to be a tremendous danger, while to others he represented the soul of freedom for their country. Wallace had been gaining more and more followers in his quest against the English here in the southern half of the country, while Andrew de Moray had been putting forth a fair fight to the north. Wallace fought for a country for Scotsmen, and for the Scottish king, John Balliol, in his captivity, no matter how weak Balliol had proven to be. Though Arryn thought little of the captive king, he had come to know Wallace through his cousin, and he admired the man very much, and had joined with his band on many an excursion against the English.

Wallace continued to respect the imprisoned John Balliol as king, but he didn't live under the assumption that the king would be released. He fought under the flag of the lion triumphant, the symbol of their country. Arryn led his own group of knights and freemen. He was respected as the leader of his group, and he led with his own stern set of ethics. Far too much that was true butchery had been done by both sides in this wretched war, and thus the way he fought, and the understanding among his men that they would not massacre their own people or the English peasantry in battles in which they had no voice. As Jay had said, he allowed no man to be put to torture, but fought fair battles. He slaughtered neither women nor children. His men were free to ravage what property they might; God knew, they had to survive, and survival was getting harder all the time. He had burned fortresses to the ground, seized supplies, relieved great ladies of their jewels—but not their lives.

A little more than a year ago, soon after Edward had forced Balliol's abdication and demanded that all Scotsmen sign an oath of allegiance to him, Arryn had encountered Lord Angus Darrow, cousin to Kinsey, and they had fought upon a bridge. Arryn had bested the man, but Angus Darrow had flown at him in a rage and plummeted to his death far below. Arryn and his men had still granted quarter to Darrow's followers, doing nothing more evil than relieving them of the gold, jewels, and fine woolen goods they had been attempting to bring south to England from Scottish coffers.

Not long before that fight, Arryn had married Alesandra MacDonald, his friend's young cousin and ward. He hadn't really thought that he'd had the time or the right to take a wife, but he knew that she had cared for him and trusted him since they'd been children. She'd been orphaned as a child, and she was always there, smiling, gentle, eager to see him always.

His father had been dead then, having perished on a journey northward some months earlier. What had happened to Sir Robert Graham, they didn't know. His body had been found on the side of a cliff. There had been no witness to his death. Arryn missed him bitterly. He could only guess that his father had been murdered, accosted as he had been himself. But he could prove nothing.

Alone, he had become what they called the Graham of Hawk's Cairn, a knighted, well-to-do, and well-respected land-owner; it was time to start a family. He had known different women in his life, in different places: landed widows, buxom maids, the lonely, the passionate. But now he wanted a wife, someone to love and cherish—a gentle touch, someone with whom to talk at night, to keep his house, bear his children, laugh with him, grow old with him.

He and Alesandra had been children together, but she had changed. Shy and slim as a girl, she had grown into a beautiful, self-possessed young woman with dark doe eyes and a wealth of rich brown hair. She had captured him in a way he had least expected, slipping beneath his skin with the softness of her voice, the hesitancy and tenderness of her touch. She had seemed to him to be everything that he was not: patient, courte-ous, balanced, thoughtful, and kind. She embodied all the honor and innocence for which they fought. Her outlook on life was bright and optimistic and ever cheerful, and little had made her as happy as the knowledge, soon after their wedding, that they were going to have a child. At Hawk's Cairn, she had turned his grand but nearly deserted manor into a home, given it elegance, made the whole of his holdings seem richer than they had been.

Then, while he was in the north, meeting with Moray, Darrow had ridden in. Arryn had heard from the few survivors that his wife had been seized and raped by her tormentors, then left in an upper bedroom of the manor, stunned and bleeding, when the fire had been set.

Even now, nearly a year since, his flesh went cold when he thought of what his wife had suffered. He had left her to that fate! She had died so because she had been his wife! Guilt plagued him when he lay awake, and it tortured his dreams. He would see her walking toward him, see her eyes so wide, hear her whisper his name ... and when he would look up, she would suddenly begin to burn before him, and he would hear her screams.

Even now his hands began to shake, and he felt hot and cold, and sick! He couldn't bear the thoughts that tortured his mind, that would do so until his dying day. . . .

And yet men would ask him for mercy!

He lowered his head, closing his eyes against the beauty of the country for which it seemed he had sold not only his soul, but Alesandra's as well.

Darrow and his men had killed his wife. Darrow had been guilty of heinous cruelty and brutality, as King Edward had been, but it was true, as Jay had warned, that to become like them would be his defeat, and their victory. He would not slaughter men needlessly, inflict agony upon the innocent ... brutalize women or children.

But neither could he let Darrow's betrothed go in peace! God knew what role she might have had in any of this, no matter what her passion and pleas for others. And did it matter? Of all that belonged to Darrow, she needed most to be taken away. She was the slim thread that gave him any power in Scottish affairs; her family had the position and the wealth. And if he hesitated in taking revenge, all he had to do was close his eyes. . . .

And the dreams would haunt him, waking, sleeping. He would see the flames rise. . . .

And hear Alesandra's screams in the silence of the night.

He turned away from the view, looking up to see that one of his men duly guarded the open tower above the master's chambers. He saluted his man, walked the circumference of the parapets, then hurried down the outer stairs to the courtyard below.

He summoned his squire, Brendan, a second cousin, and one of the lads he had found half-dead outside the manor walls at Hawk's Cairn. Brendan had been struck with a battle-ax while defending the door to his lady's house. Amazingly, he had survived the blow. The lad was sixteen, the age Arryn had been himself at the king's death. He had shown amazing courage, readily risking his own life for others'.

"Fetch Pict for me, Brendan."

"Aye."

Pict, aye, he still had Pict, the great destrier King Alexander III had given him on the day he was knighted, fighting as the king's champion in a border skirmish that had been determined by his victory. His father had still been living then; that was before men were found mysteriously dead along the wayside for refusing to sign an oath of allegiance to Edward of England.

Brendan returned with his horse. "Shall I ride with you, Arryn?"

Arryn hesitated. This cousin of his was very much like him: a tall, strapping lad with very dark hair and serious deep blue eyes. He had spent hours training with weapons of war at Hawk's Cairn, and listening to the words of the rebels when they met. Most of his family had perished beneath Edward's pounding fist in one way or another, and he was destined to wage war against the English as well.

"It's always well to have a man at your back," Brendan told him.

Arryn grinned. "That's true, and you're a good fellow for a man to have at his back. But right now, Brendan, I think I'll ride alone."

"Aye, Arryn."

So he rode alone, circling first the inner walls of the tower at Seacairn, then calling to his men on the portcullis to raise the inner gate, and seeing that the outer defenses were as secure as the inner defenses. Seacairn was an admirable fortress, begun back in the days of the Norman conqueror, enhanced during the realm of David I to the exceptional fortification it was now, with two walls to be breached to secure the innermost tower.

Dawn was breaking by the time he had ridden the whole of both walls and spoken with the people who remained awake to tend to the wounded, and to his own men, who had taken over the key lookout points on the walls.

Returning at last to the inner courtyard, he chose to brush Pict down himself and stable him with a fine supply of English grain.

Then he returned to the main hall, where Ragnor waited for him, standing now by the hearth, ready to give him a report. Another friend since childhood, Ragnor was a tall blond man with a red beard and light eyes, coloring that betrayed his Viking ancestry, something to be found frequently among the Scots, as in his own ancestors—just as Norman and English blood was common among them as well. The Scotland they now so passionately loved as one country had formed from native tribes that had come long before Christianity, just as it had also formed in more recent years with the addition of more would-be conquerors, invaders—and neighbors.

"You've been riding the fortress?" Ragnor asked.

"Aye, we're secure."

"I've seen to the men, and the servants here, the injured, the priest. We've seven wounded, three dead," Ragnor said. "The wounded are in the priest's house, just by the outer wall."

"Aye, I went by and spoke briefly with one of the women tending the wounded."

"The dead are down in the vault in shelves, the cold will

keep them, as we should have time for Christian services later. The defenders lost five only, with another ten suffering severe wounds, five minor injuries. The servants have sworn allegiance, acknowledging that their fate will be swift and irrevocable if they betray us in any way. In all, the bloodshed has been light for this victory, and it is a tremendous victory.''

"Aye, but Darrow was not here—he deserted the castle.''

"He didn't know we were coming; he answered to his overlord.''

"Aye, but still . . .''

"Arryn, God knows, we're all aware of how badly you want to kill Darrow. But though he has slipped through our fingers, we've still seized an important castle, and no matter how fierce Edward's rages and those of his men, this is our country. We don't want it to become a rotting graveyard, not by our own hands. There is something within Scotland that Edward himself doesn't see. His armies may be well trained, powerful, and numerous, but victory over a countryside is in more than the armies.''

"Oh?''

"Arryn, this castle had an English lord before, but I don't think that ever made the people here English. I think that the majority of them wanted us to seize the fortress. Perhaps they did not feel so when the old lord was alive, but they do now. The old lord might have been an Englishman, but he knew that this castle was Scottish, that Scottish law was ingrained in the people.''

"Let's hope,'' Arryn said. "I don't want to diminish what our men have done here, but what real victory have we actually taken? If Edward were to come now with his army, we would have to abandon this place. We don't begin to equal his might. He remains a threat, and he remains a power. And God help us, but it's true: Scotland is a land of different factions, and too often our own nobles are concerned with what they will gain individually, rather than with the good of the country. That's our true weakness against the English king. Our richest and most powerful nobles have aspirations to be king, and so they vacillate like branches in the wind rather than cast their fates against Edward. If we continue to fight in the name of a weak and powerless Scottish king, I fear that we fight for nothing," Arryn said, and shook his head. "Even Roger, who is a member of his clan, knows that is truth. Balliol bowed down before Edward, renouncing his claim to Scotland. Such a man is not a rallying point for warriors!

"We fight for Scotland, and not for a king, and we fight because we have no choice. What else is there? Edward has given everything he touches to English lords, and the English lords take everything Scottish, including our wives, daughters, and lives. What men can live with so little honor? What man can look to a man to whom he owes homage and not demand that his wife and daughters be given dignity? Ah, but that sounds noble, doesn't it?"

"Aye, of course—" Ragnor began, frowning.

"Yet it's not even honor that drives us on, I'm afraid," Arryn said. "If we don't fight, we fall prey to slaughter, again and again. We must fight; it is simple survival."

"But do we fight all our lives?" Ragnor asked wearily. "Is there hope for us other than homes beneath the trees in the forests where we run when we can't outfight the might of the English? For surely you realize you have been an outlaw, you have refused to sign the oath—but with this siege you will make a real enemy of the English king. You will find all your holdings seized."

Ragnor was basically right. It had been soon after the sacking of Berwick that Edward had demanded that every landholder in Scotland sign an oath of allegiance. Many men had refused to do so—though more than two thousand had, among them most of the men who would be claimants to the throne when the time came for a new king to rise among the contenders. Many men who had not signed the oath had been slain by English officials planted in Scotland. Arryn remained certain his own father had been murdered by Englishmen, though he feared he would never have the proof of it.

Just as Angus Darrow had meant to murder him.

But some had avoided the oath and survived, and like him, were becoming more open daily in their rebellion.

"No," he said to Ragnor. "The king can seize what he will. Taking land and holding it are two different things. One day Scotland will be ours. And besides, what can any man now take from me? Nothing is left of my land but charred ruins and burned fields. Even our people who have survived have sought shelter in the forest at the base of the mountains."

"You still provide for them."

"We steal for them."

"We plunder English baggage trains and take back what is ours."

"True. But eventually we will regain our country."

"Is that a dream we live or a truth to be hoped for?" Ragnor queried.

"Are you becoming a pessimistic poet rather than a warrior?" Arryn demanded.

Ragnor grinned. "I? I come from a long line of reckless berserkers—men who would fight when they didn't even know what they were fighting for. So I say, let's pray we live to see this Scotland for the Scots."

"Aye!"

"And we'll drink to life, eh?" Ragnor said. "The ale here is exceptional." He poured from a large keg of ale into two tankards, giving one to Arryn, then raising his own and drinking deeply.

"To life!" Arryn agreed, and drained his tankard. His head, he realized, was beginning to split. He had been awake all night. It was a new day. He wanted nothing more than a deep and dreamless sleep for a few hours of forgetfulness. He was crusted in blood, and he longed for a steaming bath as well. "Ragnor, summon a servant, whomever you have found most trustworthy. Who guards the tower above?"

"Young Niall of Perthshire. Thomas Grant watched until dawn, and now it is Niall who is there."

"Good. Have him keep the watch until midday; then give it to Joshua Martin. Keep the men with the sharpest eyes on the wall as well. I don't expect trouble by night, but ..."

"I'll stay awake myself until midday, then have Jay keep watch over all. You need have no fear, Arryn. We'll watch your back well for you to get some sleep." He hesitated. "You're taking the tower?"

"Aye. Why?"

Ragnor stared into the flames. "Well, I do not deny you the business of revenge, but ..." he hesitated again. "I find her very strange, the lady of Seacairn. Not what we expected."

"Really?" Arryn inquired, annoyed that anyone's opinion of Darrow's betrothed should matter to him.

"Come, Arryn, we thought to find either a simpering, inbred idiot or a cold, calculating shrew determined on pushing Darrow into taking every last drop of blood possible to increase their worth to Edward. She is neither. She is intriguing, the men agree. Courageous, passionate—the most determined warrior in this castle, one might say."

"So you all have been discussing the Lady Kyra?" he asked, and didn't know why the idea irritated him so.

"Aye."

"And you find her winsome?"

"Almost noble."

"Well. There are those who consider Edward I a noble king. And he is, to us, nothing more than a noble butcher."

"Aye, and that's true. Arryn, we've admired her, but ... we

are cautious for you as well. There's not a man who does not share your anger and pain, not a man who will ever forget Hawk's Cairn. So, aye, you should take what is Darrow's; he should die a thousand deaths and rot in hell for eternity. And the woman is justly yours. But aren't you afraid you'll awake with her knife in your throat?''

"I intend to take no chances; have no fear," Arryn assured him. "There is no possibility that I will be taken off guard.''

Ragnor stared at him, nodding; then they both turned, hearing footsteps as a sprightly man with dark eyes and graying hair came into the room. He wore a simple bleached muslin tunic and warm woolen hose; Arryn had the feeling he had recently stripped away an overvestment that would have carried Kinsey Darrow's arms. The man seemed vaguely familiar.

"My fine sirs, I have come to see if—'' He broke off, staring at Arryn, then began again quietly, "Sir Arryn?''

"Aye? Do I know you?''

"That you do, sir, though you may not remember me. I was a young groom when you came here years ago, riding with your father. My name is Gaston; I'm the Briton who tended the horses back then. I came to the household after nearly being trampled." He grinned with good humor. "You, good sir, dragged me from the courtyard when a dappled gray would have made mash of my face.''

Arryn grinned, remembering the occasion. "They shouldn't have had you in the stables. You did not like horses.''

"Still hate the creatures, sir, mainly because they hate me.'' His smile faded and he went silent. "Forgive me for speaking. Morning has come. I came to see if there was something else you required.''

"You are welcome to speak, Gaston. Tell me, have you become head of the household servants here?''

"At times.''

"At times?''

"When Lord Darrow is in residence, sir, he has his own company of retainers."

Arryn glanced at Ragnor, tempted to grin. Dissension in the household might be good for their current cause.

"But they have gone with him?" Arryn said.

"Aye, sir, they accompany him everywhere. I am a Briton, you see, and to Lord Darrow, nowhere near so competent as his own man from Sussex. However, sir, I would have you know that not only am I exceedingly competent, I am also remarkably grateful that you have chosen to seize the castle, take its wealth—and refrain from slaughtering its inhabitants."

"Well, Gaston, I'm not at all fond of slaughtering servants, and I am convinced that you will be remarkably competent. I want a very hot bath drawn in the east tower room, and I'd also have a large tankard of Seacairn's fine ale brought there to be savored while I steam. Can you manage such comfort for me, and quickly?"

The Briton was frowning. "Aye, sir, that I can, but I've been told that the Lady Kyra is residing now in the tower."

"That she is," he said flatly.

For the first time it seemed that the Briton hid resentment. "Well, then, sir . . . you should remember that I came here under the old lord; his daughter is a Christian lass—"

"We're all good Christians here, aren't we, Gaston? If you wish to be of good service, do as I say."

"Aye, sir," Gaston said, bowing and backing away. "Immediately."

He left the great hall, hurrying toward the kitchens. "The lady has her supporters!" Ragnor said softly.

"So she does. Pour me more ale."

Ragnor filled his tankard. He lifted it. "To Scotland. To our slain brethren."

"Aye, to those we've lost!" he said, and watching Arryn added, "And why not drink to vengeance?"

"Fine. To vengeance." Arryn drained the tankard. Finally, finally, he could begin to feel the soothing effects of enough ale in his blood. He walked to the fire in the great hearth, leaned against the mantel, and watched the blaze. Red flames, gold, yellow, crimson, even blue. Leaping, falling, warming the hall. Man needed fire. Fire warmed, fire heated, fire cooked. It staved away the sure death of the bitter cold that could come to the land. And yet . . .

Fire burned. Fire killed. . . .

He could still close his eyes and smell the smoke, the rancid smell of burning flesh.

"There must be vengeance!" he said softly.

"Aye. And Darrow's woman should know that vengeance."

Ragnor spoke with no conviction. She had bewitched them all.

Arryn spun around, his teeth gritting in fury. "I should simply give her to every soldier who breached these gates and leave her thus for Darrow to find."

"But you would not."

"Aye, and why not?" Arryn demanded bitterly. "Tell me, why not? Why do we stop where our enemies would not?"

"Well, knowing Darrow as we do, he would marry her still, and thus gain her wealth and many estates, both English and Scottish."

"If he kills enough Scotsmen, the king will reward him with estates and riches anyway," Arryn said bitterly. "He probably rose miraculously in the king's eyes, simply by burning men—and women—to death."

"You have taken this place, and his intended. You will drain him every time you're able. In time you will catch up with him. And then . . ."

"Then, so help me, if I die in the effort, I will see that he meets Satan."

"The time will come."

"Well, then!" He strode back across the room and poured himself more ale. "I am to duty, and to bed."

"Good night, Arryn, and take care! You must know that she'll fight back. That . . ."

"That?"

"That she'll want to kill you."

"Aye, I am aware." He paused, placing his hands over Ragnor's red-bearded cheeks. "She has already tried. Though it seems that this castle is filled with fools who fall quickly to her feet, I will not fall prey to the lady, my friend. Trust me," he said earnestly, looking into Ragnor's eyes.

Ragnor watched him go. "Would that I had your duty!" he whispered softly, and yet he knew that demons plagued his friend, and that this was a strange vengeance indeed.

Arryn walked up the steps, tension knotting his limbs. He felt a new surge of anger, and couldn't help wondering if he would be so bitterly determined if Lady Kyra had been the broad servant girl, Ingrid. As in the words of Julius Caesar: "I came, I saw, I conquered!" That simple. Have her brought to him, brought away. Over and done . . .

Why wasn't he doing that? Why was she residing in the tower room already? He would have to take his longed-for steamy bath with her there; he wouldn't dare shut his eyes—she'd be ready with a knife. . . .

He paused, frowning, forgetting his dilemma for the moment as he heard a thumping sound from the area of the parapets. Rather than taking the twisting steps on up to the tower room, he walked out to the parapets once again.

The drop from the tower to the parapets was perhaps thirty feet. There was a guard above her, but as long as she had stared at the circular walkway below, she had seen no man make a single pass by. There was nothing to guard from here; the man atop the tower above her head could see riders coming from any direction.

The castle and the village had been duly subdued.

And already the dead had been cleared from the courtyard; the wounded had been taken away to be treated. Morning had come, another day, a new day. Things changed, and things stayed the same. The merchants were at their business again—grateful they had been spared the last battle to plague them.

Locked in the tower room, she had paced through the night, waiting, and at every little sound, jumping—certain that he was returning at last.

She had paused before the fire and, unbelievably, drifted to sleep, then awakened once again with an ungodly feeling of urgency. She had paced like a fool, making no attempt to escape.

But then, realizing the night was ending and day was coming . . .

It had been time for sheer desperation.

If she could make it down to the parapets below, she could make it to the courtyard from there, mingle with the bakers' daughters and the fishwives—and disappear.

So thinking, she dragged her hastily created escape sash from the bed. It consisted of linen sheets wrenched from beneath the rich furs on the bed, her torn undertunic, the tassels from the tapestries, and the towels that were always set by the washstand. Her overgown had been left in little better shape by her tormentor than the tunic beneath it, but she'd found one of her father's old mantles to tie around her shoulders, and thus she could escape with both decency and some anonymity.

She had carefully chosen the structure of the escape rope she had created, with the tassel cords at the top end to be tied around the legs of the heavy oak chair she had wedged by the window. When her knots were carefully completed—very carefully completed, for she didn't intend to die in this endeavor—she took a deep breath.

She started out the window, then looked up. She could see the top of the guard's head, but he could not see her. The overhang protected her from his vision.

Slowly, slowly, slowly . . . she started down the rope.

It was painstaking—so difficult! She feared that one of the knotted garments would slip at any minute. She had to move more quickly . . . and yet so carefully. The day was chill; sweat beaded on her forehead.

Another foot . . . another foot . . .

And she could jump.

She did so, landing softly, her knees buckling slightly, both feet on the ground. She paused then, eyes closed, hands against the cold stone of the tower. She was shaking, very afraid, aware that she might well have plunged to her death.

But she hadn't.

She had made it.

And she was almost free.

And yet . . . what then?

Don't think about it, she warned herself. *Don't dare think about it, not now; just figure out how to leap down to the ground below, to join with the workers in the courtyard. . . .*

She opened her eyes. They flew wide. A gasp escaped her.

He was there—the damnable, wretched, invading bastard so bent on her destruction. He was quite at his leisure, and had been watching while she struggled with a desperate and precarious attempt to elude him. He leaned against the wall quite casually, one arm across his chest, sipping ale, staring at her with his deep blue, ruthless gaze.

She started to turn. His fingers snagged her hair, drawing her back. She met his deep blue eyes, his shaven cheeks beginning to show stubble. He was weary, drawn, and sarcastic, his deep voice pleasant—and biting.

"How very rude. You intended to leave without saying good-bye."

"Aye, I'm afraid so. I didn't know your whereabouts. So, now, sir, how very rude of you to detain me when I am so anxious to be away," she replied, reaching for his fingers in an attempt to persuade him to let go of her hair.

"So you missed me, and wondered about my whereabouts. I'm so sorry. Seizing and securing a castle are time-consuming. But I was just coming to join you."

"How unfortunate. I was just leaving."

"But I think not!" he said, and his light tone changed in such a manner that she knew he meant his words.

"You are hurting me," she told him, tugging anew at her hair.

"Good," he said, and his stare was so cold, his rejoinder so flat and honest, she felt a swift siege of chills. "That is my intent."

"Perhaps your intent should be delayed for the sake of logic, as this is most awkward. Be so good as to let me go, and I will precede you back up the stairs," she suggested.

"I will not let you go, and you will still precede me back up the stairs."

He had the most piercing eyes she had ever known, and a strange way of speaking in a manner that left no doubt as to his intent. When he spoke, there was no room for argument or negotiation. His statements were cold, chilling—and irrefutable. He absolutely despised her, she was certain; yet she would go with him and be . . .

Used and abused! His words!

He was as cold as ice, but his limbs and eyes burned with a strange passion. He had given mercy to the men, to the servants, but he was still covered in blood from the battle.

She bit her lower lip, staring at him. He gripped her as if he would far more willingly throw her from the parapets than drag her up to a bedroom. There had to be some way to argue him out of this; he had but one intent, and that was revenge against Darrow.

"You think to threaten me, and so strike out at Kinsey? My dear sir, you don't understand us. We are both ambitious to a fault, and therefore will still wed. I am aware of his fondness for damsels in distress; he is resigned to my hunger for variety. I—"

"Were you aware that he has murdered those 'damsels' when he is finished with his own amusements?" he queried sharply.

She bit her lower lip again. "He never meant to kill your wife—"

"I'm sure his remorse was deep, that he has prostrated himself on his knees to God daily since the event."

His dry sarcasm was biting.

"I still say that it was not intended," she protested, "and since you are so obviously appalled by me, I can't think what you hope to accomplish here! Did you think to soil his virginal bride? Dear sir, you're so sadly mistaken. There's nothing you can do, short of murder—"

"Ah, but," he interrupted, "we have not yet discarded that as an option, I must tell you in all fair warning."

"You don't want to kill me!" she accused him.

"No," he admitted flatly, those impenetrable blue eyes never wavering from hers. "But that will not stop me from doing so. Let's go back upstairs, shall we?"

"Why don't you just finish it here? Go ahead. Prove your brutality. Do it now. Throw me over the parapet!"

"Alas, I dare not. I might hit someone below."

She tugged afresh at her hair, as frightened by his coldness as his heat, and not at all reassured by his dry humor. "Please . . ."

He suddenly released her hair. "Get upstairs."

She walked in front of him, then turned on him again. "I'm telling you, this will mean nothing at all to Kinsey."

"Indeed? Well, good, then. God knows, there is nothing wrong with enjoying vengeance. I see that you are so anxious to get to it that you have already discarded half your clothing."

Her cheeks reddened. "Sir, you might remember that my clothing is in dishabille due to your less than gentle touch!"

"Ah, but that was hours ago—last night, as a matter of fact. You had no time for repair?"

"I was busy with important work," she told him.

"So I see," he replied, surveying the tied clothing and bed sheets that had supplied what should have been her escape route. Then he stared at her again, touching the garment that cloaked her shoulders. Your father's mantle?" he asked politely. Then his eyes narrowed darkly. "Or Kinsey's?"

She didn't know why she answered with the truth so quickly, but she did. "My father's."

His eyes stayed hard on her. She started to walk again, then spun around, anger and despair welling within her. "I will not walk ahead of you like a lamb to slaughter!" she exclaimed, and, slamming both hands hard against his chest, she tried to push by him. She made it to his left side before she was dragged back. His fingers tangled in her hair again. Tears stung her eyes. Step by step, she was dragged inexorably toward the tower room.

And there stood Jay. "Thank God!" he muttered, and the way he now looked at her, she thought that she had lost a friend for certain. He was furious with her for trying to escape.

Yet what did they expect? As they had come against her in Darrow's place for vengeance, so they must realize that it was equally a matter of honor for her to refuse to accept the fate they intended for her as well.

Yet Jay was furious. She had made a fool of him.

"Arryn! I tell you, she did not leave by the door! I just discovered her absence when the servants came with the bath—"

"She departed by the window, Jay," Arryn said, and she felt his gaze. "Not suspecting her capable of such idiocy, I discovered her quite by accident."

"Idiocy!" she protested, fighting his tangled hold upon her hair again "Not idiocy, but sheer desperation. It is my *duty,* sir, to escape you!"

"She is very eager to return to Darrow, so it seems," Arryn said.

He had come from behind her, placed his hands upon her hips, and thrust her forward into the middle of the tower room.

Gaston was there with several strapping young lads. He had brought the old, deep, Norse-carved hip tub from the kitchen. Water steamed from it while a kettle bubbled above the fire. Fresh towels had been laid out on the tapestried chair by the side of the hearth. A deep, thick, brown bear pelt lay on the floor by the tub and before the fire.

It was a charming domestic scene.

To make it all the more comfortable, new linens were being hastily arranged upon the large bed, with its carved oak head- and footboards.

Gaston met her eyes with sorrow. She realized that he had come here, seen her escape attempt, and had tried to keep quiet the fact that she had been absent from the room. But Jay had burst in behind him, and when Gaston could not pretend that she was still within the room, he had hastily tried to repair the damage she had done, hoping that by doing so, he might help soothe the temper of some savage beast.

She ruefully smiled her thanks to him, then quickly lowered her eyes. She didn't want the invaders seeing any exchange between them. He was her friend, trying to help her. It was a pity that he could not.

Gaston was quick to spring to action. "Ah, sir, ah, my lady!

The bath awaits, and all is fresh and clean. And there is a large flagon of ale here, sir, with two of the castle's finest silver cups. I shall pour for you.''

He offered ale first to Kyra; she took it gladly, draining the cup before he had turned to Arryn. Arryn didn't notice.

Gaston quickly gave her more ale. Again she thanked him with her eyes. She would never give up the hope of escape, but it seemed to dim. Drink was all that was left.

"Shall I serve you, sir?" Gaston asked. "Help you to remove your mail—''

"The lady will help me," Arryn said.

"The lady will not!" she protested, then felt his eyes. She wanted to scream, but she found herself smiling sweetly instead. "The lady could not possibly give you the assistance you require. Why, the weight of your mail—''

"I'm sure you'll manage very well. Gaston, leave us.''

Jay had hovered at the door. "I'll remain on guard.''

"It will not be necessary. Gaston, if you please . . .''

"Ah, but Lady Kyra is right! The weight of your mail—''

"Gaston. Get out.''

The Briton had done his best to defend his lady; he had lost. "Aye, sir," he said softly. He looked at Kyra, apology in his eyes.

She lifted her chin, trying to show him that she would be all right.

He left the room. Her friend was gone. She was not going to be all right.

Jay looked in on them a minute longer. "Good night," he said simply.

Then he, too, quietly departed and closed the door.

And she was alone with the man who had sworn vengeance against her.

CHAPTER FOUR

"Come over and help me," Arryn demanded.

Help *him?*

"No!"

"I need your assistance with my armor, my mail."

"You want me to undress you?"

"Aye, dammit, get over here."

"Shall I rape myself as well?" she inquired far too flippantly.

"Madam, get over here."

"I haven't the strength—"

"You have considerable strength, as you demonstrated by crawling down that wall. Now get over here."

To her surprise she found herself obeying. He directed her in unbuckling the leather lancets that held his mail at his shoulders. When she was finished, he ordered her to lift the coat of mail.

He was captured within the mail, his arms held in the prison of links. He had ordered Jay from his post at the door. It suddenly seemed her last chance for escape.

"If you'll hold just a moment here . . ." she murmured, and leaving him with his face covered by the coat of mail, his arms encompassed by it, she stepped away.

Then she sped for the door.

She had barely reached it, grasped the large brass handle, and begun to drag at the heavy weight of the wood, when she felt his hands upon her. He caught hold of the sturdy fabric of her father's mantle; it did not tear, but gave to his grasp, falling from her shoulders. She tried to gather the remnants of her torn gown around her, standing, shaking, her back to him. She winced, eyes closed, aware of her bared shoulders.

He didn't touch her. Nor did she hear him. At last she could not bear not knowing anymore. She turned.

He had rid himself of the mail coat, and more. Hose, shoes, tunic lay on the floor. He seemed completely unaware of her, a naked man in the prime of strength and life, covered in the dirt and blood of war, muscled like a Greek god, and oblivious to all else except his desire to step into the tub. If he would just do so . . .

"Take a step toward that door again," he said quietly, "and I swear I'll drag you downstairs and have done with this in the company of the entire castle, friend and foe. Now that, I believe, would disturb Lord Darrow if he hears of it—and I promise, it will disturb you deeply."

She stood then, her teeth clenched hard, wishing she had the courage to defy his words and bolt.

She stared at the door, not bolted and not guarded, and did not move. And she despised herself for it.

And still, she spun around, biting hard into her lower lip.

He lay in the tub, his head back, soaking, eyes closed, ebony black waves of hair drenched in the steam of the water. Tiny scars flecked his chest and neck. The structure of his face seemed strong and undaunted; yet his eyes remained closed.

Vulnerable.

She turned wondering if he would leap naked from a tub to pursue her before the whole company of the castle.

"Aye, milady, forget the door. I will do it, and with great irritation."

His *r*s rolled softly with his language. He was weary she thought. And yet . . . he read her mind—and assured her of his intent.

His eyes opened, pinning her where she stood clasping her gown to her chest. She couldn't read his thoughts in the least.

He looked away, lifting a hand.

"Bring me ale."

She stood still.

"My lady . . ."

"I am not your servant!"

"Servant? Nay, too kind a word. Slave, madam, better suffices for the moment. Bring me ale."

She strode across the room in an instant fury, forgetting the state of her clothing, and stumbled as her torn gown tripped up her feet. She cried out, falling. To her distress, he was instantly out of the tub, lifting her from the pool of her clothing. His wet naked flesh brushed her own. She was mortified, red as a sunset. His eyes pinned hers. Are you all right?"

"Leave me be!" she whispered miserably.

To her amazement, he did. He stood, striding back to the tub. His leg muscles were as taut as steel. His buttocks were more so. She looked away quickly, shaking, burning inside, wishing that she had simply leapt from the parapets.

She heard him plunk back into the water. Then a moment later: "I'm still waiting for the ale."

"You must wait until you rot!"

He was silent for a minute. "What an intriguing person you are, my lady! One would think that you'd strive to please me in little ways to abate my obviously foul temper."

"And would it make any difference?"

"Not a whit!" he assured her. "And still, one would think . . ." She was startled then to see something that was almost a smile curve his lips. "I am willing to share."

"You, sir, are in good health and able; you could help yourself—and serve me as well," she said with all the haughty disdain she could summon.

"You want me out of the tub again?" he inquired politely.

No, she did not. Yet she was not in much better shape herself with her gown nothing more than tatters. She tried again to gather the pieces.

"It's quite useless, you know."

"What's useless?"

"Any attempt at modesty." She suddenly felt his eyes again. "You've been with many men. . . ." His voice trailed suggestively. "Well, what difference is one more?"

She should have managed to cast aside every last strip of garment remaining to her, walk boldly naked about. She couldn't quite do it. But she did pour cups of ale for them both. She came as near the tub as she must and handed him his. She even managed a tight-lipped smile.

Maybe she'd imbibed a bit too much ale already. She was feeling reckless, and perhaps had too much false courage.

"What difference is one more? No difference at all except, sir, I always choose my lovers, choose them carefully. Great lord or stablehand, I choose only those who intrigue me."

He stared at her a long moment, shrugged and smiled with a certain amusement. *"Slainte!"* he said softly, imbibing all in a swallow. "You too, my lady," he said gravely. "Take it all."

She stared at him hard and drained her cup.

"I'll take another. You must join me again."

"Because I am so unappealing?"

His smile faded. "Because you are not," he murmured.

Her eyes did not leave his. She walked back to the ale;

poured his, then poured her own. She returned to stand before him. "Then . . . are you attempting to make this more palatable for me by forcing me to drink myself into a stupor?" she demanded.

But sunk within the tub, his hard, cobalt eyes upon her, he shook his head—and drank again deeply. "No, my lady. I am trying to make it more palatable for me."

His words and manner were confusing, and yet . . . they could not have cut more deeply, and for that she hated him all the more. Here she was, about to face force and violence, and *he* was shuddering at the thought of it!

Despite herself, she had never felt more . . .

Insulted!

"Then, perhaps, sir, if this is all so *unpalatable,* you should give up this quest to hurt Darrow! I've been with half the castle; you needn't bother trying to ruin me as a bride. I am common, vile—absolutely filthy!"

He studied his cup. "Half the castle?"

"Every stablehand," she assured him. She should keep him drinking, she realized. He had to be exhausted.

"Every single stablehand?"

"Alas, every single one."

"But I thought you chose your lovers carefully?"

"I carefully chose them all."

"Ah, then! More ale, my lady! More—more!"

He frightened her and infuriated her. And yet . . . there was something about him that made him a worthy enemy—although a man with whom she wished she were not engaged in such wretched combat. She suddenly felt her temper soar. *Common sense be damned; survival be damned.*

This was not to be borne.

"Ale? More ale? You would have more, then fine! Aye, more ale, sir!" she exclaimed, seized with a reckless fury. She grabbed the container, determined to dash it and its contents upon his head.

He was up like a flash of lightning, his hands snaking out and capturing her hard before she could elude him. He shook her like a rag doll, and the remnants of her clothing fell from her like autumn leaves from a tree before winter. Their naked bodies, sleek and wet, were suddenly together, and she had never felt such tension, nor felt so strange at the touch of a man's eyes pinning her own. He held her as she gasped for breath to speak, yet she did not manage to do so, for she was suddenly plopped down before him in the tub. "Filthy, my lady? I have said that I will share. You must then bathe as well."

She tried to gasp a protest; she could not—because he was touching her. His eyes were suddenly hot as blue fire; the soap and his hands were suddenly everywhere, moving over her breasts, her hips, her abdomen, between her thighs. Where he touched, she quivered. She was furious and indignant.

And she was burning.

She tried to rise; he dragged her back down. His hold was rough, hard, powerful.

His fingertips moved again over her breasts, stroking her nipples. The wicked blue fire of his piercing gaze seemed to seep through her, ignite her limbs. Chills and tremors swept through her. His hands moved again, deep below the surface of the water. She reached out to stop him. She touched his chest. Muscle constricted.

His hands slid between her thighs again. His fingers were slick and ungodly intimate. She wanted to shriek, to scream. She tried to catch his hands, wind her fingers around him, stop him, press him away.

Stop, no, cease, damn you, bastard. . . .

The words that she wanted didn't leave her lips.

Breath escaped her, as worthless as her valiant attempt to

stop his touch. She was shaking inside and outside, alive with a rage that swept like thunder with every brush of his fingers. It was anger, of course, that he dared touch her so, fury, fear— more—fire, simply fire. . . .

"Wait!" she managed at last. It should have been a scream; it was a gasp, a whisper, a plea.

And he did so, but she quickly realized that he hadn't really heard her at all, or if he had, he did not mean to give way. He had halted only because he was up again, dragging her with him. She shrieked, clinging to his shoulders to keep from falling, and yet he meant for her to fall to the rug beneath them. Their wet, naked bodies came together and apart; she felt the muscled heat of his every movement and twisted, writhed. But he was pure speed and fierce passion, anger, and emotion. He was above her, then atop her—between her thighs. She became abruptly aware of the state of his arousal as she felt the hard length of his manhood against the intimate portals of her sex. Then she bit hard into her lower lip, trying to keep from shrieking aloud as he suddenly penetrated her, moving deeply, more deeply within her. She would not cry out, she swore, but the pain was stunning, shattering, then numbing; she couldn't move, couldn't breathe, could only feel him move, his flesh, hot, wet, the power of his hold against her, the slick movement, the pulsing, beating, pain. . . .

He went as still and tense as a longbow; then heat seeped into her, filled her like a river, swamped her, and with it the pulse began again, a slow pain of memory. She wanted to hurl him from her, move him, yet he didn't budge, and she was suddenly aware of his blue eyes, as invasive as his body, pinning hers. And there was no apology, just anger, and a single demand: "Why?"

"Please . . ."

"Why did you lie?"

"Please . . . oh, God, please—"

"Why did you lie?"

"I knew you didn't really want me! I thought that you would . . ." She closed her eyes and swallowed hard. "I thought that you would leave me alone."

He moved from her at last. She closed her eyes; her whole body seemed to continue to burn.

"You bloody little fool!" she heard him say quietly. "I thought you were goading me, challenging me. I believed that you were quite adept at what you were doing, that you were accustomed to your power, that you were tenacious, cunning—and had known half the men in the castle."

She rolled away from him, aware that tears were seeping from her eyes, ready to fall down her cheeks. Her back to him, she whispered, "What difference does it make? You wanted to hurt me, didn't you?"

He was quiet for a very long moment—so long that she was almost tempted to look back at him again.

He rose and walked away from her. He seemed as restless as a tiger, sleek and powerful in his every movement, and still. . . caged. And yet he was the one who had made himself master here. He paused at the mantel and was still, staring at the flames.

"I felt . . . obliged to take everything that was Darrow's—including you. Did I want to inflict pain? No, not really!" he said very softly at last. "What I have wanted is to stop the anguish in myself, my dreams, the hauntings. . . ." he said, and added bitterly, "Nay, what I really want is to kill Kinsey Darrow. I want him to die slowly—by flames."

There was a tremor in the very deep cadence of his voice. She winced, shivering, her back still to him. "I know that perhaps you can't believe me," she whispered. "But I'm sorry about your wife. So very sorry."

"My lady, I have just violated you. You need not apologize regarding the fate of another woman at this moment." He was quiet again; then he must have seen her shaking, for he rose and reached for her.

"No, I—"

"I am taking you to the bed, nothing more—to the warmth of the furs."

Despite her instant and instinctive protest, he lifted her and carried her to the bed. She was so very sore, wounded to the core. She couldn't have fought him then; she hadn't the will. Her arms curved around his neck. His eyes held hers; she trembled still harder, suddenly aware now as she hadn't been before of his great, sword-yielding strength, the perfect honing of his body, the way that he moved—against her, touching her. He was the enemy who had come to her house and invaded; and she should have been fighting still, slamming against him, protesting even his lightest touch with the last breath in her body.

Her body remained in too much anguish.

He ripped away the furs that covered the bed and slid her onto the smooth cool sheets before covering her in the furs once again. Shivering, teeth chattering, she drew the furs tightly to her chin.

He studied her. She watched him in return, trying to keep her eyes glued to his and not let them fall to the portion of his anatomy that had so tormented her just moments ago. Then he slid into the bed beside her. She clutched the furs more tightly, ever guarded. But he kept his distance, lying back, lacing his fingers behind his head as he stared without really seeing up toward the ceiling.

"It is strangely hollow," he said at last. "Kinsey Darrow stole everything from me. And here I lie in the handsome chamber he would have made his own, with the wealthy and titled heiress he would have had as his wife! But nothing has changed; the pain has not eased!"

He looked at her suddenly, sharply, eyes narrowed. "Ah,

but there is something of a victory in this; I have taken something that will not be his.''

"You think that you will hurt Kinsey through me?" she whispered.

He turned away from her again. "He loves you so that it will not matter? Well, lady, God help you both then, for I cannot stop until I have ridden him down and to death at last. Would that he had seized Alesandra—and nothing more. If he'd kept her at his side for a year, she'd have still been my wife, and love would have been far stronger than any damage he would have tried to cast upon my pride. But he killed her! The bastard killed her!''

She held her silence then, wincing. She realized his rage, and felt the anguish that tore at him, and began trembling again.

Perhaps it was amazing that he did not seek to slay her in return.

She moistened her lips. If she were to tell him the truth, he would surely never believe her. "If I were to die now, I'm afraid that Kinsey would not too deeply mourn—I believe that the king would grant him my estates.'' She didn't add that the king had arranged the marriage to reward Kinsey Darrow and that she'd been allowed no argument in the matter. In fact, she'd been told quite simply that she'd marry Kinsey on her own two feet, or bound and gagged and held bodily before a priest so that she could be forced to nod at the appropriate moments.

He glanced at her sharply; then the smallest curve of a smile molded his lips. "My lady, I don't think that you will die now. I intend to try very hard not to kill you. But upon occasion, I'm afraid you tempt one to throttle you.''

"And what did you expect? That because a woman had been left in charge of her own father's holdings that I would surrender meekly like a mouse and forget all thoughts of freedom myself?" Tears were suddenly stinging her eyes again. *How foolish*. It was a violent world; she knew it. King Edward of England believed himself supreme—it didn't matter in the least that he destroyed lives with a word or the wave of his hand. Why should it matter when he was ready to kill at any given moment?

"I had not expected . . . you," Arryn told her, and turning toward her suddenly he said, "I'm sorry that I hurt you."

"But that was the intent."

"The intent was to take what was Darrow's."

"An interesting concept, for anything can be taken from any man at the whim of a king."

He shook his head, staring at her. "I don't think you, and certainly not your betrothed, begin to understand the swell of rebellion that has begun."

"If you speak about the outlaw Wallace."

He laughed interrupting her. "I do speak of Wallace."

"He is an outlaw, a brigand."

"And why is that?" he asked harshly. His eyes were narrowed on hers. She inched back as the passion of his anger caused him to raise up on an elbow and stare at her. "He is an outlaw! Because he protested his father's murder? His father refused to sign the oath years ago, you know, and amazingly, he was killed. And then what befell . . . Marion . . . well, perhaps what he suffers is even worse than the dreams that haunt my sleep, because he feels his guilt is even greater."

"I have heard the minstrels. I know it is rumored that the woman he loved was killed, but I have heard as well that the story is nothing but the outlaw's defense because your William Wallace murdered the king's agent Heselrig—"

"That was no rumor!" he snapped angrily. "My cousin John was there that day, with William. They had skirmished with soldiers, and disappeared through Marion's house. Heselrig retaliated by killing Marion—a very sharp blow to the head, sent her way in anger, ended her life. And now, can you imagine? Her house was burned to the ground as well.''

"Wallace is not a man known for his mercy!'' she protested. "He has burned men to death as well.''

"Once!'' Arryn said his features constricted as he stared at her. "And I know that occasion, for I was there myself. The English tricked several hundred Scotsmen, calling them to a meeting at Ayr. Each man was hanged as he arrived. Our party was forewarned, and the tables were turned, and aye, when we arrived, he was in a rare fury, and the murderers were locked in—and the barn that hosted both the living and the dead became a funeral pyre for both.''

She bit her lip, staring at him, shaking her head. "Still!'' she said softly. "It is a band of outlaws! I'm sure that your estates are forfeit after this attack on Darrow, and the seizure of a castle King Edward would claim. Scotsmen still continue to side with the king. Robert the Bruce and others with claims to the Scottish throne side with Edward. Men with wealth and power side with the king. You would fight a war against a mighty power with rocks and sticks!''

"I would fight a war with the hearts and souls of men. But it's not just Wallace here in the south—Andrew de Moray, a rich baron, has tumbled the English in the north. He has taken a number of castles in his ancestral lands. The country will rise; nay, lady, the country is rising.''

"Yet if Edward came here, you could not hold this fortress!''

"Edward is fighting in France.''

"If the king were to send an army—''

"The king will send an army. Mark my words,'' he told her.

She closed her eyes, turning away from him, feeling a sense of pain and loss again, and damning herself for arguing politics on such a wretched night as this. "Aye,'' she said, her back to him. "The king will send an army. And you will be killed and captured. And Edward is brutal with men he calls traitors.

You will be hanged, disemboweled, castrated, and drawn and quartered.''

"He can call me traitor all he likes, but I cannot betray a man to whom I swore no allegiance. John Balliol may be a sad puppet who has abdicated his crown, but by law he was declared king. We ride to his banner—and to the flag of the lion triumphant. Robert the Bruce—the young Robert the Bruce—grandson of the competitor, is the hope of his family. He would sign a pact with the devil to be king. Maybe the day will come when he rises to claim the throne, but he cannot be king of the Scottish people and lackey of Edward. Aye, lady!'' She was startled when his hand suddenly fell on her shoulder, and she lay very still. "Wallace is an outlaw and a brigand. He has nothing at stake. No great lands or titles in England to make him vulnerable to an English king. He wants nothing, no riches, no gain—just freedom for his country. He is a man with nothing to lose, and that makes him very dangerous indeed.''

"Wallace will be killed or captured, hanged, drawn and quartered—''

"My lady, do you ever shut up?'' he demanded, his voice suddenly harsh, his grip upon her shoulder suddenly relentless as he forced her back around to face him.

"I would gladly keep silent!'' she assured him, "were I to be left in peace.''

"I am trying to make you understand what is happening in this country.''

"You are trying to excuse your behavior to me.''

"I owe you no excuses!''

"Then why did you apologize?''

"I still owe you nothing! You played the role of the talented whore, my lady, assuring me you'd slept with half the castle.''

"Had I slept with every man and beast in the castle, sir, it did not mean I was willing to sleep with you!''

"Willing?'' he inquired. My lady, this is not a courtly masque or other entertainment. We have taken the castle. This is a war. I have taken the castle and I have taken you.''

"To be used and abused and discarded in a very tarnished manner—so that Kinsey can take for his bride a woman who was yours first! You are just like him!"

He stared at her, his eyes cold as ice. "You should thank God, madam, that I am not just like him. But tell me! What does your Lord Kinsey say to your ceaseless conversation?''

She inhaled, gritting her teeth, taken by surprise. She looked away. Could he even begin to imagine that she had been praying for escape from Kinsey when he had come upon her? Could he begin to understand how she despised the man to whom the king had said she must be married? Aye, Kinsey was just the warrior Edward needed for Scotland. He was vile and cruel, and though he had said that he'd never touched Graham's wife, she knew him, and she had known that he had molested the woman. . . .

Before he killed her.

Only the fact that Kyra was sworn to him as wife, though the ceremony had not yet taken place, had kept him showing a pretense of courtesy for her. What had he thought of her words? He had hated them; he had nearly struck her upon many occasions for telling him that he could not practice such heinous cruelty upon a people he meant to subjugate. Eventually a man would rise and strike back, and if Kinsey ever fell, God help him. But he had told her that the Scots were beasts, animals, barbarians. No matter that her mother had been among them.

"I will not discuss Kinsey with you!" she said, afraid that he would read her thoughts. "Nor will I argue the fate of Scotland. You're a fool, and you'll die a fool's death, and I will dance at your funeral, sir, for what you have done here. That is the way of it, right? *Willing* means nothing, and women are just things, and men have only won when they have taken the most *things* from their enemies. You have taken the castle;

you have taken me. And so, when the king takes you, it will be the justice of your outlaw war, will it not?"

"You know what Kinsey Darrow did. That we've taken Seacairn is justice."

"Justice, sir, is a matter of opinion."

They might have argued it all endlessly, except that they heard a pounding at the door. Alarmed at her state of undress, Kyra clutched the covers to her and leapt from the bed, backing away from the door.

Arryn watched her with narrowed eyes.

"Aye!" he called loudly.

They heard Jay's voice. "Arryn! Your cousin has come."

She knew from the frown that knitted Arryn's brow that he had not expected the arrival of his kin. He leaned back, studying the door.

"Do you hear me, Arryn?"

"Aye, Jay. I'll be down."

He stood and walked to Kyra. She swallowed, staring at him, the fur clutched to her breast. It didn't cover much; it exposed more.

"What in God's name is the matter with you?" he inquired.

"I was startled, that is all," she murmured, aware of the way he stood there, aware of her own nakedness, so barely covered by the fur. Suddenly she felt a strange burning, as if the whole of her body heated, as if he were too close, as if she couldn't bear the heat. As if he would touch her again. She couldn't stand it if he did. Yet she could see his hand, large, strong, slashed with a few scars. His chest, his eyes ... she was shaking, aware of him, his being, his touch, her own.

He'd hurt her! He'd attacked this castle, told her his intentions, and carried them out! And strangely ...

She didn't hate him as she should. He was striking and compelling; the tone of his voice was deep; his arguments were solid and intelligent.

He had come for revenge. . . .

She felt the strangest urge to be touched again. She denied the urge, felt his eyes.

"Your cousin is here!" she whispered. She tried not to look over the length of him—muscled, tensed. . . .

Aroused.

"Your cousin—" she began again.

"Aye."

He reached out and took the fur from her. Her fingers curled tightly around it, then eased to his force. And she knew, and she felt tremulous within.

"You don't want me!" she protested in a desperate whisper.

"I don't want to want you!" he returned.

"Your cousin—"

"Will remain. Would that you had just stayed down, my lady, hidden in a bundle of begging! But then . . . it is war, isn't it? And I am here and the castle is mine . . . and so are you."

He hadn't moved from her. He didn't touch her still, but she could feel him. Something seemed to burn in the air between them. His muscles were so tense, rippling as he stood watching her. . . .

She tried not to let her gaze slip.

Oh, God, his eyes the way he looked at her . . . she seemed flushed, trembling, shaking, on fire, denying, and yet . . .

There was something about him, this, the intimacy. . . .

He caught her to him, lifted her.

Fight!

She didn't.

His eyes kept burning into hers.

He laid her upon the bed. He came over her. Some kind of a terrible groan seemed to rake through the length of him.

And still, his eyes pinned hers. . . .

He was within her; she closed her eyes, moistened her lips. . . .

She didn't feel the pain, just something strange, burning, building.

She should have been twisting, turning. . . .

She couldn't have stopped him.

She hadn't tried.

But she wasn't in any pain! Indeed, there was that something. . . .

And then it was over. And he didn't apologize or explain. He didn't speak to her at all. He smoothed back a tangle of her hair, pulled a fur back around her as she shivered.

Then he rose.

The fire still blazed, but the light outside had succumbed to the darkness and shadows of night. His body was a silhouette, muscle, tone, and agility somehow stressed by the silently moving dark figure he had become. He walked toward the tub and found the length of tartan he had worn, wrapping it around his waist and throwing it over his shoulder. He paused long enough to retrieve his hose and shoes, then started to exit the room. She thought that he had forgotten her entirely, that he would leave without looking back.

But when he reached the door he paused. His back remained to her. ''Make one move out of that bed while I'm gone and suffer the consequences.'' he said.

The fur was warm.

She kept shivering.

''Mark my words, lady!'' he warned softly.

And then he opened and closed the heavy door, and was gone.

CHAPTER FIVE

It was past midday, Arryn realized; his men had come in from their duties to dine in the great hall.

A number of their captured enemies were among them—the Irishman Michael Corrigan, the Seacairn priest, and the captain of the guard, Tyler Miller. The priest seemed to be listening and observing; the young captain of the castle guard was asking questions of the newcomer, Arryn's cousin, John Graham. John sat at the edge of the long oak table, his legs folded beneath him. All eyes were on him, as if he had been entertaining the company with heroic tales.

"Ah, lads!" John was saying, addressing mainly the men who had survived their capture of the castle, but also the Scotsmen among them. Brendan had come in, eager to listen to the tales of his adventurous kinsman.

"Aye! You can talk about King Edward being a fine specimen of a man, tall and great, known as Longshanks, aye. He's a Plantagenet king, my friends, and aye, they can be fine enough in appearance, good enough to look upon, and he is a long, straight fellow, honestly a warrior; now that cannot be said of every king! So it's not that he's a fool, or an embarrassment. But did you know that the Plantagenets have a curse upon them? They're known for being evil men, men of vile temper and fury—and dishonesty. Why, when good King Alexander died in 1286, the king swore to be our friend while planning to wed his son and heir to our little Maiden of Norway! Alas, the child died as well—God sparing her a marriage to that boy, perhaps! But then Edward claimed again to be our friend, overlooking the choice of king, and he must have been glad indeed when the law agreed that John Balliol had right to be king over the rest of the thirteen claimants, all heirs through various daughters of true kings. So he raised up a king—and how lucky for Edward, since this king was married to the daughter of John de Warenne, Earl of Surrey, one of Edward's most efficient and ablest commanders on a field of battle! So Edward made a king, and made that king swear fealty to him, and when Balliol had been crowned, the Great Seal of Scotland was broken into pieces—and taken to England. And bit by bit from there, Edward tore down the king he had created, and made himself overlord of a country not his own. Ah, good fellows! We should have seen what was to be. Too many of our influential lords were willing to lie down with Edward for the sake of the titles and lands they claimed in England. But sleep with the devil, and the devil will have his due! We have seen what this king had intended all along. Take note of Wales—in 1282, Prince Llewelyn was defeated in battle and killed, and, ah, there you have it; Wales is annexed to England. Will we let this king win such a victory over us? Never. Men will fight for the Crown; they will sleep with the devil again and again to achieve riches and land, and the king will think that Scotsmen can be bought—he doesn't realize that there is a man among us they call an outlaw, but who fights for no personal gain, and seeks only one reward—the freedom of a country!''

"Do we drink then to William Wallace, cousin?" Arryn inquired.

John turned quickly toward him.

They were nearly of an age, and similar in height and stature and coloring; eyes of a deep Nordic blue had come into the family at an early age, and it seemed that most of its men carried the trait, along with thick, wavy, very black hair. John had a pleasant sense of humor about himself, and a flair for the dramatic; he was charming, but never shiftless. He had given his loyalty to William Wallace with an unshakable conviction, and like Wallace, he had determined that he would live to see Scotland unbridled from the yoke of the king of England—or die in the trying.

"Arryn!" John hailed him in return "Indeed, cousin!" He leapt from the table, standing and walking toward Arryn. They embraced briefly. "We can drink to William Wallace—or to you! My congratulations! What a victory you've seized here!"

"Something of a victory. The rat I'd hoped to capture departed before our arrival. So, John, we've seized a castle for the time being," Arryn said.

John was searching his eyes. "But *Darrow's* castle," he said with meaning.

Arryn was tempted to correct him, to tell him that the hereditary rights to the castle came through Darrow's betrothed. Yet before he could speak, he remembered Kyra's comment that the lordship of any castle came at the whim of a king.

"And Darrow's woman," John said quietly, with a small smile on his lips. "I did not mean my interruption to be ill timed, yet riding in your wake, I learned along the way that you had come here."

"Aye, I made my intent well known," Arryn said. "Why

were you riding after me? Were you eager to be a part of this? Where rides Wallace?''

John's smile deepened. That's why I've come. I'm seeking men to fight a real battle against the English.'' He half sat and half leaned against the end of the table once again.

''A real battle? Is the English army on the move?''

''Indeed. After William killed Heselrig, there was no going back.''

''I heard that William Wallace dragged the bastard right out of his bed and slit his throat!'' Captain Miller said with surprising relish.

Arryn stared at the young man whom they might well have cast into chains or put to the sword.

Miller cleared his throat. ''Kinsey Darrow has never been my laird, sir!'' he told him. ''I was duty bound to his lady, but . . .'' His voice trailed.

''So, young man. Would you ride with an outlaw then, for Scotland? Have you the balls, son, to ride against the English?'' John demanded.

''Aye, sir!''

''Aye, sir, so you say, yet I faced this man with my own army of brigands today,'' Arryn said, walking farther into the room and studying the young man suspiciously. ''Captain Miller, young sir—how do we know we could trust you to ride with us?''

''The lad tells the truth of his heart!'' the priest interrupted. He stepped forward into the center of the room. ''Tyler, Justin, Joshua, Julian, Conan . . . and more, sir, have long despised their duty here. If William Wallace raises an army against our oppressors, they will be passionate warriors for our country.''

Arryn listened, arching a brow doubtfully, crossing his arms over his chest. ''To defy the king of England is certain death if a man is caught.''

''We know what depths of cruelty kings and their lackeys

fall to, sir!'' Tyler told him. ''We have seen the handiwork of the English.''

''Don't fool yourselves that you'll ride for a man who will not take such brutal retaliation,'' Arryn warned. ''What you've heard of Wallace is true. He didn't start the war with the English; they murdered his father, and his brother, for refusing to bow down to a foreign prince. And they murdered those who gave him assistance as well, including women and children. But for all who enter this war . . . be aware. The conclusion could be grim.''

''So, cousin!'' John demanded. ''Does this mean you will leave behind this glorious homestead you have seized and ride for Scotland as well, when you are needed!''

''Did you ever doubt it?'' Arryn asked him.

His cousin grinned and shook his head. ''Trust me, William Wallace is not a learned general such as some of the men in the king's command, but he knows this country, and knows how to use every brush and tree and strip of river to our advantage. He has raided and triumphed. But he has learned as well that to truly rid us of the English yoke, there must be more. He is anxious to have you, Arryn. He asks that you join him for a meeting at—''

''We'll drink to the endeavor!'' Arryn interrupted firmly.

His cousin gazed at him, arching a brow. Then he realized that Arryn was not yet ready to trust everyone in the hall, no matter how passionately they stated their convictions.

''To William Wallace's endeavor!'' John agreed.

''Aye, let's drink to a free Scotland!'' Arryn proclaimed.

Gaston was in the hall, bringing pitchers and tankards of wine and ale. How much attention did the Briton give to what was said? Arryn wondered. Were these men all against Kinsey Darrow in truth? It was easy to believe because of his own hatred of Kinsey, and yet, in this outlaw war against the king, men were ever treacherous. The richer or more powerful a man, the more he had at stake to lose if he defied the English king.

His thoughts he kept to himself, pretending to drink and enjoy the revelry. With his men and those who attended John— and with those who had fought them and now claimed to love Scotland with equal passion—he drank, yet now far more moderately. They hailed the future, Wallace, dead Scottish kings, and the kings to come. Drink flowed freely.

"Hail to all outlaws!" the priest called out.

Arryn looked at the priest, and found the man's eyes enigmatic. "Aye, Father, hail to all outlaws who would seek honor and freedom!"

"Hail to the Lady Kyra!" someone called.

And the room was suddenly silent.

It was a disturbing matter. Men who claimed to despise Kinsey Darrow were not so hostile when it came to the man's betrothed. Yet every man here knew that it was her position and her riches that had aided Darrow in every turn of his brutal rampage against the borderlands in the name of the king—and the lady of Seacairn.

And every one of Arryn's men had known what had befallen his home and property—and his wife. There had been no pretense about the fact that he had meant to take Darrow's castle and his intended bride.

And so men stared at him now. Surely, some of them, such as Father Michael and passionate young Tyler Miller, must be pondering her fate—and feeling shame that they should so readily betray her to the enemy and join with that enemy.

He smiled, lifted his own glass, and inclined his head. "Indeed. Hail to the Lady Kyra!" he said politely.

Then the rough-hewn humor of seasoned warriors came to the fore. I came, I saw, I conquered! he thought again. The reward of victory. Seize and take. It was what they had done. What he had done.

And still she had ignited his temper—and his appetite, making it easy to carry out what he had seen as a duty. Revenge. The victory now seemed hollow. How much easier it would have been if she had been the broad blond servant woman, if she had been a fool, a trembling schoolgirl—a far different lass! Yes! He had meant to hurt! And now he was . . .

Shamed and guilty himself, and it infuriated him that he should be so. He hadn't begun to imagine that he might want her. That she might slip beneath his skin. She was the enemy; he had loved the wife he had lost! Alesandra still walked in his dreams; he saw her face. . . .

Heard her screams . . .

And yet . . .

She had leapt up, afraid again at the pounding on the door. And he had watched her pulse race, her breasts rise and fall, and what she had awakened in him . . .

He hadn't meant to touch her again! Not then, not that night, and now . . .

He was alarmingly eager to return to the tower room above.

Well, he would not do so. Not for hours. It was day; there were things to be done. He had conceded enough to her already. And she still argued for King Edward, and was quick to tell him how he would be hanged and disemboweled if caught.

Let her remain in her tower alone awhile.

Loyalty be damned, he thought ruefully, for the men—his and hers—seemed to think that his acquiring of the lady was a manly pursuit to be cheered.

So much for the defense of her honor.

Laughter rose, cheers, taunts, bawdy jokes. Among his men, it was understandable. His men were warriors—they had become outlaws, and the spoils of victory were theirs. They expected no less than that he take full measure of what spoils the castle had delivered. But the castle guard seemed too willing to change sides. How could they turn so quickly from their lady?

Arryn felt the priest's eyes on him, and turned toward the man of the cloth. He stared at him boldly. With cheers and drinking chants rising around the great hall, he found himself by the priest.

"Look, will you!" the priest said. "They fought yesterday; they drink in one another's arms tonight." Not even his mind seemed to be on the welfare of the lady of the castle.

"Such is the nature of drink, Father! And we do know that such camaraderie may fade with the coming of another dawn."

"Ah, Sir Arryn! It's a difficult life, to wonder at all times whom you may trust."

"Ah, Father! I do not wonder at all times whom I may trust. Yes, this is most curious. Can this great change of heart be true? Do you not damn me, then, in your heart, for the invasion here?" he demanded.

The priest studied him thoroughly in return. "No, sir, I do not."

"Now that I must question. But you say you are honestly a Scotsman—and against the king of England?"

The priest grinned. "I am honestly an Irishman—and against the king of England."

"Ah! But what of your lady, Father?" he asked blandly. He set his tankard down, crossed his arms over his chest, and stood boldly before the priest. Have you no heart for the innocent? No rage for what we have done—against her? We seized the castle *and* the lady. Would you not defend her against the heathen likes of me?"

Again the priest studied him for a long while. "She has remarkable powers for defending herself, sir. And yet . . . she has said nothing to you?"

"She has said many things, Father. What exactly should she have said?"

"It is not my place to speak, Sir Arryn."

"Oh, I'm quite sure you speak quite freely, when you've a mind to do so," Arryn said dryly.

"As you say, sir. Perhaps. Tell me: what is your intent when you ride from this castle? Will you torch it, set fire to the crops and the countryside to assure yourself Darrow receives no bounty from it?"

"I've not yet decided. I've always had a fondness for Seacairn."

"But you'll not leave the lady to burn?"

"That was never my intent."

"Not even in vengeance?"

"Not even in vengeance."

The priest studied him for a very long time, then shrugged. "Perhaps there is a greater toll you can take against Lord Darrow."

"A greater toll than murder? Do tell me, Father."

"Marriage."

"What?"

"Marry the lady yourself. Keep him from these lands."

"Father, I had a wife."

"Aye, that I know. The lady perished. At Darrow's hands."

"I want no other."

"But it's not in you to execute the lady, even in revenge."

"Don't imagine that you know me so well, Father."

"I do believe that I know you—I see living men here tonight who would have been put to the sword by Darrow—and even others among your Scottish outlaws. Don't look at me so—mercy does not make a man weaker, sir, but stronger. Still . . . don't you see the wisdom of what I'm telling you? Marry Darrow's intended. Then he is left without the promised riches that give him his power to raise funds and men. Granted, he is among Edward's favored barons, and the king will eventually find him another bride, but such a treasure as Lady Kyra is difficult to find. Many rich lasses come with bulbous noses, broad backs, pinched eyes—or they're old enough to be a laird's mother! If you would really infuriate Kinsey Darrow, take not just his woman but his *wife.*"

A deep, conflicting sense of betrayal burned in Arryn's heart. He could not. Yet the priest's words did have wisdom.

A wisdom he would deny.

Nay, he wouldn't kill her.

And God help him, he would be gentler.

But he wouldn't leave her, and he'd be damned before he'd marry her.

"To demand a night in retaliation for crimes far more heinous is one thing, Father. To wed the enemy is quite another. If you'll forgive me, I'll leave you and all these newfound friends who may or may not prove loyal. I've business at hand. Tomorrow may bring another battle, sir, as easily as it brings another day."

"God protect you, sir," the priest said. "Through the day and the night to come."

Arryn nodded and started from the hall again. He saw his cousin across the room and nodded.

John extracted himself from the company, leaving the men to their meal, and joined Arryn. "Come, John, let's ride and talk."

"Aye, and that we must," John told him.

Twenty minutes later they were beyond the outer gates, riding north to look back at the castle.

"I still say it's quite an accomplisment," John said.

"It would be—if we had the power to keep it."

"Aye, Edward will come soon enough," John said. A breeze stirred his hair as he looked at Arryn. "But we're going to best him this time."

"Edward has trained and disciplined archers. Cavalry. Foot soldiers who have waged campaigns in France and Wales. We have an unruly—and often untrustworthy—group of freemen, tenants, farmers, and a few barons, far too many of whom will watch the way of the wind before striking a blow. If it appears we have a chance to take the battle, they will be on our side. And if it looks as if Edward will win, they will swear loyalty to the king of the English, and say that they were with him all along.''

"Some men will waver," John agreed. "But," he added, and excitement was evident in his voice, "look what we have accomplished. We've learned from the massacre at Berwick, and from the rout at Dunbar. Men have risen, important men!''

Arryn arched a brow skeptically; then he shook his head with disgust. "The most powerful and probable champion we could have is the younger Robert the Bruce—but it's true that he believes his loyalty to Edward may cause the king to place him over John Balliol. And the heart of our rebellion, William Wallace, still recognizes Balliol as king. John, as long as the Scottish are at odds with one another, we'll not find freedom.''

John smiled. "But you see, many very good men are coming together. Wallace and de Moray are ready to combine their forces and fight together. Wallace has asked to see you. Can you meet with him in Selkirk Forest in a fortnight?''

"Aye, that I can, but I remind you, you must take care—''

"Aye, cousin! I realize that you've allowed men to live— who may not be all they vow to be. I'll take greater care with my words—especially since any association with William is like a death decree.''

"I don't imagine I need any association with any man for a death sentence, were Edward or Darrow to get their hands on me," Arryn said.

"Like as not. Look there, will you? There comes Jay Mac-Donald.''

Jay, on his large gray mare, was riding bareback and hard toward their position. "Arryn! Arryn! A group of Darrow's men were spotted from the tower. They're coming toward the castle with carts of supplies.''

"Is Darrow among them?"

Jay shook his head. "I'm afraid not, but they seem to be heavily laden with arms and armor, food, kegs of ale."

"Then I think we should greet them, don't you?"

"Aye, the men are ready to ride. But, Arryn, we could trick them into returning to the castle, and take them in the courtyard," Jay began.

"But their arrival could be a trick as well." John murmured.

"In what way?"

"A Trojan horse," Arryn explained. "They may know we have taken the castle. The supply wagons may carry more men, armed men, prepared for an assault. It would be best to plan an ambush there, at the rim of the trees. They'll not expect us there, and we'll have good cover against them if they're prepared for an assault. Jay, hurry back and order our men to seize up their weapons; I think that armor will weigh them down where we fight. Make sure our archers are well supplied with arrows. John, ride with me to the end of the trail there, we'll mark our positions."

God protect you, sir, through the day and night to come, the priest had said. Had he expected Arryn's attack, and had he known Darrow's men would return? Or had he been referring to the danger that might be encountered at night?

From a beautiful woman, the most dangerous of all enemies?

"Arryn!" Jay said, steadying his mare. "What of the men of Seacairn who have vowed that they will fight with the Scots?"

He hesitated "Allow them to come. If they falter in fighting the enemy, strike them down immediately."

"Aye, Arryn!"

He turned his mare and galloped back hard to the castle.

Arryn looked at John; then together they raced for the trees.

* * *

Kyra awoke suddenly, startled to realize that she had been sleeping. Deeply.

She lay on the great master bed with its fine linen sheets and warm furs, then twisted quickly, afraid that he might be there with her.

But he had not returned.

She gazed at the fire, down to embers in the hearth, remembering that he had warned her not to leave the bed when he had left. But surely he did not mean for so long!

Then she suddenly swore with a soft fury. Was she going to listen to him?

He did hold her life in his hands, she reminded herself. She had feared death. But he hadn't killed her. Not yet . . .

And he was going to try not to! He had said.

But . . .

This . . . this had happened. She had fought, attempted flight, reason, violence, and flippancy, and nothing had availed her. Her lies and flippancy had only goaded his temper and instigated the speed of force against her.

She had fought, aye!

And then . . .

And then she had not fought!

Fool!

What good would it have done?

She'd never know, because she had allowed it.

No! It was not that simple; she had given him nothing!

And denied little.

She couldn't think about it. She could think of nothing else. She hurt; she was angry . . . and yet . . .

She had prayed to God and the Virgin Mary never to have to marry Kinsey, never to give in to his demands, never have to lie with his arms around her. Well, at least now she would never have to lie ignorant and vulnerably innocent in Kinsey's arms.

Tears stung her eyes—just briefly. She grew angry with herself.

Crying about this would solve nothing. Her life was a disaster. Perhaps she could use this situation to make her life *less* a disaster.

She wondered how the invader of Seacairn would feel if he were to know that she had abhorred the idea of being with Kinsey.

Surely there must be some way to use this event to get out of the marriage. She had prayed to the Virgin, and Arryn had appeared. Apparently the Virgin had a mischievous sense of humor. "What now?" she whispered aloud, addressing whatever trickster in heaven had brought her to this predicament.

She walked away from the bed, suddenly determined to rid herself of the reminders of what she could not change. She walked to the tub and stepped into the water. She cried out in shock at first from the feel of it, for the water had grown cold. She clenched her chattering teeth together. Goose bumps formed on her flesh. It didn't matter. She scrubbed strenuously.

The door suddenly burst open. She froze in fear, suddenly afraid that his vengeance would go further still, that he had simply said to his men, *Take her, use her, abuse her! She is Kinsey Darrow's woman.*

"My lady!"

But it was Ingrid who cried out her name and came running across the room, falling down at her side by the tub, casting her plump arms around her shoulders and hugging her despite the water. "Oh, I would kill him for you if I could, the brute! The wretch. The barbarian. Did he beat you, hurt you, threaten to kill you?" She swallowed, barely halting her speech. "Burn you? Oh, my lady, if I could only help you! Have you wounds? He didn't hurt your face. But what man would mar that beautiful face? No, no—''

''Ingrid, I am well enough.''

Ingrid pulled back, her huge blue eyes very wide ''He didn't cut you . . . whip you . . . beat you?''

''No, Ingrid, I am not injured.''

''Well . . .'' Ingrid said, and her voice trailed. ''Well, we must somehow kill him!''

''Kill him?'' Kyra repeated. She should at the very least want to kill him, shouldn't she? The thief of her honor! But oddly enough, though she might want the strength to put him in his place—and maybe that place was being tied to a whipping pole—she didn't want him dead.

She said, ''Ingrid, are you mad? If we kill him, there are a dozen more with him.''

''But there is the matter of honor, my lady! They are outlaws, nothing more than ruffians, men who defy the king and kill and pillage and . . .'' Ingrid went still, allowing her tone to imply all the other wretched and awful things their uninvited visitors did.

''Ingrid, forgive me. I don't want to die,'' Kyra said, then held silent for a moment. She had run to the chapel soon after Kinsey had left, and in sheer desperation she had actually contemplated death rather than marriage to Kinsey. But the outlaw invader who had come here today couldn't know such a truth.

She felt a sudden chill and wondered what Darrow's reaction would be to the events that had taken place here. That was the point, of course: that Darrow would know that the Scotsman had come for him, and not finding him had seized the castle— and her.

Darrow would probably be more than happy to kill her himself. The Scotsman would be right: Darrow would be furious that she had become "used goods"—and used by his greatest enemy. He had hated her frequently enough, but he had coveted her as well. She had used all her wiles, her standing, the Church, her priest, every power she could conjure to keep him at bay this long. Would he still want her now, or would the thought of her with another man twist his thinking? It wouldn't be unlike Kinsey Darrow to find a way to snuff out her life, pretend to go mad and smother her in a rage, throw himself on the mercy of the king . . . God knew! He might find sympathy from the king, and be rewarded for her murder with her title and lands.

"There will be nothing to live for if these heathens take over the land!" Ingrid said with a sniff.

"Ingrid—it's their land. As it was my mother's," she said softly. Good God, she was defending them. "Ingrid, a towel, give me a towel, please."

Ingrid did so; Kyra stepped from the tub, twisting a large linen bath sheet around herself. She walked over to the fire, but the blaze was burning low. It gave her little warmth. She stretched out her hands in an attempt to feel some heat.

"What is happening below?" she asked, then turned to face her maid. "What of the men? I know several were killed; they must have been. But Father Corrigan . . . and Tyler, what of them?" She hesitated. "Were they put to the sword?"

Again Ingrid sniffed—a very loud, very contemptuous sniff. "Nay, lady! The wretches changed their colors. Why, last night, they drank with the rabble in your great hall! Those that lived are now bosom friends to the rogues who came here to do such evil!"

"But—they are alive?"

"Alive—the wretches!"

"Ingrid, I didn't want them slain."

"They betrayed you, lady."

"I ordered them to surrender. I had thought I had a chance to escape when they came to the chapel . . . but there was no chance. No man down there betrayed me. They did exactly as I ordered them."

"You are too kind, my lady."

"There is nothing kind in justice, Ingrid," she said. "Life is a far more precious commodity than most men seem to know."

"But, my lady! What will Lord Darrow have to say?" Ingrid demanded with real distress.

"I don't know. I don't at all," Kyra admitted. "But tell me quickly, what is happening now? It's well past midday."

"Aye, and maybe we'll be back to normal again, my lady!" Ingrid said. She looked around herself, as if afraid that the castle walls had suddenly sprouted ears. "There was a huge cry and scuffle going on below. Men arming themselves, running out of the gates, some of them going for their horses! Something is surely taking place. Why, my lady, I believe that Lord Darrow is coming back to rescue you from these heathens!"

"What?"

"I'm quite certain the guard saw something . . . there was much activity in the courtyard! Why, who else could it be, but Darrow coming back for you?"

Kinsey! She had warned the outlaw that he'd be gutted and quartered—she'd had no idea it might happen so quickly.

Maybe he could best Kinsey. Or maybe it wasn't Kinsey who had come at all. He would certainly not come riding rashly to her rescue!

She had to find out what was happening. She stared at Ingrid for a moment, then whirled around. In a large trunk she found an old pair of her father's breeches, a shirt—far too big, but what matter?—and a tunic. She dressed quickly, winding her hair in a knot at her nape.

"My lady, what are you doing?"

"I'm going out."

"There's a guard on duty at the door."

"Um . . . they thought they could spare a man, did they?" she murmured. "Still, it will not be one of his best men. Here, help me!"

She rushed to the bed and began to plump up pillows beneath the linen sheets. She covered the long mound she had created with furs. "There . . . now, Ingrid, you must call to the man to help stoke the fire. And keep telling him to be quiet, that I am sleeping, that I must be rested when Sir Arryn returns."

"Oh, my lady! You want me to act out such a fabrication? Oh, I cannot!"

"You must! Now, Ingrid, I'm going to the door. I'm opening the door, see; Ingrid, you must help me!"

Ingrid was still flushed and afraid. Shaking her head, Kyra threw open the door, hiding behind it. "Aye, woman, what is it?" came a male voice.

"The fire has died. My lady sleeps, but I see her shiver now and again. You must stoke up a new fire; Sir Arryn will not want to return to a sick and sneezing . . . companion."

For all her protesting, Ingrid did very well. The man who walked into the room was tall and lanky and had a limp; Kyra realized that he was probably recovering from a battle wound. He wasn't a young man, nor one of the outlaws she had seen as yet, but his features were sad and serious, his eyes deep brown like his hair, and she was almost sorry that she meant to cause him trouble.

When he walked into the room, she sped out. She started down the stairs, but at the exit to the parapets were two men on watch. She bit her lip, weighing her chances of getting past them.

She could see better from atop the tower.

Down ...

She couldn't go down!

She turned and fled—up, rather than down, yet all the while she was thinking that there was no escape from the heights. . . .

Other than a plunge into the river.

CHAPTER SIX

Arryn had taken a position on the steady branch of an old oak, watching. His men were within the trees and around them. William Wallace had made something of a base for himself in Selkirk Forest, and Arryn had learned, from disappearing into the forest on many an occasion, that it was a good place to be when numbers were suspect. He could accost the party when it reached the end of the road. He didn't intend to lose the day—he wanted the supply wagons. But just in case . . .

He and his men could disappear into the forest as well.

"Arryn!" Patrick called down to him from a higher branch.

"Aye, Patrick!"

"They'll be perhaps another twenty minutes. They've a bad wheel on one of the wagons. It's bogging them down."

"How many of them are there?"

"Twenty . . . thirty maybe. That I can see. There's a large covered wagon as well—could be covering a number of men."

"Will you order our archer to fire before they reach us, to

give us that element of surprise?'' John, on the next branch, asked him.

''Nay, we'll give them a chance to put down their arms.''

''We'll have more prisoners than men of our own,'' John commented.

''Aye, and we'll need to see what our new companions do as well!'' Arryn said softly, indicating Tyler and some of the other men from the castle. He had purposely kept them grouped together to keep an eye on them. They were, however, a short distance from his archers, downward and southward, should they repent their newfound loyalty.

''Arryn!'' Jay called quietly from across the road.

''Aye?''

''What if we must flee?''

''Then we shall flee.''

''But . . . but . . .''

''But what?''

''What of Lady Kyra?''

''She will be rescued into the arms of her betrothed.''

''You mean to leave her to him?''

Arryn wasn't sure if John was aghast that he would give up such a prize—or that he would leave the ''poor'' girl behind. He frowned, feeling a strange tension. He did not want to leave her behind. He didn't intend to lose this battle; they had men at the castle still. But a prearranged signal, a burning arrow, would warn them to leave.

And still . . .

''Tyler! Tyler Miller.''

''Aye, Sir Arryn?''

''You and Ragnor ride back to the castle quickly. Come back with Lady Kyra.''

''Aye, sir!''

Was he making a mistake? If Tyler meant to cause trouble . . .

Ragnor would be with him. He was allowing one of his best

men to leave when battle was imminent. But maybe this was more important.

Ragnor seemed to think so as well. He leapt down from his perch in the trees, lifted a hand and nodded, and mounted alongside Tyler. The two started off toward the castle.

Arryn looked up. The sun was already beginning to set.

"Arryn, they're coming!" Patrick called down.

And he could hear them: the whinny of horses, the sound of the Norman French that was still the accepted language among these men. They sounded at their ease. If this was a trap, they were not expecting one in return.

He stood, balancing on the branch, looking down as they reached a point in the road right before him.

"Bon soir!" he called.

Their leader wore a conical helmet with an open faceplate. He reined in quickly, searching the woods for sight of the man who had accosted him.

"Good sirs, good evening!" Arryn called. "We are all around you, and would spare your lives if you would share your treasures."

"Outlaws! Heathen Scottish outlaws!" one of the men shouted, drawing his sword.

"Surrender your arms!" Arryn offered.

"Surrender!" the leader with the conical helmet roared. He began to laugh, studying the Scots where they perched in the trees. "Surrender? To a band of outlaws who will soon be carrion for vultures?"

"My lord, you are laughing at us. In all fairness, I should warn you: I have taken the castle. Is Darrow among you?" Arryn inquired.

The man's eyes narrowed on Arryn. "My lord Darrow is not with us, but he'll be pleased when he returns to find you spitted and roasting over an open fire."

"It's the Graham!" another of the men said, recognizing Arryn and urging his mount closer to the leader's.

"Aye, not *a* Graham, my fine English sirs—there's two of us!" John called out, his voice deep and dangerous. "And we shall see who will burn this time!"

"To arms!" the Englishman thundered.

John looked at Arryn, who nodded quickly.

"Archers!" his cousin shouted.

And before the English could do more than draw their arms, a rain of arrows flew across the darkening sky.

Men screamed, shouted, roared with anger. . . .

"Now!" Arryn cried.

And one by one, like hail from the sky, they began to drop down on soldiers below, who broke ranks, stumbling for cover as they tried to dodge the rain of arrows while drawing their swords to counterattack. They were well trained and well disciplined, and reinforcements did come bursting from the large, canvas-covered conveyance in the middle of the line of supply wagons. Arryn was glad of his order that they wear no mail, for in the confined space they had the advantage of speed and maneuverability; his men had learned from the very beginning to find the weaknesses in English armor, going for the throats of men, beneath the arms where the plate was divided, along the sides where mail did not completely mesh.

Arryn met two opponents, big, burly fellows both, huge and awkward in their heavy plate armor, and both snarling and overconfident, until they fell to the speed of his sword. When he turned as the last fell, he nodded a grateful acknowledgment to his cousin, who had stopped a third man at his back; then he saw the leader of the men charging toward him on foot, and he let the man come, and come closer, and closer. He deftly moved in time to let the man come crashing into the oak; then he ducked swiftly when the Englishman turned with his sword swinging wildly.

"You're still welcome to surrender," Arryn said, jumping back.

The man swung again with a roar.

"Does that mean, sir, you'll not give in?" Arryn inquired softly.

"I'll see you in hell, heathen!"

"So let it be," Arryn said. He rose with his own weapon pointed skyward, and caught the man dead center in the throat. The defiant braggart fell without a whimper.

Arryn retrieved his sword and spun just in time to slash a man through the middle who had meant to render him through the head. He stepped aside quickly, drawing his sword back at the ready once again, but saw that the battle had ended. He stood in a forest of blood. Men lay in a tangle of dirt, mail, mud, and flesh. Looking across the road he saw Jay grabbing a man who would flee for his horse; his men seemed to be standing for the most part. Patrick nursed an injured shoulder, but he nodded that he was all right as Arryn looked to him with an arched brow.

He quickly surveyed the men standing, mostly his own. The men who had been the castle guard at Seacairn had not turned against them when it had appeared that the English would have the superior force.

At the sound of hoofbeats, he turned quickly.

Ragnor and Tyler had returned to the scene of the skirmish. Arryn sheathed his sword and strode toward the two of them as they reined in their horses.

"Arryn! She's gone."

"Gone?"

"Gone!" Ragnor said.

Arryn couldn't help but rivet his eyes quickly on Tyler. "Sir! I swear, I knew nothing of it! Nor did the man you left on guard."

Arryn shouted for John to see to the survivors and their own men. He called for Pict, and his well-trained war-horse trotted in from the copse where he'd been left. Leaping upon the stallion, he slapped his thighs against the animal's haunches, and they tore back toward the castle.

Kyra had never been afraid of heights—she did, in fact, love to be high. Although her father had been granted the lordship of Seacairn soon after her birth, she had still spent much of her time growing up in London, and there she had loved to visit the beautiful Norman churches and explore the lengths of the catwalks. She'd been a guest at the Tower frequently enough, and loved the view of the landscape from there, just as she loved to visit the castle at Stirling, and look across the distance of the rolling fields as they undulated into the more distant mountains.

Even at Seacairn, this view from the highest point of the tower was magnificent. The river stretched away forever, so it seemed, and in the sunset, it was cast into a dazzling display of sparkling color. Darkness came quickly once it settled, but in the late afternoon, the colors were glorious as they painted water, field, and sky.

Tonight was especially beautiful. It was a pity she could not take time to enjoy the simple splendor and deceptive peace of it all. . . .

For there was a man upon the tower, naturally, keeping a keen eye on the surroundings of Seacairn.

Careful not to make a sound and to keep her distance from him, Kyra tried to surmise what was happening. The high tower here gave full view to all of the surrounding countryside. She looked anxiously to the road from the northeast, and felt fear settle in. The trees shielded most of the activity, but between branches and trees she could see that men had returned to Seacairn, that baggage wagons littered the roads . . . .

Along with bodies.

Her heart shuddered and seemed to skip a beat. Kinsey had returned, she thought. And even as she watched, riders broke out from the trees. Their heads were bent and they rode hard, two at first, followed by more.

Who?

The guard at this high point had moved close to the low wall. Kyra moved silently behind him, and far to his right, using one of the four brick pillars that supported the low wall as a shield. She bent over the wall, trying to see.

If the sun were only still out . . .

God in heaven, *who* was coming?

"My lady!"

Startled that she had been seen, she twisted around. She saw Arryn's man coming toward her.

And, to her horror, she felt the wall behind her giving. She tried to straighten, tried to catch herself.

No one had leaned against this sector of the wall in a hundred years! she thought in dismay.

She reached out instinctively; brick crumpled in her hands. She hadn't intended it, but suddenly she was pitching over the wall.

From the outer wall, Arryn saw Kyra go sailing toward the water.

It appeared to be a perfect dive.

"She's mad!" he cried, reining in Pict. Then he spurred his horse, certain that the fool had broken her neck, and if not, then she would plummet to the depths and drown—freeze.

He raced around the outer wall, reaching the river where it veered from the castle. He couldn't see her. He looked up. Guy of Wick stared down from the tower, pointing. Arryn saw where she had landed; he cast off his mantle, scabbard, and sword and plunged in.

The river was bitingly cold, deep, and swift, a fact for which the inhabitants of the castle were usually grateful, since it removed the waste that might be stagnant in a protective moat. But the water was dark as well, thick with undergrowth in places, and in plunging from such a height, she might easily become entangled and trapped. She might be knocked unconscious. . . .

Fool! If she died, she deserved it! he told himself, furious— and afraid. And ever more furious that he was so afraid. Was she trying to kill herself? Or was she so desperate to reach Kinsey Darrow that she would attempt any idiot's scheme?

He dived into the water, searched in the stygian darkness, then surfaced. Again, and again. He refused to give up.

He was vaguely aware that Ragnor had reached him, and others, and that they, too, had plunged into the river after her.

Then he heard shouting; Guy from the tower high above. He spun in the cold water and saw her. On her own she had risen and swum to the opposite bank. She had emerged and, soaked and panting, stood on the embankment. She rose to her full height, still gasping in air. She was dressed in some ridiculous male's outfit she had surely seized from her late father's coffers, and the material molded to her form as she stood there shivering, regaining her breath.

And then she saw him, met his eyes, froze as they stared at one another.

And at that moment he wanted to throttle her. There was far too much defiance in her, and far too much that . . .

Appealed. The brilliance of her eyes, catching the dying light of the river. The clothing that clung like a second skin to her perfect form. Even the length of her hair, tangled with sea grasses.

She turned to run.

In seconds he was out of the water. She was fast and fleet, but she had made a death-defying dive and surfaced in ice-cold water and swum hard against it. Despite the lead she had on him, he was quickly behind her. She cried out before he touched her, aware that he was there. He threw his arms around her, bringing them both down. They fell on the hillside and tumbled down the grass. In the end, he pinned her down, staring at her. She was soaked, covered in grass now, and shaking. And still her eyes met his with that same green defiance.

"Get . . . get . . . get . . ." She gasped, and could say no more. Her eyes closed.

"I should just let you kill yourself!"

Her eyes flew open. She shook her head. "I wasn't trying to kill myself!"

"Then you're an idiot, pulling such a stunt to reach Darrow. Why? To warn him? Of what? He'll know we're here soon enough. Just to get away?"

"Oh, you're an idiot! I wasn't trying to kill myself."

"So you were trying to reach Darrow!" he lashed out angrily.

"No!"

"Liar!" His anger was such that he almost struck her. He pulled back and realized that he was mostly angry with himself. Damn him, why the hell did he care? Why was he still shaking with relief just because she was all right?

She flinched, still shaking, her teeth still chattering. "I fell!" she cried out, her voice tremulous.

He realized the depth of his own cold, but he didn't let her up, not then. "You *fell?* If you weren't trying to reach Darrow, why did you run?"

"Because of your face!"

He arched a brow, startled. "Ah, lady, it may not be so beautiful, but it isn't a face to make a maid run!"

"You looked as if you meant to kill me!"

He was silent a moment. "Maybe I did."

He felt and heard the hoofbeats at the same time. Ragnor was next to him, leading Pict. Ragnor's teeth were chattering, too. The glance he cast the Lady Kyra was not a kind one, either.

"She seems alive and well, Arryn."

"Aye," he said simply, and, reaching a hand to her, he pulled her to her feet. She did, at last, seem too worn and weary to fight him.

"My lady, you are like a cat, landing on her feet at all times," Ragnor said. "Darrow was a fool to leave you. What woman would plunge into a river for her lover?"

"You may ask your own man—I fell!" she snapped.

Arryn caught her around the waist, lifting her to a seat before Ragnor on his horse. "Take her back to the tower. See that she is thawed. I will tend to Darrow's men."

He turned away, but she called out, "Wait!"

He turned back.

"You fought Darrow?"

"Many of his men lie dead, lady."

"But he was not among them?"

She sounded anxious, and yet he wondered at the strange tension in her eyes.

"Nay, unfortunately, Darrow was not among them."

She lowered her lashes, hiding her gaze. She didn't seem to be rejoicing in the fact that the man hadn't been slain. And still . . .

Her lips were turning blue.

"Get her to the castle," he said to Ragnor. "And, of course, warm yourself."

"Aye, and that I will; my very balls are frozen, and my future dynasty may well be at stake!" Ragnor muttered.

He spurred his horse. Arryn leapt on Pict, swearing. He was freezing as well, and tired to the bone.

But there were dead men on the forest road.

And more worrisome still, there were living men there as well.

"They are saying that you are mad, they are!" Ingrid proclaimed indignantly. "And they whisper, and some say you were trying to kill yourself, and others liken you to Boadicea, the Briton queen who fought the Romans with such fury and passion."

Kyra inhaled, then gave up. She'd told Ingrid a dozen times that she hadn't been suicidal—or heroic.

She had fallen.

No one was going to believe her.

Despite Ragnor's anger, she hadn't said another word in her defense on the return to the castle—or to her tower room. When she asked him about the battle, his look told her he assumed that she was concerned only for Darrow's men—and Darrow himself.

He had little to say to her. She'd kept from freezing on the return to the castle by worrying about the men who now lay dead.

Seeing Arryn emerge from the river, she'd known instantly, of course, that once again he'd been the victor. But he'd never believe she had been more afraid that Kinsey Darrow might have returned. . . .

And that he might have been victorious.

At the castle, she hadn't in the least protested the arrival of fresh steaming water or her immediate plunge into it. Ingrid brought mulled wine, and it was warm and good, and the simple luxury of warmth had been sweet as well.

But now . . . the time was passing.

She had emerged from the tub into one of the huge snowy bath sheets, and wrapped in it, stood before the fire. She had heard the men below, heard as a meal was served, as conversation flowed. She wondered what had happened to Arryn; he had been soaked and frozen to the bone, and surely he had dried and warmed himself somewhere—but not here. Had he given her up as a madwoman? She could only hope.

"My lady," Ingrid said firmly. "You mustn't try to reach Lord Darrow again."

"Ingrid, I fell."

"My lady . . ." Ingrid began, then she fell silent. She stiffened. "Footsteps!" she said softly.

"Footsteps?"

"On the stairs, he is coming back!"

"He will not hurt you, Ingrid," Kyra said, and wondered if she wasn't a fool to make such an assurance.

"But he hurts you."

Kyra smiled, walked to her maid, and touched her face. "You are good and loyal, and I love you. But don't be afraid. I'm not hurt."

"There must be a means of escape!" Ingrid said passionately. But then her blue eyes went very wide. "Except not now. He is nearly here. I will think all night, lady, I swear. If you can survive just a few more hours . . . It must be so horrible for you. But we will help you; the right time will come. Oh, my lady, I will think until I have a solution. I will pray and pray . . . don't give thought again to taking your own life. It would be a terrible sin, you know."

She didn't need to contemplate suicide, Kyra thought dryly. Darrow—or this Scotsman—might readily do the deed for her.

"I will survive another night, Ingrid. I don't know what else to say. I was not trying to commit suicide. I fell."

"You think you fell, perhaps, God love you, lady! You were just so desperate to escape the heathen outlaw brute that . . ."

Ingrid had started toward the door, but as her voice trailed, she hesitated. "But if you get so desperate again, my lady, or if you must . . ." She pulled a small, glittering knife from a pocket at the side of her overgown. She gave a grave nod to Kyra, and set it under the mound of one of the down pillows.

"Ingrid, don't leave a knife."

"You may need it, my lady!"

"Ingrid—"

"Bless you, my lady—oh, my God, take care of your sweet self!" Ingrid said, anxious then to depart.

She reached for the door.

It opened before she could touch it.

And indeed, Kyra realized, shivering anew . . .

The conqueror had returned.

CHAPTER SEVEN

Aye, Arryn was back, indeed, pausing curiously in the doorway. He had bathed and changed elsewhere. He appeared in a fresh tartan, his dark hair sleek, his cheeks freshly shaved.

Ingrid, caught there before him, stared at him, mouth agape, and turned so miserably red that she was nearly purple.

"Sir!" she cried, and bobbed a curtsy.

He seemed to fill the doorway. Ingrid remained as if frozen.

Arryn stared at the servant for several long seconds, then looked at Kyra where she stood by the fire. "What ails her?" he asked sharply.

"She is afraid to move."

"Why?"

"You are blocking her path."

He stepped aside. Ingrid fled as if demons from hell might come flying after her.

He watched for a moment, then closed the door behind her.

"Why is she so afraid?"

"You would ask me that? Sir, you attacked the castle!"

"I have offered her no harm."

"Well, at one point, you did mean to ravish the poor lass."

"Thinking she was you."

"And I was preferable?" she queried with what she hoped was a regal and icy demeanor.

He stared at her a long moment, then slowly walked around her, hands clasped behind his back. "I'm not so certain," he murmured.

"Oh?" She said, and could have kicked herself.

"Were she you, it would have been far easier to do the deed and walk away. Run away, perhaps."

She lowered her head, determined that she wouldn't smile, or find the least bit of humor in her enemy. He was speaking pleasantly enough now, but she was sure that he hadn't forgotten her last escapade, and that, like Ingrid, he failed to believe the simple fact that she had fallen.

He sat at the foot of the bed, removing his hose and shoes. "Well, my lady, a dive into the river—and a steaming hot bath. Which was the greater attempt to scrub away the stench of an outlaw from your noble person?"

"Both, perhaps. I did my best, but I believe such a stench is impossible to wash away completely." She was sure some dreadful payment was intended her for drawing him directly from the scene of a bloody battle into a cold river.

Especially when he believed she was either trying to kill herself because of him—or to escape to reach Darrow.

"Well, I'm sure you'll keep trying." He stood again, blowing out the lamp that sat on a bedside table. The room darkened into a gloom lightened only by the dying embers of the fire. She watched as he cast aside the yards of tartan wrapped around him, certain that he meant to come after her once again. His back was to her. She noticed again the muscle and sinew of his build, and the scars that lined his body.

She tensed, unnerved, certain that he had to mean some violence toward her.

But he did not come after her. He did not even turn toward her.

He crawled into bed, stretching out. She remained where she stood, watching him warily. He didn't speak for a very long time. She was almost certain that he had fallen asleep. She took a step, a single step, just to see if he had done so.

His eyes did not open as he spoke. "Attempt to leave the room or raise a hand against me, and you will regret the rashness of such a choice."

Startled, she bit her lip. "So . . . what am I to do? Stand here all night?"

"If it pleases you."

"I may do what pleases me?"

His eyes opened and fixed on hers. "As long as what pleases you pleases me. You're welcome to come to bed. It's quite large."

"Aye, indeed, but never quite large enough, thank you." She tossed her linen towel over her shoulder and turned her back on him, approaching the fire. She lay down on the large fur before it, then rued her action, remembering too clearly that this was actually where *it* had first taken place the night before. And now it was so late, the fire was low. She shivered, and she didn't know if she shivered because of the cold, or because no matter where he was in the room, it seemed that he was with her.

Time passed. It seemed that eons went by. She felt that he had to be sleeping. She rose again slowly, watching him. He must be beyond exhaustion. He had come riding out of the woods with his band of men, his foot soldiers in his wake. He had planned his strategy, and fought past Seacairn's defenses. He had dealt with the men who wouldn't surrender—and those who had. And he hadn't slept.

And then he had fought the men who would have seized it in turn.

And he had dealt with her.

He had to be exhausted. Sound asleep.

It wasn't so much that she wanted to test his temper, as she wanted to know just what her situation in the castle was. Did he sleep with guards on duty, making sure that she didn't leave? If she did leave the room, was she to be stopped? He hadn't said that she must stay.

She padded softly to the bed, barely daring to breathe, careful to be silent each time she put a foot down.

She reached his side and paused again, standing very still, like a wading bird in the marsh, listening, waiting. He lay on his side, facing away from the door.

Dangerous way to sleep, for an outlaw, she thought. And especially for a man so wary and careful. He must be so tired that he wasn't thinking logically.

His face, in repose, seemed young, some of the lines even smoothed away, and she realized that his strong features were attractive and compelling. Even in sleep, however, he seemed knotted with muscle, and she thought that he must train very hard with his weapons of war to come to such a very honed state.

He breathed . . . his chest rising, falling. Muscles twitched slightly. She froze. She waited. He didn't move.

At last she turned, tiptoeing for the door, ready to test her boundaries.

She never heard him rise; she knew only a whoosh of motion, and then he was in front of her, barring the door.

He towered at the door, very large, and very grandly naked, and she stepped back instinctively, but it did no good. His eyes were wide open now, very alert, as blue as the sea, and promising no quarter once again.

"I thought that it was open; I was checking for a draft," she murmured.

"Excuse me, but, my arse, my lady!" he said softly. And before she knew it, his hands were on her, and though he only lifted her, she felt as if she were flying. He didn't set her down with any particular cruelty or force, but it seemed that she hit the straw mattress very hard. Instinct caused her to inch away; his fingers landed on her jaw and he looked down at her. "One more move and you spend the night tied to the bedpost."

His fingers hurt. She remained defiantly silent, her head high, until he released her. She worked her jaw, trying very hard to keep her eyes on his. "Why?" she demanded. "I don't understand this! You need sleep. You don't trust me. I have a room; why not let me go to it? You've accomplished all you wanted—"

"Kyra, you may shut up or I'll tie you and gag you," he said flatly.

"Why are you doing this? Must I stay here through an endless eternity for both of us?"

"It will not be endless, I do intend to sleep."

"To sleep! So you intend to sleep, and I am to stay, and that is it?"

"Ah, so now you're the wounded damsel!"

"I have been the wounded damsel since your arrival, sir."

"There was no need for it."

"Really? You came here for vengeance. For Darrow's intended."

"Perhaps I had changed my mind. But when you insisted on taunting me with the extent of your experience . . ."

"Now you make your force my fault?"

"My God! You are in no position to argue here, my lady! Still, I'm merely suggesting—strongly!—that you would be far better off if you would learn to keep silent."

"I'd be very silent if I were just out of this room!"

"You will be silent, and you will stay."

"Again, I remind you, you are exhausted, and need to sleep."

"Aye, lady, and that's the truth."

"So you don't need me anymore!"

"I never *needed* you, my lady."

"Then let me leave!"

"Do you realize, lady, I am really tired, but you are awakening me?"

"Good, you should not sleep so easily!"

"Oh?" His brow arched. "Not to allow you any more arrogance, but you are quite capable of keeping me awake."

"You deserve to be kept awake."

"It would not be to listen."

Her cheeks flamed. "You do need to sleep. If you'd just let me out of here . . ."

"No."

"But—"

"Perhaps I'm afraid you'll try throwing yourself in the river again."

"I didn't throw myself in the river."

"Maybe I'm afraid of you *falling* again."

"I'll not fall again, I swear it."

"Neither will you leave this room—I swear it."

"But if you would just be logical . . ."

"Logical? I want you here. Where I can reach you at any given moment."

"Ah! So I must remain here wretchedly in case an urge for further vengeance suddenly seizes you in the night?"

"My lady, many urges have plagued me already."

"I am aware of that."

"Many more urges than you have imagined."

She knew that she flushed. "But you—the conquering hero—have now failed to act upon those urges?"

"Are you suggesting that I do?"

"No!"

"But then, did I even say just what the urges were? Alas—I've somehow controlled myself," he said, and she was furious to realize that he was laughing at her.

"Then don't keep me here!"

"Ah, dear Kyra! Are you afraid of yourself? That you may wake in the night with uncontrollable urges?"

She was astounded and further enraged that he could mock her so.

And afraid. Afraid of the trembling inside her. Rage, yes. Indignation, definitely.

What else . . . ?

She didn't know.

"You are beyond low, sir; to cast a term such as 'rat' or 'wolf' your way would be to insult thousands of animals. And I can promise you, there's not a single urge that touches my heart, soul, mind, or senses regarding you, sir. There's anger, loathing, more. You have seized my castle. You have seized me. You assault, kill, plunder . . . ravage. So forgive me if I fear like treatment again if I remain."

"If you will just go to sleep, you'll need fear nothing." The teasing tone had left his voice. He was worn and irritated, and the threat was back in his words.

The very fact that she seemed absolutely powerless set fire to her rage. She gritted her teeth hard, knotted her fingers into her fists, and tried to remind herself that she was testing a barbaric outlaw who'd had his home and family burned to the ground. Yet she'd never felt so at a loss; no matter what tactic Kinsey Darrow had used to get his way, she had subtly reminded him that she was her father's daughter, that King Edward had honored her father, that even his Scottish tenants had obeyed him, and that the power of loyalty from any of her lands lay with her. She was not wed to him yet, she would not share his chambers, and she did remain a free woman with a title in her own right, and though the king honored him, she could still place a case before Edward and . . .

Kinsey always backed down. She did stand in high regard with the king of England.

Edward had always shown her the greatest courtesy. She had been his first wife's godchild. Though she never deluded herself that the tales she heard about his ruthlessness were false, she had always wanted to believe in his motives.

And yet . . .

He had done vicious things. He fought hard; he had slaughtered his enemies.

Edward had annexed Wales to England. He had all but done the same thing here, but the Scots kept fighting. And even if he had humiliated John Balliol and forced him to abdicate, many of the freedom fighters fought in his name, for he had been crowned the true king.

Edward meant to destroy any sense of nationalism here. He had stolen the Stone of Scone, the ancient piece of rock on which Scottish kings had been crowned for decades. He had taken it to England, all to prove his mastery of this country, all to break the Scots.

And still . . .

She had known him differently than the Scots. She had known him as a man capable of generosity and charm.

And she had used the king of England against Kinsey Darrow. She could not use him against this man. She could not escape this Scot, or rid herself of him. Her words meant nothing to him. She just wanted to be away from him—she wasn't even certain that she wanted to escape the castle anymore.

And she couldn't even tell him that she was afraid of Darrow, now that this had happened.

She had only despised Kinsey Darrow before. Now she feared him.

But she couldn't explain that to this outlaw.

Nor did it matter to him.

Sir Arryn was apparently quite confident in his own strength and command. He stared at her a moment longer, then crawled over her to reach the other side of the bed. She shuddered, feeling his flesh brush her own. But he settled a distance from her. He lay on his back, though she wondered why he bothered. He could see with his eyes closed, from either side of his body, so it seemed.

For a moment there was silence.

But she couldn't endure his proximity.

"I don't know why you won't just let me sleep in my own chambers."

"Ah, lady!" he warned. "Those lovely lips will be sadly bruised by a gag!"

She turned her back on him, pulling her sheet around her shoulders and trying to delve down deep into the furs. She told herself that he meant to sleep, and she should do the same. Yet her hand slipped beneath the goose-down pillow, and she felt the knife that Ingrid had left there for her, certain that she'd be ready to sacrifice her life for her honor. Her fingers curled around it.

Maybe she could sleep . . . just touching the blade, believing she had some control over her life—or death. Some sense of protection, no matter how false!

Again, it seemed forever that she lay there, her back to him. At last, uneasy that he lay so close, not touching, she turned with as little movement as she could.

She was startled to see that a sheen of sweat had broken out over his face, chest, and shoulders. His breathing was rapid; his heart seemed to thunder. He began to twist as he lay on his back; then he cried out the word "No!"

He swung toward her, reaching out, his eyes wide open. In terror she shrieked out, digging beneath the pillow for the knife, hastily bringing it before her, ready to strike. Yet the sound of her voice suddenly froze him, and she realized that he was looking at her, really looking at her, as he hadn't done before. And the tense look of anguish that contorted his features was gone, replaced with simple fury.

"English witch!" he swore.

"No, stop!" she cried, edging back against the pillows, brandishing the knife before her. "Stop it now; I'm warning you—"

He didn't seem to appreciate fair warning.

He moved with such swift violence and force that she cried out again, instinctively making a slashing wave toward his chest with her weapon. Instinct betrayed her, for he hastily jumped back, then lunged forward, capturing her wrist. She cried out again, certain her bones would snap.

She was dragged back down flat on the bed. The knife was wrenched out of her hands. She gasped for breath, struggling wildly against his weight pressing her down, even if she struggled with no hope that she could ever so much as shift his hardened frame.

He crawled over her, straddled her, pinned her wrists flat down to the mattress, and forced her to lie still beneath the pressure of his thighs. She was very afraid again, because it was evident he thought she had meant to attack him. She had pushed him too far too often now, perhaps, and now that she was actually innocent of malicious intent, she was afraid that she had learned his temper too well, and the consequences she now faced were dire. And then . . .

His violent tossing in the night had been so disturbing. He had been asleep; he had been dreaming! But she knew he would never believe that she had thought he was attacking her, as he might have attacked whatever demon had haunted his dreams.

Kinsey, of course. Kinsey had been that demon.

"Don't! Please!" she whispered.

She felt his eyes more than saw them, for the fire had died low and the night was dark.

"Don't what?"

She inhaled deeply. "Kill me!"

"Um. You meant to stab me in the heart, but I should offer you no violence. I was warned that you would try to kill me. Quite frankly, I didn't think you were so stupid."

"I'm not stupid! I never meant—"

"If you hadn't *meant,* you wouldn't have wielded a knife."

"I swear to you—"

"God, quit lying!" he cried with enraged aggravation. "Tell me, did Darrow ride *to* war, or *away* from your ceaseless tongue?"

"It's a pity I didn't kill you!" she retaliated, then rued her words. Stupid, oh, God, aye, if she didn't realize the fury of this man who held all the power!

She closed her eyes, wincing, waiting for some awful blow to come her way.

But he didn't touch her. To her amazement, he rose. She heard him moving about in the shadowland that was almost complete with the dying of the fire. Yet a minute later he was back, and he carried one of the long leather bands that attached pieces of plate to his coat of armor.

She inched away again, backing against the carved headboard. She tried to leap up; she succeeded in losing the linen sheet at last. If he noticed, he gave no sign, but pressed her firmly back, capturing her wrists, smoothly slipping them into the noose he'd created, and tying it then firmly to a post on the headboard. Amazed, she tried to free her wrists, protesting passionately. "Don't, please, don't, I wasn't trying to kill you!" she whispered. "You attacked me—"

"I attacked you? Never, my lady."

"I beg to differ!"

"Beg to your heart's content," he told her. "I am bone weary, and need to sleep."

"Then you should have slept alone!"

"I'm afraid that it would not have the same effect on those who know that I came here specifically for you."

"But I didn't try to kill you. I'm telling you the truth. You were dreaming, you spun on me, I thought that you meant to . . . strike me, strangle me. . . ." Her voice trailed. His deep blue eyes were on her.

"Do the ties hurt? Are they too tight?"

"Am I to say 'aye'? Then you can tell me that you've come to hurt me?"

He smiled suddenly, and shook his head, and she became disturbingly aware of him, every inch of him, of his flesh against her own, of the burning it created. With the sheet gone, she was humiliated to feel as if her breasts swelled, her nipples hardened. She was in pain, but not from the leather that bound her to the headboard. She hated herself for not hating him; and she despised the way that she felt, her flesh, so incredibly sensitive, vulnerable to his every movement, each brush with his flesh, the touch of his hands, the movement of his thighs.

"I'm tired. I don't want to hurt you; I do want to sleep."

"You were dreaming!" she repeated.

"Perhaps. But you had a knife."

"I didn't mean—"

"How can you not mean a knife?" he asked softly.

"I will never be able to sleep so!" she told him.

"That is your misfortune this evening, my lady."

He crawled from her. She should have been glad. He lay down again, his back to her—safely now. She tugged at her wrists, wondering if she could possibly writhe her hands from the ties.

She could not. He had definitely learned how to tie a knot. She lay there, miserable, cold, shaking. She would have pleaded with him again if she thought she had a chance. As it was, she suddenly feared to waken him again. She didn't know if he might have believed her that he had been dreaming, but still . . .

He could waken and try to strangle her, and she would be a lamb to slaughter. . . .

She'd lost her sheet and the furs. And the fire was gone, and the castle was drafty. Her shaking increased. She'd awake very ill, she thought, and then he'd repent his cruelty.

Or would he? If a man came in vengeance, would he ever repent?

He moved suddenly and she went dead still in terror. Then she realized that he was walking to the fire, looking around, finding the pile of logs, restoking the blaze. She could see the breadth of his shoulders and back as he hunkered down before the fire, assuring himself that the wood was catching, the flames were rising.

He rose, waited a moment longer, his body bathed in the red of the flames.

He returned to the bed. "Better?" he inquired.

"Warmer," she said softly.

He pulled the furs up around her.

"I wasn't trying to kill you."

"Maybe I'll believe you—in the morning," he told her. "At the moment, I really am exhausted. I dare take no chances."

"You *were* dreaming."

"Maybe, lady. I often dream."

"I'm . . ."

"Aye?"

"I'm sorry."

"For trying to kill me?"

Her temper started to soar at the question. "I'm sorry for what happened at Hawk's Cairn. Sorry that your wife died."

"And I should release you for those words?" he asked sharply.

"Fine, sir! Leave me be then!"

"My lady, that is my intention for the night. And I am sorry, but I cannot release you. Only a fool would do so."

She jumped, startled when he reached out to touch her.

He only adjusted the covers again, then walked around to his own side of the bed.

At least she was warm. And she was exhausted herself. And the ties that bound her were not too tight, and she wasn't actually in any real pain.

Eventually, she slept.

CHAPTER EIGHT

It was her turn to dream. The world was soft, gentle. She lay entwined in furs, comfortable furs. She curled against them, slid along them, savored the feel that seemed to caress her spine, touch her nape, bring a sweet warmth all around her. Delicate strokes eased along her flesh, teased her neck, back, breasts, belly. Liquid warmth, slow, erotic, feathered over her, seduced, elicited, demanded response. She arched, moved into the touch of fur, the fiery wetness that brushed her with a greater urgency, a greater strength. Liquid seared her throat, her breasts.

Her eyes flew open. She was staring at the expanse of his chest. She was no longer tied to the bedpost, and her arms didn't ache. He must have released her almost immediately after he had tied her. Despite her denials, she had fallen asleep quickly.

Her hand lay upon his chest. Her leg was cast over his body. She was curled against him as if he had been her lover for eons. Her fingers even moved upon his chest, her fingertips brushing through the dark mat of hair. And the way that her leg was angled . . . she could feel far more about him than she wanted to know.

How had she done this? She had slept with her entire length cast intimately against him.

His arm was around her. Amazingly, his touch had been the seductive stroke of fur that had so teased her in her dream. He had lain awake for some time. And amazingly he was still touching, his fingers moving through her hair, his body curving now to hers. . . .

She tried to pull away. His arms tightened around her.

"Did you think you were with him?" he inquired, and she could hear the hardness of his words vibrate in his chest as she lay against it. "With Darrow?"

She was certain that she was flushed the color of sunset, yet he could not see her face, just the top of her head. Had she thought she was with Darrow, and thus responded? What a foolish, foolish man!

She tried again to free herself from his grasp, struggling against his arms and the length of his body. She felt as if she grew hotter and hotter with her every effort. Surely she did not want him repeating what had been, and yet the fever in her made her long to touch him, explore the strength that lay against her. She had to keep protesting, fighting. It was the only honorable, noble, proper thing to do. Yet he didn't ease his hold; she felt a certain tension and anger in him.

"Did you think I was Darrow?" he repeated harshly.

"What on earth difference would that make to you?" she cried in return, going rigidly still. He pressed her from him and down to her back, leaning over her intently.

"Perhaps I'm simply curious. They say that men can bed anyone who is warm."

"Including sheep, so I've heard," she told him, eyes narrowed. "Especially Highlanders."

"What aspersions you cast upon Highlanders! I have heard it is the English, especially royalty and nobility, who are fond of sheep. From the first Plantagenet on down. Ah, but I'm not actually a Highlander myself, though Stirling is the gateway and I ride with many a man who is a Highlander. As yet none has requested that we travel with sheep. You still haven't answered my question. You slept, you dreamed. Did you dream of Darrow?"

"Will you let me up?"

"No. Answer my question. You were comfortable, my lady, nay, more, you were seductive, and so I am curious. Men, as you have agreed, can sleep with anything. They say that women must feel something to want a man."

"I don't want you; this conversation is ridiculous. If you'd please—"

"So did you want Darrow? Is it he who intrigues you?"

"Release me."

"I won't release you until you've answered my question. Tell me, must a woman be intrigued at some level to lie so with a man?"

"Sir, your questions are absurd! Most women are wed at the whim of a father or an overlord to men they despise. Or—" she began, then broke off.

"Or what?" he queried.

She shook her head.

"Or what? Tell me, and I'll know if you're lying!"

She still hesitated, her lashes falling. "Or . . . they are simply taken by relative strangers . . . and I've heard many poor girls are forced into the arms of the landed lords on their wedding nights because Edward has said that his men in Scotland were free to practice the droit de seigneur."

The right of the lord. It was an archaic feudal custom in

which a lord could take the bride of any tenant for the first night following her wedding. Edward had decided it should be revived in Scotland; he was not kind regarding the people he would conquer. He had been known to say that they would simply breed the Scots out, just as he had been quoted as saying, on leaving Scotland, "A man does well who rids himself of a turd."

She opened her eyes, meeting his again. This wasn't an easy thing for her to say, especially due to her current situation. What had made her bring up such a thing, more sins on the part of the English lords sent to rule here in Scotland?

He was staring down at her thoughtfully. She wondered what he would have been like if they had met under different circumstances.

"Please, I've answered you," she murmured, meeting his gaze. She had to break free from him. She flushed, remembering the way he had looked at her when she jumped from the bed. Now she lay touching him. The same such situation would arise. . . .

"No." His eyes narrowed on her again "No, you haven't answered me. Did you think I was Darrow?"

She felt the stirring of her temper and a deep sense of aggravation. "How could I be dreaming you were Darrow when I wouldn't have known what I was dreaming!"

"My dear lady, was I remiss completely? There's far more to the act of love than . . ." He looked at her, and she thought that surprisingly, he broke off the words he had first meant to say. "There is far more to the act of love than . . . the act of love. But then, I'm sure you know that well enough—you may have managed to maintain innocence, but it's unlikely that you're ignorant. If you're wise enough, and sardonic enough, to bring up sheep, you're hardly unaware of the ways of the world—and men and women."

"If you don't mind . . ."

"I do mind. I want to know the truth about you."

"What does the truth matter?" she inquired, beginning to feel desperate.

"We're talking in circles; I won't do it."

"And I have nothing to say to you! Will you beat the truth out of me? Torture me?"

"Ah, perhaps there are different ways to discover . . . let's see, we know what you and Darrow did *not* do. But what did you do? Two cunning and ambitious schemers . . . and a man with such a betrothed, such beauty and promise awaiting in what he is anxious to claim as his house! He was just awaiting the words of a priest for all to be his. It has been a long betrothal. So just what did occur between you two young lovers? Tell me."

"There's nothing to tell."

"Ah, you're shy of description. I shall help. We'll start with basics." His face lowered to hers. His thumb stroked slowly over her cheek. "Did he touch you this way? Is that why you're as quick as a cat to lean in to be stroked? Did he cherish your lips, kiss you so . . . ?" he inquired politely, and before she was fully aware of his intent, his lips were on hers, opening them, forcing, molding, sensual . . . his body was pressed to hers, and the feel of his lips seemed to touch the length of her. Pride caused her to twist; his strength defied her pride. His fingers held her face to the slow leisure of his lips. The kiss was markedly slow, sensual; he tasted, teased, delved. The way that his tongue moved . . . aroused . . . stirred . . . . She tried again to shift, alarmed at the fire that seemed to seize her, the way her tongue slid against his . . . simply to find room in her mouth, so she told herself. But it was something else—tasting in return. She became aware of the scent of him, and found herself liking it, the feel of his body blanketing hers, and liking it as well. His hands, the way they touched her, held her to the kiss . . . .

It was a feeling of being cherished, wanted; it was sensual, sexual, an intimacy she hadn't known, and hadn't known she could want.

Ridiculous.

It was the way he had probably touched every whore he had known since his wife died.

Men could bed sheep, so they had agreed.

Why didn't this bare and brutal logic keep her from feeling that . . .

The way that he kissed her was tender, languid, meant to seduce. As if he were bewitched by her, hungered for her, touched her with longing. The feel of his lips tantalized, and the warmth of him beside her made her pulse within.

Fight him this time; don't be such a fool!

Aye, fight him!

But she never did so. What was this insanity? There had never been this question before; she had simply hated Kinsey, the sight of him, scent of him, nearness of him. She had hated him, as she should hate this man who touched her so.

Protest, move away, don't allow yourself to feel this . . . this . . .

Hunger, aye it was a hunger!

No . . .

Deny it or not, she was the one who was startled when he suddenly broke away. His finger moved over her cheek. It was damp with her tears.

Aye, tears. Touching her cheeks.

And he read them wrong!

"So you did love him!" he said, and his voice sounded like death.

She did love him? Kinsey Darrow? The very thought made her shudder!

He rose, pushing away from her as if he had just discovered her to be poison.

At a table near the hearth, he found washwater and poured it from the ewer to the bowl. She noted the length of his body again.

He was leaving her.

Was she such poison that a man holding all the power would simply walk away?

He had dismissed her entirely, so it seemed. In minutes he was dressed and gone.

Arryn was angry, and he didn't know why. *She* had the ability to goad his temper, and it was ridiculous, and bizarre, and he shouldn't put up with it, not for a minute.

He could leave her; he could walk away from her. She meant nothing to him. She was a little fool ready to throw herself from a tower rather than risk any chance of not finding Kinsey Darrow, warning him of danger. He should tie her to a stake in the courtyard, build up a pile of rushes, and set fire to it all.

She was the least important factor in all that he was doing.

Downstairs in the main hall, he found that it was late again, that his men had eaten, that Ragnor had ordered them to various tasks. A mason was on the tower, repairing the wall.

"You know, Arryn, it looks as if the lady might actually have fallen."

"Then why did she try to swim away when she saw me?"

"She's our prisoner. What would you do as a prisoner?"

The truth of Ragnor's words didn't improve his mood toward Darrow's lady. "It doesn't matter. Have you spoken with John?"

"Aye." Ragnor was quiet for a moment, surveying the main hall, but they were alone. "Wallace believes that we can strike at the English and win."

"I think the time has come."

"So we'll meet and find out his intentions in a fortnight."

"Aye. But if . . ."

"Aye?"

Arryn smiled, showing his growing sense of excitement. "If Andrew de Moray is really bringing down a force from the north, if we can really gather together such strengths . . ."

"The barons will still be against us. Aye, our own."

Arryn shook his head. "They will fear for their own holdings, but they won't be against us. But what we have needed is a real coordinated effort. Oh, aye, we've taken this castle, Wallace has taken castles . . . Andrew has made even greater seizures in the north. But when John Balliol abdicated . . . those who survived the English retaliation were left to be outlaws. We had no common banner. If we can create a real force, a great force, it will not matter that the Bruces stay away, fearful that Edward will never see their line as kings! What we have is the people—when Wallace flees, he is hidden. Men risk their lives for him. Women, too, see death, and are willing to die for him. He has nothing to gain, nothing to lose—except his life. He compels belief; his power is in his love for his country, in his willingness to die for Scotland. That is greater than any title, Ragnor!"

"Aye, and it will be good." He was quiet for a moment.

"Ragnor, it's good to have men fighting for their beliefs, for their country. But it's also good to have men who are disciplined, who know how to do battle, to form ranks against an enemy. We need to work, to train."

"Your men are warriors, fierce, brave."

"We need more against the English. We need the greatest skills we can accrue."

"Then we will train."

"Aye," he said, and was thoughtful for a moment. "We will train, and take care with that training. John knows now to be careful about what is said, and we must all be careful here, always, about what is said regarding any plans."

"Why is that?"

"We are within miles of the forest of Selkirk."

"Aye?"

"Traitors would have but a few steps to go to discover Wallace before he is ready."

Ragnor nodded. "Aye, then we'll be silent." He smiled. "Fierce and silent."

Arryn grinned. "Summon our new men—those we've acquired from conquest here, along with those of our own not on duty. We shall see how they do with schiltrons on the far north field."

"Aye, Arryn. The priest has suggested sunset to bury the dead. The bodies have been wrapped in shrouds and kept below, but . . . even so, they grow ripe."

"Fine, they'll all be buried with Christian dignity. The Englishmen who would seize Scotland may lie now in Scottish soil."

"They would seize Scotland."

"And now they will have it."

"For eternity," Ragnor said. He shrugged. "Like as not, it's the way we all will end."

"Like as not, the way we're going, it will be a kind enough death to die in battle," Arryn said. They both knew the punishment for men Edward of England considered traitors.

When Ingrid came that day, she was accompanied by Gaston and several of the household servants; they had brought trunks of clothing from Kyra's own room.

Ingrid seemed tired, asking her anxiously about her welfare, but then falling silent and saying no more about their heathen conquerors. Kyra was offered a steaming bath once again, and Ingrid washed her hair with rose water, and spent an hour brushing it out before a fresh fire. She dressed in a soft gold undergown and pale yellow tunic. The sleeves were furred, as was the hemline, and when she was dressed, she was surprised to realize that she felt very much the lady of Seacairn once again.

It had been like this when her father was alive. When she believed that her father would have some say in her marriage. He had refused to allow her to be wed as a child; such marriages were a common enough occurrence. She had known that Edward had long considered Kinsey Darrow a good match for her; Darrow had his own ruthless determination, since she was hereditary heiress to great tracts of land. But Edward had not committed her to the betrothal until her father's death. She wondered what would have happened had her father lived. And then she knew that he would have fought, and he would have died. He had been an Englishman, and his liege duty had been to Edward of England.

When Ingrid and Gaston had both been gone some time, she paced the tower room, feeling like a bird in a cage, and growing angry with herself because she could not help but wonder about her captor. Every so often she grew flushed and uneasy, thinking that she would not have fought him with any sense of noble pride if he had remained that morning. But he had left her, in an obvious state of . . .

Wanting.

Not able to bear her own thoughts any longer, she strode firmly to the door and threw it open. As she suspected, she was not alone.

Jay stood guard, staring at the door to the parapets.

"My lady. I was about to come for you."

"Oh?"

"We bury the dead this evening; the ceremony begins shortly." He stretched out an arm to her. She hesitated, then accepted it. He led her down the stairs.

Gaston and a number of the servants were busy in the great

hall, setting the table for the evening meal. The hounds gathered by the hearth, awaiting the bones and crumbs that would come their way.

"Come, my lady."

She followed him out to the courtyard. Jay's mount awaited him, and she found that someone had known which horse was hers, for her mare was saddled and awaiting her just past the great doors of the inner court, held there by one of Arryn's lads.

She mounted her horse, watching Jay.

"You're not afraid I'm going to gallop for the trees?"

"If you do, it will not be my affair," he said. And, looking toward the portcullis gates, she saw that Arryn blocked the way to the fields beyond the castle.

"Lady Kyra!" he called politely. "Father Corrigan buries all men alike. Come, join us. The dead will surely cherish your prayers."

How could he sound so polite and so mocking, all at the same time?

She rode ahead of Jay, irritated and aware that she would not try to run at the moment. The people were gathering: farmers, smiths, fishwives, attending Christian burial for those who had fallen in her defense!

And, of course, those who had fallen to bring her down.

She reached Arryn's position and did not slow her gait. He watched her go by and followed. They rode to the great copse at the beginning of the woods; she knew where, for it had been a hallowed ground for many years, from long before the days when the conqueror had come to England, and their world had just subtly begun to change.

The people were gathered; Father Corrigan was in his robes. The corpses were neither English nor Scottish in their shrouds.

She dismounted from her mare without assistance, and strode to the crowd. She was glad when cries and smiles greeted her.

Because, of course, the people here were the people she knew. The villagers. She had come and gone as befitted the daughter of a nobleman, but she had shared their lives as well. Her father was a man aware of his position, and the responsibility of it rather than the honor. He and she had joined in the May Day dances, baptisms, weddings, and funerals before. On saints' days, she had humbly washed the feet of their poorest tenants, brought food to the aging and aid to the injured and sick.

These were the people she had known all her life. It was good to be among them.

"My lady!"

"Lady Kyra has come!"

She knew the faces of the people: tenants, servants, artisans. She smiled, greeting them in turn; many of them touched her clothing as she passed among them. They gained strength from her, she knew, and comfort and courage. She touched them in turn, a child's face, an old man's shoulder, a mother's hand. Alistair, a farmer, now limped and leaned on a cane. She touched his shoulder.

"The outlaws did this to you?" she whispered.

"Nay, they did not. And I'm well, my lady." He flushed. "I fell in my haste to clear a path to the river yesterday. I—I was running from them."

She nodded. "It will heal, I think. And you should have run. You had no weapons, no armor; you could not fight."

"Perhaps not, Lady Kyra. And I pray we all heal."

She smiled. "Indeed." She hesitated, ready to tell him that these conquerors would not rule long; Edward would come down upon them with a mighty blow.

She said nothing.

She felt cold. Cold and afraid.

She saw Father Corrigan come to stand in the copse with the corpses. He spoke to the crowd, saying that God welcomed all men who believed, and then began funeral rites in Latin, his voice rich, blanketing the crowd. He prayed for the whole of their community, for the people of Scotland, for men who had died fighting. He said nothing overtly against Edward; his prayers were for the dead. When he had finished with the basic rites, he went from corpse to corpse, sprinkling them with holy water, making the sign of the cross over each body.

Then the men lowered the corpses, one by one, into the graves that had been dug for them.

The sound of the bodies thumping into the soft, newly turned earth seemed very sad and final; the smell of that same earth was rich and redolent. Then there were tears, as soft this morning as the sound of the earth as women cried for the men they had lost.

Darkness seemed to fall just as the last man was buried. *Ashes to ashes. Dust to dust.* Kyra found herself watching Sir Arryn. His features were grim. He was surely thinking that this was a kinder scene than that which he had encountered when returning to Hawk's Cairn after Kinsey Darrow and his men had come through.

Dust to dust. These corpses would decay.

Ashes to ashes . . .

He'd found nothing but charred bodies to bury upon his return.

Father Corrigan intoned a few more prayers, then told the living to go in peace.

It seemed a strikingly sad epilogue to funeral rites taking place in the aftermath of battle.

She was startled when she realized that Arryn was staring at her. When he started through the people to reach her, she instantly backed away, then turned and fled for her horse. She managed to leap up just as he reached her, catching her mare's reins.

"You're joining us for dinner, my lady?" he inquired politely.

She hesitated, wanting desperately to strike him and get away from him.

"You're giving me a choice?" she inquired.

"What I meant, my lady, is that you're not thinking of leaving, are you? It's been a long day. I'm not in the mood for a chase."

"If you're giving me a choice—"

"Aye, that I am. There is dinner, or there is none," he said politely. "But then, it's interesting. Do all your people love you so? The men-at-arms who have joined us, who eat in the hall as well? The servants who bring the meal? You've been so warmly greeted here. You're missed. I would think that you'd want to be among your people."

She smiled, leaning low. "And you'd have more influence and power here and with these people were I to pretend to tolerate you?"

"But you do tolerate me, my lady," he said smoothly, a cobalt shield seeming to cover his eyes so that they were like glass. "You've actually done far more than tolerate me."

She lowered her eyes, trying to draw her horse free from his hold.

Of course, she could not.

"Look at me, my lady."

She did so, her jaw clenched, her lips pursed.

He smiled. "You needn't worry that you'd give anything to me. I don't give a damn about my power here. I've not come to stay."

"What good is seizing power you cannot hold?"

"I'm not trying to seize power, lady; I am merely gaining strength. I will leave this place in time."

"After you've plundered it of goods and riches and anything you can steal."

"Goods, riches, plunder—and men, my lady. We have gained many things here indeed."

She was surprised to feel a strange sense of fear. He hadn't mentioned anything about her. He meant to stay here, methodically strip her home, and when he must—simply leave. He didn't covet the lordship of Seacairn—he had no illusions that he might have won such a victory here.

"So what does it matter, Sir Arryn, if I stay, if I come to dinner, if I do not?"

"A matter of convenience. If you run, I come after you, we fight, you're hurt. I'm weary, dirty, and aggravated."

"But what if I outrun you?"

"You can't imagine what a good horse I ride."

"My mare is a good horse."

"Aye, that she is," he said, smiling, and she felt another streak of fear sweep through her. He could look at her and keep his every thought a total secret.

And he could look at her in such a way that she knew exactly what he was thinking.

He meant to steal her horse. She was worthless once he left, but he wanted her horse.

She thought about slamming her heels against the mare's flanks, trying the strength of her horse's bolt against him, but even as the idea entered her mind, he tightened his grip on the mare's reins.

"Don't do it."

"And why not?"

"Because I'll see that you suffer far more for my pains than I will."

She stared into his eyes. "Don't steal her. When you leave, please don't take my mare."

"Please? Did that word come out of your mouth, my lady?"

"You've heard me say it before."

"Um . . . the circumstances, however, were different."

She flushed. "Oddly to you, sir, it is a word I know well. I cannot stop you from plundering the castle, robbing us blind. Please don't take my horse."

He watched her for a moment. For one reason, he smiled. Had he forgotten whatever anger she had stirred in him this morning?

"Come to dinner. Willingly. Sit by me. Courteously. Politely. Be the lady to the manor born!"

She didn't respond; she continued to meet his eyes.

"Ah, think on it, my lady! The choice is not so hard. Race the mare, I come after you, I catch you, we roll in the dirt, another gown is ruined, you are bruised and humiliated, I am left in a foul temper, I am rude and irascible throughout the night and God knows for how long after the night, or just how wretched the night becomes—and I take your horse when I go."

"And how long will that be?"

"Not soon enough for your liking, I'm certain. I will be here long enough to make you very miserable—should I choose."

"You must realize that you make me quite miserable—whether you do or do not choose."

"Ah, but with conscious effort, I can make you *very* miserable."

"But all I have to do is come to dinner and you promise not to make me miserable and to leave my horse?"

"I promise to think about leaving your horse. I said that you should come to dinner and be polite—no, lady—be charming. I've heard you're quite capable of kindness, wit, and such charm to soothe even such a savage beast as the English king."

"You're bribing me?"

"Is that how you see it?"

She smiled back at him with narrowed eyes and pursed lips. "I am not for sale, sir, at any price."

"So you did choose Kinsey Darrow." His eyes seemed like glass again, masking his thoughts.

She froze, feeling trapped. "I never sell myself, sir," she said, not allowing her voice to falter.

"Intriguing, my lady, whether true or not. But I'm not bribing you. I am cajoling you. I'm quite bereft that you cannot tell the difference."

"I would be allowed to say no to cajolery. Am I allowed to say no?"

"Are you so fond of remaining locked in a tower?"

"The company is at least pleasant."

"Dear God! You are flattering me!"

She flushed. "When I am alone in my tower, sir, the company is pleasant."

He arched a brow. "Um, so you insult me."

"If all enemies did was insult one another, sir, we would not be standing in a graveyard now."

"True. So . . . we are in a quandary here, my lady. Do I let go of these reins, or not? Never mind. I've risked your pride again. You would fight unto the death! I won't force you into any desperate measures for the moment."

Wary of his intent when he was so pleasant, she asked, "Out of respect for the dead, Sir Arryn? The men slaughtered here."

"My men lie among yours," he reminded her, and with a sudden smooth movement swung up on the mare behind her.

"What about your horse? Perhaps he'll take this opportunity to run away," she said. He was at her back, his arms around her, his hands on the reins.

"Old Pict? Nay, he'll never run. We've come too far together." He nudged her mare. "So . . . dinner, or none?"

"The great halls—or a great stone cage?" she inquired, trying hard not to feel him there.

"Those are the choices."

"Once again, I ask you why?"

"Because as of now, I am lord here, and it is what I say."

"As of now . . . you know that you are beaten, that you can hold nothing."

"You never give up fighting, do you? You await any opportunity to inflict a blow. But don't worry; I am aware of the strength of your king. And in truth, I don't want to hold a 'great stone cage,' as you say."

"Then what do you want?"

"Scotland. Scotland, for the Scottish. Here we are—dinner, or your cage?" He dismounted from her mare and reached for her. She hesitated, met the steady probe of his dark blue eyes. His hands settled around her waist. She placed her own on his shoulders, allowing him to sweep her down to the ground. He turned away from her.

She was left alone. The breeze stirred, cool and fresh.

Men dismounted from their horses all around her; grooms came out to take the mounts. She stood very still in the courtyard as night descended, and life went on. The people who lived within the walls of Seacairn were returning, some sad and quiet, somber, some already moving forward—masons discussed the walls, a knight commented to a young squire that his saddle needed repair. The dead were buried, tears had been shed, and they all knew they needed to pray for tomorrow.

"My lady! May I escort you in?"

She turned. Jay stood there, smiling, a query in his eyes that went beyond the question he had asked.

"Aye, Jay."

He came and took her arm, and started for the great doors to the inner tower. "I am sorry about your guards, slain in defense here. They died for duty."

She gazed at him curiously. "You think that all the men who defended Seacairn should have changed sides, abandoned fealty to Edward so easily?"

"You lost very few men," Jay said. "And so did we." He didn't actually answer the question. He meant to be tactful.

"Aye, many surrendered. I commanded them to do so."

"And it was a mercy," he said simply.

"But, Jay, if Darrow's forces had remained . . ."

"It would have all been different. We can't know the outcome, can we? Because they didn't remain. Do you think that he might have known that we had enough strength to take the castle?"

She felt strangely uneasy. "Of course not. He'd have never left the castle to be taken by his enemy."

They had reached the hall. The great table was filling with plates of venison, eel, fish, fowl, and mutton. Gaston had directed the cooks well, and all the serving platters were attractively prepared, adorned with greens and berries. Arryn's men were aligning themselves down the length of the table. Two seats at the head remained. Jay escorted her there.

"Perhaps I would be best off down the length of the table some. I haven't had much conversation with some of your companions."

"Ah, my lady! There you are. We're quite delighted that you've decided to join us."

The voice seemed to sweep around her. Deep, husky, pleasant. And with a warning mockery.

Arryn had come. He was so close that she spun directly into him as she turned, and it seemed that he swept around her, encompassing her air and space.

"I was just saying that I should sit elsewhere."

"But this is your place."

"Oh, I wouldn't presume to claim a place when you have claimed the castle. As I said, I should enjoy getting to know some of your men."

He pulled out her chair, his eyes steady on hers. "How well did you wish to get to know them, my lady?"

Despite herself, she flushed. And again despite herself, she sat. She was immediately irritated with herself. She should have held her chin high and started down the length of the table.

He sat beside her. "Perhaps you should reconcile yourself to getting to know me."

"I know far too much about you already."

"How curious. I don't feel that I know you at all."

"Well, you are the conqueror, you know. Fond of making entrances and exits at your will alone."

"Alas, that's the way of it. Wine?" He reached for a trencher and the goblet that sat between them, filling it.

"I would love some. Dulls the senses, you know."

"Sometimes, I've been told, it sharpens them."

"I believe you've been told wrong."

"Perhaps."

"But then, I believe you've been told wrong about many things."

"Such as?"

Me! she might have shouted.

But she did not.

She shook her head, fingers reaching for the goblet. She drank a long swallow. The wine was cool, but it seemed to send a strange heat snaking throughout her limbs.

"Now, see, my lady, you don't feel comfortable completing a thought, even after goading me. We don't know one another at all."

"Oh? Perhaps that's true. But I was not under the impression that you came here to get to know me at all, Sir Arryn."

"I did not. But then, I am here. And so are you. So perhaps we should get to know one another better. I was reflecting upon just such an idea this morning."

"Were you? I'd not have known. You left quickly. I thought that maybe you left with such haste to go out looking for a sheep."

The minute the words were out of her mouth, she regretted them.

She pretended to be busy with her meat, wondering what on earth had prompted her to say such a thing. She felt his eyes on her, and wondered if he would explode with anger. But he was amused, she realized. He leaned back, studying her, a strange smile curving his lips.

He leaned close to her suddenly. "Oh, good God, my lady! Were you distraught that I might have left *you* for a sheep?"

"Distraught? Never! I'd have pitied the poor sheep."

"Oh, but I'd never have left you for a sheep!"

She felt her cheeks flaming, but chose to ignore her own discomfort. She ate a piece of meat, chewing slowly, aware he watched her all the while, wishing she were not feeling so painfully uncomfortable.

"Sir," she said, speaking lightly, "you will have to cease with such chivalric words; I could become far too confident in my appeal, and I will begin to believe that I am preferable to domestic stock."

He laughed softly. She had reached for the wine; he had done the same. His fingers curled around hers.

"My lady, I believe that I am done with this meal."

"Oh, but we've just begun—"

"Indeed, we have."

He rose and pulled out her chair. It scraped against the floor. Loudly.

The room had been filled with conversation.

It ceased. She felt a dozen eyes turn to her.

Arryn spoke out, addressing the assembly.

The assembly had all gone quiet, all staring at them.

"My friends, I'll say good evening. The lady and I have decided to retire for the night. Please, enjoy the excellent food at Seacairn, and indeed, stay, enjoy the meal, store the taste of this fine food in your minds for less affluent days to come. I know that I shall certainly remember all that I have enjoyed and known here in the leaner times ahead.''

She could scarcely breathe; she felt a tremendous sense of humiliation, every one of them watching her, knowing. . . .

She would have run, would have turned, would have doused him in the wine, she was feeling so desperate. She would have done almost anything.

But he knew it. One look in his eyes, and she was aware that he knew she was feeling furious—and reckless.

Oh, he mocked her, taunted her—knowing she was powerless!

And still, she made a reckless movement for the wine to douse him.

She didn't make it. No matter how swift her dive, his reaction was faster. He caught her, spun her around.

"Nay, my lady, I think not."

"One day, sir, I will make you pay."

"Perhaps. But the day hasn't come."

"Did you have to make all eyes turn to us?"

"Aye, that I did."

She stared at him, her eyes damning him.

While the way that he looked at her . . .

She had seen the look before—the morning when she had stood before him, when he had taken the fur away. . . .

Her breath quickened.

He swept her up into his arms. She struggled; his arms tightened. She longed to scream; it would have made it all the worse.

Her eyes met his again.

And he strode from the great hall, his purpose far more than evident.

CHAPTER NINE

"Lord Darrow!"

Kinsey Darrow stood in the center of the manor house at Clayton. It was a lesser manor as such places went; the master here had been from the clan MacDonald, a stubborn old bear of a man, knighted by the guardians while the Maiden of Norway still lived, an irascible fellow if there ever had been one.

Had been.

He'd never signed the oath of allegiance to Edward of England. Naturally, when they'd come here, they'd claimed he had, that his name had been on the Ragman Rolls, a legal document stating that those who signed recognized the king of England as their overlord. This made the man a traitor, and eligible for a traitor's death—and they had given old Sir Tigue MacDonald such a death. He had been a huge fellow, dark haired, tall, and old but muscled like a bear. He had brought down eight Englishmen before he'd been taken. But then, by God, they'd had their revenge. They'd only half-hanged him before they started cutting out his entrails, and when they castrated him, they used his own organs to gag him before they finally struck off his head.

It now sat on a pole before the manor house.

They'd only mowed down half of the old lord's men—he'd used temperance, having learned in the past that if he slaughtered whole villages, there was no one left to serve him and his men. Kinsey was convinced that a good number of the people here were half-wits as it was. They didn't seem to understand much about the conflict going on around them. It was a poor stretch of flatland with some farming, some sheep, even a few cattle, but little more. The house was clean and neat, and the hearth was sound, creating a good enough fire. It was, though, hardly the kind of place he would have considered worthy of such military action, but the old lord had been a vassal of the Earl of Harringford, and he had summoned Kinsey because he'd wanted an example made of the old man. The earl was growing uneasy; the tide of nationalism among the Scots seemed to be rising at an alarming rate.

But as for this place . . .

At the death of Sir Tigue, the people had stood numbly. Some of the women had cried. He hadn't forced the old man's pretty dark-eyed daughter to watch the show; she had understood immediately the implications of everything that had happened to her home, and she had been a pretty piece in his bed the very night following her father's death. She had understood her choices, and she had wanted to live. Nor had she been unfamiliar with the role he had expected her to play. He thought, perhaps, she had even been glad of his coming. She was not a nationalist herself, Kinsey realized, but an ambitious young thing, who might well be plotting to use her association with him to move into a different circle of society.

"Lord Darrow!"

Hearing his name so anxiously repeated, he strode across

the room to the door, which stood ajar, and threw it open wide. Giles of Chester stood there, panting, breathing very hard. He had just ridden in from the south, having been sent with a message to Lady Kyra that Darrow would be returning in a fortnight.

"What is it, Giles?"

"The castle."

"What castle?"

"The castle has been . . ."

"Damn it, man, quit blubbering! What has happened?"

"Arryn Graham has taken Seacairn!"

For a moment, Kinsey stood dumbfounded. He had believed that not even Arryn Graham would go after the castle at Sea cairn. Not that he had left it heavily defended; he had not. He had been sure that the walls of the place alone would dissuade such a savage as Sir Arryn. The man's audacity to attack such a fortification!

Kinsey gripped the messenger by the throat, shaking him. "What are you saying?" The man gasped, unable to speak. Kinsey released his hold.

"It's true; I swear!" Giles gasped out, rubbing his neck. "He rode in soon after you rode out."

"What of the men I sent back with supplies?"

"Taken on the road, my lord."

Pain struck Kinsey's head, his fury was so great. He turned from Giles, so angry he was ready to impale the man with his sword. He drew his weapon anyway, and slashed down on the table. Wood shattered and groaned and cracked. Kinsey's arm shook, and the impact seemed to reverberate through the length of him.

He spun back to Giles.

"What of Lady Kyra?"

Giles hung his head. "She tried to fight him. They said she

nearly bested him at arms, waging war with him in the chapel. Then . . ."

"Aye, then?"

"She threw herself into the river."

Kinsey stood dead still. If she was dead . . .

He suddenly saw Kyra: beautiful, proud, *disdainful* Kyra. Always keeping her distance from him. Always courteous, always correct, always so cool and untouchable, and always, always seeming to burn beneath. It was there, something rich, warm, lush, and passionate, something always held away from him! Somehow she was superior; somehow . . . she used the king against him, but he had forced himself to reason, knowing that in the end she would be his. And when the vows were spoken, and the woman and the titles and property were all his . . .

Well, he would quickly teach her who was superior in marriage, and in the world. He had thought that often, lying awake at night. Wanting her beauty, wanting to break her, wanting more, whatever it was he couldn't touch, whatever it was he couldn't take. He could never walk away—and he could never seize her in a rage, because there were men—his own men!—who would defend her, just as he defended all that was English, in the name of the king. Somehow she drew their loyalty, their admiration. And their love.

But now . . .

If she was dead, she would never have the power to make him feel like a lesser man again! If she was dead, the king would know his sorrow, his pain, his rage . . . and the king might well reward him. . . .

Aye, that much was true. But he suddenly doubled over, thinking that Sir Arryn, his greatest enemy, had taken Kyra. Taken what Kinsey could not take, seized what he could not have!

Kyra had thrown herself into the river. . . .

"Is she dead?" he whispered.

"Nay, my lord, thank God; the lady lives! She swam right out of the river—"

"And escaped him?"

"Nay, my lord, she remains his prisoner."

Kinsey turned around, placing both hands on the simply carved wooden hearth. His prisoner. His whore. She remained his whore. She'd be better off dead.

"By God . . ." he began, and his voice thundered with emotion. "Damn him, damn him, damn him! We'll ride against him."

Sir Richard Egan, second in command of his men, burst in behind Giles. Richard was a very tall man, deceptively lean. At thirty-five, he had watched a great deal of the world, and was as hardened a warrior as a man was likely to find to fight beside him. "Kinsey! I've heard about the events at Seacairn. But you've got to think, my lord. Word has traveled here, and we're all furious, and your men pray for your lady; yet as your friend, and a man who would die for you, I beg you, don't throw all our lives away. My lord, you must realize your death will do her little good! He has a great many men with him. And he holds the castle. He has garnered support with every day he has traveled. He has gained the respect of such powerful traitors as Andrew de Moray and William Wallace. We need greater strength. The earl will come tomorrow, and tomorrow you can appeal to the king for the army you will need."

Kinsey spun around, ready to strike out, but one look at Richard and he suddenly controlled his own temper. Richard knew about ambition—power, revenge, lust, and fury. He had to fight the sick rage seizing him now. He couldn't throw himself blindly after the outlaw—his own life was of greater importance.

He lowered his head, hating Kyra, hating that she had the power to make him forget reason for rage.

For longing . . .

Hating that she could make him feel as if he were not superior. As if he were . . .

Inferior.

He clenched his hands into fists at his sides. He lowered his head. "Leave me."

"Lord Darrow—"

"Leave me!" he shouted, and he raised his sword menacingly at Giles.

"Come," Richard told Giles, and urged the man out.

"You, too!" Kinsey grated to Richard.

Richard shook his head. "You will use this to your advantage. The king will know your rage, and know your sorrow! The world will hear that she cast herself into a river to be free from such a savage. All men will want to join with you for revenge. We will be justified in all that we do."

"Richard, you don't understand what has happened here."

"Indeed, I do. Listen to me; pay heed to my advice: you are a smart and cunning man—you are no fool, and you mustn't behave rashly."

"Aye!"

He turned back to the fire.

"Kinsey."

"Get me ale, and leave me be."

"My lord—"

"Get me ale, and leave me be!"

Richard wisely turned aside.

Kinsey drank heavily, tankard after tankard in a matter of minutes, wanting to spend the night in oblivion. The poor ale went straight to his head. He felt ill.

He retired to the master's chambers when it was late. The ale had not eased the rage that gripped him. He felt dull and angry still.

Night. She was with him.

Impotent rage filled him anew.

The buxom daughter of the dead master of this house he had claimed came to him. He looked at her dispassionately as she shed her tunic and undergown and approached him. She crawled atop the bed, rubbing her body over his. She seemed to have grown more wanton with the passing days. He didn't touch her. She continued to move against him. With no encouragement, she shifted his clothing. Her hands closed around him. She whispered things, pressed her lips to his, smiled, eased down the length of him. He inhaled sharply as she serviced him.

Enough . . .

But she moved up the length of him again, touching him, kissing his lips. She suddenly made him want to vomit.

He gripped her by the hips and was unhappy with the flesh he found there. "You're built like a cow," he told her.

"My lord?" she murmured, as if she hadn't comprehended his words. Maybe she hadn't. "Cow!" he repeated, and he gripped her by the shoulders, throwing her forcefully from the bed. He didn't understand his own rage. Kyra. He had hated her at times. She was all he could see now. The fine detail of her features. The smooth, graceful, effortless way she moved. The green of her eyes, the gold in her hair. He thought of her, and of this whore he had taken.

And all others paled in comparison.

And as he had so many times, he hated Kyra.

And wanted her.

And raged impotently.

He thought of Arryn Graham's lady wife. The woman he had taken who had stared at him, not fighting the inevitable, but ignoring him. As if he didn't matter in the least. As if he hadn't even really touched her. . . .

Alesandra! What a ridiculous name for such a timid maid.
She had barely fought him, and still . . .

She left him feeling as if he had taken nothing. Nothing!

He hadn't meant to kill her. But when the fires began and he saw her face, he had remembered the way she had looked at him. He hadn't even touched her. He didn't matter. He hadn't bruised her, harmed her, violated her in any way because he just hadn't mattered. Her husband would come home, and she would love him, and he would love her still. . .

And so, when the flames had risen . . .

He had let her perish.

Aye, she had died! She had burned in agony! She had died, pregnant with the outlaw's whelp. But not even that seemed enough now. He had thought Sir Arryn a savage, like a High-lander, a man accustomed to the petty family and clan feuds of the chieftains, with no knowledge of real warfare. He had managed to murder his kin, aye, but that had been the kind of fight that such barbaric men could win, hand to hand, muscle and brawn, no strategy needed. He had considered him a baying hound with no real bite.

But now the man was moving, and moving against him, and Kinsey Darrow couldn't help but feel rage.

The outlaw had Kyra. And God help him, he couldn't help but wonder . . .

Was Kyra not glad of it all?

Jay left the great hall after Arryn had done so, feeling restless and anxious. He walked toward the stairs to the outer wall. Summer. Such a beautiful time here, with warmer days, cool, soothing nights. There were times in winter when the snows were so fierce and cold that no fire seemed to warm a man, but summer, ah, summer was the time for Scotland. The land was so rich, verdant, striking in its roll of meadow and valley, green grasses, bright wildflowers, rich, dark forests. Aye, summer was lush. And the moon would sit high in the sky, and the stars would sparkle, and it was a good time just to be alive.

That thought always made him grave, because so many of his friends and relations were dead. Not many of the people who had been friends, kith, and kin had survived the massacre at Hawk's Cairn. Brendan, left for dead, was with them now, a strapping and handsome lad, grave beyond his years.

And his own sister, Katherine.

She had been in the manor when Darrow and his men had come.

It had been summer as well, then. Early summer, the freshness of a season just turned from spring, with warmth, richness, a redolence in the earth. The shaggy cattle had grazed in the fields, sheep had huddled on the hills, and the river had sparkled under the warmth of the sun. The old family manor, begun before the country was even formed as it was now, sat in the center of thatched-roof houses, fields of activity, valleys of produce. Orchards surrounded them, and the forest, alive with game. It was a great place, where the old spirits had lived in hollowed-out tree trunks, maidens had fallen in love with strapping lads, toothless old wiccans had cast spells, senachies had told daring tales of long-ago fights, and men had waged fair trade. This was where Kinsey Darrow had ridden to repay his kinsman's death, and he had done so with a vengeance. There were few men-at-arms there, for none had been needed; they quarreled with none of their neighbors, fought no family feuds. And they should have been deep enough into the country, close to warring Highland chieftains, to be far from the demands of such men as Warenne, the old Earl of Surrey, Edward's most able commander in the field—and Cressingham, the king's tax collector, a man hated even among the English.

They should have been far from danger. . . .

But danger had come. Darrow had ridden up, his men herding farmers and shepherds into the barn, gathering masons, smiths, artists, musicians, mothers, children. Some had screamed and run, and of those, a few had escaped, and more had been slashed down by the armed and armored horsemen who had hunted them. And in the manor, Kinsey Darrow himself had gone to search out the mistress, and he had found her, and when he had finished with her, he had left her.

They had set fire to the manor, and to the barn.

And it was said the cries of the dying could be heard into the Highlands and beyond; they were howls that tore day and night asunder, and would remain forever in the hearts of those who had heard them.

Jay had not heard them; he and Arryn and most of their fighting force were in the north, helping de Moray as he cleared a castle of its English general. The fighting had been fierce; the surrender noble. Rich men had been taken hostage, and poor men were allowed to return to their lands in England— if they had the nerve to do so. They had been in good spirits.

Until they had ridden home.

There was nothing in the world so horrible as the smell of burning human flesh. And they had seen the smoke, and smelled the death, long before they came to Hawk's Cairn.

Arryn, at the head of their forces, had spurred Pict and raced ahead. Men had tried to stop him.

He had found Alesandra himself, the remains of Alesandra; they could tell only because of her wedding ring, the family insignia ring she had worn on her third finger.

The cries of rage and pain could be heard clear to Ireland, so the stories went. Not true, certainly. But not a man of them would ever forget, or forgive, Jay knew. Alesandra had been his cousin. Katherine, his sister, had been in the manor until Alesandra, under attack, had ordered her to go. She had escaped by striking one man with a pan, stabbing another through with the dirk she had never failed to carry in their treacherous times, and riding another into the ground. She made no pretense about the situation; she had killed, and gladly, to live.

But she remembered. . . .

They all remembered.

Jay saw a figure upon the parapets. John Graham, looking toward Selkirk. With uncanny hearing, he sensed Jay and turned, then waved.

Jay joined him.

"A fine night," John said.

"Aye, beautiful."

John laughed suddenly. "And ye'd think we'd be at court, eh, Jay?" he said softly.

"You're restless tonight."

"So are you."

John glanced at him. "I can feel, Jay, can ye not? I can feel it; it's in me bones! My heart feels it, my limbs feel it . . . the time is coming."

Jay studied John's face—deep blue eyes, handsome, but with a hardened and rugged profile. "We all know well that Edward's men seek Wallace's army. What we question is if they know how many men de Moray brings. Can they find Wallace while he strikes across the countryside and slips into the forests?"

"Few men can find Wallace," John said.

"Aye," Jay said, with no other comment. John was one of them. He had gone through more close calls with Wallace than perhaps any other man.

After a moment he asked, "Can we win, John? Can we take back our country from such a man as King Edward?"

John was quiet for a long moment. "Aye, it can be done. I believe it can be done. We weren't ready for the English at first. We showed that at Berwick, and at Dunbar. But we've learned. We've taken back so much, Jay!"

"If we win a great battle, will we win Scotland?"

John stared at him. He shuddered suddenly. "Will we win Scotland? Aye, most of it. Will we keep her? God help me, man, I do not know. But I will fight until I cease to draw breath, Jay. I will never forget . . . what was done."

Jay kept studying him, then looked across the slope to the great forest beyond the castle. "We have begun here. It's a fine place, a great, sturdy fortress. It could be well defended."

"The staunchest castle can fall."

"Aye, but . . . I wonder if Arryn sees what he has taken."

"Does he see it . . . will he want to stay? Or will he fight with Wallace when we make our great blow for freedom?" John said. His eyes narrowed on Jay. "You, my friend, seem content enough to be here."

Jay started. "As I said, it's a fine fortress—"

"Held by a fine lady?"

Jay felt a flush color his cheeks. "John, she never rode with Darrow—"

"She's betrothed to him."

"But, still . . ."

"You're seduced, lad," John advised.

"Not from my senses! I tell you—"

"Don't fear, my cousin is seduced as well. And not from his senses, I pray."

"You feel nothing when you see her?"

"Aye, but I do. I admire the bonny lass, I do. She's a rare beauty and spirit, and damn, my friend, but I am alive and well—and I feel lust! If my cousin were to tire of her . . ."

"He will not!"

"Jay! You rush so quickly to her defense! Arryn seized the castle to take it, to plunder it—and to have revenge. He will ride from here—and she will be left to her English fiancé, forever changed, but alive, and assumably bitter against him for the rest of his days—which will be numbered, we hope— for the fact that he deserted her with a madman on his way!

She will be left behind, Jay. To her own people, and her own allegiances.''

"But can he leave her? For the love of God, I could not.''

"Jay, Alesandra, your cousin, his wife, was murdered. Viciously. Your sister Katherine uses her hatred of Darrow and everything and everyone associated with him as a crutch to live. How have you found such forgiveness?''

"I haven't. I never will. But was Kyra at any fault?''

"Does anyone really know?''

Jay didn't answer. He looked over the wall. "He intends to leave her . . . but he can't. He really can't.''

"He must.''

"Why?''

"These are treacherous times.''

"For her, as well. She was raised English, and so she defends the English king. But she has seen things, and she is compassionate. She knows what happened; she was sorrowful, I'm sure of it. She has come to know Arryn.''

John arched a brow and grimaced. "Aye, she's been forced to, one imagines.''

"She can become one of us.''

"Jay, she is not a maid, a shepherdess, or a farm wife. She is Lady Kyra Boniface, godchild of the deceased queen, pawn in Edward's game. She will never be one of us.''

"Why not?''

"She could betray us all.''

Jay shook his head. "If Arryn chose to bring her—''

"Not to Wallace! Not to Wallace. Besides, he won't.''

"Why not?''

"She is his revenge, nothing more. As you loved Alesandra, so did he, many times over. As you feel guilt for her death, so does he—many, many times over.''

"Why am I the only one who sees this? She really mustn't stay. Surely, in the end, Arryn will realize it and bring her.''

"I'll wager you my fine black stallion against the jeweled sword you took from the fat English tax collector that he will not!"

"I'll accept the wager! Arryn will bring her."

"Though you'd win a fine horse, if you're so beguiled by the lass, you should perhaps pray that he doesn't," John said, somewhat sharply.

"Why?"

"Because if he did, and if she even thought about betraying us to Kinsey . . ."

"Aye?"

"Then I would slay her myself," John said bitterly. "Slice her to ribbons, and set her afire. Good night, Jay."

John started down the steps.

Jay looked out on the warm, beautiful night.

And shivered.

CHAPTER TEN

By the time they reached the tower room, Kyra was struggling in earnest, utterly humiliated, far more enraged than frightened.

Her flying fists had no impact on him, her words—commands that he set her down immediately—went unheeded. Then her fist connected with his chin, her nails caught his throat, and he was swearing back at her. "Wretched little wildcat! Take care, lest you reap what you sow!" he warned her, but she was incensed, and desperate—and hopeless.

He kicked open the tower door, kicked it shut.

"Set me down!"

"With pleasure, my lady!"

She landed on the bed with a force that swept the breath from her. When she managed to gasp in air again, she rose, leaping to the other side of the bed, wound her hands into fists, and prepared to face him.

But he had already turned away from her. He was studying

the fire. It burned warm and bright; the servants, it seemed, were more than willing to please him.

To provide for his comfort.

She should have kept her mouth shut, maintained her distance. But she did not.

Her voice was deep with her fury and emotion—a threat, she thought, that she was powerless to implement. Still shaking no matter how she clenched her fists, she cried, "You wretched, barbaric bastard! My God, you have no right to humiliate me so, to—"

"Humiliate you?" He spun on her, staring at her. "People do not die of humiliation."

"What you do is cruel, and you are wrong! People do not die because of humiliation? You—you and the rest of your stinking outlaws! Your pride is wounded. Edward has wounded your Scottish pride—"

"Edward has massacred Scottish people in huge numbers."

"Because they would not bow down."

"That's right, my lady. We will not bow down."

"Well, forgive me then for refusing to bow down to you!"

He watched her for a long moment. "Ah, but you have no choice, do you?"

"Why are you doing this? Why did you have to make such a show before your men, treat me like . . ." Her voice trailed off. She turned away from him.

"Perhaps, my lady, what I did is the greatest kindness."

She spun back around. "And how is that?"

"Perception is an all-important element in life."

"That I am perceived as your . . ."

"Whore?" he supplied pleasantly.

"Aye, that you treat me so. Is that an important perception?"

He nodded. "People perceive that you are mine. Therefore, you are left alone and held in regard."

"Aye! Sir Arryn, I can feel the regard! Every time your men

look at me and speculate about the revenge they know you meant to take.''

''Aye. They speculate. Would you have them do more? Besides, this is all your doing, my lady.''

''My doing!''

''It sounded as if you were distressed with the concept that I would leave you—for a sheep. I had to make it quite plain that you were preferable. Ah, but then, you would throw yourself from a tower, death being preferable to me.''

''I didn't throw myself from the tower!''

''How flattering, my lady. So I am preferable to death?''

''Death, such a death, would be a surrender, Sir Arryn. I don't surrender in any battle. I will survive this—since you've informed me you'll do your best *not* to throttle me. But you, sir, will eventually lose. You'll be taken, and a very sorry fate will await you.''

''Then I must live every moment—and survive you, of course.''

''Survive me? Oh, aye, I'm very dangerous!''

''That you are, my lady. But then, there are ways to avoid the danger you would offer.''

''Oh?'' she inquired, but then, meeting his eyes, she remembered the way she had fallen asleep—tied to the bedposts.

''Aye.''

''So you think I would try to kill you in your sleep?''

''Have you grown so fond of me that you would not?''

''Nay, fine, let it be as you say! Perhaps you will not survive me! You should value life and safety and sanctity. And as to me, well, have done with the threats and the warnings and the torment!'' she challenged him. ''Perhaps I would rather survive a dozen—nay, two dozen!—of your men!''

''Would you?''

With shoulders squared, she started toward the door. She didn't run or look away from him, but glared at him as she walked with long determined strides to exit in fury and dignity. He watched her as she walked by, watched as she threw open the door. Hesitating just slightly, she turned to him. But he bowed, indicating that she was more than welcome to leave.

She started out, her heart beginning to hammer. Afraid to go on, afraid to go back, she picked up her skirts, ready to run.

She was appalled to find herself relieved when his hand landed on her arm. A shriek left her as his fingers wound tightly around her flesh. She met the grim resolve in his eyes as he stared at her coldly for one long moment before he none too gently tossed her over his shoulder.

"Why don't you let me go!" she grated, slamming her fists against his back.

"Because you are—"

"Darrow's!" she finished in a hiss, banging against his back. "Damn you, I am not brick or stone or a jewel or a piece of land or—"

"Nay, lady, you are something far more important!"

Once again she landed ignominiously on the bed.

"Damn you!" he told her.

"I will try to escape you every minute of every day."

"It's good to know," he said coldly.

She rolled from where she had fallen, standing once again, looking at him stubbornly, her gaze slipping toward the door.

"Go ahead. I dare you, my lady!" he challenged.

Thus goaded, she gritted her teeth and started by him again. This time his fist landed against the door before she could fully open it, and she was over his shoulder without having ever departed. "Stupid bastard. *Dead* bastard, you are a dead man," she cried, knotted fists pounding his back once again. "You'll be sorry."

"You'll be sorry if you don't stop!" he roared. "I'll strip you naked and blacken and blue your backside before the whole of the village if you don't cease pounding upon me!"

She landed on the bed again but rose on her knees, still in defiance. "Do it, fine! Just do it, try it in front of the villagers and see if—"

"If they don't rise against me, so that my men can hack them down like so many armed enemies?"

"Oh!"

That time she slammed his chest. And she didn't have to rise to try to make a departure again, because he dragged her up, one arm around her midriff, and started for the door himself.

"No, no! What are you doing? Stop, you can't, you can't! Stop, you must—"

He was halfway out the door. She grasped the door frame. "Please stop; I don't want more dead men. I . . . damn you!"

She took a wild swing at him and managed to connect hard with his jaw.

She gasped, stunned at the feel of her knuckles hitting bone— then panicked. He was dead still for a moment, as stunned as she. Then he plucked her up by the waist, lifting her back into the room. He slammed the door shut with a vengeance that reverberated. He reached for her, dragging her toward him, half lifting her then, half dragging her, approaching the bed.

"There is an alternative; we can deal with this right here!"

"What? No . . . I didn't mean . . . I . . . I . . . stop . . . I . . ."

In horror, she found that he was sitting, wrenching her over his knees, tugging at her tunic and undergown.

"No!" she shrieked, struggling against him. She managed to slide back; she was on her knees looking up at him, her face flooded with crimson color.

Shivering, she lowered her eyes.

"I-I don't want anyone fighting for me, dying for me."

"Were you expecting someone to burst into the bedroom here?"

Her eyes rose to his. He arched a brow. "Kinsey Darrow?

Do you think he's coming now to rescue you, that you'll get to see me hanged, drawn and quartered, and disemboweled?''

''No!''

He was quiet for a moment, studying her. ''Nay!'' he said softly. ''You don't think that's going to happen . . . but it's an enjoyable concept, eh?''

''What do you want from me?'' she whispered somewhat desperately.

''Indeed, what do I want from you?'' he murmured, then rose. He strode toward the fire and remained there for several minutes, watching the flames. ''Surrender, unconditional surrender!'' he said softly, then moved away. ''For this wretched night, at the very least!''

He began to disrobe, his actions unhurried. His sword and scabbard were carefully placed on a trunk; his long stretch of tartan was folded. He made no movement toward her then; she might not have existed. She should have inched away to a distant corner of the room; she might have kept far from him. Yet she found herself asking in a whisper, ''Why do you hate me so much?''

He was still for a moment. Firelight played off his naked shoulders. Muscle and sinew seemed to ripple in shades of crimson and gold. His head was lowered, and she could read nothing of his expression.

''Because you are—''

''Don't!'' she protested.

But he continued. ''Because you are Kinsey Darrow's,'' he said.

''But I am not!'' she insisted passionately. She rose, carefully backing away from him. ''People do not own people!''

''You think not? Among your English, lady, wives are but property.''

''Wives bring property to a marriage.''

He still hadn't glanced her way, but continued to undress as casually as if they had long shared chambers, maintaining his argument as he did so. He cast shoes and hose aside, his patience coming to its limit as he glared at her. "Aye, and you brought Darrow quite a bit, didn't you? The vast income that allowed him to train and arm a legion of men. And it is said that you are a favorite of King Edward, and would goad Kinsey into any action that would please Edward."

"And you believe that?" she whispered. She did not turn away from him.

"Should I not?"

"I am not a murderess."

"Are your hands stained with blood? Perhaps not—though you are quite adept at handling a sword. An interesting talent for so innocent a lass."

"I learned at court for the entertainment of the lessons."

"There was no one to show you needlework?" he inquired dryly.

"I learned many things at court."

"Aye, King Edward's court?" he inquired.

She lowered her head.

"I learned many things at Alexander's," he murmured. "Including the fact that no man is greater than the country, though the country can be run by the dictates of one man. Edward did not murder every man, woman, and child at Berwick—but he gave the order, and thus he is drenched in all that blood. Indeed, the rivers of blood that flow here are all of his doing, whether he strikes the blows that kill or not."

"What is it I am guilty of, then? A betrothal made in my name?"

"You have never sworn fealty to King Edward?" he demanded, sitting upon the bed. He stared at her a long moment before bending to blow out the bedside candles. The room darkened, but the glow of the fire continued to grant both light and shadow.

"Aye, but that—"

"And you will wed Lord Kinsey Darrow, knowing the blood that he has shed?" he inquired, throwing back linen sheets and furs to settle into the bed.

She stood still, not answering as he turned his back on her. She felt a strange sense of weary exhaustion sweep over her. There seemed no way to explain to this man that she had grown up as Edward's subject, but that no matter what loyalty she had sworn, there was, in life, the matter of humanity—and a difference between right and wrong, battle and brutality, warfare and murder. Yet how could he condemn her when so many of the great Scottish barons still feuded with one another, when they were willing to kill each other for the crown, and when the most powerful men in the country vacillated continually in their loyalties, wanting to honor the tradition of Scotland, but ever fearful of Edward's strength and power, and fearful they would lose their holdings?

He remained with his back to her. She had been dismissed, so it seemed.

"Surrender the night, Kyra; let it go."

She lowered her head and said softly, "Nay, please let *me* go."

He remained still for so long that she thought he hadn't heard her. Then he turned, staring at her from the dark shadows on the bed. "What is it that I'm doing to you that is so brutal and so cruel?"

She couldn't see them but she felt his eyes. "I don't know what will happen, sir, from one moment to the next."

"Ah, lady, then you stand as all Scotland!"

She walked to the hearth and stood before the fire. She felt the warmth of the blaze against her face, heard the crackling of the kindling within. "I never know when you will choose to put on a pretense of courtesy, when you will hate me for the actions of others, when you will lose patience and seize me up—''

Her words broke off, for she heard something, a whisper of swift movement on the air. He was up and striding toward her quickly with sure purpose. She cried out softly as he reached her, lifting her into his arms with a determined force that brooked no opposition. But when her eyes met his, she was surprised to find no anger. In fact, something within her froze the protest she would have issued.

''I would not torture you with wonder as to when this would happen, my lady. So I have seized you up; courtesy is lost. Come to bed, because I am weary still, and anxious for comfort.''

''But I am not comfort.''

''Tonight you will be.''

''You're wrong; I do not give in so easily. I will never surrender, even for the night.''

''I don't believe you,'' he said softly.

She burned. And why should he? She had not fought him so desperately before. . . .

''Tonight you must believe me.''

''If I do or do not, it will not matter. I will continue the conquest, and as before, my lady, offer no quarter. That's what you need to hear, isn't it?''

''No! It has nothing to do with what I need to hear!'' she told him, but her arms were around him as he carried her.

If he dropped her, she assured herself, she could break bones. She had to hold fast to him.

''Then why fight?''

''Because it's wrong; you're wrong.''

''I don't think that you really hate me so much.''

''Ah, but, sir! You loathe me.''

''I loathe many things. But not you. Nay, not you, not at this moment!''

She had protested, but she was too weary to struggle against him.

Her words were the best fight she could manage, and though she wanted to deny it, her fight was all for her pride.

Somehow, at that moment, it felt ridiculously good to be held by her enemy. She was sorry that he was the foe, and sorrier still that any gentle touch from him would mean less than nothing—she was Kinsey Darrow's, and that was all, like the castle, the produce, the riches here.

He laid her down and stretched beside her, and the firelight flickered against the stone walls of the castle, and strange patterns and shapes were cast there, and the room glowed in night currents from the blaze in mists of crimson and blue. His fingers brushed her cheeks, and suddenly he was leaning over her, staring into her eyes, studying her face. She wondered what he could see, for the room was so deep in shadows, and yet she was aware of the shape of his face, and the length of his form, and she closed her eyes. Even then she was aware of his heat, his scent, and the force of his length beside her own. She was acutely aware of him, of the linen of the sheets beneath her, the tickle of the fur pelts that covered the bed. She was so aware of his touch. Aye, she had closed her eyes, but she did not shut him away at all, but brought him closer, and it was difficult to breathe, and she wanted to escape, and . . .

There was something so compelling about the way that he touched her. Just her face. The whisper of his fingers against her cheekbones. The pad of his thumb stroked her lower lip, and then she felt his mouth against her own. A sound formed in her throat, and perhaps she managed the slightest moan of protest. But his lips were firm, not brutal, forming to hers, parting them thus, and his tongue seemed to invade with a sensual stroke of pure liquid fire. *Twist away*. Aye, she tried, surely, but his palms fell on either side of her cheeks, he seemed to quest and drink from her lips, and his kiss was slow and leisurely and she was not fighting it . . . rather the sensations seemed engulfing, like heady wine, sweeping her into a spiral that whispered of wonders untold. When his mouth parted from hers at last, she inhaled on a long and ragged breath, her lips remaining parted and ever so slightly swollen, cold now to the air in the room, and hungry, and she still knew the taste of him. She hadn't wanted to open her eyes; it was so easy to deny him in self-imposed darkness. But her lashes betrayed her, streaking upward, and he was studying her again, and there was something deep in the cobalt of his eyes that first made her want to run . . . and then want to stay. His fingers threaded into her hair, and he murmured then, "Darkness is always best, isn't it, my lady?"

But before she could respond, he was kissing her again, and there was a subtle change to his touch. Though not brutal, it demanded; where his tongue had quested, it now invaded. She lay busily trying to field and fend sensation when all was already lost. He awakened something within her. He was the enemy and he should have repelled her, but rather he seduced.

And she wanted to be held.

She felt his hands upon her, at the laces of the brocade tunic she wore, at the ties of the linen undergown. Her fingers curled around his, yet each time his lips parted from hers, they returned, and when she would have stopped him he paused, and stroked her cheek again, feathered his touch over her face, found her hands again. She wasn't conscious of exactly when she discovered that her clothing had melted away like so much ice at the coming of spring; she knew only that when she shivered, he touched her, that she was close to him for warmth. The memory that she owed it to herself, king, and country to fight him stirred within her, yet she was still able to tell herself it would not matter. Would it?

She had used this argument before.

Yet could she have changed anything?

Again, she realized she would never know, for she was being seduced, and she was allowing it to be so.

And more . . .

She did not lie still.

She did not tolerate him in an effort to save her life.

She *anticipated*. . . .

She felt his lips against her throat, and the pulse of her own heartbeat in the slender vein that beat against his kiss. The tip of his tongue teased her flesh, a brushstroke of blue fire, and it seared a path between her breasts, then followed around the fullness of one, a slow, flickering voyage, until his caress centered upon the peak of her nipple. The graze of his teeth, the brush of his tongue, the fullness of his kiss played there, and through that touch, streaks of lightning seemed to enter within her. It was her breast he so encompassed with the liquid fire of his mouth, yet the flames he ignited seemed to burn deep into her being, to find a center like the sun, radiate there, burn back into each limb and each inch of flesh, mind, soul, being. She stirred against him, murmuring, no words, just whispers that were as incoherent as the thoughts and desires arising, all that she struggled against, all that she struggled to find. She meant to protest in some small way; her fingers fell upon his shoulders, and through that simple touch she felt the fire that burned in him, felt the ripple and pulse of muscle, scent, motion, and life, vital beneath her. She meant to press him away; she pressed him downward. Her nails stroked over him; her fingers dug. She twisted, turned, tossed her head upon the pillow, and murmured anew. Protests . . . oh, God . . .

His tongue laved her navel. His fingers stroked down the length of her thigh, rubbed over her belly. Her hips twitched and moved. The hard heel of his palm moved low on her abdomen. Her fingers moved in his hair. She gasped in a breath, moving, rocking, writhing, twisting away . . . twisting back. His touch sliced between her thighs, his thumb pressed, found entry, rotated, caressed. And then his mouth was upon her, low, intimate. Tongue teasing, penetrating. Searing wet heat seemed to burn straight into her. She arched and writhed in protest and astonishment, in protest and on fire, the length of her crimson, and still . . . such a sea of lightning streaking through her. Her fingers clutched convulsively, burying themselves in his hair. He clutched her wrists, breaking her hold, never breaking the intimacy of his seduction. Words tore from her then, and still they meant nothing, cries and whispers in the blue shadows that played upon the castle walls, and nothing more. Then suddenly he was on top of her, and her limbs were parted, and he sank deeply within her, and again his lips caught her own, and the intimacy between them was in his kiss. His fingers entwined with her own; he drew her hands above her head and pinned them there, and met her eyes, and her breathless stare, as he began to move.

She allowed her lashes to fall.

No surrender.

No quarter.

He did not hate her so much!

Nay . . .

Not then.

He moved like fire, and she was aware of the feel of his flesh, and his touch, and the fullness of his sex within her, the pulse of his heart and muscle and sinew. She knew his strength, his texture, the feel of the linen beneath her, the touch of his flesh. She was so aware of every detail of the man, and yet she was not; she was aware of the thunder, the fire, the blaze that centered where they merged, the hunger, the longing. Nothing real mattered; the hunger mattered, the aching, the reaching, the fire . . . and then . . . the moment that burst upon her in a startling blaze, just a moment, yet blue fire, sweet blue fire, burning into her, searing sweet, staggering, sweeping breath away, steeling her limbs, plundering all logic and reason. . . .

She heard the snap and crackle of the fire. She saw the shadows play against the stone walls of the castle. She felt him, rock muscled, still against her, flesh still fire, but passion spent. Sprawled. He was sprawled atop her. Weary, satiated— self-satisfied. He'd set out to seduce; he'd seduced. And suddenly the fact that she'd been so easily and so completely seduced dismayed and infuriated her, and she wanted nothing more than to be free of his hard, sleek limbs and the very casual way he remained spent, but draped upon her.

The way he lay there was almost like . . .

A swagger.

She burned. She blushed through every pore of her body.

"Off, dear God, off!" she cried out, pressing desperately at his massive frame.

"Jesu, my lady—"

"I can't breathe!"

He shifted instantly, but he was still at her side, and his arm was around her, pinning her. His eyes were on hers, narrowed and sharp.

"Please . . ."

"Ah, there you go. You do use that word well. Please . . . what?"

"Get away from me. I—I told you. I can't breathe."

"I think that you're breathing just fine."

"No, I'm not. Please. Get up, go away! Let me up. You've had what you wanted."

"Ah, Kyra, indeed, poor lady. You were so wretchedly seized! I have been cruel to you in the extreme!"

"You are cruel."

He laughed softly.

She gritted her teeth, tried to strike out at him. He caught her arm, still smiling. "No surrender, my lady? Who meant to seduce whom?"

She gasped, staring at him. Newly infuriated, she struggled like a wildcat.

"Stop!" He laughed. "You're furious with me because—"

"I was wretchedly seized!"

"Because you dropped your sword before the first blow was delivered." He tried to smooth a tangle of hair from her face. She tossed her head to avoid his touch, but he caught her cheeks between his hands and met her eyes and warned her, "Ah, Kyra, take care. You'll come to crave my touch, and I will be gone."

"Hanged, drawn and quartered!" she retorted.

He laughed softly, and his reply was as quietly spoken. "Maybe."

She went dead still, staring at him. "There's no maybe about it; Edward will hunt you down. He means to have Scotland from east to west and north to south."

"Then life should be lived to the fullest."

"Your life, sir, is your own to cast away."

"But I am very much alive tonight."

"I am not; I am exhausted."

"Amazing. I'd not have known."

She struggled again, dying to strike him.

"If you're truly exhausted, we can sleep."

"I don't want to sleep with you. I don't want to be with you; you're mistaken in what you think was acquiescence."

"I thought that it was more than acquiescence."

"I cannot stay in this room!"

"You must stay in this room—you will stay in this room. You may have your charms, Lady Kyra, but you remain the enemy. Seduced though I may be, I don't forget who I am for a minute, or that you are Edward's beloved subject. But I'd not make you any more wretched tonight. Feel free to rest on the floor, my lady. You can always sleep on the furs before the fire.''

"I can sleep on the furs before the fire! You are incredibly rude, so discourteous! You go sleep on the furs by the fire.''

"But I was not the one complaining, my lady. I am content where I am.''

Blue shadows, blue flames, and all seemed to reflect the blue in his eyes. "I am content where I am," he repeated. His expression was grave. He smoothed back her hair, and she didn't protest, but met his gaze.

"Shall I make you stay with me?" he whispered.

"If you would have me here—aye!"

A small, grim smile curved his lips. "You can live with being forced, my lady. But you cannot live with any form of surrender?''

"If there is force, one can only fight.''

"Or bide one's time," he pointed out.

"Time, sir, is not with you.''

He stroked her cheek. "That much is true. Sleep with me, my lady.''

She closed her eyes.

"I am forcing you," he whispered.

He pulled her against him. She made no protest. It was absurdly comfortable to feel his chest at her back, his body curved around her own.

"Don't love me too much," he murmured, and his voice was teasing at her nape. And yet, she thought, there was an edge to it.

An edge she felt as well.

"I do not love you at all!'' she protested, stiffening.

The tension seemed to leave him. He laughed, and the sound was soft and low and pleasant in the night.

"Alas, my lady, how cold. When I am truly beginning not to hate you at all."

"For being Kinsey Darrow's?"

"Um." His arms tightened around her. "Indeed," he murmured, "I am beginning to forget that you were ever his."

CHAPTER ELEVEN

Mounted on Pict, Arryn watched as his men drilled with schiltrons, a formation in which they formed tight ranks and used sharpened pikes. With ten men in each group, they created a bastion effective against English cavalry. His men, and the armies of such men as William Wallace and Andrew de Moray, were made up of what the English called rabble, except for Andrew de Moray himself, who was a rich and powerful man in the north, as his father had been before him. Many of his family members had been seized at Dunbar, and now counted down the hours imprisoned in England or forced to fight for the king in France.

But what the armies were really made of were the people. Customarily, it was the magnates—the rich men, the aristocracy of the country—who fought. They paid their armies, made warriors of them, and knighted them on the field. But in this fight for Scotland, most of the aristocracy and the rich were compromised—they often held lands in England and in Scotland, and even if they did not, they might well have signed the oath of fealty, the ragman rolls, and thus had to take great care with what they did. Many of Scotland's great barons had fought the king of England at Dunbar after the slaughter at Berwick, and there they had been beaten and imprisoned, taken to England to the Tower, or forced to fight for Edward in his eternal battle against the French. Some had to take care, lest they give Edward a reason to execute their imprisoned relations, and though Edward promised relief to the Scotsmen who fought his continental battles for him, it was said that he didn't intend to keep his promise there any more than he had meant to keep the promise he had made before John Balliol became king— that he would leave Scottish matters to the Scots.

Nay, the men with whom they now fought were not typical. They were not the sons of rich men and barons, taught from childhood to wield heavy weapons. Some were the sons of nobility, aye, the younger sons of lesser nobility, but most were simply Scotland's freemen, her landowners, farmers, merchants, masons, and fishermen. They had risen because of such atrocities as the massacre at Berwick; they had banded against the English because Edward had given his noblemen their daughters. They were the very soul of the country.

But the soul needed training.

Against many of his men was the fact that when the English came with a full army, that army was always accompanied by exceptional Welsh bowmen—Edward knew how to flatten a country, and how to draw from it. The Welsh had perfected the art of the longbow, and they could cause a rain of death to fall upon the enemy. Arryn's men needed to learn the use of the crude shields he had them carving daily as shelter, just as they needed to learn to use them against the English swordsmen and cavalry who would come to slice and hack them down as if they were so much wheat in the field.

"Run it again . . . hard, fast, form rank, fall!" he shouted out, watching as the second group he had chosen for the schiltrons came forward. They were dedicated; they were good.

They were ill paid because they were not the soldiers of a great overlord; they took their chances when they rode against the English. Here, at least, they had sacked the riches of the castle, and it had contained a great deal of value. They had seized silver, gold, jewels, fine fabrics, and more important here and now, they had seized weapons, harnesses, horses, and food.

He looked up suddenly, feeling as if he was being watched. He was.

She stood upon the parapets of the outer wall and watched. He frowned, perplexed, wondering how she had escaped her tower room. They had been here five days now, and at the moment he was feeling particularly at odds with her, and irritated with himself that he should let her cause him to feel anything at all. In the nights since they had buried the fallen dead, she had refused to come down to dinner. He might have forced her down; he had chosen not to—though her absence had irked him. Still, it had seemed important to him that she not overestimate her own worth to their efforts. He had thought her more than resigned to his company after the night they made love—aye, made love; he had taken great care to seduce her—but the morning had brought her a greater distance from him than ever, and though he had thought he understood, her distance made him aware that he had given in far more than she. His wife's murder had been brutal. He had been with other women since then, had seduced, been seduced, even laughed since then. But this was Kinsey Darrow's betrothed; he was not supposed to be gentle and kind, nor give a damn as to her feelings on the matter. Yet she left him shaken, and still . . . beguiled. It was not surprising that such an exceptionally beautiful woman could create a wealth of lust, but it was irritating, a chafe to his temper, that he should find himself not at all appeased, and wanting to hear the sound of her voice, the soft peal of her laughter, feel the touch of her fingertips against his flesh . . . see her smile, hear her protest, feel her in the night as she slept against him. She was just a woman; Kinsey Darrow's woman, at that. He lived far too often with haunting dreams of Alesandra calling his name, of her screaming as the flames rose around her. . . .

He lived, he breathed, he fought, he was human, he risked all for his country. He needed companionship. But Scotland was filled with beautiful women, rich and poor, ardent for freedom, fond of such a passionate rebel. Those who knew they played a wretchedly dangerous game, that life was fickle, easily ended. While this one . . .

She had said that she always fought. He had thought she had given in. Maybe a battle, but never the war.

Don't love me too much! he had taunted, because she had given in, or been swept away, or perhaps just shown the age-old wonder of what existed between men and women. Had he been too pleased, gloating?

I don't love you at all! she had assured him.

And she had spent the last two nights curled in a ball on the furs before the fire. He had left her there. It had been painful. She would have come if he had forced her into bed. She would have had the luxury of keeping her pride intact, but he had found himself pitched into a battle of wills. Still, he had stubbornly determined that he would not allow her to consider herself so unbearably appealing—and he had put up a good pretense of ignoring her completely. Except that last night, he had managed only half the night, departing in the middle of it to sit brooding before the blaze in the great hall. She had sworn her fealty to Edward—and to Darrow. He had taken the castle, he had taken her, and now he could be done with both.

Why did he let her bother him so?

Guilt?

He suffered enough guilt every time he thought of Hawk's Cairn.

He had come here with such venom in his heart. His vision had been clear: destroy Kinsey Darrow, his riches—and the woman he had loved. But she wasn't what he had expected, and sometimes he remembered that he had known her father, and sometimes he realized that she was a child of the aristocracy, and marriage was a bartering system, not a union entered for love. Sometimes he admired her, and liked the way she fought, and wished that he had more men who had her constant supply of courage and determination against all odds.

Aye, he thought dryly, they needed more warriors such as this lady.

Don't love me too much. . . .

He was coming to admire her too much. He couldn't forget that, though he had liked her father, Hugh Boniface's loyalty to Edward had been steadfast and indisputable. He had given homage to Alexander as well—in a time of grace and peace now gone. Sad indeed that the king of England should be so greedy, wanting the island to be his from north to south, east to west, and France as well. Maybe that was for the best, since the king himself remained in France, and he might have able warriors, but none so ruthless as himself. He was near sixty; he was still nearly seven feet tall in his full armor, rough, rugged, and ever ready to fight. If only he had not been born with the streak of cruelty that seemed to run among the Plantagenets, he might have proved to be an admirable king.

But there had been Berwick. . . .

Arryn kept his eyes on Kyra. She appeared restless. Perhaps she was growing weary of the confinement she had set upon herself. Perhaps she was trying to distract him from his training. She was capable of distracting men; that much was certain. And therein lay the danger. It would be far too easy to forget that she owed her loyalty—and gave it freely—to the king who had massacred almost the whole of what had been a great and thriving town.

His eyes narrowed as he stared at her. She suddenly realized that he was watching her, and she started to back away from the wall. She knew that he would come for her, that he would have to quit his training session and seek her out. Had she intended her escape just to be of further irritation to him? To cause one of these very important sessions to be disrupted?

He would not allow her to do so. He would send one of his men instead.

"Jay!" he shouted. Leaving his position on the field, Jay mounted his horse and came loping toward him.

"Kyra is upon the wall. Will you see that she returns to the tower?"

"Aye, Arryn, if you wish," he began, but then paused, looking past him toward the forest. Arryn had already heard the hoofbeats coming from the direction of the northern forest. As they watched, John Graham, with two companions, came from the trail, riding hard toward them, waving a hand in greeting.

His cousin had left at dawn just a few days ago, riding back to report to Wallace regarding Arryn's men and his strength— and his promise to fight. Now John was back, and though they bordered the forest of Selkirk, Arryn thought that his cousin had ridden very hard and fast to have returned so quickly.

"See to Kyra!" he said briefly to Jay, and lightly spurred Pict so that his battle horse flew into motion, and he raced the distance to meet his cousin.

"There's news?" he shouted.

"Aye! News, indeed." John straightened in his saddle, looking around. The fields were filled with men. Arryn's—good Scotsmen—and those who had begged mercy and sworn to his cause at the taking of the castle. Indeed, the Irish priest, Michael Corrigan, had proven to be something of a swordsman himself, and worked with a number of men now, teaching them about the weight of the weapon they carried, the art of retreat—and the art of a thrust to kill.

"We'll head to the castle," Arryn said.

John nodded to his companions, who broke off to remain in the field, watching the sessions. He and Arryn rode for Seacairn. The portcullis was open, and they traveled quickly through the outer and inner defenses. They left the horses with Brendan in the courtyard, and entered the main hall. It was empty. A carafe of ale sat at the far end of the table, and John helped himself liberally after the long ride.

"What is it, what is happening?"

"Good news is this—Andrew de Moray has become a powerful weapon for us here, even in the south. He is a man of vast means, a true baron, an aristocrat—and a man defying the king, and even the fact that the king holds so many of his kin hostage!"

"Aye, we've known that de Moray is a fine man for a rebel cause."

"What we've not known is how many fine men he has compelled to follow us! Knights, Arryn, fellows who know the skills of warfare."

"What of the king?"

"He has sailed for France, but his armies are on the move. They think they will crush us quickly in a decisive battle that will break the Scottish spirit once and for all! But, Arryn! Our successes have been so vast that Wallace and de Moray are ready to meet the armies." He began to draw on the table, indicating events. "Aye, look here! We took Perth—I rode beside Wallace myself at this turn of the tide—and here at Dunottar, we took a large contingent of the English, many who had fled there! Then on to Aberdeen . . . We returned to Selkirk, but de Moray continued attacks. All these castles fell . . . Elgin, Forres, Nairn, Lochindab—at Aberdeen we destroyed English shipping. My God, Arryn, we've a good fighting chance, but we must move ahead more quickly. You'll need to ride to Wallace within a few days' time—he is choosing his ground for a major battle. See here, the English commander Cressingham moves thus, and Warenne rides along here. Word has it that Cressingham is so certain of his strength that he has told Percy to disband his army in the west!''

"I'm told Wallace offered no mercy whatsoever at Dunottar.''

"The barns of Ayr were sharp in his mind, Arryn. Don't forget, the English trapped a good three hundred and sixty men there, tricking them to an eyre or council, hanging one and all, even the lads who served them, and burning them to ash. You know well how easily the English set blaze to both property and people!''

Arryn steeled himself against the pain that never failed to wrap around his heart at the reminder. Aye, they'd done enough in revenge, and God knew, the English had warranted it. It was no good claiming the Scots had struck first when John had still been king and invaded the north of England—not when the English army had crossed the border within two days to inflict the terror at Berwick.

"Still, cousin, if we're ever to best the English at battle, the bickering amongst us will have to stop. I was nowhere near Irvine when our good nobles finally decided that with Edward busy in France, they might make a stand—but then argued so fiercely that they backed down before the battle!''

"Aye, well, it boils down to this often enough—the Bruces, who have wavered a few times too often, believe that a nationalist victory will have us rallying to stand behind John Balliol as king, and if not John, then another member of the Comyn family. Bruce is likely to give up the honor of Scotland for the honor of a throne. This Robert the Bruce is a pup—''

"So is Wallace. So are we all, John.''

"Aye, but Wallace has lightning in his eyes. He draws men. His passion is what binds us. Even at Irvine, while our nobles squabbled and sued for Edward's peace, Wallace's men found an English baggage train, killed its defenders, and made off with immense treasure, which we will need. Nay, we'll not back off again. It will be de Moray and Wallace leading the men when we face the English now, and that I swear to you! De Moray is a wealthy man, Wallace the second son of a small landowner, a lesser knight! They will come together, and others will join them, and cousin, I beg of you, you must!"

"Aye, I intend to fight, and you know it, John."

John nodded, watching him. "Good. There's more."

"Aye?"

"Kinsey Darrow has learned of your being here."

"Does he ride here even now?"

John grinned. "One would think! I was told his fury was so great that he nearly went into apoplexy. He almost killed his own messenger. But he was warned by sounder minds to wait for greater force; last I heard, he was awaiting the Earl of Harringford and his forces."

"Powerful forces."

"Aye, but they'll be called to join the English as they hunt down Wallace. Cressingham is a fool who believes himself up against no more than rabble, but he knows it to be a large rabble, and the command from the king is that the Scots be crushed."

"Where was Darrow?"

John looked down for a moment. "At the manor of old Tigue MacDonald." He hesitated a moment. "He had the old man meet a traitor's death, strung him up before all his tenants, hanged him, gutted him, chopped him into fours." John spoke bitterly. "Pillaged, robbed, murdered, raped."

MacDonald. A good man, a fierce old fellow without a moment's compromise or doubt in all his life! Arryn thought.

Another hatred against Darrow that burned at his very soul!

"He is not so far."

"Still, I believe that the Earl of Harringford will command him to join with the army before coming here."

"Perhaps. Still, I'd best see that the guard be far more than just wary."

"Aye, and Arryn, we need all that you have seized here! Our men are fierce fighters, rich in spirit, yet poor in weaponry. Have you stripped the armory here?"

"That I have. And we've the smiths working day and night to repair swords, finish those begun, repair what plate and mail were left. . . . Aye, there was fine armor to be had here, and we have stripped it all. My men will be armed."

"Is there more?"

"Aye, there are those who still have hand-hewn pikes, nothing more."

Arryn lifted a hand, hearing footsteps on the stairs. Jay came into the main hall. "Arryn," he began, then paused, arching a brow with a hopeful grin. "Aye, John, a great war council! Tell me, for the love of God, that all goes well?"

"Aye, Jay. And will, by God, be better. Tell me, man, can you fashion a sword?"

Jay shrugged. "Well, I have fashioned an opposing swordsman, upon occasion."

"Lady Kyra has returned to reside above?" Arryn asked sharply.

"Arryn, as you commanded, I returned her to the chamber, demanding to know how she had escaped, of course. She said that she did not escape, merely left the room. You left no man on guard, and did not slide the bolt."

Aye, he had grown precariously lax! He had not slid the bolt because, at the back of his mind, he knew that they could be counterattacked at any given time.

And the castle might well be set to the torch. . . .

He'd have no one else burn, no more of the scent of charring flesh to haunt his dreams; he'd not have her die. . . .

As had Alesandra.

"Did you slide the bolt now?"

"Nay, I came to ask what means you would take to keep the lady within."

"I will see to her," Arryn said. Jay was a good friend who knew him well and seemed to understand him at times when he didn't understand himself. "We were discussing the urgent need for arms," he said to Jay.

"Well, we have plundered this castle."

"And you have fashioned many a swordsman . . ." John murmured. He stared at Arryn. "What of the fallen?"

"Aye, John, we took every sword, knife, and blade from the fallen—the enemy, and our own."

"But have you really taken weapons from all the fallen?" John inquired, a touch of humor in his eyes. "And those who might not have fallen quite so hard?"

"What are you talking about?"

"What of the great men of this fine edifice who have found their eternal rest in their shrouds in the shelves of the crypt?"

Startled, Arryn looked at Jay, then at John. He shrugged. "I admit, cousin, we had not thought to rob the dead, though the dead have the least use of mortal weapons!"

"Shall we to the crypt?" John queried.

"No!" The sudden cry was cast down as an indignant gasp. Looking up, Arryn saw that Kyra had decided to depart her tower prison once again. Had she meant to slip by him, or simply to spy on him? Either way he felt his temper simmering. He looked at Jay, but Jay shook his head, and he realized he was the one in command.

"Lady Kyra!" he said coldly. "So you have chosen to join us again."

"No!" she repeated passionately.

"No?" he queried, his voice deep and grating. "Ah, lady, it is a word I hear from you too often, and so strangely, for you are in no position here to give command!" Arms crossed over his chest, he sat at the end of the table and watched her as she came down the last of the stairs.

Her head was bare; the length of her red-gold hair rippled down her back, and her eyes had never appeared a deeper emerald. She ignored his reprimand. "You would stoop so low, sir, as to rob the dead?" she demanded. Passion and indignation were in her voice; her breasts rose and fell with her words and her fury, and he was struck with the thought that she was indeed far more than a beautiful woman—she was a rare one, with fire and spirit, and something within her that he wanted still! That Darrow hadn't had apoplexy at her loss did not seem at all to make him a stronger man, just a greater fool.

"Do you hear me, Sir Arryn? It is a vile crime indeed to steal from the dead, sir! God will not forgive you such an act."

"Oh? God discusses what He will and will not forgive with you, my lady? Have you taken to communing with Him in the self-imposed exile you have enjoyed the last few days? How curious, for I believe He will forgive me. This will be a lesser crime, I think, than that of which we are all guilty—robbing the living of life," he said flatly. "Come, John, as you suggested, to the crypts. Kyra, you must join us, and pray for us in the good Christian spirit with which you gave warning—or, lady, do the dead rest in the chapel above us?"

She was not about to answer him. He rose swiftly, catching her arm as she started up the stairs. His fingers wound around her wrist. Up a few steps, she looked down at him with her eyes surprisingly filled with tears, and all the more dazzling for them.

"If you think that I will help you—"

"No matter. But you will accompany me." His eyes locked

with hers. "Jay, call for Gaston, and ask him where we will find the castle's revered dead."

Gaston, bobbing and ever courteous and cheerful, informed them that the dead rested deep below in this tower. All they need do was take the back set of stone stairs, yet they must take a torch, for the caverns beneath were as dark as any pit of hell. "But Lady Kyra could have told you that," he finished, smiling at Kyra.

"Aye, she could have, but she did not."

"Why would you see the dead?"

"We would borrow their weapons."

"Borrow?" Kyra spit out.

"Ah, lady, they were mostly good Scotsmen, I'd imagine, and would be glad to lend a hand to a cause of their country! Bring a torch then, Gaston," Arryn ordered.

"Aye, Sir Arryn."

John took the torch; Arryn took Kyra's arm, keeping her wrist locked firmly in his grip.

The stairs were damp. Though it was summer, the region tended always to be cool, and as they went lower the stone became cooler still, and the air around them became all but frigid. A good way to preserve the dead, he thought. The esteemed corpses of Seacairn would be all but icicles.

They reached the ground floor and an archway that surely dated before the arrival of the Normans. Deep within the cavernous hallway that opened to them next was a room filled with stone shelves, and upon those shelves, the nobility of centuries—ladies in elegant gowns, men in arms and armor, the fragile texture of their shrouds shielding them from the living. Arryn saw immediately that John had been right—many of the old lords and privileged knights of Seacairn had been laid to eternal rest with their weapons. Swords glittered in the firelight of the torch that John carried to lead the way.

"There are many, many!" Arryn said, pleased at their discovery. Dragging Kyra along, he walked to the wall. He didn't think of the bodies that haunted their vision, of the dozens of men and women, some hardly changed in the cold of the cavern, some decayed to bone.

He pulled the shroud from a dead man at eye level, taking the handsome claymore at the corpse's side in his left hand. Kyra wrenched at her wrist, trying to free herself from him.

He gazed at her, startled. In his pleasure at the cache, he had almost forgotten her.

Her face was ashen.

"Do you know, my lady, what Kinsey Darrow has been doing?"

She froze, refusing to answer.

"He has just murdered an old friend of mine. And I am the one committing a crime here? Come, though, we'll leave the crypt behind; there are so many weapons here that I will have to send my men to retrieve them."

He started from the crypt, pulling her along. To his surprise she pulled back. He turned to meet her eyes.

"Not my father's!" she whispered. "Please don't disturb my father's site!"

He arched a brow and turned slightly. Into the rock that made up the shelves, the names of each of the dead had been chiseled. He saw that the old lord of Seacairn was just a corpse away from the dead man he had disturbed.

He looked back at Kyra. "Why, my lady, isn't your father's sword the weapon you used against me when I came to find you in the chapel?"

She shook her head. "It was my own."

He arched a brow again. But of course. If she had learned swordplay for her own amusement, she would have had a weapon made, one less heavy than the blade that such a man as her father would have carried.

"Please!" she whispered. "Don't disturb my father's grave."

John, behind them, cleared his throat. "Perhaps one weapon will not make a difference."

Arryn continued to stare at her. "Give me your sword, then, my lady, and we will let your father's be."

"You have it. Your men took it after you bested me in the chapel."

"I still say, lady, that it is up to you."

She searched out his eyes; then her gaze fell. "Don't take my father's sword."

He watched her for a moment, then looked to John. "I'll send men down now to assist. You'll get all the weapons we can supply. See to it that the body of Lord Boniface is not disturbed."

"Aye, Arryn."

"And you, my lady . . ."

"I will return to the tower, Sir Arryn," she said.

He nodded to her, a slight, grim smile curving his lips. "Aye, lady, that you will."

Ragnor kept the bulk of the men at work in the fields; John and Jay supervised the removal of all the available weapons from the corpses in the crypt.

The corpses held more than weapons. Many of them had been laid to rest with jewels, medallions, gold and silver chains, brooches, and more. John appealed to Arryn; the men had asked if there were not riches to be sacked from the castle as well. Since Edward—and even de Moray and Wallace—had been known not just to sack churches but to burn them to the ground as well, he determined that the men fought for an uncertain future, and God knew, some small piece of jewelry might buy them an escape sometime, when the tide of war did not go their way. He allowed the riches to be removed, but the corpses were to be respectfully shrouded once again, and when they were finished, Father Corrigan was to give a blessing. Father Corrigan reported tartly that he wasn't certain just what prayer was used for the ravaged dead, but that he would find something. It was when the day's work was done, when the training in the field had ended and the dead within the crypt were left in peace again, that Father Corrigan found Arryn upon the parapets, and reported that he had asked God's blessing on the dead again, just as he had requested.

It was late, very late. The night guards remained awake, and few others, and Arryn had not expected the priest to search for him that night.

"You're appalled, Father, that we've robbed the dead?" he inquired, leaning back against the wall. He had come here for his own peace. The summer night was beautiful—the warmest so far. If it were not for the very cold stone of the castle, they might not even need a fire for warmth, even into the wee hours of the night. The stars were out against an ebony background in the distant sky, and the breeze that touched his flesh was balmy.

Corrigan shrugged. "I heard about your earlier comment, Sir Arryn, to Lady Kyra. The crimes we commit against the living are far greater."

"Ah, Father! You're a man of God. What crimes, sir, do you commit?"

"Sir Arryn, what do you know of any man? In my past, sir, there remain sins untold."

The priest was a striking dark fellow, as tall and well built as any warrior. A curious man, Arryn had known from the beginning.

"Against the living—or the dead?"

Corrigan leaned against the wall, looking out at the night. "There are all manner of sins, sir. Pride is one."

"Murder another."

"Lust . . . vanity. But I would say, sir, that pride is among my greatest, and the dangers it causes! But I am the priest— I have no desire to unburden my soul to a layman, sir, no matter how powerful and wise."

"Ah, so you would mock me, Father."

"Nay, Sir Arryn, I do not. Nor do I condemn you for your sins against the dead!"

"Only against the living."

Corrigan hesitated. "Only against the Lady Kyra."

"That is all, Father?"

"It's the greatest sin of all, Sir Arryn, to refuse forgiveness."

"Lady Kyra has not asked my forgiveness."

"She has not sinned against you."

"What of Kinsey Darrow?"

"One day he will have to answer to God."

"Nay, Father, one day he will have to answer to me."

"Perhaps."

"And what of King Edward? What will he say to his maker?"

"All men must face a final justice—even kings."

"Vengeance is mine, so sayeth the Lord, eh, Father?"

"Aye, Sir Arryn."

"So . . . we should all prostrate ourselves before Edward?"

Corrigan smiled slowly. "Nay, Sir Arryn. And thereby my own sin, my own pride, for I cannot, will not."

Arryn nodded slowly. "I have told you, Father, that when I leave here, I will leave the lady in good health. That is a promise. I swear it."

"That's not enough."

"What would you have me do?"

"Take her with you."

"To the battlefield? Nay, Father, that would be madness! God knows if we can win this . . . and God knows as well, she is loyal to Edward, and to Darrow."

"Sir Arryn—"

"That is all, Father. Good night."

He did not expect the priest to leave, but departed himself.

He entered the tower room, certain that he would find Kyra there—after all, they had made a deal, even if the promises had been subtly given. He thought that she would be in the chair before the fire, as she had been the past nights.

But the fire burned low, and the chair was empty. Nor did she sleep upon the rug before the hearth.

Puzzled, his temper already beginning a slow boil as he wondered what trickery she might be about, he carefully entered the room, and quietly closed the door behind him. He looked about in the shadows of the room, then realized she lay beneath the sheets and furs upon the bed. He felt an instant quickening in his groin, a constriction of his muscles, a hunger in his very soul.

He determined he would not betray it so. Striding into the room, he began to disrobe. The mound within the bed did not move.

She would feign sleep, he thought.

The last of his clothing tossed aside, he approached the bed. He sat by her side, then drew back the covers. Her back was to him—naked, sleek, her flesh gold perfection in the dying firelight, the curve of her buttocks enticing, the scent of her sweet and feminine. She tormented his senses, haunted his loins, teased him as no woman had before. He found himself running a finger down the length of her spine and speaking to her mockingly.

"Do you think, my lady, that in life, your father would have so willingly traded his sword for your honor?"

He was stunned when she flipped with uncanny speed—a sword clutched in her hands and pressed instantly to his throat.

Her emerald eyes were alive with fire, with triumph. And he was ever more the fool. He froze at first, damning himself.

He was not going to die for Scotland, or for glory or freedom. He was going to die for being a fool.

The point of her blade pressed against his flesh. His eyes met hers, filled with rage.

"Up, Sir Arryn!" she commanded.

With little choice, he clenched his jaw and rose—the point of the blade led him to rise. She followed.

"This is one weapon you failed to steal, sir!" she told him.

Standing, feeling the point of the blade, he returned her stare. "Your sword, my lady? You lied, I see, and my men failed to retrieve it when you lost it in fair battle?"

"Fair battle! You would talk about fair battle!"

"I wouldn't talk at all. If you're going to kill me, I suggest you do it, because if you lose that sword to me, you will rue the day."

"I imagine I will rue this day one way or the other, sir. But kill you? So quickly? Nay! When I suggested you hang me quickly, you commented that a hanging would be far too kind, far too merciful! Nay, Sir Arryn!" The blade moved from his throat, teased his midsection, set upon his abdomen, very, very low. He felt the touch of her steel, almost a caress.

"Traitors, sir, are hanged until half-dead, disemboweled, castrated, and then cut up to be sent to the four corners of the world!"

"I'm not a traitor. I never gave my allegiance to an English king. But then, murder and mutilation are punishments your people enjoy inflicting. Is such a death one you would enjoy doling out, my lady? Are you trying to keep pace with Kinsey?"

"I want but to bargain with you, sir. Your life for my freedom!"

The passion and emotion in her voice startled him; she stood before him, naked except for the sword, so very beautiful, her hair reflecting fire and gold from the hearth, her eyes . . . so vital, so alive. Yet . . . she wavered. Just a sign of weakness. Enough . . .

He grabbed the blade itself, felt the sharpness with his fingers, even the sting as he cut his own flesh to seize the weapon and steer it from its present course. She gasped, struggling to retrieve control, but with the threat removed from his person, he caught her hands where they held the hilt of the blade and nearly crushed bone until she cried out and her hold eased. He seized the weapon from her and hurled it toward the far corner of the room. He caught her by the hair, wrenching her face to his. "Do that again and you had best kill me very quickly! A warning—never, ever hesitate. If you threaten a man, be ready to kill!"

He pushed her from him, then stepped past her, walking to the low-burning fire, hunkering down before it to study the deep cuts on his fingers and palm.

"Get over here!" he commanded sharply. She didn't move. His anger was such that he strode back by her again, catching her by the hair. She cried out, startled, as he drew her by its length to land on the fur before the light of the fire. He stared down at her. "I'll need your care for these wounds, lady. Now!"

She stood, coming to his side, her heart pounding. "I have a salve," she began.

"Poison, I imagine."

"I didn't mean to hurt you."

"Castration is not painless, my lady."

"I meant to bargain, nothing more!" she whispered. "Don't you see, you fool, when you hold the sword, you have the power. When I hold the sword . . ."

He stared at her. Aye, she'd held the sword. But she hadn't used it. Because she was a woman who could not commit cold-blooded murder.

Was that the truth of it? Or had he merely taken her by surprise?

"Get your salve."

She nodded and swallowed hard, backing away from him. "Perhaps the cuts should be stitched."

"Perhaps you are trying to be gentle and kind so that I don't decide a simple hanging would be just fine!"

"I can stitch. . . ."

"The cuts are not so deep. Get your salve. And if these wounds fester in any way . . ."

His voice trailed off. She went to a trunk and returned with a jar. He sat on the chair before the fire; she knelt before him, the firelight playing on her hair as she lowered her head to tend his wounds. The salve she used was soothing. Her scent was intoxicating. She carefully wound linen bandages around his hand. When she looked up at him, she saw his eyes. Her own fell quickly. He saw that she was shaking.

"I'm sorry."

"Of course you are. You don't want me to kill you."

"I never meant—"

"Did you, or didn't you? Since I seized the sword, I'll never really know exactly what you meant."

Her eyes remained downcast. He caught her chin with his thumb, forcing her to raise her head, to meet his eyes.

"Have I been so brutal, so vile?"

She swallowed hard. New life flickered into the emerald of her eyes. "Nay, you fool, you are not so vile!"

"Fool?" he asked, his voice dangerously pleasant.

"Nay, you are not so vile."

He rose, drawing her up with him.

"I would have demanded nothing for your father's sword; I knew the man, and admired him."

"You made me bargain."

"I didn't make you do anything, if you'll recall. I let you bargain."

"My God! And that means—" she began, her temper flaring.

"My hand does pain me, my lady," he cut in quickly.

"The salve is good, I swear it," she replied.

"I believe you, though that, indeed, might make me a fool."

"I have tried to make it better."

"You will try harder." He turned and walked to the bed, drawing the covers back again with his good hand. He lay down.

She hesitated, standing before the fire. "Oh, you didn't make me bargain!" she murmured.

"Nay, lady, I did not."

"But now . . ."

"You tried to kill me."

"I swear, it was not what I meant."

"Why not?" he asked abruptly, sitting up in the bed to watch her.

"Because . . . I . . ."

"It would be perfectly understandable if you did want to kill me, right? I came here, seized your castle—ruined you for your precious fiancé, who is scouring the countryside, killing off old warriors! I have made your life wretched."

"You have!" she said softly, with surprising passion.

"Then—"

"I never wanted to kill you. Remember, sir—I showed you mercy."

"I seized the sword."

"Because I hesitated."

"Aye—you hesitated."

"So we are back where we started. You tried to kill me; I triumphed. I'm sorely aggravated, and my hand really hurts! The choice, however, remains yours."

"The choice?"

Bargaining. She was always bargaining.

But there was a true plea to her voice.

"So you have surrendered your sword to me this time. I haven't just seized it from you; you have given it to me?"

She didn't answer.

He didn't force her to do so.

Pride was a great sin, so Father Corrigan had told him.

But if it was a sin, it was one he understood far too well, and one he knew that he shared with her.

"Don't tie me, please."

"Obviously, my lady, I would not dangle you from the parapets."

"I know, but . . . not here, either. Please."

"You tried to kill me."

"Before God, I did not wish to kill you."

"Or disembowel me."

"Nay."

"Castrate me!"

She flushed. "I swear, it was not my intent."

"Your blade, my lady, was most deceptive then."

"I meant to show you—"

"Power. Ah, yes. The power to negotiate. All you sought was freedom!"

She didn't reply.

He watched her for a long moment.

"You want freedom so desperately?"

"Wouldn't you?" she queried.

He shook his head. "You can't ask that question; there is no comparison to our position words were cold; her eyes were curiously damp, glittering, deeply emerald.

"You know I can give you no date!" he said impatiently.

"Then, sir, why wouldn't I want my freedom?" she whispered. "Am I to stay, be charming, cooperative . . . until you decide that you have robbed me of all that I have and it is time to move on?"

"That is the way of things, aye," he said wearily. But he stroked her cheek. "You'll have your freedom," he told her. "That is all that I can give you. You'll have it—in time. In time, my lady."

"Aye!" she murmured. "I will have it."

She agreed with him, but she had conceded nothing. And still . . .

He threaded his fingers into her hair and drew her head back down to his chest, cradling it there.

And thus they slept.

CHAPTER TWELVE

William Wallace was a huge man.

Tall, burly, muscled like steel, his strength of will lay in his eyes, and in his soul.

Andrew de Moray was not so large—few men were—yet he seemed no less powerful, and all that he had accomplished thus far was probably greater, for his name was well known even here in the south. He had come from power and wealth, had much at stake and much to lose, and by God, would risk all to be free from the shackles of Edward of England.

The call was out for men, and many had come, and more would come. Despite the disaster at Irvine, the successes of these men—and others, such as Arryn, who had also seized great English holdings—were so great that the barons of Scotland, frightened as they might be, were still ready to cast their lot with a battle that might be won.

Men were encouraged to come, to fight. Some were trusted, some were not, and yet as both Andrew de Moray and William

Wallace, who met with Arryn in the forest at Selkirk, told him, they might be in the midst of battle, and still not certain of whom to trust.

"You have a large number of men, so I've heard," Wallace told him, his foot upon a log in the clearing where they gathered. "And I have heard that you have worked them with schiltrons, taught them what battle against English cavalry might be like."

They spoke alone that night, a meeting arranged by John so that Arryn might be assured of the intentions and determination of the two leaders here, just as they might be assured of troops that would bring an assured loyalty—something not likely to be had from the nobles with their knights who promised to fight but might not do so if they didn't see victory in the offing.

They sat on logs around a small fire that burned in the center of the copse—Andrew de Moray, Wallace, John, Jay, Ragnor, and himself. The surrounding forest was filled with men, those who rode with Wallace now, those who had ridden south with de Moray, and those who were beginning to come to the banner of their country.

Wallace and de Moray themselves had just met, and though most men in Scotland were wary of the nobles and the clergy, Arryn was certain that Bishop Wishart, an old Scot to the bone no matter what the church or a king might claim, had set in motion this chain of events. He had found the two men most responsible for rebel activity in the country, and he had surely been the one to suggest the union. They came from far different lives: de Moray wore fine clothing with rich armor, while Wallace remained a rough-hewn knight. Arryn, knighted when Alexander still lived, and a landowner of rich enough estates until Darrow had scorched his people and place, was better equipped for the battle to come. Yet Wallace, with his great successes against the English, might have seized any form of weapons and armor he chose, but he knew, as well, that speed of movement was often a far greater asset than the weight of plate and mail. He would choose carefully in the battle to come, Arryn knew.

"Aye, William, we've worked formations, trained with pikes, shields, swords, battle-axes, more. They've learned to gather weapons from fallen enemies; and they've learned to stand their ground against English cavalry—and to take care against Welsh bowmen. Some men with me are knights such as myself, trained and ready; some are farmers; some are fishermen. I've an astrologer, a cook, and a teacher of Latin among my men. Many of the men who fight with me were merchants, masons, goldsmiths . . . they lived and worked at Hawk's Cairn, little of which remains, as you well may know."

"Aye, indeed!" Wallace murmured bitterly. His retaliation against the English had often been brutal, but the atrocities committed by the English well warranted his fury. He'd seen men go before the king of England in good faith, only to be weaponless and powerless, and betrayed: hanged, slain, skewered, beheaded.

And like Arryn, he had lost the woman he had loved, in his case to the English lord Heselrig, the bastard who had crushed Marion's head in his determination that she give away Wallace's whereabouts. There were those who whispered it had been her fate to die, for it had been Wallace's furious murder of Heselrig in return that had spurred so many rebels to join him.

"So there is nothing left of your Hawk's Cairn, eh?" Wallace asked.

"Aye, well, the land remains. And the ruins. When the time is right again . . ."

"Aye, when the time is right. When Scotland is for Scots," Wallace said. He lifted the skin of ale that they had shared between them. "And to your clan, my friends, for it seems there are many of you, and the lot of you fair fighters, and loyal to a cause."

John and Arryn looked at one another and shrugged. "I believe we have been a fairly proliferate clan, and so I cannot speak for all our numbers. There are many branches of the family now, most from the area of Stirling, but we've kin in the isles to the west, and through marriage, up into the Highlands," John said. "My father, you'll recall, William, was not so ready for this fight!"

Wallace affectionately slammed John on the shoulder. It was meant to be a tap, but Wallace was a powerful man, and John grinned, nearly toppling from his log. "Your father kept his peace, and bought us time, and gave us cover. He's an old man, and this may well prove to be a young man's war. He signed the Ragman Rolls, John; we did not."

"Still, bear in mind, we are many, and some honor the Comyn claim to the throne, while others think that Bruce must be king," Arryn said.

"For now, I need only know that a man is for our freedom."

"That you have from us both," John assured him. "As well you know."

"Aye."

"Sir Richard de Lundy has gone over to the English, I am told," Arryn said.

"Aye," Andrew de Moray said, "and 'tis more than true that we'll not know who fights with us until we begin to take the battle."

Arryn studied Andrew anew, impressed with what he saw: a man with a firm, deep voice, steady hands—and steady eyes. He was a great tactical commander, Arryn had heard. He had beaten the English by attacking—and disappearing. He knew what ground to fight on, how to trap cavalry in bogs, how to avoid bowmen by slipping into the cover of thick forests, and, most important, how to inflict heavy damage on the enemy while retreating in time to prevent retaliation. From strategies of striking and melting away, he had gained strength, enough strength to attack castles, seize them—and hold them.

"There's no help for it that there are factions," Wallace said, leaning forward. "For the most part we are one people, the layman and the cleric, the rich man and the poor. We are Scots, and weary of English oppression and the lies of a king who claims to be an overlord and would be a conqueror. I'm sorry that young Bruce is more concerned with a crown than a country, but God knows, he'll learn soon enough that Edward intends to give no man this kingdom."

"When the battle comes now, we'll be ready, as we never were before," Andrew said firmly.

Arryn looked at him sharply, knowing that he referred to a number of the tactics that King Edward had taken. Since Alexander's death ten years ago, Edward had taken step after step—and those first steps subtle—to secure Scotland. Some said that the Scots had asked for trouble when they'd sought his guidance as an arbiter among the noble contenders for the Scottish crown, but seeking his guidance and opinion had appeared to be a sound decision made by the regents—a decision that might help prevent civil war. Naturally, the Scots saw it as the worst kind of betrayal when he had used this invitation as further license to demand homage from Scotland.

That was in 1291, and Edward had summoned a great many of the nobles to a meeting at the border—he had summoned his own northern nobles there as well. The Scots had arrived expecting a council, not war. They had not ridden in with weapons or troops. When they arrived, King Edward demanded that they recognize him as lord paramount of Scotland. The Scottish power and aristocracy asked for a delay; they were given twenty-four hours, and then three weeks. But even with three weeks' time, there was no way they could successfully deny Edward of England; they were well aware of the power he would soon have at the border, and that three weeks' time did not allow them to gather any type of opposing army, especially for the magnates who had come from the north of the country.

The infamous oath of allegiance the English king demanded was to begin to be administered on July 13, 1291, and to proceed for the following two weeks. Any man who came to the appointed place to sign the oath, and then refused to do so, was to be arrested—and not released until he complied. Any man who sent a good excuse as to why he couldn't come at the appointed time and sign was to be given to the next parliament. Any man who ignored the summons to sign the oath of allegiance was to be dealt with severely.

And so the English given power in Scotland were all but granted the right to rape, murder, and pillage at will—all in the name of King Edward.

John Balliol had been crowned king at Scone, in 1292. In 1295 he rebelled against Edward's demand for troops for France—and in 1296 he was forced to prostrate himself before Edward.

In the matter of a few years, Edward had stamped down on the country with a mighty heel, and then he had begun to grind. Stunned at first, led by factions, beaten viciously at Berwick and Dunbar, the Scots had floundered in their rebellion, anger and fear vying in the souls of a people and a nation.

There was only so long any people could be so subjugated.

And here they were, summer of 1297. They had become outlaws, rebels, striking daring raids against the giant English war machine.

"We'll be ready, and we'll fight, I'll swear it," Andrew de Moray said with quiet passion. "We watch the English now, as they watch us; we are still moving about the countryside, foraging, stealing English supplies. But the time has come when the armies have begun their real movements. They intend to encounter us soon. We have decided our positions. Word will come to you when and where to join us; if yours are trained as you say, they'll meet the first wave of English cavalry, fighting on the left flank. Aye?"

Arryn watched de Moray draw patterns in the dirt. De Moray's eyes met his. "We'll not back down. Cressingham will naturally demand that we do so, thinking that we will sue for peace. He will want to break us, take hostages, humiliate us. But we will not seek peace."

"Nay, there will be no peace!" Wallace said. He rose. Again Arryn, not a small man himself, was impressed by the sheer size of the man. The sword Wallace carried was almost as large as the man, a weapon to deal out the bitter justice Wallace never hesitated to deliver.

Arryn rose as well, along with his cousin and the others. He gripped Wallace's hand, meeting the man's eyes, and he knew that his pact was made. They needed no oaths, no written agreements of allegiance and loyalty. De Moray gripped his hand tightly as well. They were all aware of the consequences, should they fail.

As he prepared to ride for Seacairn, John was beside him.

"How goes life at the castle?"

"Well. It's a fine fortress, with good people."

"Aye, maybe. But keep in mind, they are not all to be trusted," John said.

Arryn looked at his cousin sharply. "Aye?"

John patted Pict's nose. He looked back to Arryn. "The battle comes soon enough, but while Wallace still awaits the whole formation of his army, it wouldn't be good if the English were to stumble upon them."

Arryn leaned forward. "So who knows exactly where Wallace and de Moray wait? The men with me—"

"I trust implicitly," John said.

"Then . . ."

"Be careful with her, Arryn."

"Your pardon, cousin?"

"Tell her nothing, ever."

"Her?" he queried tensely, though they both knew of whom they spoke.

"Lady Kyra."

"I share little enough of my thoughts and plans with my own men, John. I'm not likely to have council with a woman sworn to the English king."

"Arryn, you're angry with me! Don't be. I just warn you to take care. She is beautiful and charming . . . no, she is much more. She is clever. She understands much of what is happening. She is extraordinary, and therefore frightening. There are men and armies ranging all about now. If she were to know anything at all about you . . . about Wallace, this battle . . . and if she were to escape . . . well, she could be very dangerous, that is all. Don't forget her loyalties while you fall beneath her spell."

"I am under no one's spell," he said irritably. He leaned low, telling his cousin heatedly, "I never forget Hawk's Cairn."

"It will be your battle cry," John agreed. "As I said, don't be angry. I just warn you because I do admire the lady. But I would not hesitate to cut her down for a betrayal. I have not known her, as you have."

"I'm not a cold-blooded murderer, John," Arryn said. "But I've not forgotten. Trust in that: I've not forgotten!"

John nodded and stepped back.

Arryn turned back to Jay and Ragnor, who patiently waited a few lengths back.

They rode for Seacairn, leaving the forest of Selkirk behind them.

From the parapets, Kyra looked down longingly at the river below. Aye, the water was cold, frigid. But it was summer, and the cold could be borne. If only she could jump ... how much more difficult could a jump be than a fall?

Of course, God knew what she would do then, where she would go. If she was going to escape, she must do so carefully, with grave thought given to her every move. She didn't know where Arryn had gone now. She had awakened late yesterday morning to find him gone, which she hadn't known at first because he had never sought her company during the day. She had found out only when she had ventured from her door to find Patrick on guard, and inviting her to join the men in the main hall for dinner. Somewhat warily she had done so, afraid that perhaps she had been left to the devices of Arryn's rabble, but too curious about what was to come to refuse any chance for information.

She'd learned nothing, except that John Graham, Jay, and Ragnor were with Arryn, that they were expected to be gone no more than forty-eight hours. But though he'd been gone the length of the day already, she still had ample time to think, to plot, to plan, to make good an escape. His men were not rabble at all, she discovered that night, but earnest young fellows, dedicated to their cause, and kind to her, despite the many degradations they had suffered. Patrick, who had apparently been assigned her guardian in Arryn's absence, sat by her side and looked after her needs. A juggler had found his way to the castle, and he entertained. A senachie, or storyteller, traveling with the men, played a pipe, and gave the sad lament of King Alexander III, so fine and robust a man, and so tragic a figure, losing his beloved wife, his sons, aye even his daughter, who died in childbed, then dramatically plunging to his death in the pursuit of his young bride—and an heir for Scotland.

At her side, Patrick sniffed.

She looked at him, arching a brow.

He had dimples, rich brown hair, and bright hazel eyes. He smiled wryly at her. "Ah, there's no disrespect intended, for

Alexander were a fine enough king, and a sorry enough man for all his losses, but he was a fool the night he died!''

She must have gazed at him with some astonishment at his words, for he quickly defended himself. ''Ask Arryn, if you would! The night was wretched, and the king were warned! Arryn rode with him, and was among the men who found his battered body below the cliffs. And he said they knew, the lot of them knew, somehow, even then, that we were in for it! The sky burned red, they say, foretelling of the blood that would run.''

She shivered slightly. ''Then Arryn knew Alexander well?'' she inquired.

''Aye, he was given over to his household as a lad; he was knighted by the king himself. Alexander admired Arryn, taught him, and gave him many opportunities. Once, rather then send armies to war, he and an old border lord agreed that they'd have their champions joust to settle a dispute. Arryn fought for Alexander, no more than a lad at the time. He won the day, and the king rewarded him. Aye, some things were civil then! An agreement had been made, and it was honored. Alexander suffered much, you see. His wife—Edward's sister—dying, then his young son, and his older son, and even his daughter, giving birth to the Maiden of Norway. I think that he saw the sons he might have raised in Arryn. The king gave him that great dark horse of his as well. One day Arryn brought down a boar that might have gored the king. He saw the danger and went hopping right down on the creature and wrested it to the earth with nothing but a wee knife. He rode with the king, admired the king, and yet was furious with him for giving up his life and setting us all on this trail! It was Alexander who told Arryn that no one man was Scotland, that the people were a nation, that there was a pulse and uniqueness all our own.'' He grimaced. ''So you see, lady, we cannot so easily give homage to another! Especially so heinous a monster as your Edward!''

She hesitated, lowering her head. Then she looked up at him. ''Patrick, have you heard the tales about your William Wallace?''

His eyes narrowed. She trod on dangerous ground. And still, there was a point to be made. ''Wallace has conquered castles and towns—and put all good men to the sword, whether bishops and priests begged for their lives or not!''

''You must know what was done—''

''Aye, that I do, Patrick. But you must see then, to English children along the border, your hero is seen as sent from Satan himself. And as to Edward . . . you see, the queen of England was my godmother. And I spent several years as a child living in London. The king I saw was a great man, resplendent in his armor, and often merciful to men brought before him who begged for his forgiveness!''

'' 'Tis said that many a dying maid and child begged for their lives at Berwick, my lady,'' Patrick said.

She lowered her head. Aye, it was true. The massacre at Berwick had been so brutal and terrible that it would forever stain the reputation of Edward I of England. And still, the king was all she had, she realized. The king of England was the only man who could salvage her situation now—and dear God, save her life.

Arryn did not understand. He would give her her freedom— when he left! She couldn't stay and remain with him.

And she couldn't stay . . .

To be imprisoned once again. By Kinsey.

Escape . . .

She would do so. She had to.

But that night, she almost fell asleep at the table.

With the room spinning, she leaned heavily on Patrick to

reach the tower. Ingrid was there to help her to disrobe. And she slept alone, slept like the dead.

Patrick, she surmised, had drugged her. Far easier to drug a dangerous enemy than spend a night fearing her treachery!

So it was already afternoon as she stared at the river. Time to plan her escape was slipping away. She realized, ever more fully, that her only chance to survive the brutal thrusts and parries of the Scottish war was to somehow escape all the way to London—and throw herself on the mercy of the English king. That he was away in France made her future frightening and difficult; she could never go to Kinsey. Most likely he would find a way to wed her, and then to rid himself of her. Nor could she even try to find Percy, Warren, or Cressingham, Edward's commanders in the field, searching out the rebels here in Scotland. They would care for her, of course; they would be obliged to honor the daughter of Lord Boniface, godchild of the late queen of England, and betrothed of Kinsey Darrow. They would be delighted to help rescue her—to turn her right over to Kinsey Darrow.

No, she had to get away. Far, far away. To London . . .

Or in the opposite direction. Far, far away from it all.

"My lady, just what are you doing?"

Father Corrigan had come to the parapets. Tall, rugged, and good-looking, he hardly seemed a proper soldier for the church.

"Nothing!" she said quickly.

"Suicide is a sin."

"Oh, my God, Father, not that again. I never tried to kill myself."

"Don't do it."

"Don't do what?"

"Dive into the river and attempt an escape."

She hesitated, staring at him. She had always suspected that his sympathies lay with the rebels.

"And why not, Father, what will happen to me? If I fail, he will come after me."

"If you fail in your dive, you die."

"Well, that would solve the dilemma."

"Kyra—'"

"And if he comes after me—"

"What if he does not?"

She froze, frowning. "If he does not, then I am free."

"And Lord Darrow might well find you."

Startled, she stared at him. It was chilling to realize that the priest seemed to think her in greater danger from her intended husband than from the outlaw who had seized her. Pride made her stand tall and reply to him curtly.

"Then, sir, I will be safe from all rebels, and Darrow would find them, and hang them all for what they have done here."

She turned, walking swiftly away from him, dismay filling her. She had no one. Her priest was an outlaw. Her captain of the guard had turned to the enemy. Her maid was a scared creature who had no understanding whatsoever of the thoughts of men.

And the outlaw who had taken the castle . . .

Wanted her only so long as he remained. There would be other battles, other walls to breach—other women.

"Is that what you want, Lady Kyra? Would that please you, would you see it as justice?"

She spun around, staring at Corrigan. "What?"

"Do you really wish to see them all hanged—or worse?"

She stared at him a long while. "No, Father. I wish no man's death. No man's."

She left him and hurried back to the landing before the steps to the tower room. She froze; Patrick was there, of course. She had forgotten that he watched her, every step she took. If she had tried to leave, he would have stopped her.

What had he heard of the conversation between her and the priest?

Suddenly angry and disgusted with all of them, she wagged a finger beneath his nose. "I will not come to dinner tonight, Patrick. And I will not be drugged again; it is a coward's way to keep a prisoner!"

He stared at her blankly. "My lady, I gave you no drugs!"

She hesitated, then turned around. Father Corrigan had followed her in.

"You bastard!" she charged.

"My lady! You're speaking to a man of the church!" Patrick said.

Michael Corrigan said nothing to defend himself. "A man of the church?" she murmured, eyes narrowing. "An Irish devil!"

"A preferable creature to an English traitor, my lady!" he said, bowing politely.

She turned, ignoring them both, hurrying back to the tower room.

There she began to pace. There had to be some way out of here now—before Arryn returned. Arryn's men were good, but nowhere near as vigilant as their leader himself. It didn't help, of course, that her own people were against her.

They would be watching for her to make a desperate dive into the river.

What other chance did she have?

Walking out the gates?

Walking out . . . walking right out . . .

She hesitated.

His things were still here—a mantle left on the chair by the fire, hose just laundered and left folded on a trunk. The bed carried his scent; it even seemed to retain his heat. She lowered her head. She didn't dare think about it, about him. She would want to break down, cry, despair. She couldn't admit the truth to herself; it was far too terrible. She didn't surrender—no! She had capitulated beyond belief; she *liked* him, far worse, she was compelled by him, fascinated by him, so eager now to crawl back into bed with him that it was beyond humiliating, far worse than ironic. She should throw herself into the river for being such a wretched, pathetic fool. Good God, she yearned for the sound of his voice, the way his eyes could flicker over the length of her, the brush of his fingers, the touch of his lips. If he only knew what vengeance he had truly enacted . . .

She closed her eyes tightly. She had to leave. Now. Before she was forced to see him again. He was, she realized, the man she had always wanted Kinsey to be. His strength lay in the power of his beliefs; he could be merciful despite cruelties done to him.

Shaking, she sat down. There had to be something else.

If she tried to escape and reach London, and if she could convince the king that she would die at Kinsey's hands, she would simply be made the prize for some other warrior in the king's service, another man willing to fight and kill for the king's goodwill.

The low-burning fire in the hearth flickered; she watched the shadows of the flame as they danced on the stone. She reached out.

Fire . . .

Kinsey had left his wife to burn. . . .

She rose. She couldn't leave by way of the river. If she survived a dive, she would be stopped. They would be watching for her. Father Corrigan knew her intent, and he had become her enemy, though why, she didn't know. He had to realize that she'd be in danger once Kinsey returned. Or maybe he still didn't believe that men could have such pride and be so possessive that they'd rather kill than allow their enemy any small victory.

She paced before the fire.

Late, it was so late in the day already! Day—no, it was night; darkness was falling. She'd slept like the dead. The drug had been strong, and yet tasteless. It must have been in the wine, and she had never known, never even suspected. . . .

She paused, watching the flames again, blue and crimson flickering against the stone of the castle.

Father Corrigan . . . the Irish demon!

Determined, she swung around and hurried to the door, throwing it open. Patrick sat slumped on the floor just outside the doorway. He sprang guiltily to his feet as she appeared.

"My lady—"

"I need to see the priest," she said sweetly.

"But—" he began with a frown.

She set her hand upon his shoulder. "Please, Patrick. I must see him. I have been in there thinking about my words. . . . I must apologize."

"I'm not sure where he has gone."

"Well, we'll try the chapel." He wasn't going to be in the chapel, she was certain. "And then we'll try his quarters. Please?" He stared at her uncertainly. "Patrick, my immortal soul could be in danger."

"Aye, lady, come; we'll see the priest," Patrick told her.

She smiled sweetly. And innocently.

Arryn felt restless on the return to Seacairn, despite the speed with which they rode. Accompanied by only Jay and Ragnor, he could ride far harder than usual.

He felt a strange sense of relief and freedom, and yet a deep gravity—the time had come at last when they would face a large English contingent, when they would fight a real battle, when they had a chance to make a stand that would matter.

It was in their favor that Edward battled the French at this moment, and therefore was not in Scotland. His son—Edward like him, but in no other way resembling him—was in power in his father's absence. A good thing. The young Edward was not at all the soldier that his father was; he was uncertain, and might easily make poor judgments and decisions.

But the commanders coming against them were able indeed. There was rumor that the king's men came with huge armies, troops that numbered nearly a hundred thousand. Surely those numbers were inflated. What was certainly true was that they traveled with able men, trained men, archers, cavalrymen, soldiers adept with heavy swords.

"Do we stop for the night?" Jay asked when they had left the forest of Selkirk far in the distance. They approached a grove that sat atop a high cliff, giving them an advantage if any of their enemies prowled the night as well. It was where they had rested and gathered their assault the night before they had swept down on Seacairn. From the summit, he thought, they could see the towers of the castle, they were so close.

His men were weary. Though they were close, they should rest for the night.

Still he hesitated, anxious to return.

"For an hour, Arryn, we'll break, and ride again, aye?" Ragnor suggested.

"Aye, we'll rest an hour, and continue."

But while Jay and Ragnor dismounted, leading their horses toward a small stream for water, he encouraged Pict up the narrow, overgrown trail to the top of the cliff.

Aye, he could see Seacairn. And more.

Fires . . .

Campfires burning to the far east, in a copse in the forest. Two, three, four of them.

And then he knew.

Darrow was back.

* * *

The priest's house was beyond the inner defenses, but within the outer wall. It was a simple place, Kyra thought thankfully, for after she had entered with Patrick on her heels, she somehow had to find what she was searching for without letting him realize that what she longed to do was ransack the priest's belongings.

Corrigan was organized and neat. And he was a priest; his belongings were simple and few.

There were shelves by the table where he took his meals. There was a skin of wine on the table, a plate with freshly dug greens and potatoes, and bread wrapped in linen. The shelf by the table had treasures brought back from the priest's pilgrimage to the Holy Land: Arabian coffee, a few coins, a silver relic, a number of small, blown-glass vials. There were linen bandages, for when he was called upon to help the sick or the injured. There were herbs, essences, potions, and oils.

Pretending to pour wine, she studied the vials and found what she was looking for—poppy-seed extract.

A twinge of guilt tugged at her conscience.

How much to use? She didn't want to kill anyone!

Ah, but then, she didn't want to die herself.

She thought about all that she had read on the uses of poppies, and decided a few drops were all she dared.

She poured wine and brought it to Patrick. "While we're waiting."

"My lady, thank you. I am not thirsty."

She stared at him, blinking quickly to avoid showing her frustration. "Drink with me, then, Patrick. *Slainte!*"

"To what do we drink?"

"Scotland!" she said softly.

He lifted the goblet to his lips. She smiled and pretended to drink what she had poured for herself.

"So you would drink to Scotland?" he inquired.

"My mother was Scottish. Seacairn is in Scotland. It's beautiful; it's my home. Of course I would drink to Scotland."

He smiled, wagging a finger at her. "To King Edward's Scotland—that's the Scotland to which you would drink!"

"Patrick, what if we were to drink to peace?"

"Ah, 'twould be lovely, but a foolish thing, I think!"

He smiled and seemed fine. He had finished the wine. She looked at him. He looked back at her. Nothing.

Then suddenly he slumped forward. She tried to catch him. He was muscled like an oak. The best she could do was break his fall as he slipped down to the ground, his head falling forward. "Patrick!"

She had killed him.

No. He was breathing easily. He even looked up at her for a moment. "Peace! Aye, we'll drink to peace!" he muttered.

His eyes closed again.

She stretched him out on the floor. "I'm sorry, Patrick. Really. You'll have a lovely sleep, though."

Now . . . to hurry before Father Corrigan did come back!

She rose quickly and threw open the door to the tiny bedroom that flanked the main room. As she'd hoped, she found one of his ecclesiastical robes, a hooded one. Moving quickly, she tossed aside her own mantle and donned the robe.

She could not leave here weaponless.

At the foot of the narrow bed was the priest's trunk. She opened it quickly. She was surprised at the wickedly long sword she found lying on top of ecclesiastical robes and white linen shirts. There was a sword belt beneath it, with curious designs. She didn't understand them, or their significance, but she needed a way to carry the sword, and so, she dragged it out as well. She dug again until she found a small dagger—perfect. It would fit into the pocket discreetly sewn into the skirt of her overgown.

"Sorry, Father, for borrowing without asking!" she murmured, and, looking at the crucifix over the priest's bed, she hastily crossed herself. "God helps those who help themselves; you told me so!" she whispered.

She left his small bedroom and hurried out. She knelt down beside Patrick once again and assured herself that he was breathing.

Then she stood and hurried out the door, carefully watching for who might be about.

She had to hurry. If they didn't start looking for her soon, they'd look for Patrick. It was almost time for dinner to be served in the main hall.

She could see masons, farmers, and workers ending their day's work, some heading to homes inside the outer walls, some preparing to leave. With the priest's robe covering her form, the hood protecting her face, she slipped around the side of the small house. Father Corrigan's dappled mare was munching hay in her small stall. Kyra saw the horse's bridle, but no saddle. She had no time to saddle the horse anyway, she told herself. She slipped the bridle on the mare and rode quickly out, joining a group of stoneworkers on their way to homes outside the wall. Someone hailed her, assuming her to be the priest. "Good evening, Father."

She lifted a hand in return.

"Coming out to bless the new bairn, Father?" a man asked. "And a pity his da was one killed in the fightin' here!"

She nodded, praying she wouldn't have to give a real answer.

" 'Tis a wreck of a war for most of us, eh, Father?" another man said. "We toil all day one way or the other; though, 'tis true, 'tis better to be robbed by one of our own for taxes, than for a foreign prince!"

Something was expected from her. "Aye, my man!" she said, keeping her voice low and raspy. She quickly made the sign of the cross in the air. "Bless you, my sons!" she said, and urged her mare on. She was nearly at the gates.

One of the guards was shouting, calling out to the people. "All in, all out! The gates close for the night!"

She nudged her heels against the mare's flanks. The mare surged forward.

She passed beneath the portcullis.

She was free.

In the end, it had been easy. Far too easy. She was free, thank God, free, and she had to be, for her own survival. . . .

And still, she was afraid.

And her heart felt ridiculously heavy.

They returned by darkness, aware that Darrow would plan his attack for the dawn.

Reaching the gates, Arryn shouted to the guard.

The portcullis was raised; they entered the outer defenses. In the courtyard he leapt from Pict, calling Brendan to take his horse. He called commands to the guards on duty, warning them to keep a close eye on the forest, that it was filled with the English. Men were awakened from their beds; archers were sent to the parapets; oil was set to boil to be cast down upon the invaders who would come. Fires were lit around the walls so that the arrows the bowmen sent down would ignite the oil and, hopefully, put an end to any siege machines as well as the soldiers who manned them.

With the castle set into preparedness, Arryn realized that he had not seen Patrick, and though the man had been ordered to guard Kyra, the commotion should have brought about his appearance by now. Leaving Ragnor in the great hall to continue defense plans, he started up the stairs to the tower. Patrick did not wait outside the door; opening the door, he found the tower room empty. Tension beginning to pound in his temples, he summoned Ingrid, who immediately began to blather that the lady had been with Patrick, that she'd had a disagreement with the priest, that there had a been a row, and she had gone for forgiveness.

Seeking forgiveness did not sound like Kyra. Nor was he so certain that he could trust the Irish priest who had served here beneath Darrow.

He nearly shoved Ingrid aside in his haste to depart the tower room. He found the priest below in the great hall, listening to Ragnor's warnings regarding an English attack from the outer defenses.

"Father, where is Kyra?"

He didn't think that the man's surprise was feigned. "Not in the tower?"

"If she were, I'd not be asking. I was told you two had a disagreement. And that she came to you for forgiveness."

"Kyra?" Father Corrigan echoed Arryn's own sentiment that he could not imagine a situation in which she would beg forgiveness, even from her priest.

"It's true," Tyler Miller said. "I saw her exiting the castle with Patrick; they went to your house."

"But I wasn't there. I left the castle to baptize a new babe and returned straight here, to the great hall."

Arryn stared at him for a moment, then strode quickly from the castle. Jay, Ragnor, and Father Corrigan followed at his heels.

He hurried to the inner walls, calling out to the guards as he passed the gates; they had not yet been secured, and wouldn't be until they saw the attackers coming across the open slope before the castle walls. Reaching the priest's small house, he threw open the door.

There was Patrick, against the wall.

For a moment he felt a deep, shattering rage. Patrick was dead; she had killed him. But no, Patrick was breathing; he was just slumped down.

Father Corrigan stepped past Arryn, hunching down to Patrick. He swore softly, startling words from a priest.

"What did she do to him?" Arryn demanded harshly.

"Opium."

"What?"

"It's a drug from the east, from the Holy Lands—"

"I know what it is! Where the hell did she get it?"

Corrigan looked at him. "From my shelves." He hesitated, looking up at Arryn. "From the moment you left, she was planning to flee. I used it on her the night before."

"And she knew, and that was your argument?"

"Our argument was that she planned to leave," Corrigan said, offering the truth for what it was, and not as an excuse or a defense.

Arryn swore, exiting the house, Jay and the priest still following close behind. "How long ago did she manage this exit?"

"Not long; it isn't more than a few hours since we argued."

"Do you think she saw the campfires, that she knew Darrow was out there?" Jay asked.

Arryn looked sharply at Jay, then turned to stare at the priest. "Aye, 'tis possible," he said.

"But how did she just walk out?" Father Corrigan murmured.

A young woman carrying tinder for the fires came hurrying by. "Sir Arryn!" she said, bobbing and blushing. "And thank the Lord, Father! You're back! And glad we are, for we need you, that we do, what with this trouble brewing. But you returned right quick, and that you did!"

Arryn clutched both her shoulders, startling her, scaring her. "Sorry, lass, but when did you see the priest leave?"

"Just a moment, sir, before we heard your call at the gates! Aye, indeed, for the priest went out just as they were closed for the night!"

"Thank you, lass, thank you," Arryn said, and, staring at

Corrigan, he felt as if his blood vessels were bursting within his temples. "There you have it, Father. Our lass rode out as a priest, blessing all us poor fools as she departed! Jay, have Brandon bring my horse back. Tell Ragnor to wait until the last possible moment for my return, but at the first hint of light on the horizon, the gates are to be closed, and not opened again until the danger is past."

"Arryn, don't be a fool, man; you're not going out there for her alone—"

"No, he's not," Corrigan said firmly.

"Aye, that I am. There's an army out there. I can't spare the men from the castle now; all preparations must be made against an attack. I don't want the men caught out from behind our defenses. I'd not fight a battle from the trees, since we've these fine walls here for cover. I don't intend to engage the enemy; I don't intend that he should see me. I'll need to move quietly."

"I'll move more quietly!" Corrigan vowed. "For the love of God, man, you'll need some defense at your back!"

"And a priest is that defense?" Arryn demanded.

"I didn't always intend to go into the church. I learned about warfare as a boy, and can wield a sword with the best of your men."

Arryn stared at the priest for a long moment. He didn't doubt the man's capabilities.

He did doubt his loyalty.

And yet . . .

The man might well be the one to help stop Kyra before she could reach Darrow.

"Jay, go, call Brendan; have a horse for the priest, too."

"Arryn, are you sure—"

"Aye!"

Jay moved on, still frowning, still uncertain.

"Hurry, Jay. I need all speed," Arryn said, his eyes never

leaving the priest. "If you betray me, Father, I'll see that you rot in hell."

"If I were to betray you for such a man as Kinsey Darrow, it would be just that I should rot in hell," Corrigan said.

"Then we will ride, Father. Together."

"Aye. We will ride, sir, together."

CHAPTER THIRTEEN

The greatest fear Kyra had was in traveling the distance of open ground between the castle and the forest.

Father Corrigan's dappled mare was much slower than her own sleek mount, and in trying to race that distance, she had leaned close against the horse's neck, talking, coaxing, pleading that she go from a trot to a lope, and from a lope to a gallop. By the time she reached the first trees banding the forest, she was aware of riders coming hard from the hill, bearing down on the castle. Who they were she didn't know; she didn't dare hesitate to watch their arrival, but quickly entered into one of the very dark forest trails, grateful only that she had come so far.

She knew these surrounding forests fairly well, having spent many formative years here at her father's holding, as well as in London, serving in the queen's court. Her childhood imagination had often been given free rein here; she'd not been required to be a lady, but she had fought tree-branch dragons, fended off barbarians, and dreamed of being a witch or a healer in the woods, with all good men coming to her, and even a prince coming to her rescue when she was besieged by the enemy—what enemy, she hadn't known at the time.

Now, she reflected, she didn't need to fear the tree branches, nor would an enemy be so easily bested, should he appear.

Deep onto one of the trails, she shivered, thinking that though there was a moon, and stars dotted the sky, it was very dark at night, and she was very much alone. Thank God it was summer, and though the night was chill, there was no snow, no ice, no brutal cold to be as bitter a foe as any other she might face. She knew the trail she followed led to a small brook, and she urged the mare there, thinking she had, at least, some jewels in her hem, and fresh water to drink. It was a pity she hadn't thought to steal the priest's bread; she hadn't brought food, she'd been too distracted to eat much, and she had run before supper. Such a small detail. The vicious carnage between the English and the Scots was already devastating the country-side; the English burned crops and houses to destroy a people, and the Scots scorched the earth in return to starve the English back across the borders. There might be little new in going hungry here.

And she had tricked poor Patrick and left the castle. Escaped. She was free from both men: the Scottish outlaw, the English demon. She should have felt great relief, and she felt merely empty.

The woods seemed to close around her.

Shelter her.

Her world, she realized, was lost. The home she had known, the people she had known, aye, the luxuries she had known. And that was the way it must be. She didn't seem to feel that loss yet.

The emptiness was what gripped her heart. She had run from

him. Did it matter? He would have left her. And Kinsey would eventually return. . . .

And her punishment might be slow or might be quick, but it would be sure. And he wouldn't hate her so much because she had become the property of his greatest enemy; he would hate her because she had always despised him, and he would be justified to do so.

She walked her horse deeper into the woods, warning herself that she couldn't dwell on the hollowness in her heart. It was absurd. A woman conquered and seized did not fall in love with the enemy, and such an enemy could not be courteous, polite, and thoughtful, and create such a rage of emotions with his eyes, his touch, the tone of his voice. She was nothing to either of these men except a weapon to be used against one another, and that was all, and she must now take the greatest care for her own life.

She had two choices.

The king's mercy. Never a safe wager.

Or she could simply run. . . .

And disappear into the countryside. God knew it was wild enough, and there were places distant enough.

As she walked the mare along, debating the serious question of her future, both immediate and into the years ahead, she didn't feel a sense of fear. She knew the woods. She was sheltered by the oaks. But as she walked, her feeling of comfort faded. She became aware, vaguely at first, of the mellow light that seemed to seep through the forest here and there. For a while she moved on, perplexed, speaking to the mare now and then, more curious than frightened. Then, as she came to the brook and saw that the soft light seemed to emanate from the curve in the waters ahead, she froze, aware that the strange yellow light was coming from campfires.

Dismounting from the priest's mare, her heart seeming to have leapt to her throat, she moved silently to the shadow of an oak, trying to look beyond the darkness to the glow, and discern who was in the woods, just how far they were from her, and just how many men there might be.

The distance, she realized with trembling relief, was fairly great; they were at least a quarter of a mile from her, but there were a number of fires burning, and so there had to be a fairly large contingent of men. She'd be safe enough from them, she thought, if she didn't light any fires herself. On the other side of the brook there were rocky outcrops, and those would offer her shelter for the night, and a fine place to hide the priest's horse. She had been disturbed that she had not found a way to escape with her own mare; now she was glad. If this horse was discovered by someone who knew her, they would not realize that the mount was hers, and if . . .

She didn't dare accept the thought that it might be Darrow in the woods, though such an idea was most logical. He'd had time now to serve the Earl of Harringford, time to hear about Seacairn, and time to gather forces to return.

Still, frozen by the oak for the moment, she stared down the winding path of the trickling brook to that curve. She should have noted the fires from the tower at the castle. Had the guards seen that men were coming?

She should go back. Tell them.

To what avail? Surely someone had seen the fires; they would be safe at the castle. . . .

Safe! The invaders would be safe from the English from whom they had wrested the castle!

If she did not return, then when Kinsey attacked, as he must, they would all believe that she had cunningly schemed to escape to come to Kinsey, give him warning, information. . . .

What wretched timing. Arryn had not returned. He could ride back into the midst of hundreds of men besieging Seacairn.

There was a sound behind her—the slightest sound. She spun around, her breath catching, her heart seeming to fall to her feet. She could usually hear so well in the forest, but she hadn't heard danger come. And with so many campfires burning, there had to be many men about, hundreds of them, in Kinsey's service. How wretched that this one had found her!

Sir Richard Egan stood there, Kinsey's right hand man. Tall, lean, cunning, hazel eyed and dark haired, he had a feral look about him. He was a man who enjoyed power; he hadn't Kinsey's background or family, but he was fearless and ruthless, and meant to rise to greater heights in Kinsey's service.

"Sir Richard!"

"Aye, my lady. You've escaped the bloody, barbaric bastard! Thank heaven, my lady, for God knows what he might have done to you when we stormed the castle."

She opened her mouth, stunned. No words would come. She looked around quickly. He had not ridden alone, surely. He was here, this distance from camp, with others, but she couldn't see anyone. His horse, a huge black destrier, was back upon the trail, and thus she had not heard the animal.

He had followed her, she realized. He had probably been out in the circumference of the camp, keeping watch, when he had heard her. He had watched her, probably not knowing at first who she was, shrouded as she was in the priest's huge robe. He had taken great care to accost her. He had crept up on her, and she had been taken completely by surprise. She damned herself, feeling his eyes. They raked over her in a way that made her flesh seem to burn. She could see his curiosity regarding her circumstances, and it felt incredibly uncomfortable. And she knew that he had barely endured her cool attitude toward him, and toward Kinsey; he knew, in fact, she thought, that she had despised Kinsey, and all that he did, and all that he stood for.

He strode the few steps to her, clutching her arm.

"Sir Richard!" she said in regal protest, her eyes narrowed upon him. But he seemed in no mood to endure her tone.

"Sir Richard?" he repeated his name, using her tone. "You speak to me so when you have been saved? Dear child, one would think you were not grateful that I have found you, saved you from the devils!"

"I saved myself, sir. You have happened upon me, nothing more!"

Her words made him angry, she knew.

"That is no matter. You are back with your own kind. And you will tell us everything, and we will avenge the evil done you. What did he do to you? Where is he? How did you escape? How many are in the castle now?"

"Sir Richard! Please. You're hurting me. Let go of me."

He ignored her; it was as if she hadn't spoken. "We'll go to Lord Darrow, lady. He'll be anxious to see you, be certain."

"Oh, aye," she murmured, staring at him, her heart racing. He would drag her to Kinsey. She was damned. She couldn't let him know that she was far more desperate to escape him than she had ever been to flee the "barbarians."

He moved the hood back from her head. "You think that I don't hear your tone, my lady? Ah, you've always considered yourself so much more . . . refined. But then, 'tis true, you're so beautiful, Kyra. Perfect teeth, perfect face . . . perfect form. Speech so soft, so melodic, so regal. You think that that will always save you, don't you? Perhaps, my lady, your very perfection, that which demands such ardor from those who know you, will be your downfall."

"Sir Richard, if the king were to hear you, you'd be a dead man!"

"But the king isn't here, is he?"

"Sir Richard, lead me to Kinsey. But get your hands off of me."

"Why, my lady, still so haughty? The stamp of an outlaw is all over you. But come, as you've said, you've saved yourself.

Oh, indeed. I'll bring you to Kinsey, and with him you'll truly be safe.''

Safe? She'd never be safe with Kinsey.

"Sir Richard, I tell you again, your grip is too tight; you are hurting me."

"My lady! I'm so sorry. I'm afraid of losing you again. It is a miracle indeed that you have come into the forest with us here." The sarcasm in his voice seemed blatant in the quiet forest.

Yet she had to take care in answering him. If she could not get him to cease being so suspicious of her, she'd never get him off guard so that she might escape him.

"A miracle," she said, trying to keep her eyes downcast and speak humbly.

"A miracle! Some women would not have survived so well; the horror of the touch of such a heathen outlaw would have sent them into thoughts of suicide! Yet you seem to have . . . survived quite nicely. Beautifully. But I'm sure you'll be explaining everything. Bless God, lady, you look well. Exceedingly well. Amazingly well!''

"Do I?" she whispered, feeling the ferocity of his hold as he started to lead her back to the main path he had come along, where his destrier waited.

"We heard, of course, what happened. And we were furious to know that you were seized by the outlaws, taken, abused at the hands of the barbarians. Lord Kinsey was beside himself with fear, and yet . . . you do not look abused, my lady.''

There had to be a way to break free from him. There had to be. He had found her this time because she had been careless. She knew these woods better than he did. If she could escape him, she could evade his pursuit with intelligence and success.

Desperate, she saw her chance.

She looked past him suddenly, frowning.

"Sir Richard!" she cried with great alarm.

"What?" His hold on her eased.

"Your horse has gone! Such a fine creature; we must catch him!"

She was able to reverse the tables, take him by surprise, and wrench free from his hold upon her arm. She went tearing up the trail and along the path—shooing the great destrier, who had ambled just a few feet away. Pretending to chase after the galloping mount, she burst into the trees and ran and ran.

And ran, never moving faster, or more desperately, in all her life.

"Kyra!"

She heard him calling her name.

Again, and again.

His rage growing . . .

Into the deep woods she sped, her priest's robe catching on brambles and thickets. It was hard to run; she carried the priest's heavy sword. She didn't dare discard it.

She kept moving, running hard, ignoring the fingerlike branches that seemed to tear at her hair. When she burst into a second copse, she had to stop, bend over, and breathe.

She had come far.

But she was on foot now. And they had horses.

Still gasping for breath, she tried to listen over the pounding of her own heart and the wind in her lungs. Flattening herself against a tree, she heard nothing for several minutes. Then she heard shouting and hoofbeats, coming her way.

She pushed away from the tree, avoiding the rider who went by.

But she burst into a copse, and as she did so, a rider thundered in from the opposite direction. She didn't know the man, but she knew the surcoat he wore over his chain mail. Kinsey's colors, and his family crest.

The rider leapt down from his horse, coming for her. He was a stranger, with blunt features and cold eyes. Richard Egan had told him to come for her, she was certain. To take her, no matter what. In any condition.

She realized that if she was handed over to Sir Richard, she would be dead when he delivered her to Kinsey.

She backed away from the man. "Shall we play, my lady?" he queried. "I've the night to find you. If you make it too difficult for me to catch you, I will make it difficult for you. Perhaps a less gentle touch even, than that you've come to know!"

That was enough. She drew the priest's sword. It was a powerful weapon; she just wished it were not quite so heavy. And she was facing a man in armor.

"Alone! By God, I've got you alone!" he said, inordinately pleased.

"Get away from me!" she warned.

"Oh, my lady, you rile the senses, you do!" he countered.

"You fool! Kinsey will kill you!"

"Ah, will he? He'll never know. 'Tis your word, and mine, though Sir Richard has said we'll not allow you to torment our great overlord anymore. And all know that you've become the whore of that filthy outlaw! Drop the sword, lady. I'd not have you bleeding and dying here—if I can keep from it! I'd even save your life. Come, be a good lass; drop the sword."

He stepped toward her; she raised the weapon. He laughed, and she struck. His laughter faded as he barely managed to parry the blow. But then he realized that she'd had some training, that she knew her business.

And now he was furious.

She found herself fighting in earnest. She struck him several times, but his mail deflected her blows. She couldn't allow him any strikes, for she had no defensive armor, not even a shield. She searched for his weaknesses; beneath the arms, right at the neck, and at the knees. His coat was short; if she could strike . . .

He nearly caught her in the midriff; she jumped back, catching the bark of a tree, spinning around it. He came after her; rather than retreating, she leapt toward him, her sword in both hands, at the ready.

He fell back too late. She caught him in the left leg, a good blow that might well have severed a blood vessel—it had crippled him, at the least.

He let out a furious bellow. She started to sprint back again, seeing that he could not run after her. But she froze, for now a second man had come riding into the copse. He saw her, saw her imminent flight, and leapt down from his mount directly in front of her, barring her way.

She was between the two men.

"Take care!" the first howled. "She's near killed me, she has, the bitch! She's a wild one! Strike her down quickly!"

"We're to bring her to Kinsey alive—"

"Sir Richard says that she is to be taken dead if need be!"

"Lord Kinsey wants her alive!"

"Aye, then a well-used prize already! Seize her, but slice her to ribbons if need be!" The injured man swore. "She'll pay a few more pipers, I daresay! Take her down, man! I am bleeding to death here; I need help!"

Kyra looked quickly between them. She started for the second man, sinkingly aware that the first fellow *was* bleeding profusely—but he wasn't down. He was limping toward her.

Still, she had to meet the fresh swordsman first, and hope that speed and surprise would keep her back safe from the injured combatant.

She tried to watch both. Aye, bleeding, and staggering, the man she had wounded was coming toward her with greater determination. Her focus was on the second man then; she could still see the first as he kept coming . . . coming. . . .

"Kyra! Get out of the way!"

A third man had come into the copse. His back was to her,

but she knew the height of him, the breadth of him, the raven color of his hair.

She knew his voice. Arryn.

His sword arm was raised. The injured man raised his weapon in defense. Arryn smote a mighty blow. The enemy's sword shattered, he dropped without a sound.

Kyra had frozen. Arryn turned, thrusting her out of the way of battle, taking on her second opponent.

"You bloody outlaw!" the man raged, and he parried and fought hard. Arryn kept up blow after blow, step by step, pushing the man back. Kyra heard the constant scraping of his sword against the man's armor, the clangs as steel met steel time and time again.

Then . . . he caught the man at the vulnerable juncture of helm and armor at the throat. The man clutched his neck and let out a strangling sound.

Fell.

"Go!" Arryn thundered to her suddenly.

"But—"

"Go! You little fool! You came here to warn Kinsey, but his men do not all care that you find him, do they?"

"You fool!" she protested furiously, but her anger quickly died. "There are more coming!" she cried, gasping as she heard horsemen. Two men in Kinsey's colors came into the copse.

Cavalry, yet they could not manage on their horses here. They leapt down from their mounts. She saw nothing but eyes beneath their helms.

She hesitated; she still bore the priest's sword, and blood dripped from it.

"Get out of here!"

"I can help!"

But their eyes were on her; she backed away.

Arryn attacked, striking heavy blows to their heads and shoulders. They turned from her, and both men engaged with Arryn.

"My lady!"

She turned again, hearing the cry of her name. As silent as darkness, Father Corrigan had come into the copse.

"Father, he is outnumbered. I must stay and—"

"My weapon, if you please."

"You're a priest!"

"You do well enough, but I think I can do better!"

She gave up the sword.

"Get her out of here!" Arryn cried, striking a blow that caught the first man in the side, finding a weak link through the slits of his mail. Blood spurted. "Go!"

"Go!" Father Corrigan formed the word on his lips.

She didn't wait longer, but burst into the trees once again, running. She didn't know where she was going. She had lost perspective. The woods were alive, she realized. Sir Richard was still close, God help her!

Blindly, wildly, she ran through thickets and dense stands of trees. At last, again, she could run no more. She paused by a tree and heard a trickling sound. The brook she thought. She had run right back to the brook.

She straightened, leaning against a tree. She bit her lower lip, hearing the sounds of hoofbeats, of men talking.

Sir Richard! Good God, she had run right back to him. He was mounted—he'd caught his destrier—and he was raging at two other soldiers on huge war-horses.

Sir Richard was ranting and swearing. "She's out there— and so are they! Fools, peasants, farmers. Goldsmiths, by God. Idiot wild men in rebellion! There are three of our own men down in the woods, dead, slain, and you fools can't even find the swordsmen—or the Lady Kyra!"

She tiptoed then, deeper into the dark thicket of trees, closer and closer to the water. She watched her back, then turned again, thinking to cross the water.

And then she froze.

Kinsey. Tall, broad shouldered, handsome with his dark hair bared, his features so classical they were nearly beautiful. He stood upon a ledge by the water's edge. He had been giving out commands, while searching the area of the brook himself.

He didn't see her at first.

And then he did. "Kyra."

Dark eyes narrowed on her. She saw so many things in them: rage, obsession, and something cold, dangerous, ruthless . . . lethal.

He lifted a hand. "My love . . . my poor lady love. Hounded, seized, abused. Come to me!" She didn't move; he started toward her. He was so close. He reached out.

He would have touched her, caressed her face.

She found motion; a burst of energy. She pushed herself from the oak where she had stood so paralyzed, and shoved him hard, with all the force and energy in her. He hadn't expected the attack.

He fell back, flat on his back, in the water.

If he hadn't hated her already, she had just provided a humiliation he would never forgive.

She started to run again. And she knew she ran for her life.

He was up, shouting to his men. The woods were alive.

She raced toward the cliffs, toward an arbor where the trees were thick, where she could hope to hide. She froze again, listening.

Nothing . . .

Nothing.

She nearly gasped out loud, stunned and terrified, when a hand clamped over her mouth from behind her. Tight. The fingers put terrible pressure on her lips. She could scarcely breathe.

So caught, she was dragged from the copse, along a trail.

She began to struggle. Deprived of air, she could barely see. Imprisoned so in arms of steel, she could scarcely move. He ceased dragging her. She was lifted, crushed to a muscled chest. She felt the pounding of his heart as they ran. And ran. Time whirled; terror filled her.

Then he slowed, and she heard his voice in a hushed, deep whisper.

"Not a word, my lady, not a sound, if you wish to draw breath again!"

Arryn. Relief riddled her, made her giddy. She nearly lost consciousness from the strength of it.

"Nod if you understand me. And if you do make a single sound, I'll put my sword straight through your heart, do you understand?"

Tears stung her eyes. They all hated her for betraying them, when she was the pawn in the game.

She nodded. The punishing fingers left her lips. They were swollen. She tasted blood where her teeth had crushed her lips.

She gasped for breath, and found herself set down. They were back by the water, in a pool of moonlight. Arryn was panting harder than she was. His blue eyes touched hers with fury and warning. He doubled over, gasping for breath, staring at her all the while.

"So you came here to meet Kinsey?" he demanded.

"What?" she inquired incredulously.

"Kinsey, my lady! The great and gentle English lord to whom you are betrothed. Did you plan this escape well, did you know that he was out here, did you come to give him details about the men holding the castle—and to make sure he knew that I was gone?"

She had known they would think that she had come to warn the English, and still . . . she listened with disbelief and inhaled with ragged, heartfelt anger. "No! You idiot! I—"

"Shut up!"

"Shut up? I'm trying to give you an answer, since you asked me a question."

"A foolish question."

"You saw me embattled—"

"Aye, because you didn't realize your position when you worked so hard to lay Patrick low and escape our dominion. I saw you in swordplay—and I saw the man you drugged to make good your escape."

"I'm trying to tell you—"

He straightened in a flash, and was back before her. His arms were on her, fierce and brutal, drawing her to him. "Shush!"

She went silent, staring at him. A second later she heard horses. She tensed as he did, then felt a tremendous sense of relief. It was Father Michael Corrigan who rode back into her vision, leading Arryn's huge horse.

Arryn turned her around, lifted her, and hiked her onto Pict, leaping up quickly behind her.

"We make a break for it?" Father Corrigan asked.

"We make a break for it—there's no help for it."

The priest grinned. "Now's as good a time as any!" he suggested.

"Aye, that it is!"

Arryn heeled his mount. They started along the trail at what even Kyra considered a breakneck pace. Leaves smacked her face, the ground stirred like thunder. Arryn's arms were around her, his chest pressing her down so that they were both clutched hard against the horse.

They burst into the long slope of cleared land before the castle, running hard, she and Arryn in the lead, the priest hard behind them.

The wind seemed to whine and shriek around them as they rode, biting the earth, shearing through time and space. She saw the walls looming before them, smelled the scents of leather and horse sweat and lather and the wind. Then she heard a strange whistling ... and saw the arrows striking the stone before them.

"My God!" she said softly.

"Greetings from your beloved!" he exclaimed dryly. "For the love of God, stay down, stay low, my lady!"

Kinsey had his bowmen trying to cut them down—it was true; she had been right to fear him. Her life was of little or no value to him now. ...

"Yah, Pict, yah!" Arryn shouted to his horse. The animal seemed to find a new burst of speed. In seconds, just before a second hail of arrows, they burst through the outer wall. Corrigan made it behind them.

"The gate!" Arryn roared.

He was forced to rein in Pict so sharply that the great horse reared, pawing the air. Kyra was thrown back against Arryn's chest. Still, he kept them seated. Pict landed on all fours, and Arryn instantly leapt down.

"They're coming; prepare the defenses!" Arryn shouted as his men came rushing forward to meet him.

She started to slip down, shaking. His arms came around her, lifting her. She stood before the horse, and Arryn faced her, his eyes a cold, hard, cobalt. He seemed different, harder, colder, more ruthless than he had ever been before. As if he believed that she had really meant to betray him.

"So you didn't know Darrow and his men were in the woods, my lady? You never noted those campfires?"

"I did not!"

"So it was simply by chance that you carried out a cunning charade against Patrick, and it was by sheer chance that you were escaping straight into your lover's arms?"

"You fool! Why won't you listen! You saw me waging war with them, facing his men with a sword. You saw them trying to kill me—"

"They didn't intend to kill you."

"You're wrong, you're a fool, you're so blind! They were trying to kill me! Sir Richard Egan countered whatever order Kinsey had given to the men; he told them to finish with me."

"They were nothing more than lackeys rich with the spoils of war who intended their own amusement before turning you over to their lord. You are, after all, tarnished a bit already."

She lifted a hand to strike him, her desolation and desperation were so great.

He caught it.

She thought that he would surely strike out at her, but he did not. She couldn't read his eyes, but there was a strange, restless passion and fury burning in them that caused a greater fear to seep into her soul.

Her heart shuddered with fear. It didn't seem possible, but he did suspect that she had purposely run. . . .

To Kinsey Darrow.

But why not? She had never claimed to disavow him.

Arryn had saved her life tonight, whether he knew it or not. Why? she wondered. Just to keep her from returning to Kinsey?

He eyed her now with contempt. "You would test a saint, my lady. Take care, because you have taken my temper to the edge of sanity!"

She would have answered, but she saw Jay striding swiftly toward them from the inner tower. "You found her; thank God," he said briefly, apparently choosing to ignore the fact that she had escaped the castle of her own volition. "The gates are down; the men are ready. The archers are on the walls."

"Have them fire; the English are at the edge of the woods. If their arrows could reach the walls, our arrows can reach their first wave of men."

"Aye, Arryn. And—"

"I'll be on the wall myself right now, giving further commands," he said. "Father Corrigan!"

"Aye!" The priest, having reached the inner walls and dismounted from his horse, stood quickly conveying what he knew to a group of men who had rushed to assist him.

"Escort the lady to the tower, and see that she remains there!" Arryn commanded.

"But Sir Arryn, you'll need me now," Father Corrigan protested. "I know the walls, the defenses. I can be of use—"

"Every man can be of use, and you're right, I cannot spare you. Bolt her in and return to me."

Bolt her in. She was being returned to the tower.

If he turned against her, she thought, she was done. Why this terrible fury in him, this determination that she had intended to betray him?

He didn't give her another glance, another thought.

He turned, and was quickly striding away from her, calling out commands as he went. The courtyard was alive with men running to their positions.

Father Corrigan grimaced and offered Kyra his arm. "My lady?"

She accepted his arm, finding that she was suddenly blinking furiously. Tears. Well, she had done her best to dupe them and escape.

But not to go to Kinsey.

"He's a fool!" she whispered furiously to Father Corrigan, fighting the temptation to cry.

"Ah, but you'd escaped to the forest—and Kinsey was there."

"I know, but—"

"You're a thief."

"What?"

"You stole my opium, and my sword."

"If you hadn't drugged me, Father, I'd not have known you had opium to steal!"

"Ah, well, that's true enough."

She stopped walking, twisting around to confront him. "Are you even really a priest?"

"Ordained, aye, my lady, that I am."

"A curious priest, Father, certainly."

"When there's time, I'll explain."

"I seem to have time now."

"I do not," he said, urging her along.

"But you realize I had to leave, surely you know that—"

"I do know that you didn't go out to find Lord Darrow, my lady."

"Then why didn't you tell *him* that?"

Corrigan turned, looking steadily at her. "I don't think that it's something he'd believe, coming from me. You see, my lady, Sir Arryn didn't know that you were on your knees praying for deliverance from Kinsey Darrow when he and his outlaws stormed the castle."

"How did you know that?" she demanded, stopping again.

He laughed softly. "Ah, my lady, I watched you often enough. I knew your true feelings." He tugged upon her arm to get her moving again. They had reached the great hall, and the stairs, and he wasn't going to let her stop there. "Only a blind man would not. I believe Lord Darrow knew then as well."

"If they take the castle, he *will* kill me!" she told him.

"They'll not take the castle."

"How can you be so certain?"

"He doesn't have enough men; the castle is too well defended. Arryn has prepared quickly; there are new defenses using fire and oil, ways to send down sheets of fire on any rams. Kinsey will send his men in first; he'll never risk his own neck!" Corrigan said softly. "And when he sees what has been done here . . ."

"How can you know all that?"

"I spent some time spying on his quarters in the forest. They waited for the Earl of Harringford and his men to start out, as Cressingham has summoned them to the army he leads. But the earl had ridden on already, so Kinsey has nowhere near the real forces he would need to take the castle. Here we are.'' They had reached the tower room. He prodded her in, then bowed. ''My lady.''

''Wait!'' she implored.

''My lady, I cannot!''

He closed the door and slid the bolt.

''Oh, dear God, Father, please! This is torture! I can't see the battle; I won't know what is happening, please God . . .''

But Father Corrigan was gone. And the battle had commenced. She could hear shouts, commands . . . screams.

The whinny of dying horses. Arrows striking the brick of the walls . . . the thunder of a ram. She paced; she prayed. The sounds kept coming to her.

So many shouts . . .

Clanging, cries, massive thumps and bangs . . .

At length, she pressed her palms to her ears and sank down on the rug before the fire. ''Please God, let Father Corrigan be right, please God . . .''

She barely heard a whirring sound, and did not recognize what it was at first. Then she inhaled and frowned. Smoke . . .

She jumped to her feet, whirled around, searching the room. Then she saw the fire. . . .

The whirring sound had been an arrow. A burning arrow.

By sheer accident, or with incredible precision, it had soared through the arrow slit in the tower room.

It had struck a tapestry, and now the woven wall piece was aflame.

In a second it seemed that all of the wall was ablaze.

Soon the whole of the tower would be an inferno.

And she would burn. . . .

CHAPTER FOURTEEN

The enemy came at them with a head-on assault, cavalry running hard for the walls, foot soldiers coming behind.

Arryn watched coldly. He raised a hand, then let it fall.

The first volley of arrows from his men fell on the riders, causing screams, rearing, whinnying, mayhem. "Again!" he ordered, and a second barrage of arrows flew.

The foot soldiers entangled with the riders. Many of them dropped; many kept coming. "The ram, fire on the ram!" he ordered, looking down as Kinsey's men, shielded with a wood plank roofing, neared the gates with a ram.

His archers dipped their arrows in pots of oil, lit them afire, then aimed straight down, on the war machine. Arryn heard the thuds as the burning arrows pierced the wood. The machine began to go up in flames. The men steering the contraption began to scream and scatter.

But flame wasn't a newfound weapon, and Kinsey had archers sending fire over the walls as well, though he had the harder task; only one out of every ten of his arrows stood a chance. Arryn had men on the parapets and in the courtyard below chasing after the few arrows that did make it over the walls. A few carts were hit; they were quickly ablaze, and just as quickly doused.

Some of Kinsey's men rushed the walls with ladders; Arryn and his men methodically cut them down.

The dead began to pile up by the walls.

A burly man shoved a ladder close to the portcullis; his was a deadly, suicidal intent: sacrifice his own life, but reach the lever, raise the gates.

Arryn caught the ladder and shoved it from the wall. The enemy let out a scream as the siege ladder crashed to the ground below.

A cheer went up; with his fall, the remaining men at the gate began to scatter and withdraw.

It was over, Arryn thought—for the time being. A few more arrows flew as Kinsey's men covered their retreat.

"Take cover!" Arryn shouted, watching a barrage of arrows fly.

One soared very high. He watched as it arced, flew. . . .

And entered the slender arrow slit of the tower room.

Instantly he saw a burst of flame there.

"Sweet Jesus!" he said softly and, shouting, went running along the parapets.

"Dear God!" Kyra exclaimed, staring incredulously at the tapestry that burst so quickly into shooting flames. She raced for the wall hanging, jerked it down, and tried to stomp it out, but the fire had ignited with a vengeance, and beneath her feet the flames began to leap and burn high. Her tunic started to catch. She beat it out.

She raced for the washwater, but it was totally ineffectual

against the blaze. The room was going to go up, she thought. The bed would catch, the covers and furs, the rest of the tapestries. . . .

Panic nearly seized her.

She was locked in! Locked in with the fire! No one was about; they were engaged in mortal combat. She had heard the bolt slide, and she could never budge it, never. . . .

She would die.

By flame.

But the door suddenly burst open.

She turned toward it quickly, her heart racing.

Arryn had come. He met her eyes.

How he had known that her room was ablaze, she didn't know, but she could see in his eyes that he had known about the flames, and he had come because of them. "The second tapestry!" he told her, and she saw his intent. She hurried across the room as he did, helping to wrench the second tapestry from the wall and use it to bury the first. By then some of the kitchen help had come in along with his men; they carried buckets of water. His men beat out the flames as the water was thrown upon them.

It was then just a matter of time, and the fire was out.

Arryn leaned back against the mantel, tossing down the bucket he had just emptied over the flame.

" 'Tis out!" one of his men said.

"Aye, and good work, my friends," Arryn said quietly.

Ragnor had come, and stood at his side. "Aye, 'tis out. You lads!" he said, indicating the kitchen boys. "Fine work indeed. Seize those remnants, the charred remains, and get them out. The smoke will clear then, I think."

"The lads will mop the water and finish with the debris here," Arryn said. "Ragnor, see if we've injured any of our own, and if any of the fallen by the walls still live."

"Aye, Arryn."

"Take care, lest they're planning another assault once the gates are open," Arryn warned.

"Aye, we'll be watching. I don't think the dogs will be returning this night."

Ragnor departed. The boys on the floor soaked up water with rags.

Kyra returned Arryn's stare. She had listened to his exchange with Ragnor without realizing that there were no more sounds of battle coming to the room.

"Kinsey's men have given up?" she asked.

He looked at her, watching her dispassionately. "Kinsey's men turned tail rather quickly. Perhaps they're not supposed to waste their lives here and now; I don't know. Perhaps our defenses were far stronger than they had expected." He watched her levelly.

"Sir?"

"Aye?" Arryn turned as one of the lads addressed him.

"I think we've taken the water up. The walls are scorched; if you wish, we can begin to scour them."

"Nay, lad. Not now."

Kyra stood still. The tapestries and the water were gone. It had seemed that the whole room had been golden, lit by the fire. But now, already, she could hardly smell the smoke. The walls were scorched in places, but most of the room was unharmed.

They weren't leaving it, she realized. At the least, she wouldn't be leaving it. This was the most secure prison.

Other than the bowels of the castle. Down there lay the crypts. . . .

And old chambers with bars and chains. They had never been used in her lifetime.

"Go on now; that's all for the night," Arryn ordered the servant boy.

"Aye, sir," the lad said, and departed, and Arryn closed the door in his wake.

"How did you know the tower was on fire so quickly?" she asked.

He pointed to the arrow slit. "I saw it," he told her, his tone still tense.

She lowered her head. When his real home burned, he wasn't able to stop it. When the woman he loved perished in the flames, he hadn't been able to save her.

"You came so swiftly; you saved my life."

"I was the one who ordered you locked in."

She lifted her head. Here they were, together in the aftermath of fire, alone, and facing one another. And the most important thing seemed to be that he hadn't left her to die.

And so she told him, "I don't know what I can say to make you believe me, but I didn't leave here to warn Kinsey, or to give him any information, to let him know that you were away, and that your men—your outlaws—were here without you, vulnerable and leaderless."

He watched her from the doorway for a long time.

"You didn't?" he queried, still waiting for an explanation.

"When you found me, I was fighting for my life. I saw Richard—"

"Richard?"

"Sir Richard Egan. Kinsey's second in command. He's—"

"I've heard of him. Go on."

"He isn't . . . overly fond of me."

"Oh?" he questioned, still careful. "So he didn't believe you?"

"Believe me? What do you mean?"

"Whatever you told him. What did you tell him?"

"I had nothing to say to him! I-I ran away from him and he was furious, and he told the men that it didn't matter if I was taken dead or alive."

"So you realized that your sainted Englishmen were not so gracious?"

"Damn you!" she cried vehemently. "I never left here to go to them!"

"But you did leave here. Why? If you weren't trying to reach Kinsey to rescue you from Scottish barbarians, why were you so desperate to escape?"

She inhaled with a sigh, shaking her head, looking down again. "I didn't wish to reach Kinsey, but neither can I stay here with you. Why can't you see that? There is no sense to my being here. And ... I don't wish to be here when you leave."

"My men would never hurt you. And I hadn't actually left."

"No, you went to see Wallace. To vow your aid to him!"

"Aye, I went to see Wallace, and you knew it, and you know that Wallace is very near, information you might have wanted to share with Darrow."

"Damn you, I gave him nothing."

"Neither did I actually *leave* you here."

"Perhaps not, but you hadn't discussed any plans with me."

"Should I discuss my plans with Edward's loyal subject?"

"Why do you condemn me for being English? Aye! I spent time in England—"

"At the king's court, aye."

"It's natural to honor a king you've known."

"Aye."

She threw up her hands with exasperation. "You left without explanation, and aye—it was necessary that I escape you! Soon, very soon, you will take your army of men and leave here."

"Aye, that's true. And I told you that when I left, you would be free. But rather than accept my word, you would risk your life to escape—right when Darrow's men just happened to be there."

"Aye, that is exactly what happened."

"Indeed."

He still didn't believe her. Or trust her. She'd spent years in Edward's court, honored the English king, and she had been betrothed to Kinsey. So, despite everything that he had seen, she must be guilty.

She wanted to slam her fists against him. She knotted her fingers into her palms and slammed them back against the wall instead. "Oh, you are a fool!" she cried, frustrated beyond measure, staring at him, her eyes glittering with unshed tears.

"Excuse me, my lady?" he grated.

"You're a fool! A wretched, incredibly stupid fool! Even a blind man would see—ask your new man-at-arms, Father Corrigan, if you would not believe me! I hate Kinsey, loathe him, despise him! I was on my knees praying God for any salvation from a marriage to Kinsey when you assaulted this castle! You were not at all what I had in mind, sir, but then, as we've all seen, God can be more than ironic. I had been desperately praying for some way to free myself from Kinsey. And you can be blind, and stupid, and an idiot if you don't realize what was happening out there today—did you think those men would have dared take swords to me if they didn't believe that they could injure me—or kill me—and still receive Kinsey's pardon and forgiveness?"

Her words out in a furious rush, she found herself falling silent again, now watching him very warily.

He pushed away from the door, approaching her. She found herself stumbling back, reflecting upon the words she had used.

Idiot. Fool. Stupid fool, at that.

He came closer, his blue eyes dark and enigmatic.

"Don't you understand?" she whispered, still backing away. "I never chose Kinsey. I used every means to—to keep him at bay."

He paused, staring at her, just a foot away. Arms crossed

over his chest then, he watched her, and waited. She held her silence, her eyes demanding that he believe her.

"I should believe you; I should accept all this! And if I don't, I'm a stupid, blind fool? Come, come—don't hold back now, my lady." His voice grated.

"You're blind!" she said simply.

"You remain Edward's loyal subject, willing to trick and drug your enemy and risk your life to escape!"

"I have to escape—really escape. There is nothing else for me to do."

"I never threatened your life."

She moistened her lips. "But my life is threatened."

"You are among the king's favorites!"

"The king is in France! You are riding away. You met with Wallace, and there will be a battle, and—"

"I will be a part of it, and God knows, you don't believe we outlaws could really defeat troops of your great King Edward?"

"You will leave here!" she repeated. "And I cannot be here when you do!"

He stood less than a foot from her, not touching her, studying her.

"Why are you so furious, so hateful?" she whispered.

"I was warned," he said simply.

"Warned?"

"That you are . . . what you are."

"And what is that, other than sick to death of the whole of it? A pawn, in danger with both sides now. You have to understand; you have to believe me. Kinsey . . ."

"Kinsey what? You are the wondrous prize granted to him, a bride with youth and beauty and riches untold! He loves you, so goes the rumor; he is obsessed with you."

"No more! I saw . . ."

"You saw what?"

"His face."

He frowned in earnest. "So you did see him!"

"For a second only, a brief second, after I saw you. When I ran through the trees . . . aye, damn you, I saw him, and I saw the way he looked at me, and he believes that I have betrayed him, and perhaps not until then, but at that moment I knew. . . ."

"Knew what?"

"He wants me dead."

He arched a brow, studying her. Then he turned away.

"Arryn!" she cried.

He looked back.

"I swear to you, I am telling the truth."

"Oh? You would betray Edward now?"

"I loathe Kinsey. I-I would never betray you, or your men, to him. Before God, I swear that is the truth."

He did not change; something in his face had hardened. He did not look at her any differently.

"There is soot all over your face," he told her.

She wiped her cheeks. "Aye, there is soot all over me!"

He nodded. He reached out and she flinched, and he paused slightly before he touched her cheek, his thumb running over it. "Aye, there is soot all over you. And your gown is filthy. And torn. You're quite a mess."

"A swordfight, sir, is hard on gowns such as this. And fires . . . well, they cause soot."

"Aye, and more," he murmured, and his gaze was brooding.

He turned away from her abruptly and left the room. She stared after him.

The door closed behind him.

Tense, wary, she listened. She didn't hear the bolt slide home. He had chosen not to lock her in.

She suddenly felt her knees seem to give. She stumbled toward the bed and sat. A moment later, there was a tap on the door. She leapt up. "Aye?"

Ingrid entered tentatively, saw her standing there, and then rushed in, hugging her. "Ah, my lady, you're alive and well still, though they say the wretch thinks you gave him away to Lord Kinsey! He failed this time, but I know he'll be back."

"Ingrid, Ingrid, it's all right; but I'm very tired, and—"

"Aye, you're tired!" Ingrid said indignantly, then sniffed. "But he's ordered up a bath for you, and fresh sheets, and . . . it's entirely too much bathing, you know! You'll wash away the oils that belong on your skin, you'll open up your flesh to the devil, they'll be harm come from it, you mark my words, you wait and see."

"Ingrid, I don't believe that bathing makes the devil come to you."

"Nay, lady? But then you *swim,* an ungodly capability, my lady!" she said, and crossed herself quickly.

Kyra smiled; then her smile faded. A bath . . . aye, he would not want her to smell like smoke! He must despise the odor.

Yet a burning smell was different when only objects had burned. And not people!

She shivered. She didn't want to smell like smoke. She wanted him to come back to her, no matter how foolish it was to seek his forgiveness.

His touch.

"Ingrid, a bath would delight me tonight. I am covered in ashes."

Ingrid sniffed again. "At least you are reconciled to . . . him! Ah, here come the lads again, as if they're not weary enough, fighting fires in the very middle of the night!" She stepped aside then, ordering where the tub should be placed, and the linen towels, soap, water, and brushes. When the boys had finished, the room was still filled with maids who brought furs from elsewhere in the castle and clean sheets for the bed. At last Ingrid clapped the last of the servants out, took the borrowed priest's robe from Kyra, and turned her around to find the ties at the back of her tunic.

"Perhaps it does not smell so much like smoke anymore. . . ." Ingrid admitted.

"And I will not smell so much like smoke anymore," Kyra reminded her gently. "Ingrid, I . . . Ingrid, do you know what Kinsey did to Arryn's home, and to his wife?"

Ingrid looked down. "I've heard . . . rumors."

"They were true, Ingrid."

"Wallace is a brutal man; the head of these outlaws is a very brutal man! I know that as well."

"Ingrid, nothing compares with what has been done to them!" she said very softly.

Ingrid looked at her, huge blue eyes damp. "My lady, Kinsey was to be your husband. Your right and proper husband! This rebel . . ." She hesitated. "He has no title, my lady."

"A title does not make a man."

"He will never marry you!" Ingrid blurted. "You were your father's daughter and he has made you an outlaw's . . ."

"Whore!" Kyra suggested flatly.

"Oh, my lady!" Ingrid whispered, pained.

"It does not matter, Ingrid. It does not matter. Don't go against these men, and they will not allow us to be maimed or hurt, and as to the rest of it . . . well, we will survive."

"Aye, lady, aye!" Ingrid tried a weak smile. "Come, let me wash your hair then, and let the steam ease the cares of the night!"

Kyra shimmied from the tunic, discarded her shoes and hose, and slipped from her undergown. She crawled into the steaming water, shivered, and lay back. She closed her eyes. God, but it had been an endless day and night!

"My poor lady!" Ingrid murmured. "I'll bathe your hair in rose water, rub your scalp. Ease the torments inflicted upon you!"

"Aye, Ingrid."

But it was a moment before she felt a gentle touch in her hair against her scalp. There were fingers rubbing her head, massaging, and the feel of them was wonderful, and sensual. . . .

And it was not Ingrid touching her.

Her muscles tightened; she swallowed hard.

She turned, and it was Arryn. Ingrid was gone, and Arryn had returned. His mantle and the light armor he had worn were gone; he had gone somewhere else and washed away the imprints of fire and battle.

"Turn around; let me finish," he told her, and she did so, and closed her eyes again, and felt the sheer pleasure of his talented hands against her head and hair. He worked soap into her, and the rinse of elderberries. She gripped the rim of the tub and felt both a delicious sense of being stroked and languid, and yet . . .

Tense. Little ripples of sunlight working through her limbs. Nay, big ripples, hot ripples, alive and vibrant, keeping her keenly awake and aware . . .

"It is done."

He twisted up the length of her hair, draining water from it, reaching for a towel. Yet his grip drew her from the tub, and when he found a towel it was huge, and he used it to wrap her hair and her length. Sweeping it over her head and around her, he held her before him so enwrapped.

"Don't run from me anymore," he told her harshly. "I promised you freedom. When it's safe, you will have it. I give you my word."

She nodded, moistening her lips. "Aye. I will not run. Do you believe me?" she whispered.

"Does it matter to you what I believe?"

"Aye, in this, it does!"

He drew her closer. The towel fell from her form. He kissed

her lips exploringly. His hand slid down her bare spine, caressed her nakedness. His head rose away from hers.

Still, he didn't answer her. His words were a question again.

"Can it be, my lady, that you've come to care for me?"

He taunted her, she thought, no matter what his promises. She took care with her answer. "I have decided that you are not completely a wretched barbarian."

He smiled. Despite the way he held her, there remained a distance in his eyes. "I am not wretched, and perhaps you are not such a deceitful, treacherous, and cunning witch."

Her eyes widened in protest. "You don't believe me. But what promise did you expect would simply come your way? You, sir, invaded here. You came to me! I did not come to your home and invade and demand. . . ."

He laughed softly. "Demand? Well, I will not demand. I will request. Will you come to bed, my lady?"

It was an invitation—perhaps. And what if she refused?

But she didn't want to refuse. Not tonight! She could still remember the way Sir Richard Egan had touched her, the things he had said to her. . . .

She remembered Kinsey's eyes when he realized that she did hate him, would run from him, refuse him at every turn. She . . .

She wanted to be held tonight. By Arryn.

"I have told you the truth about Kinsey, about . . . me. I don't want you to think that I would use . . . this as a means of seeking your forgiveness. I don't seek forgiveness. I did nothing against you. You, sir, however, should ask my forgiveness."

"Ah."

"Well?"

"I have absolutely no intention of asking your forgiveness. This is what is, and that is that. And, again, I cannot ask your forgiveness for something that has given me such unique warmth and pleasure.''

She felt heat rise to her cheeks.

"Do you believe me? About tonight?" Kyra asked.

He watched her a moment, but his eyes remained enigmatic. "Perhaps. I will allow room for doubt. And God help me, Kyra—I pray that giving you such benefit does not make me a fool—a stupid fool.''

She flushed again, and watched his eyes reflectively. "I should not be begging you to understand me!" she whispered.

He lifted his hands. "I am here now, and you are with me.''

"Aye. I am with you . . . while you doubt me!''

"And want you, my lady, and that is enough.''

And I want you! she thought miserably. *And that is way too much!*

But she turned from him and walked ahead to the bed.

She felt him behind her, his lips touching down upon her shoulders, his fingers gently tracing a length of flesh down the middle of her spine.

She crawled into the bed, trembling. This hurt, wanting him. This was wrong, she thought. And still . . .

The wanting grew.

The sheets were delightfully cool and clean; the furs were warm.

He joined her. Stretched against her. Touched her.

Kissed her.

Made love to her . . .

He knew how to stroke a woman, and tease, and she wanted to be stroked and teased. To caress, kiss, stroke, whisper . . .

She wanted to feel him, the ripple of muscle, the sleek heat of naked flesh, the pulse of him, the scent of him . . . she wanted so much! Needed, tonight, perhaps, this feeling of being cherished. She had been wanted before. Kinsey had wanted to possess her. . . .

This was different.

Their lips touched, met, clashed, hungered, parted, met again.

The things he did . . . moving against her body.

The sound of him, the urging of his whispers when she moved on him in return.

His touch could be passionate, then tender. Forceful, then a brushstroke she could barely feel. Volatile, then gentle . . .

And, oh, God . . .

Oh . . . God

Hours later, she lay against him, spent, soaked, sated, half-asleep. His arms were around her. He held her, protective, possessive still.

He spoke softly. "Remember, my lady, you must not come to care for me too much."

Not come to care for him? Did he mock her now?

"Don't come to think too highly of yourself!" she warned, tensing. Then she cried, "Oh, you wretched bastard! I am your prisoner, remember?"

She felt his fingers on her face, stroking her cheek. He ignored her cry and rose on an elbow, leaning over her and speaking softly once again.

"I don't speak from any conceit, my lady."

"Conceit? Too much confidence from you, sir?" she retorted. "Nay, I'd not believe it!"

She felt him shake his head. "You know all the events of our recent history, and you know the path ahead for all outlaws. I will never marry you, and I would not have you weep if the day were to come when I was hanged, drawn, quartered . . . and so on."

She'd been angry—and hurt. Nay, he'd never marry her; she wasn't his beautiful, lost Alesandra.

She was the king's favorite, Kinsey's prize.

Untrustworthy, even though the truth nearly slapped him in the face!

Nay, she remained in such great danger from them all!

His last words gave her a chill; anger faded, and fear set in. He could hold this castle; perhaps he could battle Kinsey and win.

But Edward had the might of all England. . . .

She rose against him, and maybe she didn't quite hide the stricken look in her eyes, and maybe, for once, he believed in her.

For his arms came around her and he pulled her gently back to him.

"And then again, my love, perhaps I will live forever."

She shivered still.

He held her more tightly.

And they slept as the battle-scarred night turned to day.

CHAPTER FIFTEEN

Darkness.

The Englishmen had changed places with the outlaws, retreating to those hills from which Arryn Graham had seen their campfires.

Kinsey Darrow stood upon the edge of a cliff, some distance from his men, one foot upon a rock, arms crossed over his chest, tension still wound so tightly in him he could scarcely endure it. He looked across the sloping fields to the light that emanated from Seacairn, highlighting the castle in a glow beneath the moon. He saw the shadows on the wall; his own men, fallen. Sir Arryn's men, seeing to their corpses.

Kyra had come to the woods. Had she known he was there? Richard had said she'd acted strangely, that she'd purposely eluded him.

And damn her, but he'd seen her face, seen her eyes!

She had shoved him, taken him by surprise, taken him as a fool.

She had run. . . .

Made good her escape.

But then, if she feared him, why had she come, why had she escaped the barbarians? There lay the dilemma!

He gritted his teeth. Nay, there was no dilemma. She had teased, tormented, denied him since he had first asked the king for her hand. She would have refused him; it was Edward who had ordered otherwise. Yet, even when they had been betrothed, she had cajoled the king, demanded time, and in that time she had threatened him, warned him, kept him at bay. No matter, he had thought, eventually she would be his wife. Patience, and the day would be won. Edward did not stand between a man and his wife.

But now . . .

She had been in reach! He had almost touched her, taken her, seized her. . . .

And the Graham had taken her again, riding with her across the sloping hill, and into the protection of the castle.

Where light glowed now. Light . . . aye, he'd seen the light of the fire. Seacairn might have burned to the ground, but the fires had been dampened, even as he and his men had ridden hard away, dodging the arrows that were flying down upon them, listening to the groans of those burned with oil, carrying the injured. . . .

He was a good commander, an able commander, but his anger had led him to forget restraint. He hadn't gathered his men with sound thought and careful strategy. He had ordered them after the riders, ordered them to a flat-out assault on the walls. How many had he lost?

Too many, and when Richard shouted that he must pull back or face the king's wrath for all the men he was losing so foolishly, he had done so, because he had known that his aide was right. Yet, when they had ridden away, he saw the fire. . . .

And saw it ebb.

Fire . . .

His muscles constricted; his jaw tensed. Did Arryn Graham remember his charred homeland? His charred lady wife? Had Kyra been within the room that burned, or had she been at Arryn's side, delighting in the battle that left his men bleeding and broken, herself at the castle, supreme, always, always looking down at him. . . .

The blaze that might have destroyed the tower and Seacairn was out, but still . . . a glow radiated from the tower. Aye, night, the battle over, the victor lay there. . . .

With his spoils.

If only battle could be won with rage alone, he would have emerged the winner of the conflict. But rage couldn't scale walls, raise a portcullis, ram a heavy wooden gate. How was it then that the castle had fallen so easily in his absence?

She had willed it so.

"Lord Darrow!"

He turned, scowling. In his temper, he did not wish to be disturbed.

But Richard had come to him. "What is it?"

"You are precipitously close to the edge!"

Kinsey stared at him, then laughed. "And you fear for my sanity, Sir Richard! Aye, a good friend you are, but fear not."

"You are staring at the tower, and ruing the fact that we lost her! You stand too close to an edge. Think, my lord. Scotland lies in this predicament, I'll remind you, because a king went off a cliff!"

"Ah, yes. Desperate to prove his youth and strength—and ride to his wife. A foolish loss—for him. Well, I'd not cast my life aside for any woman, Richard; you may rest assured of that. I'll not die and leave you unrewarded. Our ambition will continue to climb."

"Aye, we'll do well, and both be rewarded—if you think with your head, Kinsey."

"Take care, Richard. I remain your overlord!" he warned, his tone severe.

But Richard wasn't to be cowed.

"I take care, always. Will you? She has become an obsession with you! And you will be broken by Edward if he learns that you throw away soldiers needed in battle because you would chase what is already lost to you."

"She is not lost."

"You would marry her still?"

"Long enough for legal claim to the titles that were rightfully to be mine."

"And then?"

"I am a jealous man, a rightfully jealous man, driven to the brink of insanity by all that has happened."

"Don't underestimate her relationship with the king. His wife adored her."

"Don't underestimate the king's hatred for any man or woman who would betray him—to the Scots."

"How can you prove she betrayed the king?"

"She betrayed *me!*" Kinsey said, and at the end his voice was a roar. Then his voice deepened and grew quieter. "I will have her!" he added. "I will have her back. You should have seen her, Richard! But then, you did see her, didn't you?"

"I told you—"

"Richard, you should have seen the way she looked at me. As if I had already ordered her execution. Strange, I had done no such thing. I ordered her brought to me."

"The men see her as a witch, Kinsey. And she is fierce in her defense. . . . You must understand, she might have been hurt, fighting to free herself."

"But she wasn't hurt fleeing from you, right?"

Richard fell silent; Kinsey knew he was feeling like an idiot. She had escaped Richard with ridiculous ease.

"I did not hurt her, no. But you must realize that your men

know that she has hurt you, betrayed you . . . perhaps the men who died threatened her in some way. That is why she would look at you the way she did.''

''She has always despised me.''

''She despises us all. She thinks that we are . . .''

''What?''

''The barbarians.''

''We are Edward's men!''

''She deserves whatever punishment you would mete out, Kinsey. But . . . we must take care, the gravest care. . . .'' His voice trailed away, and he was quiet a moment. Then he warned, ''Edward broke a king, the king of Scotland—''

''A king of Scotland he created!''

''Balliol had the legal claim to the throne; even the Scots who think him a weak fool believe he had the legal claim. But that is not the point. Edward stripped him of his crown and country. Do you think he would hesitate to humiliate you and throw you in chains if you were to fail in battle because of your obsession with her?''

''I have crushed these people again and again!''

''So far, we have mostly slaughtered those with little strength to fight back.''

''What difference? The king wants them all annihilated.''

''The difference is that we'll face real battle now, and you'll need all your forces; you can waste no more men foolishly here, letting them be cut down so easily trying to scale such a defensive wall as that at Seacairn.''

''*He* scaled it!'' he said.

''But we cannot do so now. You'll have revenge in time. And if you choose to, and something befalls her . . . just remember my warnings. There must be an accident . . . or a legal precedent.''

''Aye . . . all must be legal.''

Kinsey looked from Richard back to the tower of Seacairn,

glowing in the night. Soft light radiating, from a fire, from a blaze. Aye, he slept there; his enemy slept there—with her. Kinsey could not help but torture himself, imagining them together, her smile, her laughter, what he'd never been able to take. . . .

He remembered her eyes today, remembered seeing her there, in the woods, hair a blaze of red and gold, even in the night, tall, lithe. . . .

Her eyes, emerald.

Glittering on him—with hatred.

He could not stay here. His duty was to ravage Scotland. He would do so now with ever greater pleasure.

Patience.

Firelight flickered in the tower room, he was sure, bathing their naked bodies in soft, glowing gold.

Revenge would come in time.

"We'll ride hard to reach Warenne's troops come the morning," Kinsey said. "And Richard?"

"Aye?"

"If I catch them—"

"There is no 'if,' my lord. These outlaws cannot withstand the might of the king!"

"Aye, then, *when* I catch them . . ."

"Aye?"

"Remind me that they must not die easily. He is a filthy, savage rebel. She is a traitor, and surely a witch. And she must meet a traitor's death. And . . ."

"Aye, Kinsey?"

"I think that they must burn. Feel the fires of hell, burn until they are scorched, ashes in the wind, no more, no more . . . by God! I will see them in hell!"

He turned away from the cliff.

He would have another day.

* * *

A certain tension lingered at Seacairn; everyone was aware that although Darrow and his men had given up their quest for the castle, they were all biding time.

Two of the defenders had been injured, none killed. And yet, outside the walls, there had been a pile of nearly fifty men, men in Kinsey's colors readily sacrificed until their lives became too great a price for even a madman like Kinsey when a far more important battle loomed ahead.

They were duly buried.

Kyra attended funeral services again, at Arryn's side, watching as Father Corrigan spoke the rites. His words were reverent and correct, but she felt that a restlessness had begun in him. He was not at all the typical priest, or even the typical priest that reformers might condemn. He didn't keep a woman on the side, he hadn't fathered bastards—that she was aware—and he didn't drink to excess, overeat, or seem to fall prey to the common sins of the flesh. But he had courage—and a sword. And the power and ability to use both.

She never looked at the fallen men. They were all Kinsey's people; they had ridden with him and been trained by him. They were from his home of Suffolk, or provided him by the king from men-at-arms drawn from the countryside. He had taught them how to fight with no mercy, to plunder, pillage, rape, and decimate the countryside. But most of them had lived here—she had seen their faces; she might know them by name. Death was never easy, and she couldn't help but feel sorrow. What would have happened to her had they scaled the walls? Just how far Kinsey would go against her, she didn't know.

Arryn left her after the words had been said.

The night the dead were buried, she sat at the table at Arryn's side, Jay to her left, Ragnor to Arryn's right. With summer, food was diverse and plentiful; it was a rich season, and there were times when she could close her eyes and think back to a time of relative peace. She'd loved her home then, the fields, the forests, the sloping landscape in many colors, cliffs to be seen in the distance, and mountains far beyond. Even the years right after the death of Alexander had been good, even after the Maiden of Norway died, even that first year when John Balliol had been chosen as king. . . .

All before Edward showed his true hand.

"You're thoughtful, my lady," Jay said, watching her.

She smiled, her fingers curving around her wine goblet. "I was thinking."

"Ah! Of the good old days!" he said.

"They were good. When my father was alive," she said. Her smile deepened. "Everyone loved him, respected him. He didn't yell often, or bellow, or shout, but people listened to him. He loved holidays, loved to gather the villagers and his guests and have dances, and he loved the sounds of the pipes, old tunes and new. . . ." She shrugged. "Perhaps you can't believe me. He was an Englishman, and loyal to Edward."

"We don't think all Englishmen should rot and burn in hell, my lady," Jay said. "I remember your father. He was a good man."

Curious, she frowned. Jay smiled and explained.

"Oh, aye. I've been with Arryn for years; my father owed his father feudal service, while Alexander himself was direct overlord of Hawk's Cairn. When Arryn went into the king's service, I accompanied him. We rode the countryside upon occasion, and came here with Arryn's father, in fact."

"I don't remember it."

"You would not. You were in England, in the queen's household."

"Ah!" she said, studying her wine.

"Learning the domestic toils of a lady's life—such as swordplay."

She flushed, then leaned forward toward him. "You see, Jay, Edward can be very good in many ways. He humored me in many things." She hesitated. "Jay, in truth, I am so very, very sorry about what was done. About Arryn's wife. Did you know her?"

"Aye. She was my cousin."

"Oh! You were as sorely injured then by her death! And yet . . ." Her voice trailed off.

He smiled and said softly. "I in no way blame you! And there will be justice."

He didn't blame her. Why did Arryn? Why did so many of his men distrust her?

She glanced uneasily at Arryn. He remained civil to her, courteous.

And distant. He watched her. Distrusted her, still.

"Jay, I did honor Edward as I grew up. He is a dangerous king, a very powerful one. Perhaps . . . you shouldn't go against him. When he chooses to be generous, there is no man more magnanimous. When he chooses to forgive, he is incredibly merciful. Why, you've seen! Many barons have risen against him—and many he has forgiven more than once."

"But when he chooses not to forgive, men die terrible deaths. And when he chooses not to be generous, even wee bairns are fodder for his slaughter."

"Berwick stains his greatness. That is true," Kyra said.

"And he gave you to Darrow," Jay commented.

Arryn turned at that. She felt a flush of color flood her cheeks.

"How did such a travesty come about?" Arryn demanded, leaning upon an arm to watch her, suddenly intent. She wondered how much he had heard. "You were beloved of the king and queen—and betrothed to a such a monster." He grinned at Jay. "We have all agreed that he is a monster."

"We are all nothing but pawns in the game of kings—isn't that said often enough?" Kyra murmured.

"Aye, but how did it come about?"

She shrugged, watching her wine rather than meeting the glances of either of the men.

"When the queen died, Edward ... changed. He became more ruthless, single-minded. Darrow and I were both at court. Darrow saw me and asked Edward for my hand. My father had died, my fate was in the king's hands. And then ..." Her words trailed away.

"Then what?" Jay demanded.

She swallowed wine. "Edward said if Darrow could prove himself an uncompromising weapon against the Scots, worthy of holding property here, then he should be so rewarded."

Arryn seemed to withdraw.

"He would be rewarded—so he was given you," Jay said. "Yet the wedding did not take place, while, still, word had it that you were a powerful vixen, passionate for the king's right, ever goading Darrow to greater feats and—"

"Atrocities," Arryn supplied sharply.

She stared at him, a strange hand seeming to sweep around her heart. At times it seemed he knew her so well.

And then he would look at her, as he looked at her now, and she would feel a cold chill of fear.

"I managed to delay the wedding, and my reputation for power came from my ability to avoid Darrow, not push him onward. I said I needed time to mourn my father, to remember him and honor him, to pray for guidance in all things ... and then I threatened Kinsey with the king's vengeance if he didn't respect the vow I'd made to remain chaste before the marriage. I'd told him that ... Edward could be very superstitious, and that he might believe he had failed because of just such a broken vow, were he ever to fall to the Scots," she told Jay.

Delighted with her story, Jay began to chuckle.

Arryn did not. He rose abruptly and left the table. Near the great doors to exit the hall, she saw him take his mantle from a wooden hook.

What had made him angry? she wondered.

Talk of Kinsey?

She watched him leave, feeling strangely deserted. He'd warned her not to care for him.

Because he might die.

No . . .

Because he hadn't stopped mourning the wife and unborn child he had lost, and somehow she had just reminded him that she wasn't the woman he really wanted, and this place was just a conquest, nothing more. He had turned from her, she thought. It didn't matter that they still shared the tower room, nor that he wanted her. Whatever he said, he still thought she had betrayed him. He had forged a distance between them, and it was firm.

Don't care for him!

What a fool.

Close to tears, she forced herself to smile at Jay. "How have you remained unmarried, sir? Or are you? In truth, I know nothing about you!"

"Ah, no, I'm not married. Why not? When I find a beautiful woman, it seems that she is already taken."

She flushed, afraid that he referred to her.

I am not at all taken! she might have told him. *Just . . . used.*

"But you're an intriguing fellow, Jay. So! Tell me more of your story."

He lifted his hands. "Simple enough. I grew up with Arryn, followed him to King Alexander's court—and home again." Then he paused. "We rode north with the rebellion rising; we returned to . . . ruins and death." His eyes met hers again. "So now we keep riding."

She put her hands on his. "Jay, I pray you at least believe this; I'm so very sorry."

"I know." He reached out, touched her hair, then drew back his hand, flushing. "I am one of the lucky ones. My sister survived the carnage. A few did. But still, there was nothing left to do but seek revenge. And we came to here to hurt Darrow. All we have done is injure you."

"Don't worry," she told him. "I am strong, and your coming here did not cast me to such a man as Kinsey. Fate was against me, so it seems."

"But what will happen now?" Jay asked. "We dare not leave you behind."

"God help us, we must see to it that she rides with us."

They both turned. Father Corrigan stood behind them, and he spoke firmly.

"So *you* will ride with us, Father?" Jay said. "Your flock is here."

"But life calls me onward."

"What of your calling to God?" Kyra asked.

"I believe it is God who calls," he told her, bowing slightly.

"Are you sure you're a true priest?" she persisted.

"As God is my witness."

"A strange priest, indeed," she told Jay.

"Perhaps he'll share his story."

"Perhaps—one day," Corrigan said. "My lady, Mayda, the head cook, and Gaston are going to play. Will you dance?"

"Your pardon, Father?"

"The kitchen staff will entertain; will you dance?"

"With you?"

"Aye, my lady. I am good, if you'll allow me to show you . . . ?"

She looked to the end of the long table. Gaston, the little Briton, sat with a self-styled flute in his hand. Big, bosomy Mayda, the cook, held a small stringed instrument.

"I'm for my pipes!" Ragnor exclaimed.

"You know the auld outlawed tunes, do you?"

"Aye, Briton, that I do!"

Ragnor left the table hastily. Maids began to clear. Father Corrigan reached for Kyra's hand. "My lady? If I dare be so bold?"

"A man of God is never bold, Father. He is righteous!" she said, laughing. And she rose, and Gaston began to play. Plump Mayda listened a moment, then joined in, and the tune was cheerful and light, a song played at weddings and harvest celebrations.

Father Corrigan was a swordsman—and a dancer. She dropped a curtsy to him; he bowed to her. In seconds she was spinning around the hall. And a moment later they heard the first stirring as Ragnor joined in with his pipes; the tempo increased, and Kyra went on spinning around the room.

"Father! For the love of God!" Jay cried. "Let a lonely man cut in on a beautiful lady!"

Father Corrigan bowed, and she clutched her skirt in her hand and began to spin with Jay, and the rest of the men began to join in, seeking a dance. Tyler Miller cut in, Roger, Philip, and men she barely knew. They were charming, laughing, and she was growing breathless. Elizabeth, one of the maids clearing the supper, stood at the end of the table, tapping her toes.

"Elizabeth! Here, dance with this strapping young warrior, please!"

"Oh, but, my lady—" Elizabeth's eyes went wide. "Is it proper?"

"It's a dance, Elizabeth, like May Day; that is all. Ingrid, we must summon Ingrid! Jay, go find her—" she began, turning, and finding that she turned into another of the men. He was huge, she realized, one of the biggest men she'd ever encountered. Of course, she'd seen him here before, moving about the hall—she'd just never been so close to him before.

It was daunting.

He was a giant in height, as muscle-bound and broad as he was tall, with a shaggy red beard and bright blue eyes.

"I'm Swen, my lady."

"Indeed."

"May I ask the maid, Ingrid, to dance?"

"Swen, aye, you must ask Ingrid to dance. And you mustn't take no for an answer!"

And so a few minutes later Ingrid was down, and she pro tested avidly at first, but then proved that she could kick up her heels and dance like a girl. And the ale flowed, and laughter, and the maids and soldiers and kitchen help laughed and mingled, and they were all talking, and there was a very strange camaraderie in the great hall.

She was exhausted herself, breathless; her hair was loose and wild, and still she was smiling, and she had forgotten for a moment that they were on the brink of a desperate battle, that life at very best was uncertain, and her own life, perhaps, the most uncertain!

It was amazing that this evening could come about, that there could be such pleasure, and such joy.

She looked across the room at Father Corrigan. He met her eyes, smiled, and walked around to where she stood, watching the dancers as the players began anew.

"This is Scotland!" he said softly.

She looked at him, tilting her head curiously.

"This is why, in the end, the Scots will win. It is their country." He smiled, a sure passion in his eyes. "Hear the pipes, my lady; look at them all! There will be a nation, for the pipes call out, the wind calls out. You'll see."

"Let's pray we all see," she said softly. "What is certain is that there will be a battle, and perhaps another battle, and another—for years to come."

"Rebels may die, my lady, but the rebellion won't."

"My lady! Come dance again, please!" Tyler Miller called

out. He was young and engaging, charming, and his smile was contagious.

"Aye, then," she agreed.

She had to dance, to laugh, to play. To pretend that she didn't long to run from the great hall and find Arryn.

He had gone to commune with the dead, she thought.

I will never marry you!

The words seemed to haunt her, playing over and over again in her mind.

She brought a sweet and brilliant smile to her lips.

"Aye, Tyler, gladly; let's dance!"

And she swung into his arms, and she prayed that Arryn would come back, and that he would see her, and that he would know. . . .

She would never care for him too much!

CHAPTER SIXTEEN

The night was beautiful. So why was his temper so foul? Why had her simple explanation about Kinsey made him so angry? Because she had never been Kinsey's, and he had made her the object of his revenge?

Or because she was such a fighter, spirited—and capable? She had managed to wage war with Kinsey.

Alesandra had not.

Or because his cousin, ever careful, aware how much treachery existed all around them, had planted the seeds of doubt in his head?

Leaving the castle behind, Arryn called to the guards, identifying himself, and strode up the steps to the parapets. There he walked the distance from lookout post to lookout post, greeted his men on duty, and passed them again to stand alone, staring toward the cliffs.

There were no fires tonight. Darrow's men had moved on. Arryn was glad they were gone, yet certain that his summons would come from John at any time to join Wallace and de Moray. If Warenne's men were gathering, as they had all heard, then they were following in the footsteps of the Scottish army, and the confrontation was destined to come soon.

He had never thought that he would want to stay here. That Seacairn could so quickly come to feel like home. It had been a fortress to seize; it had been vengeance. It had been a step in the war, and he had always thought that it would be easy to walk on.

And so it should have been.

He lowered his head and remembered, and sometimes the past was dim, faded, and sometimes he could remember too clearly—God, for the life of him he would never forget the smell of burning flesh. So many dead; a village decimated; what had been his home, ashes. What had been his life . . .

Alesandra. His child, who never drew breath. He had left them, and they had perished. He had forsworn his Hawk's Cairn, a family, a home. His life would be revenge, and the pursuit of justice, the pursuit of Scotland. And battle would come, and he could die by the sword, face capture, face a traitor's execution. And it had not mattered. . . .

Since then, he had lived for the passion of the fight—for Scotland. For the death of all that Edward had done. A fair bargain; they knew they must ride, find luxury at times such as these times at Seacairn, sleep in the woods as well. But now . . .

He would never forget her eyes. The green tempest in her fury, her words, the sound of her voice, the very vehemence with which she had called him a fool.

Time had been fickle; too often now, since he had come here, pictures had faded. In his dreams, he was still haunted by specters.

Alesandra.

The smell of smoke seemed real in his dreams. And yet,

when he was awake, he could not see her face any longer, for another intruded.

Green-eyed, golden-haired. Darrow's woman.

Ah, vengeance.

What would he do now? Take her to battle? He mocked himself. After all, she was good with a sword!

Never trust her! John had warned.

He'd not take her to battle.

No woman belonged on the field of battle.

Then what? Leave her here, as he thought he had intended, leave her with Darrow knowing that she had lain with him? He had thought before that such an action would be fair and just to her. He had believed that she had accepted her betrothal to the man, that they had been partners, that she might love her betrothed, yearn to be back safely in his arms.

Ah, but that wasn't what she had wanted. She had been as desperate to escape Darrow as she had been to escape him.

Would Darrow dare kill a woman who had been godchild to Edward's queen? Perhaps not. And still such a fact might not make her safe from Darrow. She might fall from the tower and hit ground rather than water, find herself trampled beneath a horse's hooves after Kinsey married her, and of course Kinsey would marry her; that would give him a legal excuse to seize her holdings.

No, it was certain. He could not leave her.

Whether he trusted her or not. He could not leave her here.

He was suddenly angry with himself. He had not meant to be so burdened; he should not have allowed himself to come to this place where he was so concerned for her welfare. There was war to be waged. She had slipped into his soul, never faltering, never losing pride, giving only when she chose to give. . . .

He owed her nothing! He had been charitable, where Kinsey had been brutal and ruthless and heedless of human life!

She wasn't dead. He hadn't seized her violently and left her broken to burn to death. That should have been all; it should have been enough.

No, he realized. If that had been all, he could have left her to Kinsey in the forest.

He suddenly heard music and turned back toward the hall. Still in a tempest between his memories, doubts, and the reality of the present, he nevertheless found himself drawn to the sound. He hurried down from the wall, across the courtyard, and back to the huge doors to the great hall of the castle. He slipped within, but stayed against the door, watching.

The maids were dancing. Good Lord, even the dour Ingrid— who always looked as if she wanted to fall to her knees and pray every time he came near her—was dancing. Some of the kitchen girls had joined in, and most of his men. And those who were not dancing were keeping time with the music, laughing, drinking, singing.

He looked for her, without admitting that he did.

And there she was. The gracious lady of Seacairn, hair red-gold and flying in the night as she wove around his men, her partners, eyes flashing. She smiled, she laughed, she chatted, she teased—charming each and every one of them as she changed partners throughout the dance.

The music faded.

She laughed at something Jay said, touching his arm, bending to catch her breath. The men grew fond of her. Too fond of her. She must know that she could charm them all. . . .

Deceive them? Was she too confident?

Ragnor suddenly switched to a sad lament, and beckoned to her. She approached him, still catching her breath.

His mouth parted from the pipe for a moment as he said, "My lady, Tyler tells me you know this song of ours, that you sing it like a nightingale."

She laughed softly. "Like a nightingale? I'm not sure, but I do know the tune; it's beautiful, and it's not just *yours!*"

"I stand rebuked!" Ragnor said, "but sing it, my lady, please."

"Aye, if you wish."

Ragnor inhaled, taking his pipe into his mouth again, and hugging the sheepskin against his breast. The flute joined in, and the stringed instrument. And in Gaelic as fluent and clean as any Arryn had ever heard, she began to sing the words to the ancient and outlawed song. Her voice was crystal clear, melodic, beautiful, a sound to tug upon the heartstrings, to bring pain and poignancy and beauty to the heart.

When she was finished, Ragnor lowered his pipes. "Lovely, lady, lovely!" he said softly, and he grinned, and he told her, "You're more of a Scot than you knew."

She smiled at him and flushed. "You have called me English. My mother's family is an old and honored one in Scotland. I was born here."

She was convincing them all that she was trustworthy.

One of them!

"Ah, yes, born here! But raised by Edward in England!" Arryn heard himself call out sharply.

The laughter in the room faded. The air seemed to grow cold. No one had realized he had returned. All eyes came to him. His own men looked at him uncomfortably, and he felt like an interloper among them.

"But don't let me disturb you. It's good to take this time, celebrate life. Play another tune, Ragnor. Something lively again."

Ragnor stared at him a moment, then nodded. The pipes wheezed and whined; Gaston joined in as the chords blended . . . .

One of the maids flew by on Roger's arm. Arryn swept by, stealing her from Roger. Her name . . . Elizabeth. She was a pretty little dark-haired thing with wide eyes and huge breasts. He danced with her, laughed with her, and when they paused, he filled a chalice and drank with her. It wasn't good for him to spend too much time with one woman. It suddenly seemed important to him that Kyra realize that.

And that she did remain at their mercy.

But when he looked around the room, Kyra was gone. He wasn't going to follow her.

He damned himself.

Aye, he was.

His head seemed to be raging, splitting. The music was still going on; the whine and wheeze of the bagpipes suddenly seemed discordant and horrible. He wanted to stop them from playing, but he forced himself to let the company be—they needed this night. More of the castle servants were joining in. It was important that they dance, sing . . . play.

He walked up the stairs and entered the tower room, and she was there, stretched out before the fire, just watching the flames. Her tunic that night was gold, and the flames caught the color of her hair. It was still such a tangle, wild, seductive, young, bewitching. She was so different from Alesandra. So passionate, vital, and vibrant. Always a tempest, quick to anger, to courage, indignance, quick to speak her mind, while Alesandra had been . . .

Gentle. Quiet. Quick to smile, eager for his every word . . .

The past haunted him, tormented him.

He had left her, such a gentle, timid creature as Alesandra, and Kinsey Darrow had come, and she had been like a lamb to a slaughter. And the horror here was that the memories were slipping, and if they faded then he had abandoned her again, and abandoned all the vows he had made in his heart, and the guilt was a greater torture than any man could inflict. . . .

No. He would not abandon his wife, no matter what he did here.

She knew that he was in the room; she did not turn. She didn't move or speak at first. Then, after a long moment, she said brusquely, "Kinsey and his men have moved on, have they not?"

Of course, she knew that his enemies had left the hill. She would have noted the movement the same as any of his men. She was quick and intelligent, knew strategy and maneuver.

She had grown up in Edward's shadow.

"So," she continued, not expecting or waiting for an answer, "it will be time for you and your men to adjourn to the battle as well."

She turned at last, her green eyes luminous. "Arryn, you will leave. Imminently. I cannot stay here, you know. I do have family northwest of Stirling, at the base of the Highlands, my mother's clan . . . cousins. A few uncles and aunts. I thought that I should leave . . . soon. You know that I must. Perhaps even tonight."

"Tonight? That, my lady, is ludicrous. It's late. Very late."

"Aye, well night and late will be the time to go, won't it? I'll need to travel by cover of darkness."

"And just how were you planning on traveling?"

"Carefully, of course. With just a servant or two; I can go as a pilgrim—"

"And ride unmolested, a great distance, with several armies scavenging the surrounding towns and villages and forests?"

She rose with supple grace, folding her hands before her. "What difference does it make to you? You tell me not to care for you. Well, you mustn't become overly concerned with my welfare."

"Or your whereabouts."

"What does that mean? Oh, yes . . . of course. That you don't trust me. I will somehow betray you, and Wallace, and de Moray, and the whole union of rebels!"

He waved a hand at her impatiently. "When the time is right, I will make arrangements."

"Why? What possible concern can you have for my future?"

"My lady, aye—you could betray us."

"I have told you—"

"You may be adept at lies."

"You have seen—"

"Kinsey is not the only Englishman out there."

"I've no intention of betraying anyone. I am trying to survive!"

"Thus far I have kept you alive. I won't have you leave here to be slain by foraging men on their way to do battle."

"Most men would not kill a lone woman."

"Many men, far from home, drunk with power, would molest a lone woman. Especially when King Edward has suggested that the Scots should be 'bred out' if not decimated."

She ignored his words against the king. "That's going to be a risk, but it's my risk, and my affair." She stared at him with her eyes caught by firelight, emerald in the extreme.

"No," he said firmly.

"Arryn, I have to—"

"You're wrong; this is not just your affair. I will see to your situation."

"Will you? You're riding off to an all important battle; you may win, you may lose, and God help you, you may well die." She walked to him and stood before him, her eyes remaining brilliant upon him. "You wanted to hurt me; you said so once, when you first came. In revenge, of course, for your wife. Whom I never knew nor harmed. Well, you have managed to do me serious damage, sir. Are you pleased, is justice served, can you ride with pride in yourself now?"

Her eyes were reproachful; her tone was sharp, goading.

He was shamed. And guilty still. And angry.

He longed to strike her, shake her, tell her that she still didn't begin to know what hurt was. He reached out for her, gripped her shoulders, gritted his teeth, fought for control. She was so vibrant, passionate, alive.

He threw her from him, threw her back, knowing he had to get his hands off her. She landed on the bed, as he had known she would, breathless and stunned, but unharmed.

"Justice, my lady? Is it served? Never. My wife is a pile of ash. There is no justice for such a loss. But as to you—you'll leave, my lady, when I tell you to. And you'll depend on my protection for your travels, because I have said it is so."

Shaking, he turned to leave her.

And he strode from the room.

The door slammed hard in his wake.

It was almost dawn. Arryn had not come back to the room.

Kyra wasn't sure at what point she had begun to cry, but she had been tired and desolate, and the tears had started, and to her horror they had just kept going. She tried to stop, and then she furiously told herself she had the right to cry, and then she told herself that she'd never cry over him again, and that she'd never, never let him know that she had. He had warned her continually not to care about him. Why had she done so? He was probably bound for a traitor's death, if nothing else, and yet she lay in knots, wanting him to return, wanting him beside her, wanting to hear his voice, feel his touch. . . .

She had goaded the fight, she thought now numbly. She had teased and flirted and tried to test his temper. She had wanted . . .

What he couldn't give.

And when he had returned, she had thought she'd gotten her emotions and her vision under control; the armies were moving. Time dwindled. Better to break rationally and intelligently; better for her to go than to watch him leave! No matter what

Father Corrigan had said, Arryn had never suggested that she ride with them!

So he had come, she had insisted . . . she had lashed out at him, and he had lashed back—and left.

She pictured him dancing with petite Elizabeth, the round-bosomed maid with the pretty young face, pictured him having gone to her when he left this room. Men needed little incentive to go to a woman; hadn't he told her that?

She had to stop thinking about him, torturing herself.

But she could not.

Maybe he had gone to find pretty little Elizabeth just to prove to Kyra that she meant nothing to him, but, oh, God, if she meant nothing, why prove it?

While she lay tired and tormented, there was a tapping on her door. She stirred herself to rise, hopeful, yet foolishly so, for she knew he'd never knock.

So who did so?

In the very late hours of the night, she had shed her clothing and donned a soft, knitted nightdress; the fabric was somewhat sheer and clinging, and she hugged the soft garment to her as she called out softly, "Who is it?"

"Ingrid."

Ingrid. Of course.

"Are you alone, my lady?"

"Very," Kyra said. "Come in."

Ingrid came hurrying in, rushing to her at the bed, then drawing to a halt, staring at her, her fingers curling around the length of one of her braids, her eyes huge as she stared at Kyra.

"My lady!" Ingrid said in a rush.

Kyra half rose, certain that there was something terribly wrong.

"What is it?"

Ingrid started to speak. Her pale features turned ashen, then brilliantly pink.

"Ingrid!" Kyra leapt up, taking her maid by the shoulders. "Ingrid, what is it?"

Ingrid managed a word at last.

"Swen!"

Kyra arched a brow. "Swen?" she questioned.

Ingrid suddenly clapped her hands together. "Swen!" she repeated.

"Ah, yes—Swen." One of Arryn's men. The huge fellow, taller than any man, as big as a small house. He'd asked to dance with Ingrid; she had told him to insist to Ingrid that she do so.

She noted then that Ingrid hadn't changed. She was still wearing the clothing she'd been wearing the night before.

Except that . . .

There was straw in it. Or hay. And there were a few little pieces of hay in her long blond braids.

She gripped Ingrid by the shoulders. "Oh, my God. Oh, Ingrid, I'm so sorry, did Swen . . . did he—Oh, he must have! Father Corrigan will speak with him, the bloody bastard! Big as a house and he acts like an animal—"

"No, no, no, my lady!" Ingrid cried, horrified.

"You mean he didn't—"

"Oh, no! He *did,* but because . . . I wanted him to."

"Oh." Kyra's mouth formed the word.

"My lady!" The maid's excitement was tangible. "My lady, he has asked me to marry him!"

"Marry him!"

"Aye, Lady Kyra, isn't that wonderful?"

"I . . . I—"

"May I, my lady; will you give permission, please?"

"Ingrid, um—you barely know him, you—"

"I have watched him, my lady. Since they came. He's talked to me before. He carried the laundry for me . . . and last night, when we were dancing . . ."

"Marriage!" Kyra said.

"Oh, please, my lady!"

Kyra shook her head. "I would never deny you, Ingrid, but—you know this, that you want to marry him, after one night?"

"One night is far more than most maidens get, my lady."

"Aye, of course, but—"

"The rich are wed as children, sometimes not even knowing one another."

"Aye, and that's tragic."

"It's the way it is, my lady."

"But, Ingrid—"

"I love him, my lady."

"Can you be so certain?"

"Will I ever have such another chance? Oh, my lady! I am no great beauty, but neither is he. He is Swen! My Swen, perfect for me!"

Kyra started to smile; then she froze, for Ingrid had left the door open at her excited entrance, and Arryn was standing there, and she didn't know how long he had been there.

He walked into the room. "What is this, Ingrid?"

Ingrid blushed, but she didn't seem so terrified of Arryn any longer. "Sir Arryn, it's . . . I . . . well, I've come—"

"Aye, Ingrid, about Swen?"

She nodded, then looked at him earnestly—and worriedly. "Oh, sir, has he your permission? I didn't think—"

"Swen is a free man, not my servant; he rides with us by choice, for Scotland, Ingrid. But aye, lass, he has my blessing."

"What say you, my lady?" Ingrid asked anxiously.

"Ingrid, he will ride off to war."

"I will wait!"

"I still say that you can hardly be so certain."

"I know that I love him, my lady!"

"You don't know him."

"It seems to me, Lady Kyra, that the two wish to wed with far greater reason than most couples who would come before God."

He was making her sound ridiculous and bitter, Kyra thought. She lifted her hands. "Ingrid, you must do what you choose. With my blessings!"

"Oh, my lady!" Ingrid threw her arms around Kyra, kissed her cheek, then withdrew. "What will I do? What will I wear? We must wed quickly. . . ."

"You are welcome to anything of mine," Kyra told her, which sent her into gales of laughter.

"Oh, my lady, you tease me; I couldn't wear your clothing!"

"Ingrid—"

But Ingrid wasn't listening. She had risen to approach Arryn, tentatively, then with a huge smile. "Oh, Sir Arryn!" And she hugged him, and he hugged her back.

"Go tell Swen to find Father Corrigan; there will be a wedding tonight. Just before dinner. And we will feast and party again."

"Bless you! Oh, bless you, Sir Arryn!"

She went running out of the room.

Arryn followed her to the door, closing it in her wake. He came back rubbing his nape, and then his temples. He gave no sign he remembered that Kyra was in the room. After a moment, he hunkered down to rebuild the fire. Flames sputtered, then blazed to life again.

He rose and began to strip off his clothing.

Kyra stood, inching from the bed. "What do you think you are doing?" she demanded.

He turned to her, surprised at the question. "I don't think— I am doing. I am going to bed. I need some sleep."

He padded by her, his eyes level with hers until he had passed her. Then he crawled into the bed, turning his back on her. "This is by far the most comfortable bed in the castle," he murmured.

As if he had tried others.

Rage and misery filled her—the latter being the greater emotion.

She ignored him, walking to her wardrobe trunk to choose clothing for the day.

"My pillow," he noted, "is soaked."

She didn't respond, but kept digging through the trunk.

"Were you crying over me, Kyra?"

"Don't be absurd."

"Come here."

"I think not."

"Actually, I think that you should think anew. Because if you do not, you know I'll come and get you."

"That will be a useless effort on your part."

"Useless, my lady? No, for the intent is that you come from there to here, and it will happen. I will simply pick you up and bring you over."

She straightened, ready to protest, but he was already out of bed and on the way. And as he had promised, he picked her up, and she tensed and her jaw clenched but he walked back to the bed. And as he did so, it seemed that the sheer white knitted garment she wore made her feel him all the more fully, the play of his muscles, tension, vibrancy, movement. . . .

He laid her down, leaned over her. His hand covered her breast over the fabric; his fingers played over her nipple and the feel, through the fabric, was torturously erotic. She squirmed, trying to twist from him.

"I told you not to love me," he said softly, his touch tightening upon her.

"I do not."

"Then why were you angry; why were you crying?"

"I don't know what you're talking about—"

"You were crying."

"And it must be over you?" she inquired, eyes flashing furiously, hands pressed against him in protest. "Why would I be crying? My God! You don't trust me, and many men want to kill me! To survive I must leave my home, all that's mine, all that I've known! Imagine, why would I shed a tear—and why would I do so for you?"

His lips curled slightly; his eyes were intense.

"Why are you trying to refuse me now?"

She stared at him, incredulous. "Why are you attempting to seduce me now, when you don't trust me, and have obviously been elsewhere?"

"Since you are among the beaten and seized, you really have no right to ask such a question. Ravished ladies have no rights, you see. They meekly obey their new masters. But since I'm in the mood, I'll tell you where I have been, and that has been awake all night with Ragnor and Jay."

"And not with another woman?" *Oh, God!* She hadn't said those words. But she had! She longed to kick herself for the question.

"I considered it," he told her gravely. "You should not forget who I am, and what I am."

"And who and what are you?"

"The barbarian half Highlander who has conquered you and this castle, and that is all."

"Then you should have let me go last night."

"I didn't choose to do so. Conqueror, my lady. I rule here, for the time."

"If I mean nothing to you, you should have taken another for the night, and sent me on my way."

"As I said, I considered such a course of action."

"Perhaps you should not love me!" she told him.

He smiled. "I do not."

"Then—"

"When I am camping with an army of men, I eat stale bread, when it is all that there is. When possible, I feast on rare, red meat, and drink the finest wine."

"And that means—"

"It would be foolish to leave fine wine for stale bread," he said.

"Oh, God, let me up."

"No," he said flatly, fingers savoring the feel of her breast. He looked at her, lowered his head, then covered her nipple with his mouth over the sheer knit. She knew that she jerked at his touch, melted with it, gave far too much away. . . .

He tormented her in a leisurely fashion, teasing with his lips, teeth, and tongue, until he knew that she felt her own trembling.

"As fine wine, my lady, you may feel free to respond."

"Alas, you are the conqueror, and as the conquered, it is my role, I believe, to scream and fight and be wretched."

His face rose above hers. "I remind you, there are tears on this pillow."

She set her hands on his shoulders and tried to push him away. "And I remind you, they are for the world around us."

"It is a sorry world," he agreed. His hand remained on her breast, so sensual through the fabric. She felt the weight of his thighs, his arms, his chest, held carefully away. He was hot; he was fire, erect, touching her. She had cried half the night— and he was back with her.

She was fine wine, so he had said.

"But still . . . give up your fight with me. I watched you tonight. Is that what you intended? I watched you sway and swirl and dance. . . . I watched men tremble just to touch your hand. Is that what you wanted? If so, I fell into your trap, and thought that two should play."

"There was no trap!" she whispered. "You left the great hall."

"And returned."

"And danced with another, shared wine . . . and then left me here."

"There is no one here I want but you!" he told her harshly.

"You have all you want."

"Aye? So what is it that you want from me?"

"Nothing!"

"Is that the truth, my lady? Or do you seek some assurance? What I can't give? I had a wife!" he reminded her, suddenly angry.

"I know!" she cried in return, and yet she suddenly wondered if the anger he felt was for her—or for himself. Was it one thing to lie here with her . . .

And another to care?

"God help me, sir! I know. You never let me forget what happened, ever! You'll never believe that I was not to blame!"

"You are the enemy," he told her.

I am not! she might have protested.

But she never had the chance.

He groaned, and his lips ground down on hers.

A sob escaped her from her lips to his. She slammed her fists against him, again and again. Then her hands went still. Her fingers splayed over his chest.

His hands tugged at the fabric of her gown, wrenching it up the length of her thighs, over her hips. She felt his nakedness rubbing against her, his body sliding low, hands catching her hips.

The weight of his form wedged his chest between her limbs. His thumb played upon her intimately, parted her; his tongue ravaged her, quickly, almost violently.

She burned with want. . . .

Shrieking, protesting, digging into his shoulders, twisting, straining, pulsing, she surged against him. Felt the hunger curl and spiral deep within. Then he was up, rising against her, his hands touching her face, his lips finding hers, his mouth kissing her, ravishing, eliciting, evoking. The hunger built. His mouth was wild, ruthless, savage, his tongue seductive as his body penetrated hers, as he rose and fell with her, sank, pinned, thrust deep . . . withdrew, fast, fast, slow. . . . He buried himself within her, shuddering. Then he was rising, nearly withdrawing completely as he lifted his lips from the ravaging kiss and his eyes met hers. He moved slowly again. Each second seemed to make her more desperate. She met his gaze, then closed her eyes, threw her arms around him, and dragged him close. She shuddered with the impact, thought she would shatter from him, burst, die. . . . *Slow . . . slow . . . please . . .*

And then he was the wind, and she rose with him, and she felt the sleekness of his body as it grew damp, felt the tension in his chest and limbs, the hard rhythm of his hips, the force of him in her, spiraling, touching, arousing. . . .

She climaxed as he went rigid, thrusting with a volatile burst of wet heat within her. She clung to him, yet felt him shudder, and shudder, and shudder. . . .

How would she live without him, now that he had forced himself into her life?

He didn't withdraw, but lay there with her, arms around her, as if he were loath to let go. And she could not seem to help herself, and she spoke to him, taunting him.

Taunting herself.

"Don't care too much for me, Sir Arryn!" she whispered. "I do not speak from any conceit, but . . ."

He traced the lines of her face. "I will not care for you, not at all, my lady," he vowed passionately. "But you will be with me until . . ."

"Until?"

"Until I say you will be with me no more."

"You're not being just or fair," she protested.

"I do not need to be, my lady. I am the conqueror here."

"Bastard!" she whispered.

"Aye, probably, but the conqueror still. For now, get some sleep. We have neither of us had any."

She slept; he did not. He watched her, touched her hair, felt the softness of her breath, stared at the beauty of her profile.

Then he rose and walked to the mantel, then the ewer of water by the wash table. He drank deeply, then walked back to the mantel and stared at the flames, then back at her.

"Aye, I had a wife!" he said bitterly. "But God help me and forgive me . . . I never loved her as I love you now!"

He walked back to the bed, knelt by it, threaded his fingers through her hair again.

"But I cannot forget, cannot forget . . . I cannot forget how she died!" he said softly.

Kyra stirred, felt his touch.

And trustingly, inched toward it.

Fine wine . . .

He crawled in beside her again. The dawn had now long since broken, but it didn't matter. He needed to hold her.

There might be no more nights to come.

CHAPTER SEVENTEEN

Once again, when the moon rose, the sound of the pipes lay over the land. Tonight the doors to the great hall had been thrown wide; the villagers had come, and everyone feasted, drank wine and ale, and danced, and wished the newlyweds well.

For Swen had married Ingrid. It was a good match. They were both the grandchildren of Viking invaders who had come to stay, which made them very good Scots, Arryn was quick to assure Kyra. Most good Scots had some Viking in their background. The Norsemen had brought terror and fury to Christendom, but here, in Scotland, the country had prevailed, for the invaders had stayed, and brought their skills with them, and become part of the forming nation.

"You've Viking in your blood, I assume?" she teased.

"Of course, the wildest, most barbaric of the lot!"

"Naturally."

"My great-great-great—I don't know how many greats—grandfather was a jarl who ruled an isle. I've still family there."

"Naturally. The clans are strong."

He sobered suddenly. "Aye, lady, you can't imagine how strong. Perhaps our very salvation—even yours."

He set down the goblet of wine he had been drinking. "You teased and tormented all my men last night lady. This evening will you dance with me?"

"I don't think the conquered are allowed to refuse, are they?"

"Not unless they want to face a dire retribution."

"What retribution?"

"I would have to take you alone and away, to a darkened tower, to show you."

"Ah, dear sir! A dance, or retribution. You do make the choice a difficult one!"

"You are not properly cowed at all, my lady."

"But I am, Sir Arryn. I am. You cannot begin to imagine. Shall we dance?"

"Aye, lady. Take my hand."

They danced, and they joined with the large crowd that gathered in the courtyard beneath the moon in the gentle breezes of the balmy night. They joined the groups, and changed partners, and returned to one another, laughing and enjoying themselves. Swen, for all his huge bulk, was light on his feet, and dragged anyone within reach into the dance. Kyra moved along a line of clapping dancers, spinning with each, until she came to the end of the couples, and then she came to a dead halt, forgetting to spin.

John Graham had come back to the castle. She saw him with several other men, dismounting from their horses. They had just ridden into the courtyard.

Arryn looped her arm through his own. Spinning her.

She looked at him, and knew that he saw in her eyes the

realization that the time had come for them to leave. "We finish it out," he told her.

He meant the dance.

The words had so many more meanings.

She spun with him, spun with the others; the pipes whirred and hummed in their unique combination of melody and wail, and soon it was over, and the others were laughing and talking, and if they were aware that their world was about to change, they gave no sign.

When the music faded, he turned her over to Jay—absently, she thought. Aye, the time had come; she was dismissed. She wished that John had fallen into some distant moat, and kept away from Seacairn.

Yet, what would that have done? Eventually, if Edward's army didn't prevail without him, Edward would come. And when he rode upon the Scots, there would be no mistakes, no faltering, and no mercy.

She excused herself from Jay; the music was playing again, but she had no heart for it. It was Ingrid's wedding, and she was glad, but Ingrid had no need of her now; she had her Swen. She walked back through the great hall, and Gaston, the sprightly Briton who had seemed to serve forever there, was humming as he picked up platters and set out more fruit.

He glanced her way, bobbed a curtsy.

"A messenger has come. The Scots will be leaving soon," she said smoothly. She realized then that whatever happened to her, she would be leaving here. If the Scots won an unlikely victory, she might return. If not, she had abandoned these people.

"Aye, my lady."

"Gaston, you should go under the stars, dance, enjoy the party."

He looked at her sadly. "Aye, lady, that I will. But you needn't worry for us here." He smiled, seeing the concern and question in her eyes. "Life goes on for the common folk, my lady. Great men come and fight wars, and they think they make great changes. Only the masters change, and some are kinder than others, that is all."

She shook her head. "When the king of England is angry, God knows what he will do. And when men fight for him, they fight viciously."

"And so do their enemies. My lady, we will prevail. If Lord Darrow returns, he will hardly slaughter us all. Who would cook for him, clean for him, serve him? He is a greedy man; he wants rich fields. He'll not massacre his own tenants or their wives." He hesitated a minute. "But you must be gone. God help you, lady."

He came to her, took her hand, squeezed it, bent low over it. He met her eyes. She found herself hugging him.

"You are a good man, Gaston. Whatever happens here, play any game you must. If Lord Darrow returns here, pretend that you are pleased, glad to have a proper lord, and that you loathed the ragged Scottish army that invaded. Live, Gaston; don't anger him."

"Aye, to live, and to take moments of joy and celebration, like Ingrid's wedding. I will dance, my lady, sing, and tell Ingrid of my happiness for her. But first . . . there must be ale here, in the great hall. And wine, and bread and meat for the men who have just come. They'll sit late in the hall, tell one another of the battles that will come, and speak of their rage— and their hope."

She nodded, kissed his cheek, and started up the stairs.

"My lady!" he said, calling her back.

She stopped and turned.

He shook his head suddenly. "It isn't my place to comment. . . ."

"Aye, but please do so anyway."

He hesitated a moment longer, then told her. "I had feared

for you, thinking them to be wild men out of the mountains when they came, as savage as the old painted people, the Picts. I had wanted to help you so badly, yet you see, I knew your outlaw before, many years ago, and knew he was quick to compassion, though embittered by the war. And we see much in the kitchens and the great halls, lady, serving different masters. It's better to be''—he paused, and, being a Briton, he searched for a kind term—''better to be the lover of the man labeled a savage outlaw than the legal wife of one who would call himself lord. The one does seek justice, while the other is fueled by greed.''

"Thank you, Gaston."

She hurried on up the rest of the stairs to the tower room. Her prison. She might never see it again.

It was not such a prison anymore.

She stoked the fire, sat on the fur before it, and waited.

John had come for them; the time had come.

They'd spend the next day preparing, packing food, weapons, blankets, supplies, everything they could easily carry that might be necessary for the fight.

They were to meet up with Wallace, de Moray, and whatever other freemen, nobles, clergy, farmers, and clerks would take to the field for Scotland.

With Jay, Ragnor, Patrick, Roger, and a number of the rest of his men, he adjourned into the great hall, urging the villagers to continue the wedding celebration.

John sketched a crude map of the area on the table. "We are to meet here, outside of Stirling. And we must take care on the journey there, for the king's men ride here," John said, pointing to a place on the map to the west, "and here! Cressingham is here, Warenne here. 'Tis true Percy's men disbanded, but they may still be riding about in groups ... lethal groups.''

"Percy's men were disbanded?'' Arryn asked, frowning. "Why?''

John looked over the table at him. "Apparently Warenne thinks that he has sufficient force to deal with a pack of pike-bearing farmers.''

"Then that's to our advantage,'' Arryn said.

"The king doesn't think we're worthy of his greatest efforts!'' Patrick said.

"We need any advantage,'' Arryn said. "His men do ride with trained warriors, cavalry, horsemen, bowmen. Mercenaries from the continent. Knights with no cause, and no tournaments to attend for their livelihood. We need every advantage we can use against such men. But then, we also fight with something they do not.''

"And pray tell, cousin, what is that?'' John asked.

"Passion, desperation—this is our home. And we fight for lives. Our lives, our country.''

"Aye,'' John agreed.

"What of the barons—will they support this fight? Have they been summoned?''

"Word has it that some will arrive—and watch. And if we have a chance of winning, they will cast their lot with us. And if the English appear to be taking the upper hand ...''

"Then they will help to tear us to shreds,'' Ragnor said.

"That is simple to solve,'' Jay said.

"And how is that?'' Ragnor asked him.

"We win,'' Arryn supplied. "There's heavy work to be done in the morning. My friends, I'm for bed.'' He started for the stairs.

"Arryn, a minute!'' John called to him.

He waited and his cousin walked over to him. John spoke softly.

"I have heard that you intend to bring the priest, many of the men from here—and the Lady Kyra."

"Aye."

"She's escaped you many times."

"She hasn't escaped *me* many times. She tried to leave Seacairn—"

"When Kinsey Darrow was in the forest."

"His men tried to kill her. I was there; I saw it."

John watched him for a long moment.

"Don't question my judgment, John. I know what I'm doing. If Darrow finds her, he will kill her. It's that simple. She rides with me."

"If you trust her, Arryn, I bow to your judgment."

"Aye."

"What will you do with her?"

"Take her to the forest village at the foothills where the families of many of the outlaws have gone. It's where we would ride before Abbey Craig were she with us or not; some of these men feel they must see their wives and babes ... before the battle. And I would leave the laundresses behind, the cooks, the camp followers."

"Do you dare leave her there?"

"Aye, and why not?"

"You leave her with the survivors of Hawk's Cairn."

"She did nothing there."

John shrugged. "I bow to your judgment; let's pray others will."

"Whatever comes, there is no choice."

John nodded. "Good night then, cousin. Sleep well. Nay, never mind, don't sleep at all. As our Viking ancestors liked to say, we can sleep when we're dead. Use the night well. Would God that I were you this evening."

He grinned and spun about to return to the table, where the

others were still engaged in conversation. They could talk about the possibilities of the battle forever.

Use the night well!

He had listened to John; now John had listened to him. He knew that he couldn't risk the lives of others, that he would always have to care what he said to Kyra, and how much he allowed her to know.

But she was coming with them; he had decided what was to be, and making the decision had put his mind at rest.

He felt strangely at peace for a man leading troops to join in a great battle.

He walked the stairs to the tower room and hesitated outside the door, then opened it and walked in.

Kyra sat before the fire, soft white gown around her shoulders, eyes wistfully upon the flames, hair falling in golden tendrils down the length of her back. A soft, clean breeze whispered in from the night, catching the flames, and they danced, and shadows played against the walls. The room was both cool and warmed, in a glow and darkened, and she seemed a picture of incredible beauty, sitting there in the light and the shadow.

She heard him, turned, and started to rise, and he shook his head and came to her by the fire. He sat behind her, enveloping her in his arms and drawing her back against his chest so that they both watched the dance of the flames.

"We ride tomorrow. When the horses are gathered, the supplies are packed . . . we ride."

"Where?" she asked.

"North."

She turned slightly, smiling. "You don't believe in me at all, do you?"

"Kyra—"

"It's all right; it doesn't matter. You said that I need to know just who you are—and I know who I am. And I am the daughter of an English lord. You should not trust me.''

"There's a place . . . beyond Stirling.''

"Will the rebels try to take Stirling?''

He didn't answer her. "There's a village that's small, quiet, where the real hills begin. The English don't bother with the tenants there, for the land is craggy and poor, and the houses are sparse, the sheep give poor wool, and the cattle are skinny. It is held by the Church, by the Bishop of Glasgow, and though he is a known insurgent, the king has thus far forgiven him his every move. You'll be safe there.''

"Thank you,'' she said quietly. "I do have kin, my mother's people. They are MacLeods.''

"I know about your mother's people; you are safest where I tell you to be now.''

"But—''

"If we fail, Darrow will come looking for you. Your mother's family could suffer for harboring you.''

"But what about the people in the little village? Your people. Will I put them at risk if . . . if you fail?''

"No. They know what to do if the battle is lost. No matter what, there will be survivors, someone to tell our families that they must escape to the Highlands. They will know where to go. The chieftains are strong and crusty fellows in the deep mountains, fiercely independent. Not even the Romans of old went after them. The English . . . will not be bothered. They will ride to recapture the strongholds in the north and to the east that Wallace and de Moray seized from them through the year past.''

"And what if the English do not win?''

"Then there is nothing to fear.''

"But what of . . . the future?''

"The future? God only knows. If we win . . . Edward will be furious, naturally; he will raise an army to come after us again—he'll lead the attack himself this time. You know him better than I, and it's what he'll do, don't you think?"

"Aye," she agreed.

"And then! As to Scotland . . . Balliol remains deposed, his Comyn relatives are would-be kings, and young Robert the Bruce, Earl of Carrick, would be king, though God knows, I doubt he rides with us against Edward now. Perhaps there will be a guardianship again."

"And what will you do? Go home?"

"Well, I have no home anymore. It is ash."

"You can rebuild."

"Maybe. I don't know yet."

"You have seized this castle."

"Aye, but . . ."

She turned her head, looking up, trying to read his features. He shrugged. "It's borderland. There will never be peace here. There may not be time to rebuild anything else. Edward may march on us too quickly." He lifted his hand. "It doesn't matter what we speculate. Only time will tell."

She nodded, easing back in his arms, watching the fire. "Arryn?"

"Aye?"

"Well," she said softly, "I would not have you accuse me of caring for you too deeply . . . but I pray with all my heart that you come through the battle safely. I would pray that you not fight, but such a prayer would be useless. And so I pray that you survive."

He rested his chin atop her head. "Thank you, my lady. That's quite a kindness from a conquest so wretchedly abused."

Her hands lay upon his lower arms where they folded around her. Her fingers tensed upon his arms. "I will live," he said softly. "Don't fear; I will live, and you will be safe."

She shook her head. "I'm not afraid for myself. Running to

the Highlands had been a thought when I escaped here to the forest.''

''Oh, you did not think to escape to England?''

''Aye, I did. But . . .''

''But what?''

''Edward would have found some other wretched soul to whom to give me in marriage.''

He laughed softly. ''So it is, with women and prizes.''

''You find it amusing because you are not a package to be bartered, sold, or given for the right price or action.'' She was quiet for a moment, then she asked softly, ''Was your wife of your choosing? Was she promised to you as a babe? She was Jay's relation, so I heard.''

Tension filled him. He could not talk about Alesandra, not to Kyra.

''I'm sorry!'' she murmured softly. ''I tread on hallowed ground. Forgive me.'' She started to push away from him, as if she would rise. He tightened his arms around her, holding her against him. ''I knew her forever; aye, she was Jay's cousin. We married because we both grew up—but not because of an old betrothal, but because we were ready to do so.''

''It sounds so wonderful.''

''Aye. Wonderful. Until she was murdered.''

She pushed away from him, turning to study his face anxiously again. ''Kinsey will be in the battle. Surely, if he rode from here, he was to join the king's army. You mustn't look for him, Arryn. There will be thousands of men on the field; you can't hunt for him to kill him, or you will wind up dead yourself.''

''I have to find him, Kyra.''

''If the Scots take the day, you will find him in time. The English will hold nothing more than borderland and Berwick— if that. Don't risk your life to find him. His death is not worth your life.''

He hesitated, meeting her eyes. She seemed so grave, so sincere. He smiled ruefully. "Aye, lady. I would give my life to take his."

"Because you feel guilty. You killed Darrow's kin, and he came after you in revenge. You didn't expect such a vengeance, and you weren't there to die for your wife! Arryn, you could have done nothing else when you met Angus Darrow. You had to fight. And you couldn't have known. My God, there has been so much bloodshed, so very much! You cannot hold yourself responsible!"

He touched her cheek, eased her from him, and rose. "But I do," he told her, and he walked to the fire. He placed both hands on the mantel and stared into the blaze.

Fire . . .

He felt her arms coming around him. She laid her cheek against his back. "It is the last night we will spend here, isn't it?"

He heard her turn away, and when he turned, she was in the process of letting her tunic fall to the floor. The undergown of softest, gossamer linen fell atop it, drifting like a cloud to billow at her feet. The fire played pure gold over the exquisite curves and shadows of her body, the roundness of her breasts, the lean hollow of her belly, the flare of her hips, the length of her legs. Her hair seemed to be an endless cape of dazzling spun metal, catching the firelight in shades of silver, copper, and gold. Her eyes touched his, emerald in the firelight.

Brilliant, glittering.

She turned and walked to the bed.

Aye, it was the last night they would spend in the tower room.

He left his clothing atop hers. He started down to the bed. But she rose on her knees to meet him. Her arms slipped around him. Her fingertips played over his nakedness. She sought his lips. He crushed her to him, met her kiss. She broke from him.

Her lips played over his shoulders, throat, chest. Her fingers followed his spine. She kissed and kissed, stroked, caressed. . . .

She moved against him.

She'd learned so much. . . .

And so much was instinct. . . .

He felt her touch, savored, soared, cried out hoarsely and dragged her to him, and down, and met her eyes, and was one with her. . . .

The fire burned. . . .

Flamed and rippled.

The night passed.

They made love again.

And again . . .

She woke alone.

She could hear the great cacophony of sound going on below. The clang of harnesses, the shouts of men, the clatter of horses' hooves. Commands given, commands received. It was surprising that it had taken so much time for the noise to awaken her.

She rose, shivered, reached for a fur to cover herself, then hurried to wash and dress. As she dug into her trunk, she realized that she was dressing to leave—that God alone knew if she would ever return.

There was a tapping on the door; she hugged the fur to her.

"It's me, my lady!" Ingrid called.

"Come in."

Ingrid entered with a flourish of energy, her cheeks flushed. "Oh, my lady, you should see it all, the baggage carts, the weapons, the activity. Oh, but you will see it. And you must pack lightly, Sir Arryn says, but remember, too, that if something is a treasure to you, well, it must come, for none of us knows . . . well . . . you know. So tell me, what shall we bring?

Your warmest cloak, for though it's summer now, we could be in the Highlands come the winter if—''

She broke off, crossing herself.

Kyra sat back, smiling. "Ingrid, you're riding with the heathens?''

Ingrid turned pinker. "My lady, you tease me so. I ride where my Swen rides, and that's a fact. And I would not leave you, Kyra.''

"I'm grateful, glad that we'll be together.''

"Oh, and Father Corrigan rides with us, and Tyler Miller, and so many others. We'll do well enough; don't be afraid.''

She wasn't afraid of leaving Seacairn, Kyra realized.

She had been afraid to stay.

And she was afraid for Arryn.

"Ingrid, don't you be afraid. We'll be just fine.''

"Oh, my lady! Can you believe it? *We* are running with the rebels!''

The intruders were *rebels* now, Kyra noted, rather than *outlaws.*

"Aye, we're running with the rebels!'' she said softly.

A few hours later, they were ready.

Between the men and the horses, the cavalry and the foot soldiers and the pack animals, they filled the courtyard.

The commotion continued, despite a semblance of order. There were many good-byes to be said. Ingrid cried, parting from Gaston. Gaston was left as steward of the fortress, and Hamlin Anderson, one of the tenant farmers, was left as something of a sheriff. Hopefully neither of them would be an offense in the least to the powers that returned to Seacairn, be they English or Scottish.

Among Arryn's men, there were many who had formed friendships with the tenants and villagers of Seacairn. A few soldiers had fallen in love with farmers' daughters. There were promises, tears, hugs ... and summer flowers thrown before the horses' hooves as they pranced in the courtyard.

Before leaving the castle, Kyra went down to the crypt.

She had never liked the crypt—she had never liked the dank, dark lower realm of the fortress in any way. But she carried a flaming torch ahead of her, and she went because she felt compelled. She had packed her father's cloak, rather than her own. His brooches, his rings, a little jeweled dagger he had worn for dress occasions. But she was leaving *him* behind, his home, the home he had given her, and though she knew that she had to leave, she could not help but feel a tug of pain for leaving this place behind.

She knelt before her father's body. "Pray for me!" she whispered to him. "Pray for me."

"Kyra."

She spun around. Arryn had come down. He walked to her, drew her to her feet. "It's time; we have to ride."

She nodded.

He glanced to her father's resting place. "He will fare well enough!" he said softly. "He rests with his sword at his side."

"Aye," she said softly.

"Come."

Tears stung her eyes.

She refused to shed them.

He took the torch from the bracket where she had set it, and caught her hand with his free one. She left her father's grave and followed Arryn up the stairs.

Gaston was at the entrance to the great hall. Kyra hugged him and drew back without words.

"God willing, we'll meet again, lady," he said.

"God willing, and God keep you, Gaston!"

She went out. Jay held her mare. She mounted and took her place in the line of men, baggage, horses, and foot soldiers.

She saw Arryn mount Pict. He shouted a command, and they began to move.

She passed beneath the portcullis, and kept her eyes ahead. She didn't look back until they came to the crest of a hill.

The sun was setting. The fortress was bathed in a red glow. Seacairn was beautiful, caught in the dazzle of the sunset and the glitter of the river sweeping around the stone. She lowered her head, afraid that she would burst into tears.

"It is stone, my lady," she heard, and she lifted her head. Arryn had ridden back to her. "You have left walls of stone behind, but you've left them to join with the soul of a people."

When he rode on, Father Corrigan reined in at Kyra's side.

"Will I find the soul of a people?" she asked him, aware that he had listened to Arryn's words.

"If not, my lady, I believe that you will find your own." He smiled. "A worthy trade." He reached for her hand, and squeezed. "God bless you, Kyra."

"Aye, and may He protect us all!" she said.

His smile deepened. "Ah, my lady, as I always say—"

"God helps those who help themselves?"

"Aye, 'tis true!" he told her.

"Um."

"There is another saying."

"Aye?"

"The lord God works in mysterious ways."

"Amen, Father Corrigan."

She looked at Seacairn against the setting sun one last time.

Then she turned and rode forward, and she did not look back again.

CHAPTER EIGHTEEN

The days on the trail were hard.

It took more than two weeks to reach London from Seacairn, and that moving quickly, with little baggage. She had traveled before, often enough. She had been to see the MacLeods, and that had often been difficult. In winter, sometimes the roads were entirely impassable. Rain could wash away trails, and baggage carts could slow down a party for days on end.

She had never traveled with an army before, an army intent on moving quickly, on reaching a goal—undiscovered by the English troops that were on the road as well.

She hadn't known what to expect at night. With her father, traveling to London, she'd received lodging in the homes and manors of other nobles, or upon occasion a tent had been raised for her, and appointed with all necessities that could be managed. Fires had been lit, food had been cooked, she'd been warm, she'd slept on a mattress.

Not so now.

There were no fires; they slept in the woods. Someone was always on guard. The first night she bedded down on her saddle by Father Corrigan's side, but in the middle of the night Arryn came to her, took her hand, and led her down by the little stream near their encampment. There, amongst the rocks and the trickling water, they made love with no words exchanged. They bathed, shivering. She stayed with him, sleeping with his warmth, his chest her pillow.

He had come for her again the second night.

Their food was cold and sparse, though water was plentiful. They rode for endless hours. She never complained. As she lay against him the second night, he asked her, "Don't you miss the down of your pillow?"

"No. The nights are beautiful."

And I am with you.

She was careful not to say such words.

"You are a true outlaw," he told her, and that was all.

During the day, she mostly rode near Father Corrigan, since their party was so big. Arryn and his close advisers, the men she had come to know the best, rode ahead, often testing the trails far in advance. The English were out there in the thousands.

There were the pack animals to be seen to as well—and the foot soldiers, the supplies, and the women: the laundresses, and the women who rode just for the men. She had not known there were so many. She mentioned the number to Arryn.

"Some are wives and daughters," he told her.

"Most are not."

"Where there are men, there will be women," he said simply.

And she did not sleep quite so well that night. She had been warned not to care for him, and she had fallen in love with him. Aye, she followed him now . . . just as the camp followers did. Their trade was really no different.

The journey was long and tedious. Summer rain washed

away one trail, and they had to go back. Some of the wagons bogged down in a stream, and it took an afternoon of heavy work to dig the wheels from the muck.

Yet in time the landscape began to change to rock and cliff and gorge, with thick, heavy forests teeming in the valleys between the rising undulations of craggy, rugged land. Still, she thought it some of the most beautiful landscape she had ever seen. Brooks traveled through rock and forest, creating delightful sounds in shaded copses. The richness of summer was all around them, with wildflowers sprouting everywhere.

At different times along the trail, certain of Arryn's men would ride on ahead. They would return, riding hard, and when they did they would speak with Arryn alone, but rumors would go about the camp. They had barely avoided Cressingham's men; they had skirted the bulk of the army; Wallace was ahead of them; de Moray was behind them. They rode on. Arryn himself left their convoy for a few days' time, and they were difficult days for Kyra, for though his men were kind and respectful, she often found his cousin John watching her with speculative eyes. Arryn was careful; he said little to her. But he was convinced that she rode with them by choice, and not to seize any piece of information she might hear and flee to the English with it.

Swen and Jay had departed with Arryn, so Ingrid kept close to Kyra. Ingrid, who had loathed the invaders with a passion at first, was now trusted as if she had been with them all along. But then her love for Swen was great, and so visible always, in her huge blue eyes. Ingrid had blossomed with marriage; she was a cheerful companion, despite their circumstances.

But she was a loud snorer.

Swen was louder, so Ingrid had told her, which set them just fine together, they were a bit like the music of the pipes—sometimes very loud and discordant.

But lying near Ingrid's side, Kyra was unable to sleep. And

she felt uncomfortable, ill, as if she had eaten bad meat or cheese, or even bread that had grown too moldy, which, of course, was possible, since what they ate had been dried and smoked, and they so seldom chanced a cooking fire that it seemed a long time since she had eaten because she wanted to, and nothing tasted very good.

Ingrid's snoring became too much. She rose from her bed of blankets and her saddle pillow and started down closer to the water, suddenly wretchedly ill. Shaking, she bathed her face in the icy brook water and felt much better, and found herself thinking that it would be horribly ironic to die from a terrible disease when she fought so hard to survive the men and circumstances that so threatened her life.

The night breeze lifted, cooling her face. She sensed a sound in the darkness and turned quickly. John Graham was there.

"I am not running to the English," she told him.

"I came to see to your welfare, not to accuse you of such evil."

"Oh?" She stared at him skeptically. "You mistrust me completely and dislike me, and you don't think that I should be here," she told him.

He walked over to her; she almost jerked away when he went to touch her, but she held still, eyeing him warily. He smoothed her damp hair back from her face. "On the contrary, my lady, I don't dislike you. I admire you tremendously."

"But you don't trust me."

"It's the mere fact of your birth."

"Well, you can rest easily for the night. I'm not running out to find Lord Darrow or any other Englishman at the moment. I'm not feeling well enough to be a threat to anyone," she told him dryly.

"So I see, my lady."

She arched a brow. "So . . . you've come to enjoy my distress?"

"I've come to see to your welfare, as I told you before."

"I'm fine, I think. I'm afraid some of our food has rotted."

"Is that really what you think?"

"Why are you playing this game of a thousand questions with me?" she demanded, aggravated and unnerved. The cousins were close, she knew, and both fiercely dedicated to their goal of freeing Scotland from Edward's yoke. She had seen John Graham with others in the hall; he could be polite, courteous, charming . . . but he always watched. She didn't care what he thought of her, she tried to tell herself. But she did. He was Arryn's closest kin.

He shrugged and smiled. "There are simply other possibilities, my lady."

Aye . . . there were. She felt her cheeks flood with color, and she was startled by the rush of pleasure that filled her with the bare suggestion that she could be carrying a child.

She looked away from him quickly. "It's too soon to know for certain," she murmured. Ah, being John, maybe he wouldn't think so. He might well assume that if she carried a babe, it could belong to Darrow. But she didn't intend to fight with John, or make any show of protesting her innocence. Arryn would know. . . .

Except that she didn't want Arryn to know. Not until time had passed, not until this hint of possibility could become certainty. And even then . . .

His wife had burned to death while expecting his child.

And more than that, they would all march off to battle, and from there nothing was certain, nothing at all.

"You should get some sleep," John told her. "Shall I escort you back to camp?"

She nodded. "Aye, thank you."

* * *

In the days that followed she felt him watching her, always. He was attentive and courteous, seeing to her needs. He came to her in the evening with fresh berries, cheese from a lonely farmstead, buckets of fresh water.

"John, you needn't be so kind," she told him. "There is nothing certain."

"Not in this world," he agreed.

"And you still consider me a danger."

"Aye, that I do."

"If you knew Kinsey . . ."

"I know of him, lady, and that is enough."

She looked away from him, angered.

"Arryn feels that you are in danger from him." he said. "Only a madman, lady, would blame you for what has occurred. And only a madman would dare violence against you, or even turn from you! But then again, I have heard that he is a madman, and the concept of mercy is far beyond him. But what of the king? What of other Englishmen you have known in your life, what of all that you believe? Can you have changed sides in this bloodbath?"

"John, you should have heard Ingrid when Arryn's men first seized the castle. She called all Scotsmen heathens, barbarians, savage bastards. But watch her now! She is a child of the forest, riding hard, ready to help out in any circumstances; why, she coaxed some of the draft horses to pull a wagon out of the mud the other day. She has become a rebel through and through. She loves her Swen, and is devoted. You trust her; why not me?"

He smiled. " 'She loves her Swen'!" he quoted. "What of you, my lady? Do you love Arryn?"

"I was strictly forbidden to do so," she told him quickly.

"And you obey his orders?"

"I am a well-behaved captive, of course."

He laughed softly. "Nay, lady, not you!"

"John, you mustn't say anything to him."

"About your being a well-behaved captive?"

"About the possibility that I'm having a child."

He was quiet for a moment. "Kyra, we're going to battle against an army serving Edward of England. The best archers in the world. Trained swordsmen who are veterans of wars in France and Wales. We all may die."

"Aye," she said miserably.

"I don't think I can let a man meet such a fate and not tell him that his line will go on." He lifted his hands. "A child is a man's immortality, my lady."

"John . . ." She hesitated, not anxious to share what was personal. "He loved his wife."

"Aye, he did."

"She died, John. He is . . . he is clear that he wants no other."

"My lady—"

"I am reconciled to that. But he may not want another child, either. And I don't know if I really am expecting a child. I need more time."

"You know, my lady. You have counted and calculated since the night by the brook, and you know."

"Whether I do or not, John—"

"Tell him, my lady. Or I must."

He left her.

She rode the next day with his words heavy in her heart. She chafed, taking her place in the endless route. They traveled so slowly, it seemed! A journey that would have taken riders just a few days seemed endless with all the supplies. She couldn't bear the slow riding, the waiting, with every day more tension rising.

Then Arryn returned.

She didn't see him at first; he met in a secluded copse with his closest friends and advisers for what seemed like hours. Then he found Kyra. By then she had left the encampment for the stream that trickled nearby, and sat barefoot, her feet dangling in the water.

He said nothing to her at all when he came to her, but drew her up to him.

She held him close for a moment, then tried to draw away. "Where have you been?"

When he spoke, he didn't answer her question. "Time doesn't remain to take you as far as I wanted," he told her. "Friends will be here tomorrow to see that you and others are escorted on."

She felt cold and alone. He had just come back to her!

No, he had come back to his men, and all the people. She simply rode with them.

"So the battle will begin," she murmured.

"Aye." He was still for a moment. "Lady, put your shoes on."

She did so, and he took her hand. They started walking through a winding trail in the trees. It brought them to a rugged clifftop; he had to help her scale the rocky heights. Yet when they were there, she could see forever. The night was clear. In the distance she could see campfires. "Abbey Craig," he said. "We ride there with dawn to meet."

"The English?"

He pointed in a different direction, toward more fires, what seemed like miles and miles of fires.

"There are thousands of men!" she said in dismay.

"Tens of thousands, on both sides, although . . ."

"Although?"

He shrugged. "I believe the English may have double our number."

She turned on him. "You shouldn't fight. Before every battle such as this, the commanders send out negotiators, do they not? Edward can be merciful. He's forgiven many men who have changed sides time and time again. You can—"

"No, Kyra." He touched her hair. "There will be no peace."

She clung to him suddenly, leaning her head against his chest. "I do not want you to die!"

"My lady, I intend to do my best to oblige you!"

"Arryn?" she murmured, looking up at him. She needed to talk to him. There were words she needed to say.

"Aye?"

Words froze in her throat. No. It wasn't the time. He had just returned. She didn't want her words to send him from her now, to cause him to brood. . . .

Remember his past.

"Aye, lady?"

"I just want to be with you," she whispered.

He smiled, lowered his head, lifted her chin, and kissed her lips. "We'll return to the brook," he told her softly, and started back down the craggy side of the high cliff that overlooked the smaller hilltops and valleys around them.

They came to the water's edge. He slid her clothing from her shoulders, and unwound the great length of his tartan. She stood in the forest, shivering as he discarded his linen shirt, shoes, and woolen hose. She listened to the magic of the water dancing over the rocks in its way. The breeze stirred, twisted, whispered around him.

She walked to him, stroked the sides of his cheeks with the backs of her hands. Her fingers moved over his chest, ran through the mat of hair there. The water in the brook seemed louder; the whisper of the wind seemed to rise in tempo. A gentle moon beamed down upon the trickling water, touched it with a glaze, gave light and shadow.

He made a bed of his tartan in the soft grasses at the water's edge. He bore her down upon it. For eons it seemed that his eyes assessed her, so dark in the night that they seemed obsidian rather than blue, so intense she felt as if they stroked her flesh. Then he touched her, caressing her with an endless tenderness, and she ached, and reached out for him, and when he suddenly drew her up to him, she buried herself against him, dug her fingers into his shoulders, her teeth against him. She whispered like the breeze itself, which had become a wind, a tempest, and it seemed to swirl around them in the night, visible in the hazy moon glow. She wanted him so much . . and so much of him, the scent and feel, stroke and touch and taste. He pressed her back, and he kissed her everywhere, and the damp touch of his lips seared, and the wind chilled, and he made her hot again, kissing her everywhere but the apex where she had begun to burn, and then kissing her there. . . .

He rose above her, and the wind blew, and the night soared, and the moonbeams seemed to streak into her, and throughout her. Then they cast her down into the field of the earth once again, where she felt the forest floor, and the brook again began to trickle, the wind to whisper. . . .

She didn't sleep. She turned to him and kissed him everywhere. . . .

And then there . . .

And the woods were swept into a tempest again, wind rising, water cascading, the beat of the thunder, the beat of their hearts. The ground remained soft beneath the wool of his tartan. He covered her with his length and with the remaining wool of his garment, and so warmed, she savored the feel of him against her, the strength of his body, the smell of him, the warmth. . . .

* * *

She woke with a start.

She was alone in the forest, beneath a great oak by the brook. Her clothing was folded by her side; she was enwrapped in her father's great cloak.

The breeze stirred, the water trickled.

She jumped to her feet and let out a cry. Then she sank back to the cloak, unable to stop a sudden wave of tears that racked her.

He was gone! Gone on to battle.

It had been best to leave as he had, yet almost impossible to do so. He had never seen her more beautiful, more tempting, than sleeping beneath the oak by the crystal water, with wildflowers peeping tenaciously from roots and rocks. The colors of summer could not vie with the red-gold of her hair; the warmth of the rising sun could not compare with the feel of her flesh.

But it had been time to leave.

And God alone knew what would come.

The men were ordered to their horses, to their weapons. The foot soldiers were ordered to form. Abbey Craig was just a few hours' ride; he would go on ahead with John, Jay, Ragnor, the priest, and some of the others. The horsemen would follow hot on their heels, and the baggage would follow more slowly.

Wallace believed that the battle would be met tomorrow. Riders had ranged the area throughout the previous nights. Negotiators had gone from Wallace to de Warenne, the Earl of Surrey, and from de Warenne to Wallace. Men had gathered, armies had formed.

Scots and English.

And those who supported each cause.

Finally the time had come.

Tonight they would sleep at Abbey Craig, and await the dawn.

And so Arryn left Kyra, tenderly wrapping her in her father's cloak.

Prepared to ride, to leave the men, he halted at the arrival of Harry MacTavish, who had been steward at Hawk's Cairn, Thomas Riley, and Ioin Ferguson, men from his homeland who had stayed behind, guarding their fellow survivors in the forest at the foothills, keeping news flowing throughout the country-side and safe havens open for those who were forced to flee at different times, and take refuge.

He greeted Harry first, then Thomas, who gave him more information about English movements through the night, and Ioin, who assured him that all was well in their craggy hideaway, where they could live simple lives, and disappear into the forests and Highlands if need be.

Arryn noted then that Katherine, Jay's sister, rode behind Ioin, and he dismounted from Pict to go to her, calling her name.

She was a beautiful young woman, fair where Jay was dark, with sky blue eyes and white-blond hair. He lifted her from her horse, greeting her with pleasure. "Katherine, ah, lass, 'tis good to see you. I'd not thought we'd be able to do so."

"Arryn!" she replied, smiling, her hands on his shoulders as he held her high, studying her. He let her slip to her feet and be greeted by her brother, John, Ragnor, Patrick, and the others.

"So you ride even now!" she said with dismay.

"Aye," Jay said gravely.

"We've arrived in time to say good-bye," Thomas said.

"To say good-bye, and tend to wives and servants," Arryn

said gravely. "Harry, I'm trusting their lives to you. If the battle should go badly . . ."

"See that all disperse to the Highlands, keep low, aye, Sir Arryn, but I'll not believe this cause lost! And God bless you, if you win, why, we'll be with you at Stirling!"

"We don't intend to lose. But we surely lose the real war if we let the king annihilate us all, eh, my friend? If we do or do not take this day, it will not be the end of it. The rebellion lies in the hearts of the people; yet if we win, I wager, Edward will not let such a victory be the final word."

"Aye, Arryn!" Harry said woefully.

"Keep special guard of the Lady Kyra," John suggested, mounting his horse.

Arryn looked at him sharply.

"She may be in the greatest danger," John said.

"The Lady Kyra?" Katherine demanded suddenly. She stared at Harry, who flushed. He'd met with Arryn a day before, arranging to come here rather than having the armed men move farther from the field of battle.

"The Lady Kyra, Kinsey Darrow's betrothed, is *here?*" she demanded.

"Aye," Arryn said. "She will be among you."

"She will not!"

"Katherine," Arryn said. "She will."

"Why?"

"Katherine, we haven't time for this."

"Arryn, please! What do you mean, we have no time for this? This is our lives, and the deaths of so many! Why is she here?"

"I couldn't leave her."

"Why couldn't you have left her?"

"She would have been in danger."

"She would have been in danger?" Katherine said incredulously. Tears stung her eyes. He was impatient to be off, but she had endured much, and so he forced himself to answer calmly.

"Aye, she'd be in grave danger. Katherine, you don't understand—"

"I don't understand?" she whispered with angry indignation. "Arryn, I was there when Darrow and his men came to Hawk's Cairn. I saw what was done, I lived what was done, I heard the screams . . . I smelled the burning, the death. . . . How can you do this, how can you bring *her* here, among us?"

"Katherine, leave it be!" Jay said firmly.

"Leave it be? I cannot!"

"Katherine, she is here. I have done what I must," Arryn told her.

"She'll betray us."

"And how would that be?" he demanded with exasperation. "We're not hiding out in a forest now; we're not a small band of men seeking to strike and run, to hide from the authorities! We're thousands, gathering for a great battle! Today, the men and I join Wallace at Abbey Craig, and from there the battle is waged. What will she do, go out and tell the English that aye, there is an army of thousands formed to meet them? My dear, they are aware of it already!"

Katherine stared at him, having no answer. "She shouldn't be among us!"

"Katherine, if it distresses you, I am sorry. There was no choice," Arryn explained. "Darrow might have killed her."

"Darrow might have killed her; Edward would have killed him. Good riddance to them both!"

"Katherine!" Jay said.

"I wish they were both dead."

Jay walked forward, taking her by the shoulders. "Katherine, I can't make you like it that she is here, but you must accept it. Be courteous; it's all I ask."

Katherine stared at her brother, her jaw squared. "She is English."

"Half English," Jay corrected.

"She is here, and that is it!" Arryn said, understanding, but impatient again. The work ahead mattered, and if it did not . . .

Well, then, all was lost anyway, and he was not of a mind to make excuses for his actions to any woman.

"So she is here! And only half English! " Katherine said. She wrenched free from her brother and came to stare at Arryn stormily.

"Katherine, no more."

"I watched your *wife* die, Arryn."

"Katherine, no more!" he repeated.

"I won't stay with her. I won't eat with her, sleep with her near—"

"That must be your choice."

Katherine gasped, blue eyes troubled and wide. "You would forget your own people?"

"Katherine, I've forgotten nothing. And I will explain no more. Don't eat with her, don't sleep near her—keep your distance from her. She is none of your concern."

He turned sharply from her then, guilt weighing down on him. But it was not an argument that could be quickly won, and it was time that they rode.

"God go with you all!" he said, looking them over as he mounted Pict once again.

"Aye, Arryn! We'll be waiting!" Thomas said.

Katherine stood stubbornly, ignoring her brother as he mounted his horse. Then she suddenly raced forward, throwing herself against his leg. "Jay, you big bloody fool, you watch yourself in battle now!"

"Aye, sister, I always do." He reached down, patting her head.

"I'll see you at Stirling! And we'll dance on the hills in victory!"

She ran along as they started to ride out; then she looked up at Arryn. "God guard you and guide you, Arryn."

"Aye, lass, thank you."

"I will not be nice to *her,* Arryn!" she cried.

"As if the lass were ever accused of being *nice!*" Jay muttered dryly at Arryn's side.

Arryn smiled, then reined in quickly. He reached down, caught her hands, drew her to him, and kissed her cheek. "Take care of yourself, Katherine."

She nodded, biting her lip, falling back.

Arryn spurred his horse. It wasn't a time to deal with domestic issues.

They started to race across the countryside.

For Abbey Craig.

Kyra rose slowly, feeling as if she were a very old woman.

She wished that he had wakened her; she wished that they had talked.

She wished that he had not ridden away, that the battle was not imminent. It was true that war was terrible! The victors would pursue the beaten, strike them down.

So much death, so much blood!

Shaking, she walked to the cool brook with her father's mantle wrapped around her. She had to stop thinking about it. Somehow she had to endure the waiting. She knelt and doused her face in the water, rinsing away her useless tears. She sat back upon the embankment and heard a twig snap.

She turned around.

A slim, angelic-looking blond girl leaned against the trunk of one of the oaks. Startled, Kyra rose slowly, hugging the mantle closer, looking at the girl in return.

"Hello," she said curiously.

"So you are the Lady Kyra."

"Aye. And you're . . ."

"My name doesn't matter. I would not want to hear it from your lips."

"Ah," Kyra murmured smoothly. "Then why have you come here to talk to me?"

"I haven't come to talk to you. I just came to see what an English whore looked like."

The girl spoke with frightening venom in her words. Kyra wasn't at all sure how to respond to her, and she realized that whoever she was, she was not from Seacairn. She felt her hands trembling, and she knotted them into fists behind her. She would betray nothing of her unease to this girl. She had to pray that the battle came. . . .

That the battle was won. And that she might quickly ride to Arryn again.

If the battle was won. *If* Arryn lived.

She felt ill, as if her heart were sinking. She wondered if she could bear the fear, and the waiting, and not knowing. . . .

And just who was this girl who wouldn't identify herself? And what did she mean to Arryn?

Would it matter, if he perished?

She clenched her hands more tightly, drawing strength from the effort. She spoke quietly, without betraying the slightest temper.

"Well, you've come, you've seen me, you've been vulgar and rude. Goal accomplished, whoever you are. So run on now, and leave me be."

To her surprise, the blond woman pushed away from the tree and started to leave. But she paused, turning back.

"You may bewitch men, my lady, but I am not so easily fooled by a face and form. Take care with me, for I know you for what you are! I can use a sword, and I'm very good with a knife, and you take one wrong step toward me, and I will kill you. Do you understand?''

Startled, Kyra weighed her answer carefully. ''I don't know what you think you know about me, but I never hurt you.''

''Oh, lady! You cannot begin to know!''

''*I* never caused you pain. But I am fond of living. And I know how to use a sword and a knife. So I've a suggestion: let's keep far apart in the future, shall we?''

''When you are in hell, Lady Kyra, we will be far enough apart, and only then!''

With that exit line, the young blond woman left her at last.

Kyra turned back to the water, feeling dull and heavy with dread. The men had gone on to battle. God knew what the day would bring come tomorrow. She might never see him again. . . .

She heard a movement in the trees and turned quickly.

She saw no one. And yet . . .

There seemed a strange whispering in the trees, as if someone had been there. She felt a tremor of warning snake up her spine.

Someone had been there.

Watching her.

Still searching the trees, Kyra frowned and wondered if the blond woman had come back to watch her. No. There was nothing furtive or surreptitious about the blond. She was angry, hated Kyra with blunt honesty, and that was that.

She was not likely to spy on her in the forest.

Watch her.

She was being ridiculous, she thought.

Because Arryn had come and gone so quickly. And because the time had come for Scotland to stand.

Or fall.

The breeze picked up, the leaves rustled, and there seemed to be a whispering in the forest again—the bare sounds of the brook, the wind, the small creatures that scurried about, that lived here. She was imagining evil within those natural sounds.

She heard humming. Ingrid was coming. Her maid came into the copse. "Ah, my lady, there you are! Sir Arryn said you were to sleep and not be disturbed, that it was better to ride to war without waking you. But they will take the day; aye, lady, don't be afraid—I know they will."

Ingrid smiled brightly, curling her fingers around one of her long braids. She smiled. Then she burst into tears.

"Oh, Ingrid!" Kyra stepped forward, putting her arms around her, hugging her closely. "You're right! They will take the day."

"His people have come, you know. To be with us, protect us. But Harry—a fine fellow, he was steward at Hawk's Cairn—says we may wait a bit before moving on. We're close here to the battle, aye, but far enough away to run with due warning. Oh, my lady! If they fail, if my Swen is killed, it won't matter if I run; he is my life!"

"Swen is bigger than five men put together, Ingrid. I'm certain he'll be fine."

"If Swen is bigger," Ingrid said, and it was apparent, even through her sniffs and sobs, that she was proud of her husband's great bulk, "then Sir Arryn is stronger. And abler! Oh, my lady, they must triumph; they must!"

Her sobs came hard again. Kyra tried to soothe her.

Yet, she looked past her. . . .

It seemed, again, that the trees were watching her. That there was evil in the whisper of the wind.

Eyes!

In the shadow and the light, branches waved softly, leaves rustled.

And again the feeling snaked along her spine.

She was being watched.

By whom?
Why?

Aye, the time had come!

He smiled, knowing that she was aware, that she was uneasy.

He had waited; he had played the game of the sycophant. And they were all such fools.

The English would win; the Scots would be ground into the dirt. Blood would run and run and run, because the traitors who were not killed would meet their fates at the hand of the law. Aye, the law decreed what became of a traitor! English law. The English law of an English king And those who had served the glory of England . . .

Would be rewarded.

He would be rewarded.

The Scots had ridden on; he had learned all that he needed to know here. It was time to join with his own kind again; men who were powerful, men who would be victors.

Oh, aye!

He would be rewarded.

He slipped quietly from the woods, and began his own journey to the battle.

The Scottish rallied to Wallace's cry.

They had been coming for days, weeks, from many parts of the country. Some of them were poor tenants; some of them were rich men. There were Highlanders and Lowlanders, Picts, Scotia, Britons, Angles, Norse, and more, descendants of all the many tribes and peoples who had come to make up the realm of Scotland. Many of the great lords, men who had sworn allegiance to Edward, did not come.

Their vassals did. Their men-at-arms came, men who could

wield swords, ride heavy destriers into battle—men who could slash and slay, and tear down an enemy.

That night, that summer's night, they encamped with great force on the heights of Abbey Craig. Old friends greeted one another. Men wounded in past fights with English embraced other scarred individuals. New faces came, and all of them the people of a country who would fight beneath a man who was not a king. He didn't fight for glory, and neither would they. They would fight for Scotland.

Gathering at Abbey Craig, they could see the fires of the English as well, stretching endlessly into the night. Thousands of them. Perhaps tens of thousands.

Arryn, as did many others, stood upon the heights and watched the fires burn. The various greetings of the men began to die down, the boasting, the laughter, the raw and bawdy jokes that sustained them and gave them bravado here tonight. They must have such energy, gusto, determination—and such desperation. Such spurs in the heart and soul were the weapons the English would not have.

He was quiet, watching as the men greeted old friends and relations. They drank, but most of them sparingly. They laughed, grew grave over friends and relatives lost, imprisoned in England . . . executed as traitors.

He hadn't joined in, but stood some distance away. His closest companions were near him, but his forces had grown so large, and were from so many towns and villages, that they were staggered throughout the encampment as well. He didn't see the priest, Father Corrigan, but then the priest seemed to be an industrious man, ready to bless men and help them with sword techniques at a moment's notice.

John came to where he stood.

"Your great army is raised," Arryn noted. "You have sworn by Wallace all this time. And he has united us."

"Aye, well, he needed Andrew de Moray. Andrew is a richly

landed fellow, with admirable lineage. But that isn't all. He's a fierce fighter, and ne'er a coward—nor has he ever vacillated for the favor of a foreign king. His raids against the English were as fierce as any Wallace took on, and perhaps better known."

"Well, then, two great men have brought us together."

"Aye," John said. He hesitated. "Arryn?"

"Aye?"

"Did your lady speak with you before you rode?"

"My lady?"

"Kyra."

"Ah." He studied John. "Now she is my lady? I thought that you did not like her—or did not trust her, rather."

John lifted a hand. "Her eyes are honest," he said after a moment.

Arryn studied him, then looked toward the gathered men again. "I did not wake her when we left," he said quietly. "Why?"

John seemed to hesitate, then shrugged. "No matter, not for now. . . . Have you watched the English encampment?"

"Aye."

"It's large."

"That it is."

"Do you think we'll die?"

Arryn shrugged, then grinned. "Nay—I've promised not to do so."

"Well, then, the clan will live on."

"The clan is prolific—there are already many of us, from many areas of the country."

"Aye, there are many of us. Many . . . to live when we are gone, to cherish, I pray, this country we would win for them."

"John, is there something more you meant to say?"

Strangely, his cousin hesitated. "No. Not unless you think

you're dying. Then call me over from wherever I am on the battlefield—you can assure yourself I will be close."

"John—"

"Excuse me, cousin; I see a fellow with whom I need a word."

His cousin left him. Arryn watched him, curious, frustrated.

Had he spoken with Kyra? To what end? Had John suddenly decided that she should be his lady, and that he owed her concern and protection?

She would be cared for, come what may. She would be safe. Harry might wait for news of the battle, but when the first hint of danger reached him, he would get the women well into the Highlands. Outlaws, brigands, wild men indeed. The Highlanders were the fiercest of the clans, and they would forever protect those entrusted to them.

Still, if they survived the coming battle . . .

He'd make John explain himself.

But John didn't return. Arryn remained apart. Friends urged him to join them. He courteously refused, needing to maintain his solitary vigil. The day to come meant so very much.

Vengeance.

Freedom.

The men, in their different groups, grew quieter. The hour grew later. The fires burned lower.

A lone piper began to play an outlawed song.

And suddenly the darkness seemed to come alive with the sound of the pipes. The haunting wail rose higher and higher in the night, like a lament to heaven . . .

Or to hell.

Amidst the wheeze and whine of the pipes, a cry began to come as well, a cry from the lips of men.

Higher, louder, a battle cry. Their courage, their resolve, anger, and passion, joining on the wind.

Come the dawn, that courage would be tested.

CHAPTER NINETEEN

He rode alone, taking care with his direction. It was easy, however, to avoid the trail of the large contingent traveling with Sir Arryn.

As he neared Stirling, evidence of the armies became abundant: trails worn by the heavy travel, bracken and trees flattened, the earth stripped bare of summer's produce. Broken pieces of harness and wagons, discarded in the heavy rush of movement, lay indiscriminately along the wayside; the waste of horses was rich and verdant as well.

By darkness, campfires lit the countryside.

There was no sense hiding them. The armies were in the process of negotiation; the Earl of Surrey, worn and ill, wanted no part of a battle, so rumor went. He was anxious for the Scots to capitulate.

They had done so often enough.

Easy enough, as well, to recognize the Scottish banners, and the English. Seeing the English camp, he rode harder to reach it. He felt a moment's uncertainty. There were thousands of troops, men who had come north, mercenaries, and Scottish lords with English estates who would fight for Edward. Rebels and outlaws defying the king and fighting for freedom. *Common men.*

He was stopped by the English guards as he approached their encampment. They immediately surrounded him, demanding to know his name and his business.

He quickly called out his name, telling the guards, "I'm liege man to Lord Kinsey Darrow, and it's important that I find him."

"Lord Darrow!" one of the men repeated, looking to another.

"Aye, Darrow's here; he pledged himself and his men to de Warenne earlier, as is right, giving his feudal duty to the king!" said another of the guards. "Darrow and his men camp yonder; follow the path there, and you'll come upon them."

So he began his trail through the multitude of Englishmen, the tassel-adorned tents of the rich, the cruder shelters of the lesser men. It was staggering to see just how many men there were, how the tents seemed to stretch forever. Knights talked and drank and gambled by their quarters; their squires polished swords and shields, and tended to horses and harnesses.

He heard the incessant clamor of bagpipes, coming from the distance.

And then he saw the banners that designated Lord Darrow's camp, and again he was accosted before entering the inner circle, where Darrow's tent was pitched.

"Who are you? What's your business with Lord Darrow?"

"Sir Richard!" he said quickly. "It's me—"

Before he could say more, Sir Richard Egan was on him, dragging him from his horse, slamming him down to the ground. Darrow's right-hand man was strangling him.

"Wait, wait!"

"You pathetic, whimpering bastard!"

"Wait! I have news!"

"Let him up, Richard!"

The noise of their struggle had apparently brought Darrow from his tent. Richard looked at him with disgust, then rose as ordered.

He dusted himself off indignantly. "Lord Darrow, I was no disloyal coward! I played the game as I thought I must—until the time when I could be of real service."

"Oh?" Kinsey Darrow stroked his chin, then extended his arm to indicate the camp. "On the eve of battle, you've come to me?"

"I could not do so before."

"We should slay the dog here and now!" Sir Richard said.

"But I have information—" he began, and broke off. Sir Richard was drawing his sword.

Darrow lifted a hand, waylaying Sir Richard once again. "What information?"

He raised an arm in self-defense, rising carefully and warily. "I serve you, my lord, I have always served you. I have watched and waited, and bided my time carefully. Now I can give you something that you want!"

"And what is that?"

"The Lady Kyra."

Darrow arched a brow, a careful man. "You have her with you?"

"No."

"I say kill him," Sir Richard insisted coldly.

"She is but a few hours' ride," he said quickly. "I could not take her myself, and assure that I could keep her alive. You do want her alive?"

"Oh, aye, I want her alive."

"So where is she?" Sir Richard demanded angrily.

"Close, and guarded by just a few men. I can take you there."

Darrow looked at Sir Richard. "A few hours . . . there and back?"

"Aye, with just a few riders."

"Where is Sir Arryn?"

He smiled. "Where else? He has joined the outlaws."

"He's lying to save his fool life—" Sir Richard began.

"Why would he lie? He didn't have to come here!"

"It's a trap!"

"It's not a trap," Kinsey Darrow said after a moment. "God, no—the fierce Scots are planning their moment, their great destiny—their great death!" he finished, and spit in the dirt.

"Aye, Sir Arryn rode out this morning with his men. I stayed behind, anxious to observe the arrangements made. She is with company from his old homestead of Hawk's Cairn; they are ordered to hurry her to the Highlands if word comes that the English have taken the battle."

"Then the matter is simple," Sir Richard said. "When the Scottish dogs are beaten, we reach her before riders can get out to tell her and her companions that they must ride to the Highlands."

Darrow shrugged, reflecting on that wisdom for a moment. Then he shook his head. "No. She might get away if we wait. I could fall, as well, be wounded, or killed. No, we'll leave now, ride hard and fast, and be back before the dawn."

"How will you explain her presence?" Sir Richard demanded.

"Explain?" Darrow asked imperiously.

"The Earl of Surrey is in no mood to brook trouble."

"There are whores all over this camp, Richard. Laundresses, God knows what else. She will be my prisoner, and other than that, subject to the king. The Earl of Surrey is well aware the lady was my betrothed, an arrangement made by the king himself. I'll worry about the lady, Sir Richard—once I have her in my company."

Darrow walked up to him. "You had best be telling the truth. If it is a trap, I'll kill you. If you've lied, I'll kill you."

"And if it's the truth and you take her into your custody?"

"Then you are restored to my service—with an ample reward in gold."

He smiled, pleased.

"Sir Richard—we'll take five men, my best, fastest riders, and those who can wield a sword and still move somewhat quietly. No armor. Sir Arryn will not have left his knights, his armored men-at-arms, behind. The Scots are too desperate to fill their ranks for the battle. We'll leave immediately."

The men from Hawk's Cairn were wary of her, Kyra had realized quickly, but they were not so rude as the woman. Katherine was her name, and she was Jay's sister, and possessive of her brother—and of Arryn, so it seemed. Kyra learned this from Ingrid, though, despite Katherine's rudeness, she had not clung to solitude in her little copse all day, but come to the center of the forest home to see the men for herself.

Harry MacTavish was tall and gaunt, with brown hair and a brown beard and deep, soulful brown eyes. He nodded to her gravely when she appeared at the circle where the three sat around a small fire, whittling pieces of wood. Then he rose, introducing himself, Ioin Ferguson, an older fellow with graying hair and a weathered face, and Thomas Riley, a young man, strong in appearance at first, but when he rose to nod in acknowledgment of her, she saw that he was missing part of his right arm from the elbow down.

She couldn't help but notice the infirmity, and to ignore it under the circumstances seemed ruder than asking about it.

"From Lord Darrow's raid upon Hawk's Cairn?" she asked quietly.

"The massacre, you mean?" he inquired politely, with no taunt to the words.

"Aye," she said.

He smiled, a handsome young man with dimples and dark auburn hair. "Lady, I was born so, and handle myself well enough, but I thank you for the concern."

Katherine returned from the woods then, stiffening as she saw Kyra with Ingrid hovering behind her. They were not the only ones who had been left behind; some small distance away were laundresses, a few other wives, one man's daughter, several men's mistresses, and a few women who were what had been termed "merchants of pleasure," along with a jester, two cooks, and a smith. But the others were some distance away, having taken up quarters in different pockets of sheltering trees and brush.

"So Darrow's whore has emerged!" Katherine said.

Behind Kyra, Ingrid snorted with a dangerous sound that caused her to smile.

"Katherine!" Thomas Riley remonstrated.

"Well, she has her clothes on now," Katherine murmured, coming among them.

"Be civil; we've all a duty just to wait," Harry said firmly.

"Aye, and who is she hoping will win but the bastard who killed all our kin!" Katherine exclaimed.

"Katherine," the older man, Ioin Ferguson, said, without looking up, "I've known ye since ye were a wee lass. There's no sense not keeping a decent tongue in your mouth!"

"How can you—"

"Arryn has said that we're to guard her from danger, lass, and that's what we'll do," Ioin Ferguson said firmly. "If ye don't like it, lass, go sit among the trees. The waiting is a toll on us all, girl; you'll not make it harder!"

Katherine stared at Kyra again, her blue eyes stormy. "He cares nothing for you, you know. He loved his wife. His *wife*.

You're nothing but the enemy, a whore to him as well, so don't go thinking that you are more to him, or that you can ever be more."

But she *was* more, Kyra thought. Aye, she was his whore carrying his child.

"I am sorry that my presence makes this more difficult for you," she said with quiet dignity.

Katherine stepped closer to her. "Traitor!" she said.

"Am I?" Kyra inquired. "To whom?"

Katherine looked as if she wanted to strike her. Ingrid stepped forward. "You little foulmouthed hussy, if you speak to my lady again in such a manner—"

"Ingrid, I can manage, thank you, really!" Kyra said. "Excuse me, I think that I will return to the copse."

"And pray?" Katherine inquired. "Who will you pray for, my lady?"

"The righteous," Kyra said simply, and turned away. Ingrid followed her.

Ingrid kept muttering in indignation. To keep her busy, Kyra found laundry, and, given a task, Ingrid went off happily. She was glad to be kept working, keeping her mind from her precious Swen.

Later in the day Thomas came to Kyra, bearing a trencher of cooked meat. She looked at him, and at the plate, incredulously.

He shrugged. "No reason not to build a cooking fire today, my lady. The English are ordered to serve the Earl of Surrey, de Warenne."

"What is it?"

"Fresh venison, my lady. Eat and enjoy."

He smiled and left her.

The smell of the meat was delicious. It seemed forever since she'd had cooked, fresh meat. She was about to take a bite when she discovered she wasn't alone in the copse. Katherine MacDonald was walking toward her.

"Cooked, my lady. *Cooked!* Roasted by fire. Just like the people of Hawk's Cairn. Just like Alesandra, Arryn's wife!"

Kyra set the piece of meat down, suddenly taken violently ill. She leapt up, made it to the trees, then stumbled down to the brook. She pressed her face into the cold water, rose, shivered, and washed her mouth and face again.

Katherine had followed her. To gloat, she thought.

But the young woman suddenly seemed uneasy. "You do deserve to be ill," she muttered, but she seemed to be watching Kyra with concern. Perhaps she'd be in trouble with her brother or Arryn when they came if they were to find her too ill to ride.

If they came back . . .

Kyra didn't look at her, but felt the girl's stare as Katherine sat down on the embankment by her. "I was there!" she said, moving close. "Not even Arryn was there. Do you know what he did? What your Lord Darrow did?"

"I can imagine," Kyra said quietly.

"No, you can't. She screamed and screamed . . . it was so horrible. And then . . . and then . . . the men were still laughing, still taking turns . . . and she wasn't screaming anymore; she was just silent. But she was *alive!* I saw her eyes . . . after. Then the fire started. . . ." Her voice trailed off.

"Where were you?" Kyra asked quietly. "Where exactly were you that you were able to see her so, and yet escape the men yourself?"

Katherine stared at her with a harsh intake of breath. Then she looked at the water and started trembling.

Kyra was tempted to reach out and touch her. The other woman would have repelled her touch, she was certain.

"I . . . I . . ."

"Never mind, I didn't mean to upset you more."

But Katherine buried her face in her hands. And she talked. "In the kitchen! I hid behind the worktable. I . . . hid. I couldn't help her! There were so many of them. But I saw them; I could see up the stairs. . . .''

"There was nothing you could have done," Kyra said. "Nothing."

"I shouldn't be alive!" Katherine said. She stretched her hands out before her, looking at them, seeing life in her own flesh and bone. "I shouldn't be alive. . . ."

"You should be alive. Someone must live to tell the story."

Katherine looked at her, nodded slowly, then jumped to her feet. "You are nothing to him, you know! Whatever you say, you are English, Darrow's woman. You deserved the same that Alesandra received. You—"

She stopped speaking, shook her head, and fled.

It was later, very late at night, when Thomas came upon Kyra again, bearing bread this time. "Katherine told me that she made a point of comparing cooked food to charred remains," he said apologetically. "I thought you might enjoy this more."

She smiled, accepted the bread, and sat with him.

"Were you there, too, Thomas, when Kinsey's men came?"

He looked at the brook under the moonlight. "Aye," he said softly.

"And you survived?"

"Some of us were quickly knocked out of the way—brutally. And we were left for dead. Brendan, a cousin of Arryn's, a lad, fighting at Stirling now, tried to stop them from entering the manor. He was struck down with such a blow we nearly buried him ourselves later. I was knocked out quickly; they didn't take me for much of a threat, a one-armed man, but I handle my weapon well enough with what I've got. But there were so many of them. . . . I was caught with a mace. I woke up when I smelled the burning. Darrow's men were already riding away.''

"It seems incredible that he is alive still!" Kyra marveled. "That God doesn't throw down lightning upon such a monster."

Thomas laughed, but with dry humor. "If God were really merciful, King Edward would fall from his horse, break every bone in his body, and die a long and agonizing death. Oh, his horse should trample his privates, and kick his intestines from his body as well."

Kyra had been about to take the last bite of bread. It seemed to harden in her fingers.

"I'm sorry, my lady," Thomas said ruefully.

"Don't be. I must be sorry, since I am held accountable for Darrow's actions."

"You are nothing like him."

"Thank you."

He looked up, through the tree branches, to stare at the moon. "They're gathered now, what men will fight. I imagine few men sleep at Abbey Craig."

Kyra shivered. "Is it so certain that they'll fight tomorrow?" she asked. Then she turned again suddenly; she'd heard something.

"What is it?" he asked.

"Eyes," she murmured. "Eyes. I'm certain we're being watched."

There was a snapping sound then, and she saw a shadow as someone moved behind an oak. "Who's there?" she called out sharply. She started forward, determined to find out who was staring at her from the woods, unnerving her so.

"My lady," Thomas called.

She stopped in her tracks; the man had stepped from behind the oak. He looked sheepish at having been caught.

"Tyler? Aye, Tyler Miller! What are you doing here? I thought you rode out with Arryn this morning. Oh, dear God! Has something happened? Has—"

She broke off as a scream sounded from the clearing. She stared at him, then at Thomas. They both started to run.

"Oh, no, my lady!" Tyler said, reaching out to catch her as she started past him on the trail. His fingers wound around her arm.

Evil!

She'd sensed evil before. What a fool she'd been.

She threw her knee into his groin with all the force she could muster. He doubled over, easing his grip.

She reached the edge of the clearing. She caught hold of Thomas just before he could draw them both out in the open. She drew her fingers to her lips. "Watch!" she whispered.

Laundresses, wives, and others had scattered.

Lord Kinsey Darrow and Sir Richard Egan stood in the center of the clearing. Three other men, in Kinsey's colors were with them. Ioin Ferguson lay facedown on the ground, Harry Mac-Tavish was beneath him.

Sir Richard and Kinsey were playing catch—with Katherine.

"My lady, you must run; I'll do what I can for Katherine!" Thomas whispered.

He would do what he could.

He must have known that he would meet certain death if he, a one-armed man, was to go against five seasoned warriors. And to do what he could . . .

He meant to kill Katherine himself before he died.

"No!" she said, yet she had no real plan.

Katherine was being tossed back and forth, her clothing caught, ripping. Kinsey and Sir Richard laughed and jested at her fear and misery, and the growing state of her undress.

"Kyra!" Kinsey's shout of her name rose loudly through the night. "Come out, my love. We'd really like to play longer, 'tis a lovely lass here, but war awaits. Come out—before we kill her!"

She was tempted. . . .

So tempted to run. To the Highlands, to the chieftains there, to their rocky little kingdoms where clans meant everything, where the English did not tread, where the Romans had not gone before them. Katherine had been nothing but cruel to her since they'd met.

Sir Richard's knife suddenly rent a long tear in Katherine's gown.

If I go to them, they'll just kill us both! she thought.

At her side, Thomas was ready to stride from the trees. She caught his arm.

"No, I'll go to them."

"Over my dead body, my lady."

"That's what it would be, Thomas. He'll definitely kill you. He may let me live. I am a survivor. I'm going to get Katherine, and you have to reach Arryn and let him know what has happened."

"My lady," he said miserably, "look, they've scattered the horses."

"You'll walk! You must live, Thomas; you must get help! Thomas, you've got to get Arryn. I'm going to have his child."

Thomas's jaw dropped.

"Kyra!" Kinsey called out. "This pretty little piece of baggage has but a few minutes of her mortal life remaining."

Behind them on the trail, Tyler Miller was beginning to stir.

"See to him!" Kyra commanded. "Thomas, for the love of God, save your life, and Katherine's, and together you'll both save mine!"

Before Thomas could stop her, she started out. She'd taken only a few steps when she heard a *tsk*ing sound.

She hesitated. Ingrid was in the trees. She shook her head vehemently, trying to tell Ingrid that she must not make an appearance. Ingrid scowled, shaking her head worriedly. Kyra started forward again.

"No, lady!" Ingrid whispered. "Your sword!"

Ingrid slid her the lightweight sword she was so adept at using. Kyra nodded her thanks, then waved Ingrid away.

"Kyra!" Kinsey thundered.

She started out, the sword behind her back.

"Ah, there she is. My dear beloved, what on earth took you so long?" Kinsey demanded. He tossed Katherine to Sir Richard. Richard clutched her against his chest, grinned, and drew out his knife, bringing it to the girl's throat. Katherine stared at Kyra with wide, glazed, terrified eyes. She flinched at the feel of the knife against her flesh.

"Let her go, Kinsey," she said, addressing the man she had prayed so fervently to elude.

"Kyra, my love, there are lessons to be learned, and you must learn them, I'm afraid. Her death will be on your conscience."

It was amazing that Kinsey could be such a striking figure, tall, powerfully built, with his aesthetically pleasing features.

Yet it was always his eyes that destroyed the picture.

"No, Kinsey," she said softly, "Sir Richard will let her go!"

And she sprang at Kinsey.

He should have been prepared. Edward had often joked with him, saying that her skill with a blade was superior to his own.

Kinsey had always laughed.

He did not laugh this time, for she moved against him with the speed of lightning. His sword was sheathed; she did not give him time to reach it. She leapt at him, causing him to drop to the ground; she pressed the advantage. She stood over him, a foot on his chest, the point of her sword at his throat.

"Let her go, Richard."

"No!" Kinsey howled with rage. "Kyra will not—"

She pressed the point. "Kyra will not what?"

A drop of blood appeared on his throat.

"I'll kill her, I will!" Richard grated to her. "And we've three more men with us, Kyra; they'll bring you down—"

"But Kinsey will be dead. And he doesn't want to be dead, now, do you, Lord Darrow? He wants to go slaughter Scots tomorrow, don't you, Lord Darrow?"

"Kinsey—"

"Kyra, I'll—"

She pressed the sword point again. She was about to slit his Adam's apple. She looked steadily at Richard. "Let her go!" she commanded.

Swearing, he did so, shoving her from himself. Katherine stood dead still, staring at Kyra, stricken.

"Run, Katherine," she said.

"Kyra, let me up now!" Kinsey raged.

"Katherine, run! Hard, fast, now!"

"My lady—" the girl began, her voice trembling.

"Damn you, run, now!"

At last Katherine obeyed.

"Kyra, let me up!" Kinsey thundered again.

"In a minute."

"My men will seize you."

"If any man takes a step, you're dead."

She waited, aware that there were five of them—and her. In a few minutes' time, one of them would rush her. It was true; if she killed Kinsey, she was dead. Sir Richard wouldn't hesitate a minute before skewering her through.

It might well be worth it to kill Kinsey. . . .

No.

She carried a child. She'd always been a survivor herself; now she had to fight all the harder, for herself, for Arryn's babe.

"Kyra!"

"A minute more," she said softly.

Kinsey's eyes darted to Sir Richard. The knights with him were eyeing one another. How much time had she given them to escape?

At last, seeing that one of the knights was about to rush her, she drew back. Kinsey leapt to his feet and reached for her sword. He snatched it from her and threw it far into the woods. Then he grasped her by the hair and drew her against his form. "Kyra, when I am done with you . . ." he began.

At that moment, Tyler Miller stumbled from the forest, still doubled over. "Lord Darrow, you have her! I told the truth; there was no treachery . . . and you have the prize."

She stared at him contemptuously, remembering that she had begged for mercy for him. He had surrendered, laid down his sword.

And Arryn had granted him mercy.

"Tyler, you are the worst kind of traitor in the world. You're a snake in the grass, a rat, a pure conniving rodent," she informed him.

"But I will be rewarded."

"Aye, he'll be rewarded," Kinsey said. "Sir Richard, reward him."

Sir Richard stepped forward. Tyler, expectant, managed to stand straight.

Sir Richard smiled. "Aye, young man, yours is a just reward!"

And with those words, he slammed his knife into Tyler's gut and ripped upward.

Surprise registered briefly in the man's eyes—indeed, shock. Then his eyes began to glaze. He clutched the knife in his gut as he started to fall. Sir Richard caught the hilt of his knife, wrenching it from Tyler's gut.

Then he let the body fall.

"Reward!" Kinsey said with disgust. "After the mess he made of so simple a capture!"

Kyra, stunned, stared at the dead man at her feet.

"A just reward," Kinsey said. With his free hand, he reached tenderly to his own throat.

He drew his hand away, stared at it, saw that it was stained with red. His eyes fixed on hers with fury.

"You made me bleed!" he said incredulously.

Then he knotted his hand into a fist and sent it flying against her jaw with a vengeance.

He was a powerful man. Aye, she had never doubted it.

Powerful. Fists of steel.

She flew back and crumpled to the ground.

Agony! He had broken bone. . . .

No, just agony, no broken bone, she thought, reeling. The earth and sky rolled, faded. . . .

She blinked furiously, worked her jaw against the pain. . . .

Blinking did no good. Eyes wide open, she saw nothing but black.

Her eyes closed. And mercifully, unconsciousness set in. . . .

CHAPTER TWENTY

The sun began to rise.

Morning came.

September 11, 1297.

The English commanders, de Warenne and Cressingham, had taken positions on the south side of the Forth; from there they could look across the river at the great army of Scots assembled. As they appeared beneath the glittering sun, the king's army was a force to behold. The soldiers rode with their armor shining in the morning sunlight, their banners flying and fluttering. Many of the men wore plumed helmets. Their horses were arrayed with lavish trappings and the king's colors or those of the great houses of England. The animals came on fiercely, prancing, snorting, harnesses jangling. They came in a long, long line.

The Scots were arrayed on the slopes of the Ochils, a colorful group of men as well, though far more ragged. Some had mail; most did not. Many rode to this battle with their faces colored like their ancient ancestors, the Picts, who went to battle in war paint, thus their name.

The Scottish position was an excellent one; the English horsemen were of little use up the slopes of the Ochils; behind them lay tangled country of more hills, dense forests, bogs, marshes, and all kind of places into which to retreat. The river protected them to the left; a bend in it protected them to the right. A soggy meadow lay to their front with a causeway to Stirling Bridge—and across the bridge lay the English.

Many of the Scots had been involved before in raids and rebel actions; many had not. Some had come here for the first time today. Alexander's reign had been mainly peaceful; Scots had battled a contingent of Norsemen at Largs in 1263—and they had faced the English at Dunbar, and met humiliating defeat. This was the first time in years that an army had been raised; the first time ever for such an army as this.

The English had at least two thousand armed and armored cavalrymen, and the foot soldiers numbered in the tens of thousands. There were perhaps ten thousand Scots in all.

But, Arryn thought, they had advantages as well.

Edward himself was in France.

John de Warenne, Earl of Surrey, Edward's senior commander in the battle, was old. Very old. Nearly his own age, Wallace's, and de Moray's combined. He was sick. It was rumored that he and Hugh Cressingham, the hated treasurer and tax man, did not get along at all. Cressingham was vain, opinionated—and a thief. Nobles for the cause of nationalism and against it hated him, and believed that he had stolen money intended for the rebuilding of Berwick.

Mounted upon Pict, rallying his forces, along with Wallace, de Moray, John, and a number of the other commanders, Arryn rode the line of his men as the dawn came and both armies assessed the strength of each other. Jay, Ragnor, Patrick, Thane . . . most of his people from Hawk's Cairn were ready, still, quiet—and grim. Behind him ranked in more of his people, those men he had collected in his travels—and many who had ridden from Seacairn. So many faces. Anxious, drawn . . .

And yet ready.

He felt vaguely disturbed, as if he should have seen someone he did not. But though men were ranged with their leaders, some were on horseback, and some were on foot. John was taking the lead with their foot soldiers, some of whom were prepared to meet English cavalry with their war formations, while he'd be leading his part of the Scots' bare-bones cavalry charge.

He dismissed a vague feeling of unease; danger was out in the open today. Death lay before them all, in the boggy meadow where the English must come to attack.

Arryn noted again that their position was excellent, and that the strategy of it was probably due equally to Andrew de Moray and William Wallace. With Wallace, warfare seemed instinctive. He had trod this ground frequently during the year, having crossed and recrossed the river many times during his raids in the spring. Andrew de Moray was adept at choosing ground; he had used bog, marshes, forests, and hills before.

And still, looking down at the vast array of the English was daunting.

The English were confident.

The Scots were ready. If they knew it or not, they had been preparing for this all summer. Andrew de Moray's revolt had given courage to others. The whole country, from the Beauly to the Tay, had taken up arms. And they had come to this moment.

"We'll not back down, men; we'll not back down! Remember Hawk's Cairn," he shouted to his troops, growing anxious on the hill.

"Remember Berwick!" someone else cried, and throughout

the lines of men, shouts and warlike keenings began to fill the air.

Did the English hear? They must.

They waited, for as was custom, all armies were given a chance to back down, to surrender. James Stewart and Earl Malcolm of Lennox and several other barons had gone to de Warenne the previous night and told him that they would negotiate with Wallace for them; they had promised him men, and said that they would desert to his cause. But they had gone back to him, saying that they could not dissuade Wallace from battle. The two noblemen had pledged themselves to Wallace and de Moray and their cause as well, and though others seemed uncertain of their motives—perhaps they were buying time for Wallace to improve his tactics and position?—Arryn was certain that they were keeping their options open, and would decide their loyalty when the battle had commenced.

Wallace sent back the answer that they had not come for peace—but for Scotland.

Two friars then came forward, suggesting they surrender— and all past remissions of the rebels would be forgiven.

They, too, were sent back.

"We fight!" Arryn roared.

And then the command was given to hold.

When she opened her eyes again, it was morning, and there was light.

Her jaw hurt; indeed, her whole head seemed ready to explode.

She stared at the sun-dappled side of a tent, and she realized then that she was in agony—and in an English camp.

She started to move. Her arms ached.

Her wrists were tied behind her back.

"Ah, Kyra, my lady! You're awake!" It was Kinsey's voice,

coming from behind her. Had Ingrid, Katherine, and Thomas made good their escape? Was there any prayer that Arryn might know where she was?

And where was she? Behind the English lines at the battle about to take place near Stirling?

Oh, God, she was awake; what would happen now?

He walked around in front of her. He was in full mail, a fresh, clean tunic in his colors over his armor. He grabbed her by the shoulders, drawing her up. "Your face is bruised and swollen, your hair is wild, and still, my lady, do you know, you have an uncanny beauty! Ah, treacherous beauty—you are a traitor! We all know what happens to traitors, but first . . . well, I think that you should see the Scottish die. Come along now; I've managed to inveigle a position in the rear of the vanguard. True, all the Scots may be dead before I take my troops over the bridge, but, alas . . . I must give up something. I'll give up killing the barbarians for the pleasure of watching you see them all slaughtered."

He wrenched her to her feet.

Pain exploded in her limbs, in her head. She staggered. He swept her up, keeping her from falling. She didn't know what he saw in her eyes as he looked down at her, but it drew out an ever fiercer fury. "Ah, my lady, fear not! You can offend my feelings no more. I promise, this is not a touch of affection— I just want to make sure that we don't miss any of the battle. I've arranged to set you on your own mare. You must be grateful, of course."

"They will kill you, Kinsey," she said.

"Dead men kill no one, dear Kyra. And they will all be dead. And you will get to see it—right before sentence is pronounced on you."

"Who is in command here?" she demanded.

He smiled slowly. "Who is in command? You think that you will escape me by throwing yourself on a greater lord? I don't think that will happen. John de Warenne is feeling ill, and Cressingham is a fool. An annoying fool, an idiot. But he has less patience with the rebels than any other man. I don't think he'll be eager to help you. Come along, my lady; it's time to watch the battle.'' He seized her arm once again, dragging her from his tent.

Many of the men had already moved into position, Kyra saw, and still, soldiers, knights, and servants were scurrying everywhere. Weapons were being honed; harnesses were being repaired; banners and insignias were carried high. Horsemen went by, foot soldiers, priests, camp followers. Kinsey ignored them all, shouting for Richard, who came forward with her mare. Kinsey set her quickly upon the animal. He smiled up at her. ''There's still going to be a wedding, my dear.''

Set precariously atop her mare, her hands still tied at her back, she tossed her hair back to be able to see him.

''I'll never marry you, Kinsey. I've always hated you. There's little difference now, except that I hate you more.''

''Ah, yes! The high and mighty lady! Did you think I meant to keep you as a wife?'' he queried, his words soft.

''You can't marry me if I won't play the game.''

''You're mistaken. There are ways to make you do anything, my love.''

''What if I die before we're married? That won't fit your plans, will it, Kinsey?''

''If you think you're going to be afforded a chance to nobly kill yourself—''

''I won't need to kill myself. My mare is no war-horse. If she bolts when I'm tied so, I am dead. It's that simple.''

He hesitated. There was a flash of uncertainty in his dark eyes.

''Don't listen to her,'' Richard said. ''She is just waiting for any chance to escape—back to her outlaw lover.''

''How can she escape?'' Kinsey demanded irritably.

"Indeed, how?" she asked Sir Richard sweetly. "I mean, you are quite certain that your might and power far exceed that of the rebels!"

Kinsey came closer to the horse. He drew a knife from the sheath at his calf.

For a moment she thought he meant to plunge it into her heart, to end things there and then, but he severed the ropes that tied her wrists together. She rubbed them, looking down at him.

"You might thank me," he told her.

She watched him wordlessly, still rubbing her wrists. He smiled.

"You make a single move in the wrong direction, and I'll flay you alive. And I mean it," Kinsey said pleasantly. "Richard, my horse! Call the men to order; it's time to wage battle."

Arryn knew that Richard de Lundy was with the English now; de Lundy should have been able to warn them not to travel across the bridge to the marsh where cavalry would bog down.

Perhaps he warned the English; perhaps he did not.

Perhaps the English commanders were too confident, too enraged that a rabble army should defy them, or both. Because de Lundy had just come over from the Scottish side, the English might have been hesitant about trusting him.

Maybe neither of the main commanders of these forces was at his best; de Warenne had asked Edward to relieve him of command in Scotland, as his health was failing, but the king had refused him.

Cressingham, Edward's tax collector, was so hated and detested that his own men had trouble abiding him—he was surely ready to squash the patriots who would dare rise against him.

And so the Scots watched. . . .

And the English came.

It was a narrow wooden bridge that spanned the Forth. Two by two, the English cavalry came.

"Do we ride, fight?" came hushed whispers.

But the signal had not been given.

"We hold!" Arryn commanded. Aye, and they were holding, all of this army, under different knights, noblemen and farmers. The discipline they had practiced was now in use. They waited, waited, waited. . . .

And the English came.

A half hour passed. More and more came.

Crossing the bridge two by two.

The Scots held.

"Arryn?" Patrick said nervously, riding up behind him.

"We hold."

Hold, aye, discipline, patience. A horsefly buzzed around Pict. He whipped his tail, stamped his foot.

"Easy," Arryn told the horse softly. "Easy."

Death could come so quickly today. And if it did not . . . ?

Would this vengeance be enough? He'd spent a year bowed down in guilt, using his fury to combat the pain. If he lived today, if he survived . . .

Another half hour.

If he survived today's battle, maybe he could bury the dead at last. He could let go of the past and become an independent man, as Scotland again became an independent nation.

He hadn't wanted to cloud his mind; he didn't want to think about Kyra. But time was passing here, with life and death in the balance. And he could not help but remember her in the copse in the forest, and the way that he had left her. He would never marry her, he had told her. He would not love her.

But he had come to love her, and to need her. And far too many times, his arguments against her had been with himself, and not with her. He had felt himself so deeply in debt to those who had died. To Alesandra. Gentle, sweet, the love of his childhood, the woman of his heart and soul, who dreamed Scotland's destiny, because it was his dream. She had died in the nightmare of that would-be honor!

He remained in debt.

He would pay that debt today, and it would be with his own life, if need be.

Another half hour's time gone by.

The English kept coming and coming. He didn't want to think about the past, and he was suddenly afraid to pray for a future.

The Scots held.

Arryn looked toward Abbey Craig. Wallace was there, upon his mount, looking down at both armies. Waiting. Calculating . . .

Nearly two hours now. The Scottish army had stood—and held.

The English came on, crossing the bridge two by two, noblemen, cavalrymen, knights with their squires, carrying their banners and crests high.

Horses prancing.

Harnesses jingling and jangling.

Colors flying . . .

Then the blast of a horn was heard.

The signal. A cry went up among the men. "On them, on them!"

"To battle!"

"Pikemen! To the flank, to the bridge. Hold the bridge; hold the crossing!"

Arryn raised his sword high. All around him, battle cries went up, bloodcurdling clan cries. Mounted, with his cavalry and infantry falling in behind him, Arryn charged down into the melee. Strategy and discipline ruled; the Scots seized the end of the bridge, creating a bottleneck.

The English cavalry who had crossed over were cut off from the rest of the army. With the weight of their armor and trappings, they began to flounder in the bog. Some foot soldiers had made it across, and some bowmen.

Now all they wanted was to return, to cross that river again. The Scots were like locusts, falling on the English.

One English commander made a determined rush for the bridge, carrying a wounded man. A few of the English made it with him.

Then there were too many; they were pushed and crushed over the bridge.

Hand-to-hand combat ensued, a cacophony of steel against steel, shouting, screaming, crying, shrieking, horses dying, men falling, dying, not dying. . . .

The fighting was bitter and vicious. Foot soldiers pulled armored men from their horses; armored men slashed, axed, and crushed the men who would pull them down. Having been among the first to enter the fray, Arryn fought from the saddle at first, using sword and shield, meeting the English upon the horses.

Men he wounded were unhorsed. He went on to meet new opponents, while the foot soldiers fell on those who had fallen. He saw, a small distance away, that Cressingham, the hated English commander who had surely expected his enemy to fold and surrender, had been dragged down.

Dozens of men slashed him, crushed him, beat upon him.

Hated, he was killed with passion, and yet, perhaps, that was an unintended mercy.

He died quickly.

The slash of a sword from behind was deflected by his mail. Arryn gave no more thought to Cressingham; he turned his attention to the desperately fighting enemies who meant to take him down.

He searched for Kinsey Darrow as he fought; he didn't find

the man. Every man he fought became Darrow. And he was not the only Scotsman to fight with vengeance tearing at his heart. By his side he heard men cry out, "For Berwick!"

"Dunbar!"

"My father!"

"My brother!"

My wife!

"Scotland! For the glory of God—and Scotland!"

Men and horses slipped in the mire. Hand to hand, it was now the English struggling desperately for their lives. The fighting was fierce and close; it was difficult at times to draw his weapon.

John was at his rear, Jay to his left. Thane fought before him. Patrick was to his right. The sword-wielding priest, Father Michael Corrigan, blessed men as he killed them. Brendan, a lad too young for such battle, was to the right, engaged heavily on the one hand with a helmeted, armored knight, down from his wounded horse, while a second man, still mounted, bore down on him with a raised sword.

"Brendan!" he roared in warning, unable to reach the lad himself.

Patrick heard his cry; he turned, shouting to Brendan. Brendan ducked; the horseman was unseated.

Brendan rose swinging, catching his armored combatant in the throat.

Arryn heard a whir in the air. He spun in time, deflecting the blow of a horseman. His counterattack brought the man down backward. Arryn prepared to step forward to finish the fight.

The fellow's horse, panicked, smelling blood, backed up. The knight screamed; then his scream was silenced as he was crushed by his own horse.

Arryn's sword dripped blood, and the marsh grew deep with blood and the fallen. English soldiers were cut down, or fell from the bridge and into the chilly waters. Armor dragged them down, and the soldiers who survived the weapons of war drowned in their haste to escape. Horses screamed and whinnied, swords clashed and clanged, the dying cried out.

He was awash in the battle, besieged from every side.

And then . . .

And then as he turned, he realized he had no more opponents.

He was surrounded by bodies in the blood red marsh—men facedown in the water and muck, unmoving.

Men . . . backs to the ground, eyes open, staring at heaven. Eternally.

From across the bridge, he could hear the rout.

"We've beaten them; we've beaten them!" someone shouted.

"After them!" another man cried.

And so the English were pursued across the river, and toward Stirling.

Arryn, starting after them, heard a commotion among the Scottish. He hurried toward the roar of activity, pushing through men, making his way over corpses.

Andrew de Moray was down. Injured, he lay among the dead. "Break way; give him room, lads!" Arryn cried.

Moray's steward and others of his men were coming to him now. "Get him from the field, carefully, carefully!" On one knee, Arryn studied the fallen commander, who, as much as or more so than William Wallace, had given his name, his heart, and his never failing, tenacious energy to the freedom of his country. The heir to Bothwell, wealthy, his father held by the English since Dunbar, he had risked everything a man might hold dear.

He gripped Arryn's hand. "We've done it, man; by God, we've done it!"

"Save your strength."

"After the bastards, after them, Arryn. Wallace . . . Wallace is still standing."

"Fought like a son of a bitch at the head of his men, and aye, he's still standing."

Andrew de Moray winced; in armor, blood, and mire, it was difficult to assess the extent of his wounds. "By God, we've done it! Noble birth does not a commander make; William has proved it! And the people of a country are a greater army than the best-trained cavalry and mercenaries without heart. We've done it . . ."

"We've a litter for him," one of his men said.

"After them, Graham, after them!" de Moray commanded.

"Aye, we'll pursue them to hell and beyond!" Arryn swore.

Andrew de Moray was carried away. Arryn shouted for his horse. Mounting, he shook slightly.

They had done it.

The English might have held.

They had not.

They scattered now, and ran, and the Scots were in heavy pursuit.

Darrow's troops had never crossed the bridge.

He had watched, swearing, disbelieving, as the English cavalry that had crossed the bridge had floundered, been slashed to ribbons—and died.

The number of dead in so short a time seemed staggering. Cressingham—who had been the main man to ignore the sensible warnings of Sir Richard de Lundy that they not cross the bridge and had insisted that they attack—was dead.

They had seen him go down.

And God knew, though rich men and knights might be held as hostages, Cressingham would not be held. The quicker his death came, the more merciful it would be.

It had been horrible to watch; no matter who the men had been, such a slaughter was terrible to see. Though Kinsey had almost forgotten her, running his horse back and forth for a better view, Kyra had had little choice but to watch. She closed her eyes and turned away, but with each new cry and sound, she found herself looking again, afraid that the tide might have turned.

It was impossible. . . .

But the Scottish army of rabble and rebels had beaten back a far superior British force. Not just beaten them . . .

Slaughtered them.

And the horsemen were coming now, ignoring the fact that the bridge that was shattered was falling in. The Scottish horsemen seemed not to note that their horses swam the cold water, plunging, floundering through it.

John de Warenne, Earl of Surrey, was shouting commands; a horn blared, sounding the retreat. The horn was not needed. The English troops were in reckless disarray, fleeing as if pursued by demons. From their position, far to the rear, they could see the Scots catch up with the English. They were dragged down, beaten, put to the sword, even as they tried to flee, crawl away . . . scream, beg, cry out for their lives.

"Lord Darrow!" called one of his men.

Despite the retreat, Kinsey hadn't moved.

He refused to believe the defeat.

"Kinsey!" Richard said sharply.

"Aye, retreat!" Kinsey roared.

Retreat . . .

Her chance for escape. To run to the Scots.

To plow into the marshes and fields of dead, and pray that Arryn wasn't among them!

"You!" Kinsey suddenly roared, drawing his horse to hers. His eyes were widely dilated, glittering with a fever that bordered on madness. "You witch!" he cried, as if the rout of the English might have been her doing.

He reached out for her. She gasped out a cry, trying to spur her mare. She was boxed in by his men.

He was more than an able horseman. He reached for her, dragging her from her mare to his horse. His fingers tore into her hair and he dragged her head back, whispering into her ear. "You think you will gloat, my lady? Dance on the bodies of English dead? Nay, I think not!"

He spurred his destrier. Her added weight seemed nothing to the great war-horse.

Among the thousands of other English, they fled.

In the aftermath of the battle, Stirling Bridge was all but destroyed, but destroyed or no, the Scots used what was left of it to pursue the English. The enemy retreated. They broke; they fled, different leaders in different directions. They raced for the borders.

For England.

Screams and shouts of triumph went up. There was bedlam at first, even among the victors.

With Andrew de Moray severely injured, Wallace took full command. There were some who urged him to forget all else and lead an immediate, full-scale assault on the fleeing English, and he did order a contingent of men to follow them, and harry them all the way. They could not really hope to follow the king's army with real success; the Scots, though exuberant, were exhausted.

There were hostages to be taken from among the injured, and rich and titled men were welcomed—so many Scots had relatives who were prisoners in England, and the hostages could be exchanged.

Then there was the matter that their own dead and dying lay all over the field.

The sooner they could separate the quick from the dead, the more chance they had of saving their own.

Thane MacFadden had been injured; how severely, Arryn wasn't certain, but his men arranged a litter, and already here were women and physicians on the field, helping with the wounded—and helping relieve the dead Englishmen of whatever riches they might have on their bodies.

Sometimes, the scavengers spit on the bodies of the Englishmen, but there was little mutilation.

In most instances.

Arryn was on the field, kneeling with Jay, Ragnor, and Father Corrigan, when Roger Comyn summoned him; they had found the body of Hayden MacTiegue among the fallen. Arryn had lost other men, and he felt sorrow for them all, but Hayden had come from Hawk's Cairn with him and traveled with him a very long way. He was a good friend, a good, steady soldier, and his loss seemed exceptionally sad. Considering the number of English dead littering the ground, they had been blessed. Scottish losses were light in comparison.

But the Scots had lost so many before. . . .

It was while kneeling by Hayden that he heard the shouts of triumph and a great commotion. He turned and saw that it was coming from the place on the field where the hated English commander Cressingham had fallen. Arryn rose, watching. He felt the others rise by him.

Cressingham's body was hoisted up and carried from its place on the field to be hung from a tree. Men shouted, gloated, sang, danced like fools as the deed was done.

Then, with a chilling frenzy, the warriors began to skin their hated enemy.

"Dear God!" Father Corrigan said. "We will become those we abhor!" He crossed himself and turned from the sight.

Arryn stood still a long time, looking over the field.

So very many dead. Cressingham skinned. Knights going onward, the castle to be taken, the English to pursue to the border and beyond. Yet for the moment, it seemed a strange victory. For as far as he could see, there were dead. At least this time, the fallen were not all his friends.

Yet he felt a disturbing sense of unease, even in triumph.

Father Corrigan, having finished blessing Hayden's body, came to him.

"What's wrong?"

"Nothing—well, except that the English will come back. Edward will return from France and fly into a Plantagenet rage. And so the English will come back—this time with the English king leading the army."

"Aye," Corrigan said, and he was smiling. "But for now . . ."

"Aye?"

"For now, Scotland is ours. Rejoice in that freedom, Arryn. Scotland is ours!"

He closed his eyes. Freedom!

And yet . . .

"Can you feel it; can you taste it?"

He opened his eyes and looked at Corrigan.

"Father, at the moment, I smell blood."

Corrigan frowned. Arryn laughed suddenly, for the first time, really feeling the triumph. He embraced the priest, pounding him on the back.

"Freedom! By God, you're right; we've done it! We've won!"

Aye, they had won. They were *free*.

CHAPTER TWENTY-ONE

Morning dawned again.

The smell of blood remained. Awakening in a camp not far from the battlefield, Arryn wondered if he would ever cease to think that he smelled blood every time he breathed.

He could hear birds chirping, and for a moment a waft of fresh, cool air moved over him, and for that moment the smell of blood was gone. There was still so much to be done. The castle of Stirling itself had to be taken; the army had to be reshaped and reformed.

There were riders everywhere now, moving information with the swiftest speed possible. Barons who had sworn for Edward were now heralding the success of the two brave young commanders Wallace and de Moray.

The latter remained severely wounded. Mortally wounded, many feared.

Wallace was ready to push on.

The English, in their haste to escape, had even deserted every position they had held, and the Scottish commanders assumed they'd be heading for Berwick, that city they had so fully occupied after having so completely slaughtered the inhabitants. If not, the first great English stronghold over the border was York. The enemy had really been pushed back—all the way to the border.

John, having slept near him, rose.

"Do ye smell that, Arryn?"

"The blood and death?"

"Nay, sir! We've wakened to an independent Scotland! It's freedom we're smelling, freedom, and victory—"

"Not to mention our lives!" Jay added.

"Aye, our lives," Arryn said.

"You're not as pleased this morning, Arryn, as you should be."

"Nay, I'm pleased. Still frightened, maybe, to really grasp the truth of our independence—my God! We won, won that battle! But . . ."

"You did not see Kinsey Darrow's body among the fallen," Jay suggested.

"There were many dead," Patrick said. "None of us could know all the dead."

Father Corrigan came among them. "Darrow was not among the dead. I saw him at one point; saw his men, his banners, his colors. He never crossed the bridge. He flew with the other wretched cowards. He remains among the living."

Ragnor, who had apparently been up some time, came riding hard over to them. "Arryn!"

"Aye?"

"Wallace would see you. When you can."

Arryn nodded. "I'm to the stream for some fresh water. Then I'll be with him."

"Aye!"

Arryn left the camp to head for water.

Not the river.

The river was still swollen with fallen soldiers and horses. There was a brook, a distance farther, but it was untainted by the death and destruction of man.

He stripped to the skin, unwilling to wear the remnants of battle any longer, and bathed thoroughly, despite the chill in the water. It was good; it was bracing. He dressed, winding his tartan around his body again in the crisp, cold morning air, and started back.

He returned by way of the battlefield, and standing high, was startled to see a young woman standing in the midst of it.

For a minute his heart raced.

Harry and the others had already heard, and had come. Victory was spreading across the country so quickly; they knew, they had come.

But who was the young woman with glowing golden hair who stood at the center of the field of dead, just staring?

Kyra?

They had taken away so many wounded last night. With Father Corrigan reading mass services, they had started to bury their dead. But so many corpses remained. Scavengers, of the human variety, had come.

Now animal scavengers came as well—buzzards, waves of them, flying, soaring. . . .

Descending.

The woman just stood there, in the center of so many dead, staring.

"Kyra?" he said softly, hurrying down toward her. "Ky—"

She turned when he was still some distance away. It was not Kyra, but Katherine. "Lass! When did you come? What are you doing here, lass? 'Tis not a good place—"

"Oh, Arryn!"

Tears in her eyes, she came running to him, throwing herself into his arms, shaking.

"Lass, lass, it's an awful sight, but sweet Jesu, lady, you've seen worse! And we've triumphed this time, Katherine—"

"No, Arryn, no, oh, God! You've not seen Thomas yet, then?"

He frowned, looking at her huge, tear-filled eyes. He set his hands on her shoulders, holding her a short distance from himself. "Katherine, what is it?"

She was as pale as a sheet.

"He came for her."

"What?" His heart shuddered in his chest.

"He came for her, Lady Kyra. Kinsey Darrow came for her. Oh, my God, Arryn, it was awful. They came out of the woods, as stealthy as foxes. Most of the people there . . . fled. And the Englishmen might have pursued them . . . but they didn't care. Harry tried to fight; he was knocked down, and Ioin, too, of course, and after they left we found that Harry was alive, and Ioin, too, but just barely, and he's old, and . . . my great-aunt Mauve came down from the village, and she says that Ioin will probably die without awakening but . . ."

"Kyra, Katherine, where is Kyra? By God, did she ride off with him willingly?" he demanded incredulously.

For a moment a thousand doubts filled his heart.

She had tricked him.

All along.

Deceived him. And when the time for battle had come, she had finished with him, certain he was a dead man, that his cause was a dead one as well.

"I'll kill her!" he said softly.

"No! No!" Katherine whispered, tears spilling from her eyes again. She started to laugh, but she was crying as well. "No, Arryn! I was the one who wanted to kill her. I didn't want her taking Alesandra's place. And I was even more hateful to her when we were talking because she suddenly made me realize that I—I didn't help Alesandra."

"You couldn't help her; you would have died as well. Katherine, she would have known that!"

"That doesn't matter now. What I did . . . well, I have to live with myself."

"We all do," Arryn said. "But, Katherine, you must tell me what happened."

He heard hoofbeats; others of his men were riding across the field, coming to where they stood. Thomas, an expert horseman despite his handicap, leapt down from a borrowed war mount. Father Corrigan, clad in his robes again, dismounted as well. Ragnor had come, Jay, John, Roger, Nathan, and Patrick. And Swen was there, with Ingrid, who sobbed loudly. Swen held her back, but she looked around at all the dead men that lay on the field, and she started sobbing again.

Swen crushed her to his huge chest. "Hush, Ingrid, hush!"

"What exactly happened?" Arryn demanded, staring at the newcomers and his own men, all who seemed to have been informed already.

Each man was white faced, grim.

"What has Katherine told you?" Thomas queried sorrowfully.

"Not very much," he said, trying to remain in control. "Kinsey Darrow came after we left. Half-killed Harry and Ioin. And then . . ."

"They played a horrible game with me, throwing me back and forth between them, wagering which one would kill me!" Katherine whispered.

"And then?"

"They started calling for Kyra, saying they would kill me if she didn't show herself."

"And so she showed herself!" he exclaimed softly.

"Aye, and they would have killed me anyway, except that she knew it, and she drew her sword on Darrow—"

"I managed to give my lady her sword!" Ingrid said proudly; then she started sobbing again.

"Lady Kyra had Darrow down," Katherine said. "And she kept the point of her sword at him until they would let me go . . ."

"I tried not to let her out of the forest!" Thomas said. "I swear to you, Arryn, I tried."

"Thomas, I know that you did. But, please God, finish this story!"

"Lady Kyra insisted that she had a chance of living, and that we did not," Thomas said. "She urged us to go for you."

"But how did he find you?" Arryn inquired incredulously.

"Tyler! Tyler Miller!" Father Corrigan spit out with contempt.

Aye. Miller! Arryn knew that there had been someone he hadn't seen among his men. That was it.

Tyler Miller . . .

He hadn't noticed because so many men had ridden with him. . . .

A man to whom he had granted mercy. Kyra had pleaded for his life, ordering him to surrender! And none of them had questioned him since.

He had fought in the forest outside Seacairn!

Aye, because he could change his loyalty as easily as a tunic.

He looked toward Cressingham's raw carcass.

"I'll flay Tyler Miller alive!" he swore.

"Nay, you'll not," Thomas said. "He wanted his reward for bringing Darrow to Lady Kyra. And they rewarded him, all right. With a knife to the gullet."

"But Darrow was here! Here at the battle!" Corrigan said.

"He must have had her with him—hoping to make her watch as we fell," Patrick said.

"And now," Jay said, "all of the English have fled for the borders."

Arryn spun around.

"Arryn! Where are you going?" Jay called.

"To Wallace!" he shouted back.

"But—but we've got to go after her!" Thomas protested.

Arryn was still walking. John stared at Thomas a moment, then came running after him. "You can't go to Wallace; we have to ride after Kyra. He'll kill her. And—"

Arryn turned to him.

"She's carrying your child," John said.

Arryn went dead still. "She told *you?*" he said incredulously.

"Not on purpose. I guessed. She wasn't certain, but . . ."

By that time, Thomas had caught up with them as well. "It's true!" he said. "If he kills her, he kills her child as well, Arryn."

A sickness seemed to grip his heart. A cold sweat broke out on his forehead; rage filled him, shook him. He turned and started walking again.

"Arryn!" John called.

He stopped and spun again. "If what you say is or isn't true, it doesn't matter. I will always go after her. But I must see Wallace. He intends to attack England. Well, by God, we'll be helping him, won't we? We'll be somewhat ahead. But it will be good to know he follows in our footsteps."

"Aye!" John said, exhaling with relief. "Except that—"

"Aye?"

John shook his head uneasily. "We have to ride ahead, and ride hard and fast. We have to catch the English before . . ."

"Before?" Thomas said.

Arryn looked at John.

"Before he kills her," Arryn said.

"She said that he would not kill her; that was why she must go to him. . . ." Thomas began, but then his voice trailed away.

Aye, Darrow would do anything. Especially now, with the English defeat.

Arryn turned and started from the hill again to find Wallace. His limbs felt numb, his heart heavy.

It seemed a bitter irony to have found freedom at last.

And lost his soul along the way.

Within hours they were ready to ride.

His council with Wallace had been good; the commander had understood the situation, but he had been able to give Arryn little hope of large forces to assist should Kinsey Darrow reach a strong castle in which to fortify himself. "The men are sorely exhausted and injured; we've the castle here under siege. I intend to take war to the English countryside, and let them have a taste of what it is, but I must return to Dumbarton, there's to be a council at Perth. . . ." His voice trailed off, and when he spoke again he didn't sound so much bitter as weary. "We hold Scotland, but I am no foolish boy. Edward will come back at us. We must maintain an army. We must, as well, send diplomats abroad, reestablish our trade rights, send bishops to Rome . . . aye, there's more battle to take place now, and though I understand why you must go immediately, you must understand why I cannot. Sir Harry and a contingent remain in pursuit of fleeing forces; other knights harry the wounded and scattered troops who have fled the main body and run alone. What men you can gather will be yours. Godspeed."

He was free to leave; free to take his men and leave.

Despite his immediate anguish, fear, and rage Arryn was aware that he must use his head. His meeting with Wallace had reminded him that he would do Kyra no good if he followed instinct and just started running . . . running after her, as fast as he could. He had experience with Kinsey Darrow. The man did not hesitate to rape, maim, torture, and kill.

And she carried his child now!

He prayed she would keep silent; such a fact might send

Kinsey over the edge. With any luck, he would remember that she had been the queen's godchild, and he might realize that Edward gave his queen's memory great respect. Kinsey would have to be careful.

Except that there were so many lies he could use! She could have an accident, riding. She could fall from a cliff. Trip, and land mysteriously with a knife through her heart.

When they were ready to depart Stirling, John asked him, "How do we find her? There are so many men out there, knights, soldiers, making their way home."

"We find every last man that we can," Arryn said.

"And kill them all?" Jay asked, troubled.

"Nay, we let them live."

"Then what do we accomplish?"

"Fear," Arryn said simply.

The good thing about the complete English rout was that the knights took little time to do anything other than run. Kinsey was distracted, at least; they rode very hard by day, and slept in the open at night.

Kyra wanted to live, and in that, she tried very hard to keep from his notice. She longed at various times just to start running from the camp. But a knife would fly into her back, she was certain, and even if the threat of what was to come her way at a later time seemed more awful than such a quick death, she refused to risk it. She wanted to live for herself, and for her babe.

The first few nights, they did nothing but sleep immediately upon the ground; there were no tents or camp mattresses for the great English soldiers then. They had been left behind in the flight.

Messengers came and went, as did men. Riders came with more news of the Scots. The Scots were besieging Stirling

Castle; the force pursuing the English was riding beneath the leadership of a man named Henry de Haliburton. Knights and soldiers were still being massacred as they were discovered.

One wounded man, an English knight from York, joined their company on the third night. His name was Sir Reginald Trotter.

The whole of his forces had gone over the bridge. He thought he had died himself, but some kind soul dragged him from the water. The horse was not his own; though horses had died in huge numbers at Stirling as well, they had also been plentiful in the aftermath—the Scots had wanted to kill Englishmen, not animals. He had come this far on a pale gray destrier he'd found with its reins entangled in a bush.

He drank ale with Kinsey, Sir Richard, and a few of their men late one night. Kyra could hear his words because she'd been tied to a nearby tree. That was how she spent her nights, tied to an oak. She didn't mind, as yet, because the men were so afraid of every noise in the woods that Kinsey had kept his distance from her.

In fact, now that he had her, he seemed almost loath to come near her. She was at times allowed to ride her own mount; she was never allowed to hold the reins.

In these few days of desperate riding, she was given brief moments alone to wash and for personal necessities, but either Kinsey or Sir Richard was her guardian; apparently they didn't trust others to guard her properly. It seemed that they might have decided that she was a witch, and that in some way she would manage to turn to smoke and elude them, if they weren't careful at every turn.

It was the third night of their southward flight when she lay awake, listening to Sir Reginald talk. Having identified himself to guards and been let into the circle by the small campfire, he told the Englishmen chilling tales of the aftermath of the battle.

"Wallace is a madman, indeed. Cressingham was strung up

and stripped of every last inch of his flesh. They say that Wallace will use a strip for a sheath for his sword. They are barbarians, all painted and wild! But my God! Why, in England, there had been trouble. Revolts against the king, especially in the north, with him demanding more and more taxes for his infernal wars. But now! Now we will be united in truth.''

"And we will rise again," Kinsey said moodily.

"Aye, when Edward returns. When the king comes, he'll lead the army." Sir Reginald was quiet for a moment. "Lord Darrow . . . I come with a message for you as well.''

"A message? For me?''

Sir Reginald lowered his head. "I was caught, captured by a band of the outlaws. They are this very minute coming south.''

Kinsey looked uneasily at Sir Richard. "Aye, go on.''

"Their leader is a man named Sir Arryn. He said that I might live—so that I might look for you as we fled the country.''

Kinsey stood in a fury. "So you've come to me as a traitor, sir!''

Sir Reginald got to his feet as well. "No. I've come to you as a messenger!''

"Aye, then, what is the outlaw's message?''

"He says to tell you that you hold what is his.''

"I hold what is *mine* that he tried to *steal!*''

"Sir, I have no argument; I only bring the words. He wants you to know that he intends to have the lady back.''

"He may 'intend' all he wants. I hold the Lady Kyra.''

"If she is harmed in any way, molested, bruised, injured . . . he says that he will find you, and that you will meet Cressingham's fate, except that he will flay you alive, skin you, and then disembowel you and feed your—excuse me, sir, these are his words, not mine—sorry carcass to the dogs.''

Kinsey's face grew mottled with his rage.

"You may tell him—''

"Sir! I beg your forgiveness. I can tell him nothing. I will not see him again. I was allowed to live with the promise that I would cross the border—and not return." He hesitated again. "There will be others. And you, sir, are free to send a man to him, to make arrangements for her return at any time. Though he thinks you should die, he is willing to let you live—for the return of Lady Kyra."

Kinsey shot a glance at her, deeply disturbed.

She thought that she should pretend to be sleeping.

Too late. He saw her eyes. And she knew that he was speculating as to why she would be worth so much to Arryn that he would let him live in exchange for her.

"This man is nothing to me. He is an outlaw."

"He reminds you that the queen of England stood godmother to the Lady Kyra at her birth. The king can be cruel, and the king can be generous."

"This outlaw has no right to tell us about the king of England!" Sir Richard stated angrily.

Kinsey walked in a slow circle by the fire, rubbing his jaw. "He thinks he is warning me that if Kyra is killed outright, the king might punish me. But that is no matter. She is a traitor—and I can prove it in a court of law."

"The king's court?" Reginald said.

"A court of the king's design!" Kinsey snapped. "I am the wronged man here, sir! The outlaw stole my betrothed. And the lady turned traitor. I will prove it, legally."

"There is one other matter," Sir Reginald said.

"Aye?"

"He sends you this."

"What is it?"

Kinsey accepted the small linen packet Sir Reginald handed to him. He started to unfold it.

He jumped back suddenly. The packet and its contents fell to the earth.

"It is his portion of the flayed skin of Cressingham, sir. He admits to being somewhat sorry that men resorted to such barbaric deeds, but then, he understands how deeply many hated Cressingham, because he knows how deeply he hates you. If she lives and is returned to him, you live. If she is harmed in any way, he will hunt you down until he finds you, and you will be food for carrion.''

''He will hunt me down until he finds me!'' Kinsey said in a rage.

Kyra tensed as she suddenly saw him coming toward her, his strides long and furious. Looking past him, she saw old Sir Reginald lower his head; he was a man, she thought, sorry for the violence, and sorry for any wrong he brought to her.

She was glad that Arryn had let him live.

Kinsey kept coming, tall, powerful, his head bare, his brown hair gleaming in the moonlight, his dark eyes sharp as daggers. There was nowhere to run, nothing to do. The ropes that held her to the tree were fast and binding.

He reached her and drew his knife. Her heart ceased to beat.

He slashed the ropes, wrenching her to her feet.

She found herself dragged through the trees. His strength, in his rage, was terrifying. His hold on her might have bruised flesh, torn muscle, snapped bone. They came to a clearing within the woods. He suddenly spun her around in front of him. She rubbed her wrists, barely daring to breathe, returning his stare.

''What? What is it?'' he flared suddenly. He walked around her, came closer, moved farther away. ''Are you a witch, my lady? What about you makes men so obsessed? Do you hold such incredible riches? Is it your voice, your eyes . . . or witchcraft? Or are you simply so good in a man's bed?''

She felt herself go pale. She might have told him that it was none of those things. Arryn cared for her, aye. She believed that. But he hadn't forgotten Alesandra.

He would come for her now, she was certain, because Thomas would have told him about the child.

Arryn would not, could not, let Kinsey Darrow destroy another of his unborn children, and live with himself. His pride was too great—and his honor.

"There . . . is nothing," she said. "I am but a part of this war between the two of you."

"You have not lain with him?" Kinsey queried dryly.

Should she have lied? She never had the chance. Her face gave her away, and Kinsey shook his head. She wondered again why she had always hated him so much. Standing in the clearing, his head bare, his colors over his coat of mail, he was an imposing figure with handsome features, sharp eyes, and a powerful presence.

His lips, she thought, pursed too thin. There was too feral a glitter in his eyes. A perfect picture that should have been right . . . but it was flawed by those slight defects that betrayed the soul of a monster.

"I never wanted to hate you, you know. The first time I saw you . . ."

"You saw my father's place in this world. Lord of the English—and the Scots. You saw my mother's wealth and family reputation here."

He smiled. "Well, aye, I saw those things. But I saw your hair as well, and your eyes. My God, Kyra, no one has eyes quite like that, so very green. You must be a witch, of course. Only a witch could have such eyes."

"If I were a witch, Kinsey, I'd not have bewitched you into obsession; I'd have bewitched you into a ditch!"

He smiled grimly, crossing his arms over his chest. "Kyra, you do play reckless games. You are entirely in my power. I hold your life or your death in my hands."

"My death could bring about your own."

"I'm not afraid of that madman outlaw," he said.

He was lying, she thought.

"Are you afraid of the king of England?"

"Let's say I'm wary of the king of England," he said. "But I can hold a legal trial; I am to be lord of Seacairn."

"It's my title, Kinsey."

"Aye, but we will be married."

"Nay, we will not."

"We'll see about that, won't we?"

She shrugged uneasily.

"I still believe that Edward would forgive me a moment's insanity. Here I am, my lady, one of his most powerful knights, ever ready to ride against his enemies! A powerful man in my prime, promised a bride of incredible beauty. And then I discover that she has been lying with one of the king's greatest enemies! My betrothed! I lost my head. My anger and jealousy were so great that I snapped her long, graceful neck beneath my fingers!"

"Perhaps the king will lose his head as well, hearing that I was so murdered."

He smiled. "A gamble indeed, my lady. I never really wanted to kill you. Except in those moments, of course, of pure jealous rage. They are real, you know."

"What do you want from me, Kinsey?" she demanded. "The hour is late. You may defy the madman, but you'll be running from him in a few hours."

"Imperious to the end, eh, Kyra?" he said softly.

"Kinsey—"

"I want what you gave him so freely."

"What?"

"You want to live; I want you."

She lowered her head, shaking. She remembered vividly the times she had been with Arryn, and the way he had spoken of Alesandra. His pride had not mattered; possession had not mattered. He would never have felt his wife ruined by Kinsey's touch; he had only wanted her alive.

He would never condemn her now for what must be. Life was important. She had to live. She bit her lip.

"I have itched to seize you many a time now, Kyra, throw you against the ground, a tree—alone, with others about . . . but we've been so busy. . . ."

"Running," she reminded him. "We still need to run."

"You were going to marry me."

"By the king's command."

"Ah, but you would have been my wife."

"I thought it was your intent to marry me still?"

His hesitation was chilling. He didn't intend it, and he hadn't intended to give himself away. He didn't mean to forgive her—ever.

He meant to marry her—and then kill her.

But he did want to do it legally—have a mock trial, see that there were dozens of witnesses to call her a traitor.

The laws were written. The king had seen to that. And the punishment for traitors was written out more clearly than any other.

"Aye, Kyra, we'll marry. It will be done."

She stood in the clearing, watching him.

"But until then . . ." He lifted a hand to her. "Come here."

She shook her head. "I'll not come willingly to you, Kinsey. I loathe you."

"What? And if I touch you, you'll be so dishonored you'll plunge a dagger into your own heart."

Now she gave away too much, hesitating.

He smiled. "There's too much spirit in you, Kyra. Too much of the fighter. What an admirable quality it might have been, had you just accepted the king's decree—and loved me."

"Had there been a man there to love, Kinsey, I would have honored the king, and done so."

"Kyra, come here, or I'll plunge that dagger into your heart and claim you did it yourself rather than lie in the arms of your future husband."

"How quickly that fact spreading across the countryside will attract another lady for you!" she exclaimed.

"Kyra, come here—or die."

Her lashes fell.

Survive! She must survive.

She began to walk toward him. "Come kiss me, my love, as if you mean it."

She reached him. She tried to keep from shivering. "I loathe you," she whispered, standing directly before him.

"You cannot know the hatred I feel for you in my heart!" he told her.

"Then why . . . this?"

"I am obsessed!" he said. His arms wound around her. His lips lowered to hers. "Make it good, my lady, very, very good. I would discover what magic you perform."

His mouth molded over hers. Surprisingly, there was no cruelty to the touch. And still she felt nothing but the discomfort of him, the feel of him, the pressure of his mail against her, the physical irritation of his tongue. . . .

A taste of onions.

Onions.

He'd been eating onions. Suddenly that seemed paramount in her mind. She barely noticed that he had his hand on her breast, that he was pressing closer and closer to her, that the whole of him was becoming overwhelming.

Onions!

They must have found them along the way, eaten them with the rabbits they had killed for their meal that night.

He was lifting her, holding her, growing more and more aroused. Carrying her down to the earth.

She tried to twist from his kiss.

She would bear him, endure him, whatever he did to her. She wouldn't try to plunge a knife into her own heart, or his.

But she couldn't kiss him anymore, couldn't bear his breath. . . .

He was making noises, fumbling with his clothing, with hers. His lips traveled to her throat.

His mouth rose above hers again.

"No, Kinsey, no, just don't . . . kiss me."

"Witch! You'll do it right, love me, as you love him."

His mouth touched hers again. She pushed against him desperately. He forced his lips down hard, grindingly.

She ripped at his hair. He rose, swearing as she leapt to her feet, staggered away.

And was violently ill.

She barely heard him rising behind her.

But then she heard his anger.

"Trust me, you will marry me!" he vowed with low fury. "And then you will die, and die your traitor's death very, very slowly for this insult!"

She heard him turn away from her.

She groped for a tree trunk to keep herself standing.

Insult! He thought that she could manage such an act of such physical misery as an insult?

She almost laughed, but she didn't.

Sir John had seen her ill, and figured out the truth of her situation.

Soon enough Kinsey would figure it out as well. And then . . .

Would he want to hasten her death, just to hasten the death of Arryn's child? Shaking, shivering, she finally realized that he had actually left her.

In the woods.

She spun around, hope flickering in her heart.

But Sir Richard was there.

He smiled. "I won't blink before killing you, my lady. I won't even blink." Then he bowed suddenly, laughing. "My lady, your bed—and your shackles!—await."

She hadn't the strength to fight him, and again, the desire to live kept her from doing so. She walked ahead of him, back to their makeshift camp.

Before the dawn, they were riding again.

CHAPTER
TWENTY-TWO

There was a group of knights, dismounted from their horses, at the stream. Brendan had found them; he was incredibly adept at slipping through the trees in dead silence, and his hearing seemed so acute that he knew when other riders were near long before the others heard the slightest sound.

They had nearly stumbled upon the Englishmen, but because of his cousin's unique ability, they had held back, Brendan had gone on, and now they circled the riders.

They were cavalry; there might have been foot soldiers in their original number, but if so, they had left the slower men behind.

Now they were encircled.

Arryn gave a signal.

Arrows flew in the forest. Perhaps eight of the thirty or so men were hit. At this close range, a number of trees were hit as well.

The men who were hit went down.

At this close range, most mail could be penetrated by a well-strung arrow.

Watching their comrades fall, the others drew their swords, turning in a panic. Arryn stepped from the trees, his sword bared. Across from him, on the other side of the water, Jay appeared. To their left Ragnor stepped out, and to the right John appeared, planting a foot on a rock and leaning upon it.

Patrick stepped forward with more of the men, just appearing from the trees. With such a show, they appeared to be more than they were.

"Hold; shield your weapons!" one of the Englishmen immediately roared. Arryn recognized his colors, and the standard on his tunic.

He knew the man. He was a graybeard, but a steady, strong man. Lord Griffin Percy was from the great northern England family of Percys, and he had met him many a time as a lad at King Alexander's court.

"The bloody Scots will eat us alive!" called one of his men. "We may as well die fighting!"

"Eat them!" Jay exclaimed. "We've not been ordered to resort to cannibalism as yet, have we, Arryn?"

"I've no taste for so tough and dry a taste as an Englishman!" John called out.

"Why, you bloody outlaws!" cried the man, drawing his sword again.

"Hold!" their leader commanded furiously. Old, Lord Percy might be, but he was a commanding figure still, and his voice could compel the very wind to cease blowing.

"Hello, Lord Percy," Arryn said.

"Hello, Arryn," Percy said, and turned to his men. "This man will not skin us, spit us, and eat us. He will not even put us all to the sword—I don't believe. Unless you have changed, Sir Arryn?"

"I've little heart for more murder, my lord. We kill enough

on the battlefield. And of course,'' he said, pausing to note the downed Englishmen, ''to surprise our foe, and allow him to see our strength. Of course, I wish to make certain as well that you are leaving Scotland?''

''Aye, Arryn,'' Lord Percy said.

''The king will raise an army against us, as soon as he returns from France,'' Arryn told Percy. ''When we let men live, we have them swear a blood oath that they will not return.''

''Well, men?'' Percy said.

''How can we swear such an oath? The king will demand service!'' one of the men cried.

''The king understands such things. He will be angry, and he will rage, and he will take his blood in my revenues, I'll wager, demanding I pay his mercenaries. But I don't care to die now, and if I give a blood oath, I keep it.'' He looked at his men a long while. Then he turned to Arryn once more. ''Sir, you have the oath of every man here. Though, for old times' sake, I would like to hear how you are faring, I believe that we should now be on our way. We may gather our dead?''

''Aye, Lord Percy, gather your dead. But we'd like to give you word as well, should you come upon a man. Lord Kinsey Darrow.''

''Darrow?'' Percy said sharply. ''He should be far ahead; his place was at the end of the vanguard when we would have attacked.''

''Aye, he's ahead,'' Arryn agreed. ''If you find him, tell him that I'm following. Closely. And that I want word of the Lady Kyra's good health, and I want the Lady Kyra herself. And if she is not returned to me soon, I will indeed roast him slowly. I will bake him while I skin him. He may send her to me, alive and well, and save his life.''

''The Lady Kyra?'' Lord Percy was troubled. ''Darrow was to wed Kyra—''

''My lord, the wedding was not of her choice.''

"But surely, Arryn, she is in no danger—"

He broke off because one of his men had cleared his throat.
"What is it, Barnabus?" Lord Percy asked sharply.

"My lord, they are not so far ahead of us. I met up with
one of his men yesterday, snaring rabbits, a fellow I had once
known."

"Aye?"

"He suggested that if we rode hard, we might join them."

"Join them where?"

"He heads for Seacairn, the lady's holding. He believes that
it is border country that will take the rebel Scots a long time
to reach, since there's so much more they must do. And he
believes as well that the fortification has been strengthened and
supplied."

Arryn felt his muscles tighten. *Aye!* The castle was fortified
and well supplied. The portcullis moved smoothly; oil vats
were full, arrows were plentiful. Walls had been repaired, and
even thickened.

"What of the Lady Kyra?"

Arryn thought that he had spoken the words himself; he had
not.

It was old Percy who had spoken.

"The lady . . . is well enough, I believe," the man named
Barnabus said. "My old friend told me that Kinsey keeps his
distance from her; he believes she is a witch. He intends to
marry her still, but broods daily, planning a trial, since, as his
betrothed, she betrayed not only him, but her king and country
when she opened the castle to Scottish outlaws." He hesitated
a moment, glancing at his fellow soldiers, then at Lord Percy,
then at Arryn. "My friend is a decent man, sent into service
for Lord Darrow. He has been appalled by many of the things
done as he has ridden with Lord Darrow. He . . . he could take
no part in the attack on your holdings, Sir Arryn. He said
that he fell behind, pretended illness. He could not stop what

happened, but neither could he take part. He spoke so openly because he thought . . . he thought perhaps Lord Percy would go to Seacairn, and perhaps temper Darrow's madness.''

"You said nothing of this!" Percy told him.

"I'd not had a chance, and my lord . . ." He paused, looking around again. "Lord Percy, sir, the Scots thrashed us roundly. They *skinned* Cressingham. Wallace is making a mask from the flesh—"

"Oh, now, that's not true!" John thundered.

"But he was skinned," Barnabus said.

Percy sighed. "Edward came and butchered men at Berwick. Now the Scots have trounced us at Stirling Bridge. And now there is little hope but that we will hate each other fiercely for all the days to come!"

"He has no just cause to slay the Lady Kyra!" Arryn said to Percy, and everyone in the woods fell silent.

Lord Percy sighed. "Arryn, by law, she is a traitor. She swore fealty to Edward. He can trump up a trial."

"The king would grant her mercy."

"The king is in France."

"Men, gather our dead. I would walk with Sir Arryn for a spell. Sir Arryn! There will be no more violence against my men!"

"Aye, Lord Percy, if your men swear the peace as well."

"Peace is so sworn."

"Then come, sir, and we will walk," Arryn said.

And the sworn enemies, now sworn to peace, watched one another warily in the forest as Arryn set an arm around the old man's shoulders, and they walked down the trail together.

She had never liked the crypts.

And it seemed that Kinsey had known it, for her prison was

the crypt, the place where her father lay shelved with dozens of other corpses.

They had come upon Seacairn on a morning much like the one when she had left it. It seemed eons ago. It was really just a matter of weeks, but the world had changed. The Scots held Scotland—and Kinsey was taking Seacairn.

When they arrived, Kinsey ordered the gates opened. The guard on the wall refused, but when Kinsey promised that he would gain entrance and create a massacre to put Berwick to shame when he did, Kyra ordered the gates open.

There was no one left to defend the castle. It was strong, armed, supplied, but there were no men left within.

They rode in. Kinsey immediately dragged her from the horse she rode. His hand on her arm, he brought her to the entrance to the tower.

When they entered, Gaston quickly appeared. "Lord Darrow! My lady." He met her eyes, and saw the warning in them. Ever quick, he bowed low to Darrow. "My lord, we have prayed for your safe return. We thank God that the barbarians left the castle, though the good Lord bless us, sir, we've heard that the Scots tore into the English!"

"The English will return and annihilate the traitors," Kinsey said. He looked around as his men filed into the hall. "See to them; bring food, the best food, and plenty of it."

Holding Kyra by the arm, he pulled her along.

She was afraid that he meant to drag her up the steps to the tower room.

He dragged her down instead.

Down into the bowels of the castle.

Into the realm of the dead.

And he left her, and after he had done so, he ordered his men down. They came with torches. As they arrived, she was afraid that they had come to rape and murder her. They had not. They had been sent to see that the iron gates to the crypt were in good repair, and that she could not escape.

Hours passed. When she closed her eyes she could not help but think of the dead rising and floating around her in a macabre dance. She could smell death, inhale it, breathe it. Rot, decay, the cold . . .

The darkness.

Her father was here! she kept telling herself. But she did not want to see his face beneath his shroud. She just wanted to close her eyes and believe that if the dead could dance, he would be with her, beside her, protecting her.

The darkness and cold were terrible. Even in her mantle, she shivered. She was so cold that she grew tempted to try to find warmer covering among the corpses. But no matter how cold she might be, she couldn't quite bring herself to do so.

So she shivered, and shivered. . . .

And no one came for a very long time.

Then, when she had nearly dozed, she heard a whisper. "My lady!"

She raised her head. Gaston was at the gate. He carried a small torch. Even his dear face was eerie in such strange light.

She jumped up, coming to him. "Gaston! You've got to be careful. He is so vengeful; if he thinks that you're helping me . . ."

"He is drunk and passed out in the master's chambers," Gaston said.

"But he has spies everywhere."

"Sir Richard is on the parapets—watching. The other men pay me no mind. They feel safe here; they've been drinking, wagering. . . . At any rate, Lord Darrow never said that I could not bring you food and water."

She nodded. He offered her a skin of water, which she accepted gratefully. He had brought her bread as well, and a piece of freshly cooked meat. She hadn't realized that she was starving. She wolfed it all down with him there, asking him to give her any news he had heard.

"Well, my lady, the countryside teems with men! Those who run, and those who run after them. There was a great council at Perth, and William Wallace has been named Guardian of the Realm. Well, he and Andrew de Moray have been so named, but word has come that de Moray travels north to his own lands, and to his young pregnant bride, for he believes that he is mortally wounded. Wallace, however, will not accept his impending death, and orders that de Moray's name be on all official papers with his own. Aye, and Wallace has been knighted, some say by Robert the Bruce, though seeing how Wallace is a stickler for Balliol being the proper king, I have to wonder at that."

"But the English continue to flee?"

"Aye. They have even left Berwick."

"My God, what a victory. And yet . . . Kinsey would come here, and hold this place!"

Gaston was quiet for a moment. "My lady, all men know that King Edward will hear of this defeat, and he will return."

"Aye, but . . . something has begun. And whether he comes back a hundred times, it will not matter."

"Perhaps not. Stirling Castle fell. The one English commander with the sense to turn his men on the bridge and salvage them from disaster was made constable of the castle by de Warenne as he went running. Sir Marmaduke de Twenge is the poor fellows' name; he surrendered the castle, for what else could he do with such power arrayed before him? The Scots could starve him out. He is a prisoner now of the Scots. My lady, so many are grateful for the prisoners alone. Some of our men may be returned from their imprisonment in England."

"Aye, that's wonderful."

Gaston started suddenly.

"My lady, I think that someone comes. I must leave you.

You mustn't be afraid. You will prevail. The dead will not hurt you."

"Aye, I know."

"Your father loved you, lady. He will guard you. God, our Lord Christ, and the Virgin will guard you as well."

She smiled in the darkness. She could remember throwing herself down before the beautiful statue of the Virgin what now seemed eons ago. *What irony!* And yet, Gaston's words did bring comfort. Maybe the Virgin would protect her now. She must have known what it was like to want to guard a babe in her womb with all the strength and power in mind, soul, and body.

"Thank you, Gaston."

He squeezed her fingers. "We're here, my lady."

"Aye, Gaston. I will prevail."

He doused his light and tiptoed away.

The stygian darkness wrapped around her.

Day came.

She knew because Gaston arrived once again. He was accompanied by Kinsey's men, and brought her washwater and more food and drink. He was also accompanied by a priest, a man from a special order with a huge black cloak and hood, a man who tended to keep his head lowered in prayer, and his hands folded before him.

He had come to receive her confession, if she wanted to speak to him about her sins of witchcraft, treason, and fornication.

She couldn't help but laugh. Sharp faced, extremely self-righteous, he looked at her severely. "My lady, confession is all that can save you. Repent, and you will be forgiven."

"Kinsey will forgive me?" she inquired.

"God will forgive you."

She smiled. "Father, if you are the man who would be my

arbiter with God, I'm sorry, but I think I would do better on my own."

"You will burn in hell. Lord Darrow remains willing to marry you."

"Lord Darrow remains willing to marry my estates."

"My lady, without confession, you will rot in hell."

"Life with Lord Darrow would be hell, not that he intends I should have life."

The priest didn't lose his temper. "There are ways, my lady, to encourage you to confess."

"I'm sure there are."

"For now, I will leave you to dwell on your sins—among the dead."

He left her.

But she'd had plenty of water, and plenty of food. And she was becoming accustomed to the dead; she even talked to them, her father mostly.

She feared somewhat for her sanity. But even that seemed better.

Kinsey had meant to break her with the corpses.

The corpses had become her friends.

The next day Kinsey had her dragged back up. He sat at the head of the table in the great hall, leaning back, ale before him, legs planted upon the table.

He eyed her narrowly, but didn't move as two of his men brought her before him, then departed.

She thanked God that castles were dim; even so, her eyes hurt from the daylight that trickled in through the arrow slits and from the glow that burned from the fire deep in the hearth.

October had come, she thought, and was surprised that she might be staring at Kinsey, and thinking about the month of the year.

She stood in the center of the cold stone floor and returned his stare. She was miserable and afraid, but yet, there seemed little sense in being afraid. Fear spoke of uncertainty.

She was certain of his intentions.

He was going to kill her. Exactly how and when seemed yet to be determined, but that he would kill her was certain. He could threaten all he wanted. She wouldn't marry him. If she did so, he would gain all that he wanted, and then brand and try her for a traitor, trump up witnesses to swear to the king that she had changed sides, and that she had slept with the enemy as well.

Then he would execute her as his wife!

Yet how strange . . .

Kinsey, for the power he now held over her, didn't seem happy or satisfied. He stood finally, and as he had done the night in the forest, he walked around her slowly.

It was unnerving to feel him at her back.

He lifted a lock of her hair. "Ah, Kyra! I could tell you that despite your captivity, your hair still gleams like gold. That your eyes are like gemstones, radiant, glittering, greener than an emerald forest. I could say you were glorious, despite all! But it would be a lie, of course. Soon you'll look like a ragged little scarecrow, your hair will lose its luster, and God knows, maybe your perfect teeth will start to fall out."

She didn't reply.

"Ready to marry me?" he asked. "I'll let you have a bath, my lady, for the occasion. A long one. I'll give you clean clothing; I'll let you sleep in a bed in a room."

She smiled. "A bed no longer holds such charms. I have found a lovely shelf in the crypt; I'm trying it out. It will await me if I die."

"If you die now, lady, your limbs will be sent to the far corners of King Edward's realm, your head will rest out front on a spike, and your torso will be burned to ash."

"Then it's good that I've made use of that empty shelf in the crypt while still alive."

He drew back his hand, ready to strike her.

But he paused. She was startled to realize that he had hesitated because someone was entering the main hall.

"Lord Darrow!" the man called.

She spun around and frowned, recognizing the man Gaston led into the hall, and trying to remember just why. He was older, with long white hair and a beard that was more salt and pepper. He had lively blue eyes, and despite his age, he was tall and robust. She had met him at Edward's court, and at her own home.

"Lord Percy!" she murmured.

Darrow shot her a quick, angry glance, then hid his expression and greeted the newcomer. "Indeed, Lord Percy."

The older man moved with sure, long strides. He reached the two of them and gripped Darrow's hands. "Your man met one of mine while hunting rabbits. He suggested that you might be coming here. I was nearly killed by the heathens in my flight; I have some injured men. I hoped to throw myself on your hospitality, not to mention the fact that you might have need of the strong, robust fellows in my service."

He didn't wait for an answer, but turned to Kyra. "My dear! How are you doing? I miss your crotchety old father, and that's the truth. A good man, he was, beloved of two kings. Are you well, child? You look a little pale. But then, circumstances are trying, aren't they?"

"Indeed, she should look pale," Darrow said sharply. "We were, this very moment, discussing the fact that the lady betrayed me—and the king."

"She betrayed you, sir? Ah . . . that's right. You two were betrothed! Well, there's a marriage that can't take place."

Kyra stared at him incredulously. She remembered him well

now, a steadfast and loyal man, one who honored the king, but was never cruel.

"Why can't the marriage take place?"

"Why not?" Percy blustered, shocked. "Why, she expects another man's child!"

Kyra's jaw dropped; Kinsey Darrow turned a mottled shade of purple. Then he stared at Kyra. Did she betray herself?

"What makes you think that?" Darrow asked Percy.

Percy cleared his throat. "Well, the heathen who nearly killed me was that wretched Sir Arryn Graham."

Kinsey was staring at her. "So that is why he wants you back so badly!" he murmured.

"Aye, he wants her back! He let me live only under the circumstance that I come to you and tell you—"

"Yes, yes, yes!" Kinsey flared, still staring at Kyra. "He'll flay me alive—"

"And broil you while he does so, if you don't immediately let the lady go to him."

"I am in a castle, Lord Percy. The outlaw is in the field. He will never reach me."

"Ah, but, he intends to spend the whole of his life hunting you down."

"Then let us hope his life will be short."

Lord Percy shrugged. "You are right. This is a strong castle. But you know . . . Stirling has now been lost. Even Berwick is evacuated by the English!"

Darrow spun on Percy. "Gaston!" he called out. "Bring our best wine for our guest!" He walked back to the table and sat down, indicating that Lord Percy should join him. "He cannot have the lady, though since I do hold the castle at the moment, I believe I know how to make his life very short."

"Oh?" Lord Percy inquired, pausing to thank Gaston as he provided him with wine.

"The lady is guilty of treason. You will sit trial with me,

Lord Percy. The evidence is irrefutable. Sir Arryn Graham, a known outlaw who refused to sue for the king's peace, came here. She ordered the men to surrender. She closed the gates against me when I tried to relieve the castle. She rode to battle with the outlaws. She has thoroughly defied the king, fought against him, caused him grave harm! And she will meet the full penalty of the law. You must agree with me—you heard yourself that she is expecting the rebel's child.''

Lord Percy nodded, watching Kyra gravely. ''Is this all true, lass? I'm well aware that you must be with child—the man was adamant, and others declared it true as well. But did you order the men here to surrender?''

''Only when certain death was imminent.''

''Did you fight against Lord Darrow?''

She opened her mouth to protest her innocence, then fell silent. ''When I heard that he had, in truth, butchered women and children, aye. That I did.''

She expected Lord Percy's sympathy. ''Ah, well,'' he said flatly. He looked at Kinsey Darrow. ''She is guilty. Guilty as charged. We must, however, have a trial.''

''Of course,'' Kinsey said.

''She'll die an outlaw's wife.''

''What?'' Darrow said.

Kyra almost said the word as well.

''So goes the word throughout the south of Scotland as we all slither and scurry!'' Lord Percy said with wry humor. ''Aye, the truth of it I can't verify, but the lady supposedly wed the outlaw in the forest as well.'' He came forward, planting his fists on the table. ''It's said they were married by the very priest who led the mass here at Seacairn—before turning traitor to join the rebels as well.''

Kinsey was staring at Kyra then with such pure rage and hatred that she thought he might soon foam at the mouth and have a fit.

"You *married* the bastard. When you were *betrothed* to me?" He made no attempt to hide his feelings from her.

It was a lie, of course. Arryn had said that he would never marry her. And, of course, it was a dangerous lie, because Kinsey couldn't torture her into saying wedding vows any-more—they would mean nothing; the whole affair would be scandalous.

And if he couldn't marry her . . .

He'd want to kill her quickly.

"We'll hold the trial tomorrow morning," Kinsey said. "I'll start the men building the scaffolding for her execution this very afternoon."

"You can't execute the lass," Lord Percy said flatly.

"And why not?"

"Well, the lass is guilty; the babe is not."

Kyra lowered her head. Good old Lord Percy. He had been on her side all along.

But she discovered she was not so easily reprieved.

"It is an outlaw's rumor only that she is with child. In fact, it is most unlikely. She has barely known the fellow long enough to be certain of such a thing. In fact, I think it's a bald lie. A lie to escape the king's justice."

"Come now, Lord Darrow! We are Christian men. We can wait to carry out justice, and be certain."

"Well . . . I must think about this," Kinsey murmured. "Still, we will hold the trial tomorrow morning. I've knighted men among my retinue; I'm sure you do as well. Six will sit in judgment. For now . . . I will call my men and see that the lady is returned to her quarters below, and we can enjoy a good English supper, eh, Lord Percy?"

"She is Hugh Boniface's daughter," Percy murmured. "Should you get to this trial so hastily?"

"Were my heart not so wounded, and were I not so outraged that she should so betray her king, I might have more patience.

Gaston, call the men on guard duty to escort the Lady Kyra back down the stairs.''

Percy's eyes were on Kyra. She returned his stare, wondering why he didn't object more strenuously to her predicament. He came to her and touched her cheek.

"I'm so sorry, my lady. Take strength. God helps those who help themselves.''

Startled by the words, she stared at him.

But the guards had come, and she was quickly dragged away.

Into the night, Lord Kinsey Darrow, his guest, and their retinues drank and feasted. The river still teemed with fish and eel, and though colder days were coming quickly, there was still an abundance of summer's produce.

Gaston served the Englishmen with a heavy heart.

The rest of Scotland rejoiced. While here . . .

He couldn't let this happen. There had to be a way to stop it.

But there was none. If he and all the villagers revolted at once, they'd be cut down by the knights with their great swords and powerful war-horses.

What to do . . .

Escape with her. He knew how to exit the castle. Not a pleasant way, but . . .

He could scurry through the drainage system, which would land him in the river. Freezing, but he was a tough little Briton.

But the gates to the crypt were huge, heavy, iron. Locked huge, heavy iron.

He tried to serve the guests and not stumble or spill a drop of wine or ale. Some of Lord Darrow's men had learned cruelty from their master; they were quick to backhand a man hard enough to loosen his teeth, should he fail to serve.

"Gaston. You are Gaston?"

It was the great Lord Percy, the tall man who had arrived today.

Kinsey had already cuffed him soundly for entering with the man before announcing him.

"Aye, it's Gaston," he murmured, eyes downcast.

"Get to the forest in the hills tonight if you would save her life. Do you understand me?"

He realized that the man was handing him a note. He couldn't help but glance around quickly.

But most of the men were drunk, and paying little heed. And Darrow, he noted, had left the hall.

He quickly slipped the note up his sleeve.

"Aye, Lord Percy. Aye."

"You can get out of the castle. Can you get men in?" Percy inquired.

He shook his head. "Not an army, I'm afraid."

"We need only bring in a few," Percy said.

"Well, aye, there's a way . . . the gates are opened in the morning. The farmers and the merchants come in with the wares, and the people shop for their meals and needs each day, other than Sunday, the Lord's day."

Lord Percy nodded.

"Bring those words with you to the forest tonight."

"Lord Percy—"

"Hush. Sir Richard is watching."

Gaston nodded and bobbed. Lord Percy cuffed him as if he had spilled something.

Gaston, head down, quickly retreated from the hall. "Steward, they would call you a steward!" Sir Richard said, catching him by the shirt collar. "You are a buffoon!"

He didn't argue with Sir Richard, but hurried on to the kitchen.

* * *

Kyra heard the footsteps, but before the torchlight appeared, she knew that it was Kinsey coming; she knew the hated sound of the way he walked.

Light suddenly flooded the crypt.

"Kyra, oh, Kyra . . . where are you? Sleeping with the dead? How soon, my love, you will be among them."

A guard opened the gate to the crypt. Kinsey stepped through.

"Can you kill so quickly, now that such a respected and learned man as Griffin Percy has suggested that you must wait until my child is born?"

"But why wait, when it's a lie," Kinsey said smoothly.

"It's not a lie."

"I say it is. And I intend to prove it. You see, I can find a physician or midwife to examine you, and I promise, by the time they are through, it will be a lie. You'll be in tremendous pain, of course, but then, you will be in great pain before you die anyway. Unless, of course, I let the executioner allow you to strangle to death before you're disemboweled."

Her heart sank; she immediately felt a weak and trembling sensation in her knees.

He took a step closer. "I can arrange for an examination immediately, Kyra. Unless, of course, you're willing to sign an oath now saying that it's a false rumor, you're expecting no man's child, and you're ready to abide by the king's justice."

She didn't answer.

"Well, then, I shall call for my physician. . . ."

He would do it, and she knew it.

"Get your document."

"It's all written. I only need your signature."

One of his men joined them. A parchment was produced. She read it quickly. It was a document swearing that she wasn't with child, and that she accepted the king's justice through a fair trial.

With no choice, she signed.

"Why not write a whole confession for me, Kinsey?" she inquired.

Kinsey's man rolled up the parchment, and exited the crypt.

Kinsey waited until he was gone; then he smiled at her. "I think a trial is far more dramatic. How fortunate that Lord Percy has come. He can testify to the proper procedures taken! So . . . you really are a little harlot! Expecting the man's child! Did you let him enter the walls before throwing yourself at him?"

"Barely," she replied. "I begged him to take me! I told him I was about to be married to a monster and a fool, and that I would know a man before being shackled to a monkey."

He hit her; she should have expected it. She went reeling, and would have fallen, except that he caught her.

"You know, I raped the last woman who carried his child. And you're not dead yet. Um, but we are surrounded by the dead. What a unique experience."

She tried to jerk free of him, but she was weak and cold.

"Lord Darrow!"

It was Lord Percy, coming down to the crypt.

Kinsey shoved her from him.

She landed against the shelf that carried the mortal remains of her father. She was no longer afraid. If his spirit existed there, it gave her strength.

"There you are! I was looking for you on a matter of grave concern."

"I'll be back," Kinsey told Kyra, and he left with Percy.

To her amazement, old Percy looked around Darrow and winked.

As if she weren't about to face the gravity of death . . .

* * *

Gaston was freezing, but he didn't allow himself to feel the cold. He had to run, and run fast.

He smelled worse than a sewer. Ah, but then, it was the sewer drains that had made him smell so!

By the time he reached the trees on the hillside, he was gasping and wheezing. It was not such a horrible incline, not for a man who knew it well, but he staggered as he struggled up.

He reached the trees.

Then, despite himself, he let out a strangled gasp.

For out of the shadow of an old oak, an arm reached out for him.

And he was dragged into the darkness of the shadows.

CHAPTER
TWENTY-THREE

Kinsey, oddly, looked like hell.

So, she assumed, must she.

But Kinsey, despite his threat, had not reappeared in the crypts. And the way he looked now was as if he had been drinking to excess through the night. That wasn't his way. He knew how to drink, to celebrate, and he did so. But he pretended to drink more than he did; he watched all the while, so this seemed very strange.

She was exhausted, having lain awake all night, praying that she should remain with the dead rather than awake to find a living man at her side.

By morning, however, water and food had been sent to her, water to drink, and with which to wash, along with a brush and clean clothing. Apparently Kinsey didn't want it apparent that he had treated her shabbily before her mock trial. Gaston had looked like hell as well, as if he hadn't slept all night, but she'd had no opportunity to talk with him, for guards had escorted him down as he brought her belongings, food, and washwater.

Poor Gaston! Loyal—to the end, she was afraid.

When he came to collect the things, she touched his cheek. "Be of good cheer, my lady," he had told her. "The priest is coming. He will be with you all the way."

She nodded, wondering if Gaston had met Father Hemming, Kinsey's strange new henchman.

Apparently he had not.

Father Hemming did appear at the gate to the crypt. "Will you confess, my child?"

"To God alone," she told him.

"Certainly, I am only his tool."

"No, any confession I would make, sir, will not go through your ear."

He didn't warn her again that she would rot in hell. He merely shook his head and walked away.

She doubled over when he was gone, afraid that she would burst into tears and sob until the execution robbed her at last of breath.

Arryn knew, and he would come after her, but it would be too late. Kinsey would have destroyed him twice over.

And she wanted to live so badly! Miraculously, the Virgin had answered her prayer—giving her a surprising happiness. But now she wanted that happiness, wanted the man who had invaded his way into her castle, her life, and her heart. And she wanted her child . . . only a tickle within her now, causing nausea at that! But, oh, God, how she wanted to live, and have her child, and love Arryn . . . whether he loved her in return or not!

"It's time, my lady." Sir Percy had come down with the guards. "May I escort you, my lady?"

"Why not, my lord?" She accepted his arm. The guards followed closely.

"Be of good heart, lady."

"Again, why not? I am about to be condemned for treason, though I do still think that Kinsey is taking the law into his own hands. The king should be the one to try me."

"You may be right; there are such fine points to the law. Kinsey is a peer, and believes he has the right to judge a peer—with a proper jury, of course."

"Of his own men."

"Naturally. How else does one find the proper jury for the result he desires?"

She looked at him sharply. "And you're to judge me as well?"

"Naturally."

"And your learned opinion, my lord?"

"Well, you are guilty of treason. And, alas, you have signed that document . . . but be of good heart, lady. Be strong."

"Strong until death, my lord!"

And so he escorted her into the hall.

Her own great hall.

She faced a table full of men, some she knew, some she did not. And Sir Richard read out the charges against her, doing his own writing great justice as he intoned and emphasized key words. She was allowed to defend herself, which she did, telling them that she never let the outlaws in. But she hesitated when she was asked if she joined with them in the forest against Kinsey.

She looked straight at Lord Darrow.

"I never meant to betray my king. But Kinsey Darrow is a strange and selfish man, with an inflated concept of his own worth. I knew that he would plot and plan a way to kill me, since I had fallen into an outlaw's path—due to his own brutality against that same outlaw! I was left to pay the price for his cruelty. Yet it was from him that I needed to protect my own life."

"Liar!" Kinsey cried out, rising. "I loved you!" he swore.

"You can love no one but yourself, Kinsey."

He pointed at her. "She is guilty of treason, by her own admission. What say you all?"

There was no surprise when she heard a roar of "Guilty!" after his words. She never looked down, never blinked, never wavered, but still, she was stunned when she was immediately grasped by two of the men. Again, Kinsey pointed at her. "Now, my lady, you will meet the king's justice!"

To her dismay, Lord Percy stood at his side, making no protest.

Yet, as the guards took her out, Lord Percy did come by her side, forcing one of the guards to give way.

"Lass, you must give confession."

She looked at him. He was so grave! Thinking of her immortal soul.

"Lord Percy, I thank you, but—"

"Give confession!"

"But—"

"I'm begging you, hear the priest!"

He moved away from her.

There had been a crowd outside the door. The people of Seacairn. Many were crying openly. They reached out for her, touching her. "My lady! Oh, God, my lady, my lady . . ."

Kinsey's men-at-arms held the crowd back. When one woman sobbed, coming too close, a man shoved her back roughly, striking her with the hilt of his sword.

"Stop!" Kyra cried.

Her courage was with her until she mounted the steps to Kinsey's hastily erected scaffolding. As she mounted it, she realized that Kinsey had planned the spectacle well. He had been threatened by Sir Arryn Graham, and he had probably let out word that she would be condemned as a traitor—hoping that Sir Arryn would come now and try to stop him. The scaffolding had been erected outside the inner wall, just behind the outer gate. It had been built high so that anyone on the hills could view the spectacle of her death.

Taken to the top of the steps, she was roughly spun around; her wrists were tied together as Sir Richard again cried out the charges against her—and the sentence.

She wished to betray the king with the vigor of a man.

She would meet a man's justice.

She would be hanged until nearly dead. Dragged down. Disemboweled.

Quartered.

A traitor's reward.

"Have you last words, my lady?" Lord Percy cried.

She stood on the scaffolding, staring out across the landscape she knew so well. It was so beautiful, with autumn approaching, the colors even deeper and richer than in summer. She felt the cool air caressing her face.

She smiled.

"Love this country!" she said softly. Then she cried out, "Honor Scotland. Arryn! If you hear me, don't fight for me— fight to keep this country yours, stay alive to come after the monsters like Kinsey Darrow—"

It was actually amazing that she had gotten so far. Kinsey, who had meant to be an observer, letting Sir Richard read the sentence and the executioner carry it out, was up on the scaffold, pulling her back.

His hands tangled in her hair. "If you would confess, my lady, do it now! For you are done speaking!"

"I'll have confession!" she cried. "You have to give me a priest!"

The crowd was growing louder. Kinsey winced. "I'd have ordered the executioner to strangle you to death, lady, but now you'll meet your God slowly! Aye, by all means! Say your confession!"

He threw her toward one of his men. She was caught.

The black-cowled executioner came toward her.

Her stomach quivered.

Her knees buckled.

She was never going to see Arryn again; she wasn't going to live to see his precious country free. She would never know her child. . . .

She was terrified. So afraid. She didn't want to die. . . .

She was suddenly ready to run to Kinsey, say anything, beg for time, forgiveness. . . .

No.

There was nothing she could buy from him.

She forced her knees to hold her. She had to die; there was no escape now. Guards were on the parapets; the portcullis was down. The people had been herded in, the unarmed people, the fishwives and the shepherds, the cow keepers, the farmers, cooks, and servants, tenants and merchants. None who could fight, except to die themselves.

She had to die with dignity.

The executioner threw a rope around her neck. Odd; she felt it chafing, so strange to feel such an irritation when so much worse would come. . . .

"The priest!" she spit out. At least she would make Lord Percy happy, and buy herself just a few more minutes. . . .

Precious minutes.

The executioner stepped to her side. His head bowed, hands folded before him, Father Hemming came up the steps. He walked across the scaffolding to stand before her. Close.

He raised a hand, making the sign of the cross over her.

"Bless you, my child."

Then he lifted his head.

Striking, deep blue eyes met hers.

Her knees buckled in earnest.

She was so stunned, she nearly shouted out his name.

He brought a finger to his lips. "Kneel!" he whispered to her.

"There's a rope around my neck!" she whispered in reply.

"It's loose enough."

She went down on one knee. He came closer.

"Am I to confess?"

"Aye, you shall confess! You kept the news of a child from me."

"I didn't intend to—"

"You may apologize later! Lean closer!"

She did so. It must have appeared as if he were listening to her whispered sins.

He cut the ropes that bound her wrists.

"When the rope pulls you up, grab it."

"Arryn! I'll still strangle—"

"You'll not! John is the executioner, and he knows how to rig a proper knot!"

"But Arryn—"

"Nay, my lady, pay me heed! It's our only chance. Catch the rope with both hands. You'll swing . . . there will be a horseman!"

Swing . . .

She'd swing!

He stood, suddenly beginning to intone words in very hasty Latin, making a strange sign of the cross again and again. Then, with his head bowed low, he stepped to the side.

"Begin!" Sir Richard snapped to the executioner.

The man in black began to pull the rope. . . .

Kyra reached up, clutching it as the noose began to tighten. The right-angled oak arm over which the rope had been thrown began to turn to the east, to the side of the scaffolding. She was off the ground, flying, holding on with all her strength.

Suddenly, the rope gave.

She fell toward the ground, unable to keep from screaming. . . .

If she hit ground, every bone in her body would be broken! And worse . . .

Her baby . . .

She never hit the ground. A man dressed in a poor linen shirt and breeches caught her smoothly in his arms. Blue eyed, dark haired, a younger version of Arryn. It was Brendan Graham. "My lady!" he greeted her, and turning, she found a horse waited for them. He set her atop the animal, and mounted behind her.

By then, a roar had gone up.

Kinsey's men-at-arms were fighting, but amazingly, they seemed to be fighting one another. The portcullis was up. People were streaming out. . . .

And riders were coming down from the hills. On the scaffolding, Arryn and John had thrown off their robes, and were battling the men in armor who leapt forward, charging for the stairs, to accost them.

They had the advantage, slicing down any man as he tried for the stairs.

"No!"

Kinsey's howl of rage was so loud that Kyra could hear it over the screams and shouts and general melee.

Then she saw Arryn. He was ready to jump down from the scaffolding to meet Kinsey.

"Come, my lady, I'm to take you to safety!" Brendan told her. He urged the horse around the crowd in front of the scaffolding. He spurred the animal toward the gate.

She tried to turn back, to see Arryn. As she did so, a man suddenly came leaping at the horse with tremendous strength. His force threw both her and Brendan from the horse. She lay stunned in the dirt.

Brendan wasn't moving.

She saw the sword just seconds before it could impale her.

"You will meet justice!"

It was Sir Richard who had waylaid them. She rolled and leapt to her feet in just the nick of time to avoid his blade. She jumped back again and again as he came swinging at her.

"Lady Kyra!"

She looked up. Jay was on the parapets. He tossed down his sword, saluting, then started to run along the wall to reach the stairs and come down.

She had a weapon now. Sir Richard smiled, coming at her harder. Jay's sword was heavier than her own, but a fine enough weapon.

And she was ready to kill Sir Richard.

He came at her, and she parried. He lunged, and she fell back. He swung, and she ducked. She took the initiative, stepping forward, again, again, again. . . . He fell back. Smiled.

Then he started for her once again. . . .

It was amazing how the ground around them cleared as Arryn met Lord Kinsey Darrow before the scaffolding. Kinsey, in a rage, was a formidable opponent. He was a tall, powerful man, accustomed to battle, ready to fight.

Indeed, he almost foamed at the mouth.

He wore a coat of mail; Arryn had none. His blade caught Arryn's arm; blood seeped upon the raw linen of his shirt.

"That's for my castle!" Kinsey spit.

Arryn smiled. "My castle!"

Kinsey lunged. Arryn let him spend his energy, countering every blow.

Then he caught the man at the buckles that held his coat of armor in place, beneath the arm. Kinsey fell back, whitening. Arryn saw the blood.

"That was for Alesandra."

Kinsey started forward; again, Arryn allowed him his fury.

This time, when he countered, he caught Kinsey at the throat. His enemy wore mail, but no helmet.

Blood spurted.

"That was for my child!" he said in a hiss.

Kinsey raised his sword in renewed fury.

Arryn did not allow it. He pressed forward, knowing that the blood Kinsey was losing had to be draining his strength.

He slashed his enemy across the throat once again.

Kinsey dropped his sword, clutching his throat.

"And that was for Kyra!" Arryn said. He swung again, and again, and again, and again.

"For Scotland! For my people, take it to hell!"

"Arryn! Arryn!"

He paused at last, breathing heavily, amazed to realize that he was nearly blinded by tears. John stood behind him, a hand on his arm.

"He's dead, Arryn."

And Arryn looked down.

Oh, aye, the man was dead.

Sir Richard's strength was greater than her own, but she could best him; she was certain.

She was not just fighting for herself.

She fought for her child.

He swung, amused, certain that he could keep her backing away, wear her down.

She saw Brendan at her side, pushing himself up from the dirt, rising. He had no weapon. Sir Richard lunged toward him.

"Brendan!"

He turned, leapt aside.

She caught Sir Richard on the side of his head. Brendan saw his sword in the dirt. He lunged for it.

Richard caught his head, but maintained his grip on his sword, though blood flowed from a serious slash.

He couldn't kill her now, she realized. Brendan had his weapon; Jay was rushing toward them as well. . . .

Then, suddenly, while taking a step toward her, his face constricted. His body contorted. And slowly, slowly . . .

He fell.

Past his body, Kyra saw Katherine MacDonald. The young woman had thrown the knife that had landed dead center in Sir Richard's back.

Katherine stared at the body for a moment. Then she looked at Kyra. "You're all right! Thank God, thank God, I didn't think we'd make it in time, survive this gamble. . ."

Kyra heard a long stride. She swung around, her sword at the ready.

But it was Arryn coming toward her.

"My lady, I know that we are ever battling, but if you don't mind, I'd just as soon not face another sword at the moment. . ."

She dropped her weapon and raced to him. She threw herself into his arms. He caught her and held her tenderly.

Kissed her lips . . .

She heard applause. She turned. Arryn's men milled around, the people of Seacairn milled around, and there was Lord Percy, leading the applause.

"Lord Percy!" she exclaimed.

"Shh! I was never here, my lass. However . . . where is that incorrigible Father Corrigan? He will fight as if he were St. Michael after the dragon time and time again. That's what happens when an Irish priest winds up nearly killed in the Welsh wars—then is sent to Scotland. Father Corrigan, where are you?"

"Here, Lord Percy, I am here!" And there he was, and she realized that he had been dressed as a fat shepherd in order to enter the walls with his sword—which he had discarded now. "Lord Darrow's men are mostly dead."

"As they should be!" Katherine whispered.

"It's over now," her brother said, slipping an arm around her.

"It will never be over!" she said.

"I'm afraid that it won't," Arryn agreed. "But for tonight . . ."

"My men will see to the dead," Lord Percy said. "For tonight . . . young sir, you're going to make legitimate issue of my old friend's grandchild-to-be!"

"Aye, to the great hall, shall we?"

He slipped an arm around Kyra's waist, leading her back to the hall. "But you said that you'd never marry me!" she whispered to him. "You said not to care for you too much—"

He stopped, pulling her into his arms. "Did you listen to me then?"

She shook her head, smiling. "Nay, sir, I must admit, I seldom listen to orders and commands. You should be warned. I didn't listen . . . I adore you!" she whispered.

He bent down and touched her lips with a tender kiss. "Aye, then, things change. Scotland is ours again . . . and you are mine. If you will have it so."

"Aye, and gladly!"

" 'Tis true about the bairn?"

" 'Tis true, though my heart did nearly stop when Lord Percy announced that we were married as well! Darrow immediately decreed that I must die."

"I'm sorry. I could wait no longer. In fact, I chafed, worried that Lord Percy would not find Father Corrigan's supply of opium, and keep me assured that he'd stay away from you in the time we were forced to wait."

Kyra gasped. "My God! Lord Percy! How shall we ever thank you?" she inquired of the man who walked ahead of them.

"You'll remember that I am a good Englishman, and keep my name from all tales regarding this noble occasion!"

She laughed and kissed him.

"Thank your man, Gaston, as well, my lady. For without him, I couldn't have gotten word to Arryn; they'd not have slipped in and taken the places of the priest and executioner!"

"Aye, he'll be guest of honor!" she cried happily. And she could not help but kiss Lord Percy again soundly on the cheek.

And then they were in the great hall, and Father Corrigan, a robe over his farmer's outfit, was marrying them.

Lord Percy gave her in marriage. Katherine stood as her witness, while John acted as such for Arryn.

Ingrid was with them; she had waited in the forest, as Swen had ordered she must do. She sobbed happily throughout the ceremony.

They were all there, all of Arryn's men, all who had so nobly invaded! They drank Seacairn's wine and ale, ate, danced. The pipes played, and she listened, leaning back in Arryn's arms. Listened to the outlawed tunes, outlawed no longer.

"My lady . . . ?" he murmured.

"Aye?"

"Well, now that we are legally wed . . . ?"

They rose together, and slipped from the great hall unnoticed. Or so they thought, though it mattered little.

The tower room held fresh flowers, fresh sheets, fresh water. The breeze rushed in while a fire burned brightly. Coolness and warmth surrounded them both.

Kyra came into his arms. "I am so glad to be your wife, but Arryn, so sorry as well. You didn't have to marry me; I'd have been glad to be with you, no matter what—"

He pressed a finger to her lips. "Ah, Kyra! I couldn't forget what had been; I couldn't forgive myself. Still, even now, I can't help thinking that if I had just been there, if I hadn't met Angus Darrow on that bridge that day . . ."

"Oh, Arryn!"

"It's all right; I'll always have the regrets, but . . . Kinsey Darrow is dead. And from the ashes of that revenge, I have been blessed. I have you."

"My God . . ." she murmured.

"Aye?"

She smiled. "That was beautiful! From such a brusque warrior, whose warning is to take care not to love him!"

He grimaced. "Thank God that you never listen!" he said.

And he swept her up.

And down.

And that night, that first time as man and wife, they made love on the fur before the fire. The golden light played on their flesh, danced in Kyra's hair, reflected as blue flame in Arryn's eyes. And later, as they lay together, Kyra murmured, "Our babe might have been conceived right here."

He rolled over her, leaning on an elbow to watch her, his eyes grave. "And not on the softness of a true bed?" he queried.

"I'm happy with you wherever we sleep," she said.

He cradled her closer. "I'm glad," he said huskily. "Kyra, we have won a great battle. Indeed, in a way, whatever we may win or lose in the future, I think that we have won Scotland. We have won the knowledge, you see, that we can fight and win. But . . ."

"Aye?"

"The English army will return. In greater strength. With greater fury. We may become outlaws again. We may give up Seacairn. Retreat to the Highlands with our wives and bairns. I never really asked you if you were prepared for such a life."

"I'm not sure that you actually asked me to marry you," she replied. "I think you just rather announced it. Prepared for such a life . . . aye. Oh, aye, Arryn! Lowlands, Highlands, I shall sleep with you and gladly, wherever we need be. I am prepared for anything—except not loving you."

He bent low, whispering against her lips, "Kyra, my love, you are my life, and my soul!"

And he kissed her.

And wrapped her in his arms.

And made love to her.

And the fire burned. . . .

And burned.

Far to the south, Edward I, king of England, stepped out of his boat, and upon the shores of his own country.

They called him Longshanks, for he was a tall man, nearly seven feet in his full armor. His eyelids drooped, an inheritance from his father. But those drooping lids covered eyes that were sharp and blue and narrowed now with the fury that had filled him since he had heard the news.

Scotland . . .

"Sire, shall we rest here for the night?" one of his retainers asked.

"God, no!" Edward swore. "We're on to London. By God! We've a new army to raise!"

And he looked to the north.

Aye.

This time, he would lead the army against the Scots.

Aye, he would lead them. . . .

Chronology

c6000 BC: Earliest peoples arrive from Europe (Stone Age): Some used stone axes to clear land.

c4500 BC: Second wave of immigrants arrive (New Stone Age or Neolithic): "Grooved ware," simple forms of pottery found. They left behind important remains, perhaps most notably, their tombs and cairns.

c3500 BC: Approximate date of the remarkable chambered tombs at Maes Howe, Orkney.

c3000 BC: Carbon dating of the village at Skara Brae, also Orkney, showing houses built of stone, built-in beds, straw mattresses, skin spreads, kitchen utensils of bone and wood, and other more sophisticated tools.

c2500 BC: "Beaker" people arrive: Neolithic people who will eventually move into the Bronze Age. Bronze Age to last until approximately 700BC.

c700 BC: Iron Age begins—iron believed to have been brought by Hallstadtan peoples from central Europe. Term "Celts" now applied to these people, from the Greek "Keltoi"; they were considered by the Greeks and Romans to be barbarians. Two types of Celtic language, P-Celtic, and Q-Celtic.

c600–100 BC: The earliest Celtic fortifications, including the broch, or large stone tower. Some offered fireplaces and fresh water wells. Crannogs, or island forts, were also built, structures often surrounded by spikes or walls of stakes. Souterrains were homes built into the earth, utilizing stone, some up to eighty feet long. The Celts become known for their warlike qualities as well as for their beautiful jewelry and colorful clothing; "trousers" are introduced by the Celts, perhaps learned from Middle-Eastern societies. A rich variety of colors are used (perhaps forerunner to tartan plaids) as well as long tunics, skirts, and cloaks to be held by the artistically wrought brooches.

55 BC:	Julius Caesar invades southern Britain.
56 BC:	Julius Caesar attacks again, but again, the assault does not reach Scotland.
43 AD:	The Roman Plautius attacks; by the late 70s (AD), the Romans have come to Scottish land.
78–84 AD:	The Roman Agricola, newly appointed governor, born a Gaul, plans to attack the Celts. Beginning in 80 AD, he launches a two-pronged full-scale attack. There are no roads, and he doesn't have time to build them as the Romans have done elsewhere in Britain. Some 30,000 Romans marched; they will be met by a like number of Caledonians. (Later to be called Picts for their custom of painting or tattooing their faces and bodies.) After the battle of Mons Graupius, the Roman historian Tacitus (son-in-law of Agricola) related that 10,000 Caledonians were killed, that they were defeated. However, the Romans retreat southward after orders to withdraw.
122 AD:	Hadrian arrives in Britain and orders the construction of his famous wall.
142 AD:	Antoninus Pius arrives with fresh troops due to continual trouble in Scotland. The Anton-

	ine Wall is built and garrisoned for the following twenty years.
150–200 AD:	The Romans suffer setbacks. An epidemic kills much of the population, and Marcus Aurelius dies, to be followed by a succession of poor rulers.
c208 AD:	Severus comes to Britain and attacks in Scotland, dealing some cruel blows, but his will be the last major Roman invasion. He dies in York in 211 AD, and the Caledonians are then free from Roman intervention, though they will occasionally venture south to Roman holdings on raids.
350–400 AD:	Saxon pirates raid from northwest Europe, forcing Picts southward over the wall. Fierce invaders arrive from Ireland: the Scotti, a word meaning raiders. Eventually, the country will take its name from these people.
c400 AD:	St. Ninian, a British Celtic bishop, builds a monastery church at Whithorn. It is known as Candida Casa. His missionaries might have pushed north as far as the Orkney Islands; they were certainly responsible for bringing Christianity to much of the country.
c450 AD:	The Romans abandon Britain altogether. Powerful Picts invade lower Britain, and the Romanized people ask for help from Jutes, Angles, and Saxons. Scotland then basically divided between four peoples; Picts, Britons, Angles, and the Scotti of Dalriada. "Clan" life begins—the word *clann* meaning children in Gaelic. Family groups are kin with the most important, possibly strongest man becoming chief of his family and extended family. As generations go by, the clans grow larger, and more powerful.
500–700 AD:	The Angles settle and form two kingdoms,

Deira and Bernicia. Aethelfrith, king from 593–617 AD, wins a victory against the Scotia at Degsastan and severely crushes the Britons—who are left in a tight position between the Picts and Angles. He seizes the throne of King Edwin of Deira as well, causing bloodshed between the two kingdoms for the next fifty years, keeping the Angles busy and preventing warfare between them and their Pictish and Scottish neighbors. Circa 500, Fergus MacErc and his brothers, Angus and Lorne, brought a fresh migration of Scotia from Ireland to Dalriada, and though the communities had been close (between Ireland and Scotland), they soon after began to pull away. By the late 500s, St. Columba came to Iona, creating a strong kingship there, and spreading Christianity even farther than St. Ninian had gone. In 685 AD at Nechtansmere, the Angles are severely defeated by the Picts; their king Ecgfrith is slain, and his army is half slaughtered. This prevents Scotland from becoming part of England at an early date.

787 AD: The first Viking raid, according to the Anglo-Saxon chronicle. In 797, Lindisfarne is viciously attacked, and the monastery is destroyed. "From the Fury of the Northmen, deliver us, oh, Lord!" becomes a well-known cry.

843 AD: Kenneth MacAlpian, son of a Scots king, who is also descended from Pictish kings through his maternal lineage, claims and wins the Pictish throne as well as his own. It is not an easy task as he sets forth to combine his two peoples into the country of Scotland. Soon after becoming king of the Picts and the Scotia, he moves his capital from Dunadd to Scone. He

has the "Stone of Destiny," recently returned to Scotland, brought there. The stone is now known as the "Stone of Scone."

The savage Viking raids become one focus that will help to unite the Picts and the Scots. Despite the raids and the battles, by the tenth century, many of the Vikings are settling in Scotland. The Norse kings rule the Orkneys through powerful jarls, and they maintain various other holdings in the country, many in the Hebrides. The Vikings will become a fifth main people to make up the Scottish whole. Kenneth is followed by a number of kings that are his descendants, but not necessarily immediate heirs, nor is the Pictish system of accepting the maternal line utilized. It appears that a powerful member of the family, supported by other powerful members, comes to the throne.

878 AD: Alfred (the Great) of Wessex defeats the Danes. (They will take up residence in East Anglia and, at times, rule various parts of England.)

1018 AD: Kenneth's descendant, Malcolm II, finally wins a victory over the Angles at Carham, bringing Lothian under Scottish rule. In this same year, the king of the Britons of Strathclyde dies without an heir. Duncan, Malcolm's heir, has a claim to the throne through his maternal ancestry.

1034 AD: Malcolm dies, and Duncan, his grandson, succeeds him as king of a Scotland that now includes the Pictish, Scottish, Anglo, and Briton lands, and pushes into English lands.

1040 AD: Duncan is killed by MacBeth, the Mormaer (or high official) of Moray, who claims the throne through his own ancestry, and that of his wife. Despite Shakespeare's version, he is suspected of having been a good king, and a good Christian—going on pilgrimage to Rome in 1050 AD.

1057 AD: MacBeth is killed by Malcolm III, Duncan's son. (Malcolm had been raised in England.) Malcolm is known as Malcolm Canmore, or Ceann Mor, or Big Head.

1059 AD: Malcolm marries Ingibjorg, a Norse noblewoman, probably the daughter of Thorfinn the Mighty.

1066 AD: Harold II, king of England, rushes to the north of his country to battle an invading Norse army. Harold wins the battle, only to rush back south, to Hastings, to meet another invading force.

1066 AD: William the Conqueror invades England and slays Harold, the Saxon King.

1069 AD: Malcolm III marries (as his second wife) Princess Margaret, sister to the deposed Edgar Atheling, the Saxon heir to the English throne. Soon after, he launches a series of raids into England, feeling justified in that his brother-in-law has a very real claim to the English throne. England retaliates.

1071 AD: Malcolm is forced to pay homage to William the Conqueror at Abernathy. Despite the battles between them, Malcolm remains popular among the English.

1093 AD: While attacking Northumberland (some say to circumvent a Norman invasion), Malcolm is killed in ambush. Queen Margaret dies three days later. Scotland falls into turmoil. Malcolm's brother, Donald Ban, raised in the Hebrides under Norse influence, seizes the throne and overthrows Norman policy for Viking.

1094 AD: William Rufus, son of William the Conqueror, sends Malcolm's oldest son, Duncan, who has been a hostage in England, to overthrow his uncle, Donald. Duncan overthrows Donald, but is murdered himself, and Donald returns to the throne.

1097 AD: Edgar, Duncan's half-brother, is sent to Scotland with an Anglo-Norman army, and Donald is chased out once again. He brings in many Norman knights and families, and makes peace with Magnus Barelegs, the King of Norway, formally ceding to him lands in the Hebrides which has been a holding already for a very long time.

1107 AD: Edgar dies; his brother, Alexander succeeds him, but rules only the land between Forth and Spey; his younger brother, David, rules south of the Forth. Alexander's sister, Maud, had become the wife of Henry I of England, and Alexander has married Henry's daughter by a previous marriage, Sibylla. These matrimonial alliances make a terribly strong bond between the Scottish and English royal houses.

1124 AD: Alexander dies. David (also raised in England) inherits the throne for all Scotland. He is destined to rule for nearly thirty years, to be a powerful king who will create burghs, a stronger church, a number of towns, and introduce a sound system of justice. He will be a patron of arts and learning. Having married an heiress, he is also an English noble, being Earl of Northampton and Huntington, and Prince of Cumbria. He brings feudalism to Scotland, and many friends, including de Brus, whose descendants will include Robert Bruce, fitzAllen, who will become High

Steward—and, of course, a man named Sir William Graham.

1153 AD: Death of David I. Malcolm IV, known as Malcolm the Maiden, becomes king. He is a boy of eleven.

1154 AD: Henry Plantagenet (Henry II) becomes king in England. Forces Malcolm to return Northumbria to England.

1165 AD: Malcolm dies and is succeeded by his brother, William the Lion. William forms what will be known as the Auld Alliance with France.

1174 AD: William invades England. The Scots are heavily defeated, William is taken prisoner, and must sign the Treaty of Falaise. *Scotland falls under feudal subjugation to England.*

1189 AD: Richard Couer de Lion (Plantagenet, Henry's son) now king of England, renounces his feudal superiority over Scotland for 10,000 marks.

1192 AD: The Scottish Church is released from England supremacy by Pope Celestine III. *More than a hundred years of peace between England and Scotland begins.*

1214 AD: William the Lion dies. Succeeded by Alexander II, his son.

1238 AD: As Alexander is currently without a son, a parliament allegedly declares Robert Bruce (grandfather of the future king) nearest male relative and heir to the throne. The king, however, fathers a son. (Sets a legal precedent for the Bruces to claim the throne at the death of the Maid of Norway.)

1249 AD: Death of Alexander II. Ascension of Alexander III, age seven, to the throne. (He will eventually marry Margaret, sister of the king of England, and during his lifetime, there will be peaceful relations with England.)

1263 AD: Alexander III continues his father's pursuit of the Northern Isles, whose leaders give their loyalty to Norway. King Hakon raises a fleet against him. Alexander buys him off until October, when the fierce weather causes their fleet to fall apart at the Battle of Largs. Hakon's successor, Magnus, signs a treaty, wherein the isles fall under the dominion of the Scottish king. The Orkneys and Shetlands remain under Norse rule for thc time being.

1270 AD: (Approximate date) William Wallace born.

1272 AD: Edward I (Plantagenet) becomes king of England.

1277–1284 AD: Edward pummels Wales. Prince Llywelyn is killed; his brother Dafyd is taken prisoner and suffers the fate of traitors. In 1284, the Statute of Wales is issued, transferring the principality to "our proper dominion," united and annexed to England.

1283 AD: Alexander's daughter, Margaret, marries the king of Norway.

1284 AD: Alexander obtains from his magnates an agreement to accept his granddaughter, Margaret, the Maid of Norway, as his heiress.

1286 AD: Death of Alexander III. The Maid of Norway, a small child, is accepted as his heiress. Soon after the king's death, Edward of England suggests a marriage treaty between the Maid and his son, Edward.

1290 AD: The Maid of Norway dies. With the number of Scottish claimants to the throne, the Bishop of St. Andrews writes to Edward, suggesting he help arbitrate among the contenders.

1291 AD: Edward tells his council he has it in his mind

to "bring under his dominion the king and the realm of Scotland."

1292 AD: November. Edward chooses John Balliol as king of Scotland in the great hall at Berwick. Edward loses no time in making Scotland a vassal of England; King John, he claims, owes fealty to him.

1294 AD: The Welsh, led by Madog ap Llywelyn, rise for a final time against Edward.

1295 AD: Edward has put down the Welsh, and the principality is his.

1296 AD: Not even King John can tolerate the English king's demands that Scotland help him finance his war against France (ancient ally of the Scots). John rises against Northern England; Edward retaliates with brutal savagery at Berwick. King John is forced to abdicate and is taken prisoner. The king of England demands that the barons and landowners of Scotland sign an oath of fealty to him; this becomes known as the ragman roll. Among those who sign are the Bruces, who, at this time, give their loyalty to the king of England.

1297 AD: September 11, Wallace and de Moray command the Battle of Stirling Bridge, a spectacular victory against far more powerful forces. De Moray will soon die from the mortal wounds he receives during the battle. But for the moment, freedom is won. Wallace is guardian of Scotland.

Please turn the page for an exciting preview
of the third book in the thrilling Graham family saga,

SEIZE THE DAWN,

available next April!

PROLOGUE

Falkirk, Scotland
July 22, 1298

Oddly enough, there could be a strange beauty to war. The sight of the arrows was, at the least, awesome.

They appeared suddenly in the radiant blue summer sky. . . .

And they were spellbinding, an arcing rain flying high into the sky, cresting, then falling with a strange grace back to the ground.

Then the hurtling, whistling sound of them suddenly took precedence.

Along with the sounds that followed . . .

Brendan could hear screams arise, for those Scotsmen who had taunted the expert bowmen of the English army with their backsides discovered too late that grace and beauty were as deadly as stupidity. Arrows connected with flesh, spewing blood, breaking bone. Men shouted, staggered, fell, some wounded, some killed. Horses neighed shrilly, animals died, and knights, not hit themselves, cursed as their horses stumbled and fell, many wheezing out a death rattle. Foot soldiers scattered; cavalry began to break; commanders shouted.

"Hold, you fools! And cover your backsides!" John Graham, Brendan's kinsman, shouted from atop his tall black steed. They'd had a certain advantage. William Wallace, their leader, knew how to choose his ground for a fight. Though Edward had huge numbers of foot soldiers and cavalry—perhaps twelve thousand of the latter and twenty-five hundred of the first— William had chosen to wage war from the flank of the Callander Wood. From there, a fiercely flowing stream met with another from Glen Village, and because of this the terrain the English must traverse was little but mire, soggy wet ground, a morass to wear down horses and men.

But today the English had come on. Mired, they had rallied.

And it was the Scots now breaking.

"Hold!" John shouted again.

Brendan saw him shake his head with disbelief, wondering what fool confidence had suggested such a show of idiocy.

Indeed! What man had not seen the arrows? They had thought to defy the deadly barrage of the English—and so life was wasted. The major assault had not even begun as yet.

Along with the rise of screams and shouts, he could hear the jangle of horses' harnesses, the trappings of some of the richer men's mounts. His own great dappled gelding, Achilles, stamped the ground with nervous impatience as a great cloud of moist air streamed from his nostrils. More arrows were flying. Men were falling, dying. Edward of England was no fool, and surely no coward, and any of them who had taken him for such were doomed. The English king had ruthlessly destroyed the Welsh—and from them, he had gained his talented longbow men. He had brought soldiers talented with the crossbow as well, Flemish, Germans, mercenaries—even some of the French he was so constantly fighting.

Even Scotsmen rode with him—Scotsmen who feared that Wallace, their protector, their guardian, could not hold against the forces of the Plantagenet king of England, self-proclaimed Hammer of the Scots.

Scotsmen who were perhaps, even now, changing sides.

"Sweet Jesu, help me!"

English riders were following their bowmen. Scottish knights were breaking. Hand-to-hand battle came closer and closer. The Scots were experts with their schiltrons—barriers created by men arranged with rows of pikes—weapons that held well against the English knights.

But even they were falling now.

Brendan quickly dismounted from Achilles, hurrying to the rugged old warrior with the arrow protruding from his thigh. He couldn't wrench out the arrow; the man would bleed to death there on the field.

"Break it!" the man commanded.

"MacCaffery, I can't—"

"You will, boy, you will." Beady blue eyes surveyed him from beneath a fine bush of snow-white brows.

"MacCaffery—"

"Haven't you strength, boy?"

MacCaffery was taunting him on purpose. Aye, and still he had the sense to know it, but the taunting worked. He snapped the arrow, gritted his teeth—and removed the shaft, immediately using his linen shirt to put pressure against the exit wound.

"Fool!" he accused his elder.

"Aye," MacCaffery said softly. The old man hadn't flinched, hadn't let out so much as a whimper. "A free fool. And I'll die that way, boy."

Die that way . . .

Did the old man feel it, too? A strange sense, not so much

of fear, but of unease and trepidation. They should not have fought that day! Many of the commanders had said it. They should not have fought. They should have continued their northern flight; they had left the land desolate, stripped; if they had just kept ahead of the English army, they could have starved it out!

Yet almost a year ago now, at Stirling Bridge, the forces of Scotland, forces truly of Scotland, rich men, poor men, diggers of soil, purveyors of gold, had faced the might of the English, and there they had triumphed. And since that time, for that precious time, Scotland had been free. The great baron of the north, Andrew de Moray, had died soon after the battle, mortally wounded in the fighting. But until the very last minute, the great survivor of the struggle, Sir William Wallace, had kept his name alive in official correspondence. Wallace had reigned as the guardian of the realm. He had gained so much power that he had pushed the tide of bloodshed into England; he had ravaged York, and given something incredibly valuable to his followers as well—pride.

Pride.

Pride had now turned to foolishness.

"Take heed!" old MacCaffery warned.

He turned just in time. An armored knight, wearing the colors of the House of York, was bearing down upon him. Brendan wielded his weapon with a desperate power, aiming deliberately for the throat. His opponent went still, hovered in time and space, clutched his neck. Red seeped through his fingers, and he fell into the mire. But another knight was coming on, riding hard despite the mire, and Brendan braced to meet him.

He had first learned the hatred of the enemy at Hawk's Cairn, where he'd fought with no talent and no experience, and he had survived because he'd been left for dead. That now seemed a lifetime ago. He'd learned. Time had given him strength and judgment—and a well-trained sword arm. He'd learned victory. . . .

And suddenly he knew.

He was about to learn defeat.

But he would never accept it. Just like old MacCaffery, who had risen to his feet despite his wound. And though the blood drained from him, MacCaffery fought on. Raising his great sword, letting it fall, raising it. . . .

Again and again.

And the mire beneath their feet turned red.

Brendan heard a shout and turned. His kinsman was down. John Graham was unhorsed, on the ground. His men flocked around him, tried to wrest him from the onslaught of men now decimating the Scots, riding them down.

"Go to him, lad! I'll cover your back!" MacCaffery shouted. Aye, he was a fierce old man, and half-dead or nay, there was no man better to cover him. So he ran, and he fell to his knees where they were lifting John, and he saw the wound at his kinsman's throat, and heard the rattle of death in his lungs.

"John, for the love of God." He reached for him, would have carried him, but John placed a bloody hand on his chest. "Brendan, run, run with these fellows! They've just gotten Wallace out. Go after him—"

"I'll not leave you!" he insisted. "I'll take you from the mire to the wood—"

"Brendan! I'm a dead man, and you haven't the time to save a corpse."

"John—"

"For the love of Scotland, Brendan! Go! This battle is lost; much is lost! But hope is alive, and freedom lives in your heart! Go!"

John gripped his hand tightly.

The grip failed. Brendan rose slowly, clenching his teeth. He looked around.

He stood in a field of dead men. Even as he watched, old MacCaffery wavered and fell at last. He had died a free man, defiant to the end.

The English were coming, hundreds of horsemen, more and more. Yet their horses stumbled over mud and corpses and blood. A knight dismounted, came at him. He let out a roar, the battle roar of the Scotsmen, a cry that sounded to heaven and earth, and gave even armored and battle-hardened Englishmen pause.

Then he stepped forward, slicing, slashing, piercing, wielding his sword with the strength of madness and rage. Men dropped before him, often felled with a single blow. He walked slowly, with purpose, rage and strength growing. John was dead, old MacCaffery was dead; by God, the dead were everywhere and the hated English were coming and coming. . . .

Too many of them.

Yet he realized he wasn't fighting alone. He glanced to the side, saw the colors and emblem of his own family, and realized his cousin Arryn had ridden in. And together they walked through the shadow of death, steel glistening in the sun, running red. . . .

Blood and haze. It seemed that there was so much on the field it was hard to tell who was who anymore. Hard to read the crests upon tunics that covered mail, and harder still to tell the woven colors of the wool on the men who fought kilted without armor.

There was a break suddenly. The English before them had fallen.

More came. . . .

Yet at a distance.

And like the arrows, they were spellbinding, horses and men in their armor and livery beneath the sun and sky, colors flying, great muscles moving. . . .

Beautiful. Awesome. Deadly.

"To horse!" Arryn shouted. Some of the men who had fought with them ran.

Brendan shook his head, eyes narrowed. "There are more of them! John is dead, MacCaffery is dead—they're all . . . dead," he said, looking at the field around him. "Freedom—or death!"

"There will be no freedom if we don't keep the fight alive!" Arryn told him. "Damn you, Brendan, to your horse!"

At sixteen, Brendan had known the sweet taste of victory at Stirling Bridge.

Now, at seventeen, he knew that he must swallow the bitterness of the defeat at Falkirk.

Arryn mounted his horse. Achilles loped behind him. Brendan hesitated but a second more. He mounted and followed.

By John's body he paused.

"Aye, cousin! For the love of Scotland, I'll ride. And I swear to you, John, I will ride until Scotland is free forever. By God's blood, so help me, I so swear! I will never surrender—myself, or my country."

The English were almost upon him.

He waited.

And with a fierce and fiery fury he turned one last time, bringing down the first knight to attack him, and the man behind him. It seemed again that there were men all around him. They had come near the wood, near the edge of the trees. As he engaged then, still mounted, striking with his sword, he found himself fighting into the cover of the trees. He was nearly unhorsed; he dismounted of his own volition, turning to fight on foot. One man assaulted him, and he pressed back hard until his attacker was to a tree, and there he killed him.

Then he turned, covered in shadow and darkness. Someone stood in the copse, wearing a dark cape over chain-mail armor.

Friend or foe?

He started forward.

The figure attacked. For a moment the enemy did so with strength and aggression. But he returned each strike of the sword with a vengeance. The enemy fell back, cried out, "Wait!"

It was a young voice—a female voice.

The cape fell from her; she wrested the mail helm from her head. Stunned, he stared at her. She was very young—his own age, perhaps? Younger still. In the shadowed light of the forest, her hair gleamed with gold fire. Her features were as perfect as carved marble, eyes as bright as stars, as innocent. . . .

He made no move against her. He just stared.

And it was then that he heard the figure behind him.

He whirled with split seconds to spare. Before the man could slice off his head, he skewered him through the gullet.

Something from the rear hit his head. He fell to his knees, pain shooting through his temples, blinding him.

"Brendan!"

Arryn had reached him. Dismounting, he drew him to his feet.

"Come on, we've got to ride harder, farther, deeper, into the wood!"

Gritting his teeth, Brendan came to his feet again. Grasping his horse's saddle, he managed to pull himself up.

The pain he felt was horrible; the self-anger was worse. No enemy was ever to be trusted!

"Brendan! Hold boy, ride!"

His vision wavered.

Then he saw a figure coming hard behind them, slipping into the trees.

And he nudged Achilles and rode hard. He was thankful his horse followed his kinsman's. And as they rode, and the English fell behind, he damned himself in impotent rage and desolation. They had lost. They had fought so long, and so hard. . . .

And he had been downed by a girl.

But he had survived.

He had been ready to fight to the death, but they had been right—death now would avail him nothing, nor would it serve his country. He would fight again.

Never surrender.

Never forget, never forgive.

Though his head pounded ferociously and he nearly fell from his mount, he kept on his horse, and stayed alive through willpower alone.

He must survive now.

For the love of Scotland!

And for vengeance.

One day, by God, aye! One day he would find out who she was!

Vengeance, anger, they were strong emotions for life!

Sanctuary . . . at last they reached a sanctuary in the woods. "Safety, lad, we've reached safety!" He heard Arryn's rough voice and fell into his kinsman's arms, and as he did so, he knew he would not stay conscious long. Darkness was encroaching all around him. A deep crimson darkness, like the shadow of blood and death. . . .

He would live.

For vengeance, and for Scotland.

Aye, to find her! And for the love of his country. He would not die.

Nay . . .

He would avenge the evil done today.

And he and his country would both live at peace, triumphant.

And free.

Keep reading for a special preview of
New York Times bestselling author
Heather Graham's
Knight Triumphant,
the continuing story in
the epic Graham Family saga.

Coming soon from Zebra!

CHAPTER 1

They were surely madmen.

From the hill, Igrainia could see the riders coming.

They flew the flags of Robert the Bruce.

They had to be mad.

She rode with a party of twenty men, selected carefully for their skill and courage—and, of course, the simple fact that they were still alive and well. They wore full armor and carried well-honed weapons with which they were very adept.

There were less than half that number coming toward them, a pathetically ragtag band, racing up the hill.

"My lady . . . ?" queried Sir Morton Hamill, head of her guard.

"Can we outrun them?" she asked.

Sir Morton let out a sound of disgust. "Outrun them!" He was indignant. "They are but rabble; their so-called king runs to the forests while his family is slain in his stead. The

Bruce is aware that he is an outlaw to most of his own people. My lady, there is no reason to run.''

''No reason,'' she said, her eyes narrowing, ''except that more men will die. I am weary of death.''

The riders were still gaining on them at a breakneck pace, racing from the site of the castle, where surely even they had realized that the black crosses covering the stone were no ploy of the enemy, but a true warning of the situation within.

Sir Morton was trying hard to hold his temper. ''My lady, I am aware of the pain in your heart. But these are the very renegades who brought the terror to your home, who cost you . . . who cost you everything.''

''No man, or woman, asks for the plague, Sir Morton. And indeed, if you ask Father MacKinley, he will tell you that God sent the sickness in his anger that we should brutally make hostages of women and children, and execute our enemies so freely. We were warned of the sickness; we refused to believe the warnings of our foes. So now, if we can outrun the renegades, that is my choice. It was not my choice to leave Langley. I want no more death laid at my feet.''

''Alas. We cannot outrun them,'' Sir Morton argued then. ''They are almost upon us.''

She stared at him angrily. ''You would fight them rather than do your duty to bring me to safety.''

''My lady, you are beside yourself with grief and cannot think clearly. I would fight such upstart rebels, aye, my lady, for that is my duty.''

''Sir Morton, I am in my full senses, quite capable of coherent thought—''

''My lady, watch! Your position here on the hill is excellent; you may view the carnage as I take my revenge on these knaves!''

Furious, Igrainia reined in her horse as Sir Morton called out an order to his men. He did not intend to await the enemy. He meant to attack first.

"Sir Morton!" She raged with fury, her heart sick as she watched the men spur their horses to his command. In seconds, the liege men of her late lord, Afton of Langley, spurned her order and took flight down the hill.

They seemed to sail in a sea of silver, armor gleaming in the sun. The colors they flew, the rich blue and red, noble colors, created a riot of shades along with the silver stream. Down the hill, a display of might and power . . .

Bearing down upon a sad rabble, scattered horsemen on fine enough mounts, some in tarnished armor, most in no more than leather jerkins to protect their hearts from the onslaught of steel that would soon come their way.

At her distance, she could see their leader. She frowned, wondering what madness would make a man risk certain death. She narrowed her eyes against the sun, studying the man. A small gasp escaped her.

She had seen him before. She knew, because he rode without protection; no helmet covered his head, and the length of his tangled blond hair glinted in the sun with almost as much of a sheen as the steel helmets worn by her own people. She had seen him dragged in with the other captured men, shackled in irons. He had looked like a wild man, uncivilized, a barbarian, yet despite the dirt and mud that marred his clothes, she had seen his eyes once, when they had met hers, and she had read something frightening in that glance. She had the odd feeling that he had allowed himself to be taken prisoner, though why, she didn't know. Or perhaps she did. Castle Langley, as her husband's home was called, had just been turned into quarters for the king's men when they had come through, bearing the families of

Scottish outlaws to London, where they would be held until their rebel kin surrendered.

And offered their own necks to the axeman's blade.

Sir Morton's men were nearly upon the riders. In the glittering sunlight, it was almost a beautiful spectacle, the gleam and glint of steel and color . . .

Until the riders came together in a hideous clash, horses screaming, men shouting, steel becoming drenched in the deep red of blood. Tears suddenly stung her eyes; Afton had wanted no part of this. He had been furious with the order to welcome the king's men, to house renegades who were his own people. He had demanded that the hostages not be treated as animals, even when they spoke with their highland language and strange burrs, and looked like wild creatures from heathen times. He had stood, a proud voice of reason and mercy, until he had fallen . . .

And neither her love nor her prowess with herbs had managed to save him.

He would have been furious at this bloodbath, had he been with her.

Had he had his way, they would never have come to this . . .

She gasped, bringing her hand to her lips as she saw that a rebel had met Sir Morton head on, ever ready to do battle. The rebel was the wild man with the tangled blond hair.

Sir Morton's sword never made contact with the rebel's flesh.

Sir Morton's head fell to the earth and bounced as his body continued through the mass upon his horse, until that part of him, too fell to the ground to be trampled upon.

Bile filled her throat. She closed her eyes, and lowered her head, fighting the sickness that threatened to overwhelm her. Dear God, she had just left plague victims, nursed the sick and the putrid and the rotting and . . .

With her eyes closed, she could still see the head, bouncing.

The clash of steel seemed to rise in a cacophony around her; she heard more cries, shouts, the terrified whinnies of warhorses, animals accustomed to battle and mayhem. She forced herself to look up.

The finest armor to be found had not protected the men of Langley from the fury of the rebels' wrath. Men lay everywhere.

Armor glinting in the sun. The shining intermittent, against the bloodstained field. Some had survived. Unhorsed, the men milled in a circle. There were shouts and commands; the blond giant was on his feet as well, approaching the eight or so men of Langley who remained standing. Watching, appalled, she didn't realize her own danger. Voices carried on the air.

"Do we slay them now?" someone inquired.

The blond man replied, then shouted at the survivors. Swords fell to the ground. One man fell to his knees. Did he do so in absolute desolation, or in gratitude for his life?

Were they to be executed? Or were their lives to be spared?

She couldn't tell. Others were talking, but they spoke in softer voices.

One of the rebels pointed up the hill.

Then, suddenly, the blond man was staring at her.

She couldn't see his eyes in the distance. She could only remember them.

He started toward his horse.

Only then did she realize her own situation, and that he was mounting to ride once again, after her.

She spurred her horse, praying that she knew this region better than he, that her mare was a fresher mount, ready to take her to greater bursts of speed . . .

For a far longer period of time.

She prayed . . .

There had been a time, not so long ago, that she had wanted to die. When the death and despair had seemed so great that she would willingly have taken Afton's hand, and entered the afterlife with him. That moment when she realized that she had lost him, that he had breathed his last, that his laughter would never sound again.

And yet now . . .

She did not want to depart this life at the hands of a furious barbarian, bent on some form of revenge. She thought of how Edward I had killed Wallace, of the horrors that had taken place, of the English furor at the crowning of Robert Bruce.

And she rode as she had never done before, flat against her mare's neck, heels jamming the beast's haunches, whispers begging her to ever greater speed. The rebel's horse had to be flagging; their animals had been foaming when they first met with the men of Langley. If she could just evade him for a distance . . .

She galloped over the hill, through the thick grasses of the lea to the north. The forest beckoned beyond the hill, a forest she knew well, with twisting trails and sheltering oaks, a place in which to disappear. She could see the trees, the great branches waving high in the sky, the darkness of the trails beneath the canopy of leaves. She could smell the very richness of the earth and hear the leaves, as she could hear the thunder of her horse's hooves, the desperate, ragged catch of her own breath, the pulse of her heartbeat, echoed with each thunder of a hoof upon the earth. There . . . just a moment away . . .

She was never aware that his horse's hoofbeats thundered along with those of her mare; the first she knew of him was the hook of his arm, sweeping her from her horse in a deadly gamble. She was whisked from the mare and left to watch as the horse made the shelter of the trees. And for a moment, she looked on, in amazement, as she dangled from the great warhorse, a prisoner taken by a madman.

She began to twist and struggle, and bite—a sound enough attack so that he swore, and dropped her. His horse was huge; she fell a distance to the earth, stunned, then gathered her senses quickly and began to run. She headed for the dark trail, desperately, running with the speed of a hunted doe.

Yet again, she was swept off her feet, this time, lifted up, and thrown down, and the next thing she knew, he was on top of her, smelling of the earth and the blood of battle. She screamed, fought, kicked, yet found her hands vised above her head, and the barbarian straddled atop her, staring at her with a cold, wicked fury that allowed no mercy.

"You are the lady of Langley," he said.

"Igrainia," she replied.

"I don't give a damn about your name," he told her. "But you will come with me, and you will demand that the gates be opened."

She shook her head, "I cannot—"

She broke off as he raised a hand to strike her. The blow did not fall.

"You will," he said simply. "Or I will break you, bone by bone, until you do so."

"There is plague there, you idiot!"

"My wife is there, and my daughter," he told her.

"They are all dead or dying within the castle!"

"So you run in fear!" he said contemptuously.

"No! No," she raged, struggling to free herself again. Afraid? Of the plague? She was afraid only of life without Afton now.

Not quite true, she realized. She was afraid of this man

who would carry out his every threat, and break her. Bone by bone. She had never seen anyone so coldly determined.

"I am not afraid of the plague for myself!" she managed to snap out with an amazing tone of contempt.

"Good. We will go back, my fine lady, and you will dirty your hands with caring for those who are ill. You will save my wife, if she is stricken, or so help me, you will forfeit your own life."

Dirty her hands? He thought she was afraid to dirty her hands after the days and nights she had been through?

Her temper rose like a battle flag, and she spat at him. "Kill me then, you stupid, savage fool! I have been in that castle. Death does not scare me. I don't care anymore. Can you comprehend that? Are such words in your vocabulary?"

She gasped as he stood, wrenching her to her feet.

"If my wife or my daughter should die because of the English king's cruelty against the innocent, my lady, you are the one who will pay."

"My husband is dead because of the sickness brought in by your people!" she cried, trying to wrench her arm free. She could not. She looked at the hand vised around her arm. Huge, long-fingered, covered in mud and earth and . . .

Blood.

His grip seemed stronger than steel. Not to be broken. She stood still, determined not to tremble or falter. His face was as muddied and filthy as his hand and tangled blond hair. Only those sky blue eyes peered at her uncovered by the remnants of battle, brilliant and hard.

He either hadn't heard her, or he didn't give a damn. His command of language seemed to be excellent, so she assumed it was the latter.

"Hear me again. If my wife dies, my lady, you will be forfeit to the mercy of the Scottish king's men."

"Mercy? There is no mercy to be had there."

"At this point? Perhaps you are quite right. Therefore, you had best save my wife."

"I, sir, have no difficulty doing anything in my power to save the stricken, though I can assure you—their lives are in God's hands, and no others. I was forced to leave Langley. I did not go of my own volition."

He arched a brow skeptically. "You were willing to serve the plague-stricken and dying?"

"Aye, I would have stayed there willingly. I had no reason to leave."

"You *are* the lady of Langley."

"Indeed."

He didn't seem to care why she would have stayed.

"Then, as you say, it will be no hardship for you to return."

"Where I go, or what is done to me, does not matter in the least."

"You will save my wife, and my child."

She raised her chin.

"As I have told you, and surely you must understand, their lives are in God's hands. What, then, if I cannot save them?"

"Then it will be fortunate that you seem to have so little care for your own life."

He shoved her forward.

With no other choice, Igrainia walked.

Yet her heart was sinking.

If your wife is among the women stricken, then I am afraid that she has already died! Igrainia thought.

Because she had lied. She had thought herself immune to fear when she left Langley. Immune to further pain. Now, she was discovering that she did fear for her life, that there was something inside her that instinctively craved survival.

She wanted to live.

But if she failed, so he proclaimed, he would break her. That was certainly no less savage than the commands given by Edward in regard to the wives and womenfolk of any man loyal to Robert the Bruce.

Break her. Bone by bone.

It was all in God's hands. But maybe this filthy and half-savage man, no matter how articulate, didn't comprehend that.

"I will save your wife and child, if you will give me a promise."

"You think that you can barter with me?" he demanded harshly.

"I am bartering with you."

"You will do as I command."

"No. No, I will not. Because you are welcome to lop off my head here and now if you will not barter with me."

"Do you think that I will not?"

"I don't care if you do or do not!"

"So the lord of Langley is dead!" he breathed bitterly.

"Indeed. So you have no power over me."

"Believe me, my lady, if I choose, I can show you that I have power over you. Death is simple. Life is not. The living can be made to suffer. Your grief means nothing to me. It was the lord of Langley who imprisoned the women and children."

She shook her head. "You're wrong! So foolishly wrong! What care they received was by his order. Those who will live will do so, because he commanded their care. And he is dead because of the wretched disease brought in by *your* women and *your* children."

"None of this matters!" he roared to her.

She ignored his rage, and the tightening vise of his fingers around her arm.

She stared at his hand upon her, and then into his eyes,

so brilliantly blue and cold against the mud-stained darkness of his face.

"I will save your wife and child, if you will swear to let your prisoners live."

Again, he arched a brow and shrugged. "Their fates matter not in the least to me; save her, and they shall live."

She started forward again, then once more stopped. She had spoken with contempt and assurance. A bluff, a lie. And now, her hands were shaking. "What if I *cannot*? What if it has gone too far? God decides who lives and dies, and the black death is a brutal killer—"

"You will save them," he said.

They had reached his horse, an exceptionally fine mount. Stolen, she was certain, from a wealthy baron killed in battle. He lifted her carelessly upon the horse, then stared up at her, as if seeing her, really seeing her, perhaps for the first time.

"You will save them," he repeated, as if by doing so he could make it true.

"Listen to me. Surely, you understand this. Their lives are in God's hands."

"And yours."

"You are mad; you are possessed! Only a madman thinks he can rule a plague. Not even King Edward has power over life and death against such an illness. Kings are not immune, no man, no woman—"

"My wife and child must survive."

He had no sense, no intellect, no reason!

"Which of the women is your wife?" she asked. She wondered if she could kick his horse, and flee. She was in the saddle; he was on the ground.

"And if I give you a name, what will it mean to you?" he inquired.

"I have been among the prisoners."

It seemed he doubted that. "Margot," he told her. "She is tall, slim and light, and very beautiful."

Margot. Aye, she knew the woman. Beautiful indeed, gentle, moving about, cheering the children, nursing the others . . .

Until she had been struck down.

She had been well dressed, and had worn delicate Celtic jewelry, as the wife of a notable man, a lord, or a wealthy man at the least.

Rather than a filthy barbarian such as this.

But it was said that even Robert Bruce, King of the Scots, looked like a pauper often enough these days. He was a desperate man, ever searching out a ragtag army, reduced to hunger and hardship time and time again.

"Who are you?" she asked

"Who I am doesn't matter."

"Do you even have a name, or should I think of you as Madman, or Certain Death?"

His eyes lit upon her with cold fury. "You must have a name when it doesn't matter, when your life is at stake? When Edward has decreed that Scottish women are fair game, no better than outlaws to be robbed, raped or *murdered*? Wouldn't you be the one who is surely mad to expect chivalry in return for such barbarity, and test the temper of a man whose rage now equals that of your king? You would have a name? So be it. I am Eric, Robert Bruce's liege man by choice, sworn to the sovereign nation of Scotland, a patriot by both birth and choice. You see, my father was a Scottish knight, but my grandfather, on my mother's side, was a Norse jarl of the western isles. So there is a great deal of *berserker*—or indeed, *madman*—in me, lady. You must beware. We are not known to act rationally—and by God, no matter what our inclination at any time—*mercifully*.

Now, tell me what I ask. Does my wife live? You do know her, don't you?''

''Aye. I know her. Father MacKinley is with her,'' Igrainia said. ''She lives. When I left, she still lived.'' Aye, she knew his wife. She had spoken with her often when the disease had brought them together, forgetting nationalities and loyalties, fighting death itself.

And she knew his little girl. The beautiful child with the soft yellow hair and huge blue eyes, smiling even when she fell ill. The little girl had gone into a fever with a whimper.

But the woman had been so ill, burning, twisting, crying out . . .

She would die. And then . . .

Igrainia suddenly grabbed the reins and slammed the horse with her heels, using all the strength she had.

The huge gray warhorse reared, pawing the air. Igrainia clung desperately to the animal, hugging its neck, continuing to slam her heels against its flank. The man was forced to [...] back, and she felt hope take flight in her heart as the horse hit the ground and started running toward the trees.

Yet nearly to the trail, the animal came to an amazing halt, reared again, and spun.

This time, Igrainia did not keep her seat.

She hit the ground with a heavy thud that knocked the air from her.

A moment later, he was back by her side, reaching down to her, wrenching her to her feet. ''Try to escape again, and I will drag you back in chains.''

She gasped for breath, shaking her head. ''No one will stop your entry at the castle. Only the truly mad would enter there. I cannot help your wife—''

''I have told you who I am. And I know who you are. Igrainia of Langley, known to have the power to heal. Daughter of an *English* earl, greatly valued by many. My God, what you could be worth! There will be a price on your head, my lady, and you will save my wife.''

Once again, she found herself thrown onto the horse, which had obediently trotted back to its master.

This time, he mounted behind her.

Even as he did so, he urged the horse forward at a reckless gallop.

She felt his heat and his fury in the wall of his chest against her back, felt the strength of the man, and the power of his emotion.

And more . . .

She felt the trembling in him.

And suddenly understood.

Aye, he was furious.

And he was afraid.

And dear God . . .

So was she.

Books by Bestselling Author
Fern Michaels

Romantic Suspense from
Lisa Jackson

Absolute Fear	0-8217-7936-2	$7.99US/$9.99CAN
Afraid to Die	1-4201-1850-1	$7.99US/$9.99CAN
Almost Dead	0-8217-7579-0	$7.99US/$10.99CAN
Born to Die	1-4201-0278-8	$7.99US/$9.99CAN
Chosen to Die	1-4201-0277-X	$7.99US/$10.99CAN
Cold Blooded	1-4201-2581-8	$7.99US/$8.99CAN
Deep Freeze	0-8217-7296-1	$7.99US/$10.99CAN
Devious	1-4201-0275-3	$7.99US/$9.99CAN
Fatal Burn	0-8217-7577-4	$7.99US/$10.99CAN
Final Scream	0-8217-7712-2	$7.99US/$10.99CAN
Hot Blooded	1-4201-0678-3	$7.99US/$9.49CAN
If She Only Knew	1-4201-3241-5	$7.99US/$9.99CAN
Left to Die	1-4201-0276-1	$7.99US/$10.99CAN
Lost Souls	0-8217-7938-9	$7.99US/$10.99CAN
Malice	0-8217-7940-0	$7.99US/$10.99CAN
The Morning After	1-4201-3370-5	$7.99US/$9.99CAN
The Night Before	1-4201-3371-3	$7.99US/$9.99CAN
Ready to Die	1-4201-1851-X	$7.99US/$9.99CAN
Running Scared	1-4201-0182-X	$7.99US/$10.99CAN
See How She Dies	1-4201-2584-2	$7.99US/$8.99CAN
Shiver	0-8217-7578-2	$7.99US/$10.99CAN
Tell Me	1-4201-1854-4	$7.99US/$9.99CAN
Twice Kissed	0-8217-7944-3	$7.99US/$9.99CAN
Unspoken	1-4201-0093-9	$7.99US/$9.99CAN
Whispers	1-4201-5158-4	$7.99US/$9.99CAN
Wicked Game	1-4201-0338-5	$7.99US/$9.99CAN
Wicked Lies	1-4201-0339-3	$7.99US/$9.99CAN
Without Mercy	1-4201-0274-5	$7.99US/$10.99CAN
You Don't Want to Know	1-4201-1853-6	$7.99US/$9.99CAN

Available Wherever Books Are Sold!
Visit our website at **www.kensingtonbooks.com**

More by Bestselling Author
Hannah Howell